UGLY

Margaret McHeyzer

UGLY
Copyright © 2015 Margaret McHeyzer

ISBN: 978-0-9943547-4-7

Interior Formatting by Tami Norman, Integrity Formatting

The past forms us,
the present guides us,
the future awaits us.

For every victim and survivor
of domestic violence.

PROLOGUE

IT'S DAYS LIKE TODAY I wish I was dead.

"Lily Anderson, you get your ugly ass out here right this minute. Don't make me come after you," Daddy screams.

He's so angry. I knew the moment I heard him come home from work I was in for it. I was in my bedroom, lying on the floor trying to do my math. He slammed the front door so hard the windows in my room shook.

And then I knew, I knew I was in for it.

"Lily Anderson!" he yells again.

As soon as I heard him yell I ran to my hiding spot. I'm inside the closet in the hallway, wedged as far into the corner as I can get. Mom's old coat hangs in front of me and I can still smell a faint waft of the perfume she used to wear.

"Lily Anderson!" he shouts. I can hear the anger in his voice and I can already feel the pain he's going to inflict on me when he opens the closet door. I know what's coming.

I close my eyes tight, scrunching them up so no light can seep through. I put my hands over my ears so I can't hear him.

"I swear to God; if I have to find you, you will not sit for a month."

My knees are folded into my chest. I'm trying to make myself small, invisible, so he forgets I'm here. I'm rocking myself, trying to block out what he's saying.

School is safe. School is safe. School is safe. I keep repeating the mantra because in a few short hours I'll be back at school. Maybe tomorrow I can go to the library after school, stay there until it closes and then sneak in after Dad's passed out, because he's had too much to drink.

It was never like this before.

I'm twelve years old and I can remember when Mom, Dad, and I were all happy. But that was years ago. It's been a long time since there's been any happiness in this house.

Well, before Mom died, and not a day since.

Mom died when I was nine. I don't remember much about her, except I remember her telling me how ugly I am. How life would be better if I were taken away from them. How I'll never be anything, because I'm stupid and ugly.

Sometimes I dream happy things. Like me, Mom, Dad and a little blond-haired boy all going for a picnic. The sun beamed down on us as we played outside and laughed. We'd eat yummy sandwiches Mom made for us, and we'd drink homemade lemonade. We'd spend hours outside, laughing and talking and just having fun. Mom would tell me how pretty I am, and how much she loved me. She would play with my hair, braid it, and then we'd go and pick bright flowers to take home and put in a vase. Dad would smile and call us "his girls", always kissing Mom and hugging me. Dad would put the little boy on his shoulders and run around the park, trying to catch the clouds.

I love those dreams, and I hold onto them; wishing they were real. But I've never had a mom like that, and my dad doesn't talk much unless it's with his fists, or to tell me how ugly and useless I am.

I feel him walking around the house. The floorboards creak and the vibrations from his footsteps come through the floor to where my bottom is. I close my eyes tighter and try and breathe as quietly as I can.

Please go away, Daddy. Please go away.

My heart is beating so fast. My hands are shaking and I'm trying really hard not to think about what's going to happen the minute he opens the closet door.

Shhh, it's so quiet. The only sound is my heart thrumming in my ears. Nothing else. Not a whisper, not a rattle…nothing.

Maybe Daddy's left. Maybe he's gone to the pub to have a few drinks. Maybe, just maybe, he's left…forever.

I take a deep breath and just relax for a moment. My shoulders drop and I finally stop rocking.

Slowly I take my hands down from my ears, and I'm so happy because I can't hear him yelling at me. I can't hear him at all.

Gradually, I begin to unscrunch my eyes from the way I've tightly closed them. But something's not right. There's light coming into the closet.

I don't even get a chance to open them fully before a rough hand reaches in, latches onto my ponytail and yanks.

"I told you it'd be worse for you if I had to find you," Dad says, as he drags me out of the closet by my hair.

I'm desperately trying to hold onto my head so he doesn't rip my hair out. My feet are trying to find traction on the dirty floorboards.

"Please, Daddy. Please. You're hurting me," I begin sobbing as I plead with him.

"Then your ugly ass should've come when I called you, you stupid bitch. You're fucking worthless, you ugly idiot," he says. But now his voice is calm as he continues to drag me toward the family room.

That's when he's most scary. When his voice is low and his eyes are filled with hate.

He throws me against the side of the sofa and takes a step back to look at me.

I look up and can see he's the angriest I've ever seen him. "You dumb, ugly piece of shit," he says, as he paces back and forth in front of me.

"Sorry, Daddy. Whatever I did, I'm so sorry." I cower into myself, trying to make myself as small as possible.

"You're just too fucking stupid, aren't you?" he spits toward me as he brings his hand up to scratch at his chin.

"I'm sorry," I say again. Tears are falling hot and fast down my cheeks. My head hurts from where he was pulling my hair, but I don't dare try to rub the spot.

"You ugly fuck." He kicks a boot into my leg.

The pain is instant and my leg feels like it's shattered. "Please, Daddy," I beg again, burying my face into my hands.

But 'please' never seems to work.

Nothing does.

I've just got to take the beatings, because that's what stupid, ugly girls do.

CHAPTER 1

THE PRINCIPAL OF MY HIGH school pulled me into his office today. He told me with how hard I've been studying and all my exam results, I'm looking at graduating high school with a 3.9 GPA. He asked me what I want to study in college, and where I'm thinking of studying.

But I know Dad won't pay for me to go to college. He's always telling me how stupid I am. His words are always close by, ready to erase any sliver of confidence I may experience.

"For God's sake, Lily, you're probably one of the ugliest and stupidest girls I know," he often says. It's usually followed by more slurred insults.

I've heard them for as long as I can remember. I'm seventeen now, and this has been going on for so long. He's right about one thing, I'm definitely ugly. I have blonde hair that sits limply on my shoulders, and my eyes are more green than brown, but they're dull and nondescript. Like me. I don't even know why anyone would want to talk to me, or be friends with me.

I don't have friends at school. I can't look at anyone, if I do they may see the bruises. Not the bruises on my skin, no, those are easily concealed. I mean the bruises hiding deep down inside me. The pain and sadness that's with me from the moment I wake, to the moment I go to sleep.

No one talks to me, because, well, I'm ugly. Ugly girls don't have friends. We simply hide away and try to blend in wherever we can, trying our best to be shadows so no one looks at us, or approaches us.

Last week as I was walking home from school; there was a boy who is at the bus stop every afternoon, waiting for the bus. He's been smiling at me. At first I thought he was smiling at the person who got off the bus behind me so I looked away, because really, who'd smile at me?

The next day he smiled again, and I looked behind me to see who he was smiling at. The girl who followed me is one of the popular girls at school, so I knew it was for her, not me. I'm not pretty and I'm definitely not popular.

Even the teachers don't know my name. Most of them have to look at their roll to check. My math and English teachers know my name, but the others don't. Even though I'm consistently at the top of the class, I still don't get noticed. Just the way I like it.

On the third day, when I got off the bus, the boy stood in front of me and said hello. But really, why would he talk to me? I lowered my eyes, clutched my bag to my chest and hurried home. He must want me to do his homework. But I haven't seen him at school, maybe he goes to another school and wants me to do his work.

On the fourth day, he stood in front of me again, and said, "Hi, I'm Trent. How are you?" He stuck his hand out for me to take and eagerly waited. But again, I just looked away, put my head down and hurried home.

That was also the night Dad came home drunk, stumbled inside, came into my room and dragged me out of bed. He grabbed me by my t-shirt and threw me against the wall.

"It's all your fault!" he screamed in his tell-tale slur.

It's also when I know to shut up, and not cry. Crying never helps, nor does pleading. I just have to take it.

"You ugly piece of shit. You're just as dumb as you are ugly. You better start sucking cock 'cause that's all you're ever going to be good for. It's all your fault," he yelled again.

All I could do was cower. I brought my hands over my head, balled my body as small as it would go and protected my head from the kicks, punches and slaps.

Dad eventually tired and stumbled out of my room down the hall to his bedroom. I would've slammed my door if I could, but Dad removed it when I was little.

I'm not sure how he's going to react when I tell him Trent tried walking me home today. I got off the bus and Trent was waiting for me. He was holding a flower in his hand and a big, sweet smile for me.

"You know, eventually one day you'll have to tell me your name," he said, walking with me toward home.

I looked at him sideways, trying to avoid his eyes, but they're so big and brown I couldn't help it. "What are you doing?" I ask as I looked around me, making sure Dad didn't see him.

"I just want to know your name." He tried to hand me the flower he was holding, but I shook my head and clutched my bag tighter to my chest. "I'd really like to give you this flower. It's pretty, just like you."

That statement made me laugh quite loudly. I knew Trent was just saying whatever he could because he wanted to use me. "Yeah, okay," I said, no louder than a whisper.

"It's true, I think you're real pretty," he said again.

But by this time I'd already switched off to his attempts to use me. "I've got to get home," I said and ran the rest of the way. When I looked over my shoulder, I half expected Trent to be following me, but he was just standing on the corner, head tilted to the side watching me.

Now I'm sitting in my room, all of my homework done, and I'm just reading. My favorite book is a play called *The Crucible*. I've read it so many times that the spine is held together by tape and the pages are completely discolored and fragile.

My stomach rumbles with hunger. I try to ignore the fact I only had a piece of bread for breakfast. Dad doesn't often bring home groceries. Only when he discovers for himself there's nothing to eat, does he buy a few bags of groceries.

Once I told him there was nothing in the fridge or the cupboards and he gave me the back of his hand and told me it's because I'm a greedy, ugly bitch who eats him out of house and home.

I get up from my bed and go into the kitchen, hoping to find something to eat. Anything, even a cracker would be better than nothing at all.

I open all the cupboards and find nothing. In the fridge there's an orange, but it's soft and on one side it's got mold growing on it. I take it out of the fridge and take it over to the kitchen sink. I cut the moldy part off and look to see how the orange is inside. At least it'll be something in my tummy.

I set the moldy part aside, because if Dad sees it in the trash, he will get angry that I didn't eat it and say I'm wasting food. When I eat the half that seems okay, I'll go bury the spoiled half in the back yard.

Bringing the orange up to my lips, I dart my tongue out to make sure it's okay to eat. It smells okay, so I take a small nibble of a segment. It's not great, but it's something.

When I finish, I go down to the back of the yard and quickly dig a hole with my bare hands to bury the evidence before Dad gets home from work.

Once inside, I scrub and wash my hands, making sure there's no evidence of what I did. I've done this a few times in the past and know how to eat, bury and wash up so Dad has no idea.

I go back to my room, sit on my bed and pick up my book.

My mind begins to wander to a time when women were considered dangerous, because they were witches. If I lived in those times, would I be considered a witch too, or would they leave me alone because I'm ugly and stupid?

"Lily!" I hear my Dad bellow as the front door shuts.

"Here, Dad," I say as I come out of my bedroom and stand looking down at my toes.

"Make me something to eat," he says, the slur in his speech only slight. "I'm hungry."

"We don't have anything. I looked earlier," I say in a small voice.

I keep looking down, refusing to meet his gaze because I'm sure he'll just yell at me. The seconds tick by, I'm so scared I hold my breath. I'm bracing myself for whatever's going to happen. He hates being told there's no food, and hates it even more when I talk.

"You fat, ugly bitch. Did you eat everything I bought?" I stay still, not moving, not wanting to be on the receiving end of Dad's wrath. "You're no good at anything. Spoilt bitch," he spits before I hear the door slamming shut.

I let out the breath I was holding, and my heart starts to calm to a normal rate. No words tonight, and no fists either. I walk back into my room and sit on my bed, picking up my ragged copy of *The Crucible* and get lost in it.

It's not until darkness starts to set in, and the temperature drops to a cool kiss on my cheek, I know Dad will return soon and I'd better be asleep. It's nights like tonight I know the bruises will be on the outside, too.

I put on my old pajamas that are too small for me, and get under the thin blanket on my bed. Clutching my book to my chest, I close my eyes and pray Dad will leave me alone tonight.

My thoughts begin to drift, and the darkness of twilight finds its way into my mind. The hopeless sting of the chilled night air keeps me hovering between the living and the dead.

Dead…such a pleasing, calming word. The dead get to sleep, to rest without being tortured by the doomed.

As my eyes close and my mind drifts into shadows of peace, I feel my book slip out of my fingers. I jerk awake and meet the angry, drunken green eyes of my father. "Dad," I startle, as I try and grab at my book.

He rips it out of my hand and begins to flick through it. "Is this what you fill your head with? Trash?" Dad keeps turning the pages slowly, as he slightly sways from side to side.

"What have I done for you to treat me so badly?" I ask. It's something I ask from time to time, and I never get an answer, other than more alcohol filled mumblings.

He slowly lifts his eyes from the book; an evil, deviant smile gradually tugging at the corners of his mouth. He moves my book so he's holding it in two hands, and suddenly rips straight through it.

"NO!" I scream as I leap out of bed and throw myself at him. "Please!" I beg. My voice is laden with pain, pleading for him to not destroy the only thing that allows me an escape from this hell-hole house on this hell-hole street; where no one hears anything, and everyone ignores everything.

Dad looks at me, his face set and his eyes frighteningly cold. He takes in a breath, and with complete clarity he says, "It should have been you." Those words are filled with malice, his tone lethal, destructive.

"What did I ever do?" I cry as I slump at his feet. The torn pages are strewn carelessly all over the floor.

"Listen here, bitch. You should've died instead of them."

Them? My eyes fly up to look at Dad. I don't even know what he's talking about. I have no idea who 'them' are.

"I'm sorry, Dad. I'm sorry for whatever I did. I didn't mean it. I'm so sorry," I sob as I clutch my hair and bring my head to my knees.

"So you should be." Dad just walks out of my room, leaving me with an ache so deep in my soul I don't think I'll ever be able to feel normal again.

CHAPTER 2

I GET OFF THE BUS and Trent is waiting for me again. He's got a cute dimple in his right cheek as he smiles at me, holding a different flower for me, a lily this time. I can't help but smile when I see him waiting.

"Hi," he says, as he takes a step toward me.

I look down at his shoes and keep my eyes focused there.

"Hi," I say in a small voice. I start walking home, my bag to my chest, the way I always hold it.

He offers me the flower, but I shake my head. His eyes look to my book bag, then he turns and watches the footpath as he walks with me. "May I carry that for you?" he asks.

"No, thank you."

We walk in silence for about fifty yards when Trent starts singing. It's a soft song, nothing I can recognize, but I don't have a radio or anything else to listen to music. Dad's television is in his room, and he keeps that locked when he's not home. I don't really know any artists or bands.

We keep walking toward my house with Trent singing and not talking to me. "So, are you going to tell me your name?" he finally says when we round the first corner.

I take a huge breath and gulp down the golf ball clogging my throat. "It's Lily," I finally say after a long silence. Trent chuckles and I peek at him to see he's shaking his head. "What's funny?"

"I think you and I are meant to be friends, Lily," he says, as he holds the flower up to me. "This flower is prettier than the one from the other day. As soon as I saw it, it reminded me of you and I had to get it." He casually holds the flower out, trying to give it to me again.

We walk a few more yards before I take the flower and bring it to my nose to smell it. The aroma coming from the flower is sweet and subtle, nothing too overpowering.

"Thank you," I whisper. I keep my eyes trained on the sidewalk as we continue to walk.

"Can I take you out to the movies?" Trent says. His tone is leisurely but controlled.

I sneak a look at him over my right shoulder, and his light brown hair is flopping to the side. "To the movies?" I ask. I haven't ever been to the movies. I don't know what it's like. I wonder if it's scary. I've heard the kids at school talk about it, but seeing as I've never been, I really don't know what to expect.

"Yeah, you know the big screen. Sharing a popcorn, watching a movie?" he says, as if I should know what going to the movies is like.

"Popcorn?" I've heard of that, too, even seen some kids eating it. But I've never had any, so I don't know if I'll like it.

"Popcorn. Made from corn. Popped with loads of butter and salt." I simply shrug and shake my head slightly. "Wait, you've never had popcorn before?" I shake my head again. "Ever?" he asks, as he stops walking and gently grips my arm.

"No," I say in a small voice. I lift my head to look at him, and now I know he thinks I'm stupid. Well… more stupid then I am.

"Really?" His eyebrows knit together. "You've been to the movies though, right?" His voice breaks in surprise when he asks.

"No, never."

"Wow." He chuckles and turns to keep walking. "I'll have to fix that problem. Tomorrow night, I'm taking you to the movies," he says so confidently.

"I've got to ask my Dad. I'm not sure I'll be allowed."

"You need to ask your Dad?" he repeats back to me. I nod my head but keep walking, head down, not looking at him. I can only just imagine what he thinks of me. Here's this ugly, stupid girl who needs to ask her Dad's permission. Why bother, when he can go find a cute girl who'll cause him less trouble? "You know, that's cool. I respect that. Can I have your number and I'll call you later tonight?"

"My number?"

"Yeah, you know your cell number."

"I don't have a phone," I say.

"That's cool, I'll friend you on Facebook."

"I don't have a computer either, so I don't have Facebook."

"You don't have a computer, and you don't have a phone?" I turn to look at him and he's got a surprised look on his face. "I'll just meet you at the bus stop tomorrow. Say about five? We'll go have dinner first."

I purse my lips together. I'm not sure what to say to him. I've got no money, how am I supposed to pay for myself. "Um," I say, struggling with how to say no to him. I want to go, 'cause he seems like a nice boy, but I don't have the money to pay for anything.

He must be sensing my trepidation, my absolute unease in this entire situation. "I mean what type of gentleman would I be if I asked a lady to dinner and a movie and expected her to pay her way? I'll meet you at five at the bus stop. If you're not there by ten past, I'll take it to mean you couldn't come."

I stop walking when we round the last corner to my house. "Okay," I say looking up into his kind, brown eyes. "I'll be there at five." I look down at my shoes, then back up at Trent.

"See you tomorrow," he says. Trent smiles then turns to walk away, "I hope you can come."

I walk home, and for the first time in years I feel something happening to me. My face feels different. Suddenly, I feel the rays of the sun touch my skin, warming me and guiding me to possibilities.

As I get closer to home I see Dad's car isn't in the driveway; which means for now, he'll still be at work. He works at a mattress factory, on the production line. He hates it there, but he hates being near me more.

When I open the front door, I'm met with the same sterile, cold silence I'm used to. Nothing inside the house has any life to it. Nothing has an air of living, it's simply dead. A lot like I usually am…but not today. Today I was asked out on a date. And I can actually feel the warmth creeping back inside of me.

My stomach rumbles, and suddenly I'm reminded how hungry I am. Other than the half orange I ate yesterday, I haven't had anything else to eat. One of the kids left their half-eaten sandwich on a table in the cafeteria today, and if there weren't so many kids around I would've eaten it. But someone picked it up and put it in the trash, so I had to go without.

I go into my room and throw my old bag on the bed. Just as I swing it from over my shoulder, the strap breaks and my books go flying across the room. Slumping my shoulders, I know I still have a couple of months left before the end of the school year. And considering I've had this bag since the second year of high school, I know Dad won't be getting me another one.

Right now though, my tummy takes precedence over the bag. The rumbling is so loud, I'm sure the people down the road can hear it. I go into the kitchen and stand looking at the empty fridge. I check the cupboards in case dad brought anything home, but he hasn't.

Walking into the family room, I take all the cushions off the sofa and dig my hand down to see if there's any loose change. I find a quarter and just as I think there's nothing I can buy with a quarter, I find a scrunched up twenty dollar bill.

I feel my eyes widen as I look around me, clutching the twenty in my hand close to my chest. I sit still for a few moments, making sure this isn't a trick. I look around again, I'm even super quiet to make sure no one saw me steal the money.

When I know this isn't a trick and I'm safe, I jump up and run out the front door down toward the small corner store, three blocks away.

I run as fast as my legs will take me, knowing soon I'll have something in my belly. Reaching the door for the small store, I pull it and go inside. The store is small, but has some basic food staples and fresh fruit and vegetables. With my twenty dollars I get three bananas, three apples, a loaf of bread and some non-refrigerated milk. I'll hide the groceries and when I'm really hungry, I'll eat something and not show Dad. He'll get angry at me because I have them, but he'll be angrier at me for not giving it to him. I know the money is his, and technically I'm stealing it, but I'm so hungry.

Walking home from the store, I eat a banana and open one of the milks. At first I drink it super-fast, but I know I'll need to slow down or I'll end up being sick.

Taking the bags inside, I hide the fruit and the milk in my room. There's a closet in my room that holds the few clothes I do have and an extra blanket for when it's really cold in winter. Dad has a space heater in his room. I have two blankets. When it snows here, it's freezing. The winter before this one, I had to go to a thrift shop and beg them for a pair of socks. The ladies were really nice to me, and could tell I needed the help. They gave me a coat, a pair of boots, three pairs of socks and a thick sweater. Dad got angry at me and told me it made him look like a bad parent. *Maybe he is.*

But I got through winter with those clothes, and I'm hoping I'll be able to get through next winter with them too. I hide the food in the pockets of the coat, the shelf milk in the boots and close my closet door. There's still a few dollars in change, and I hide that in the other boot, in case I get hungry again.

Sitting on my bed, I begin my homework when I hear the front door slam shut. Holding my breath I wait for Dad to come into my room. Hopefully he's in a good mood, although that hasn't happened much lately.

I sit on my bed, looking toward the door. *Please let him be in a good mood. Please let him be in a good mood.*

Dad pokes his bald head into my room. He looks at me sitting on the bed and snarls at me. "I'm going out," he says, with anger clear in his voice.

"Okay," I answer, not really able to say anything else to him.

His heavy footsteps disappear down the hallway and I let out the breath I was holding. Looking down at my advanced math book, I do the work set and more. As I'm lost in a calculus question, I hear Dad lock his bedroom door then his footsteps start up the hallway again.

He stops at my door, and he's dressed in jeans and a t-shirt. He just looks at me, and I watch his features change. For a split second I think he wants to tell me something. And hopefully, that something is him begging for me to forgive him. Because I would, in a single heartbeat. He's the only Dad I've got, and somewhere deep inside the anger, deep inside the hard man he is – he loves me. I'm sure of it.

"I won't be back until Monday," he says, squashing any dream I may have of him being a good father.

Today being Friday means I'll have to go without food for the entire weekend. It's common for him to go and leave me with nothing in the house. The ladies at the thrift shop had said to me, if I ever needed anything to go to them, and thankfully, they've fed me a couple of times. But I'm sure I've worn out my welcome at the thrift shop. I'm grateful I found that twenty, and have some food to see me through the weekend.

"Okay," I answer Dad. There's not much I can say. At least I know when he's not here, he can't yell at me, or tell me how ugly or stupid I am.

Dad takes a step into my room, and I brace myself for whatever it is I'm about to encounter. "Here," he says taking his wallet out of his pocket. The beautiful leather wallet is fat and holds a big stack of bills. I simply keep looking at him. "Get something to eat, I know I haven't had a chance to go shopping yet." He hands me fifty dollars and keeps looking at me.

Have I missed something? Is this a joke? Is he going to snatch it back and yell, *Gotchya?*

I keep looking at him, not reaching for the note, because I'm sure there is a part of him getting angry at me. "Here," he says, thrusting the fifty closer to me.

"Thank you," I say, hesitantly taking the money.

"You know," he begins to say, and I stop breathing, waiting for the hook. "You need to learn to suck cock, because you really are ugly and stupid, and you're not going to be able to make it in this world without some dumb fucker taking care of you." *And there it is.* The insult, the belittling, the sure-fire way to keep me so far down I'll never see the light again.

"Yes, Dad," I answer.

"When you finish high school, I want you out of the house. I don't want to feed you anymore. Or clothe you or even have to worry about you," Dad says, and walks out of my room. *Worry about me? Is this how he shows he 'worries' about me?*

My shoulders slump and I can't help but feel like nothing more than the dirt on his shoe he can't scrape off quick enough.

"Yes, Dad," I murmur, as I fall to my knees and cry.

High school is almost finished for the year.

What the hell am I going to do? I'm so scared. I'm so dumb, I'm not sure I'll ever be able to get a job. *Who'd want someone as stupid as me?*

CHAPTER 3

"HI," TRENT SAYS AS I walk toward the bus stop. "You look beautiful," he adds, looking me up and down. My jeans have a hole, my shoes are old and my blouse was something I found at the thrift shop this morning. It smells like moth-balls, but I bought some deodorant with the change of the twenty and sprayed it making it not smell so bad.

"Thank you," I say, even though I want to laugh at him. I really must be stupid. Because for a split-second, when he smiles at me, I believe him, I believe I look beautiful. What a fool I am to think I'm anything but what I really am.

"I was thinking there's a nice pizza place near the movies. What do you think?" he asks.

I shrug my shoulders and nod. I've had pizza before. They served it at school and I had found some coins in the sofa. It added up to enough for me to have a slice of pizza at school. God, it tasted awesome. I think I had it when I was little too, but I'm not sure.

"I think that sounds fantastic," I answer Trent, excited about having pizza.

"Then pizza it is. And what type of movies do you like? There's a few new ones out. Do you like sci-fi or comedies or maybe a drama?"

"I'm not sure. Maybe something to make me laugh."

We sit and wait for the bus together. Trent moves closer to me, and my automatic reaction is to flinch away. He catches the sudden jerk, I can see out of my peripheral vision how his eyebrows knit together. "I'm not going to hurt you, Lily."

I nod, acknowledging his words, though my defenses are high, just in case he tries to do something to me.

"I go to the private boy's school across town. Where do you go?"

"Public school," I answer, while I keep an eye out for the bus.

"When do you finish? I finish this year and have been accepted into college to study accounting. What will you be doing?"

"I finish this year too. I'm not sure if I can even go to college. I think I'll have to find a job. I'm going to the supermarket to see if they need anyone tomorrow."

Trent knits his eyebrows together again, and his face morphs into question. "Why?"

"I have to move out soon, and I need money."

"You have to move out?" he asks, his voice full of query. "I don't understand why you have to move out. Are your mom and dad going through a tough time?"

"My mom's dead," I say with no feeling in my voice. Or even in my body.

"Aren't you living with your dad?"

"Can we just not talk about my dad or anything like that please? Tell me about your family. Do you have brothers or sisters?" The bus pulls up and Trent and I stand to get on. With his hand to my lower back, Trent guides me on the bus ahead of him. He is such a gentleman, allowing me to go first.

"Two please," he says, handing the bus driver money for our fare. "No brothers or sisters. But my dad comes from a huge family and said he never wanted more than one child, because he didn't want me to have to fight with anyone." I look at him and nod before he finds us seats.

The bus trip is spent with Trent sitting beside me and me looking out the window. We're quiet because there are a lot of people on the bus, and trying to talk will only be drowned out by the incessant happy chatter of the people around us.

"We need to get off the bus now," Trent says, gently nudging me out of my study of the buildings we're passing.

"Okay," I say as I stand, we move to the front to get off when it stops.

"Lily, would you mind if I hold your hand?" he asks sweetly. I've never had anyone hold my hand. Not when I'm awake. In my dreams sometimes Mom holds my hand as we walk through a tall, field of bright yellow flowers. Dad holds my other hand and they count to three then swing me up in the air. A little boy is always running ahead, looking back at us and giggling.

"I'd like that," I say to Trent. When his fingers link with mine, it feels different. He's so warm. As his skin touches mine it sends a small shiver up my spine, but I can feel a smile tugging on my lips.

Is this how kids feel when they're touched by their parents? Do they smile because they know their moms and dads want to hold them, embrace them, and protect them? Is this the feeling I've been missing out on all these years?

"We're here," Trent says, as he opens the door to a small pizza shop. The smells coming from inside are fantastic. I don't think I've ever smelled anything as savory and delicious as the aroma coming from the ovens.

"Hi, table for two," Trent says to the waiter.

The place is small, fourteen booths and a few scattered tables in the center. The waiter leads us to a booth where I sit, then Trent slides in opposite me.

I look around at the walls and they're painted in fresh blue and red colors. Pictures of Italy adorn the walls, a huge painting of an Italian flag is on one of the walls, and lots of knick-knack items are on shelves everywhere.

"I've never been here before," I say, appreciating the quirky environment.

"You haven't? It's been here for so long, I used to come as a kid with my mom and dad. And my mom used to come here when she was younger. Mom says it's never changed. Everything is the same. There's a lady who makes the pizza sauce; Mom said she's about eighty years old. She still makes it, but now her kids run the business."

"Really?" I ask, as I lean my elbow on the table and cradle the side of my head as I look at Trent.

"If my mom said it, it must be true." He laughs, and I smile.

I pick up the menu and begin to look over it. These are all foreign to me, I'm not entirely sure what I'll like and what I won't.

I sense someone standing beside me, but my attention is on the menu in my hands. "Why don't you take a picture, it lasts longer," Trent says in an angry tone.

Instantly my shoulders come up and I feel an icy, cold brush of fright touch my skin as I recognize the cold, angry tone. I sit back in my seat and put my head down further.

"My apologies," I hear someone say.

Chancing a look, I peer over the menu to see Trent furiously looking at the waiter who's standing beside me. "Yeah, you better be, fucker."

"Trent," I whisper, too frightened to make eye contact.

Out of my peripheral vision I can see Trent's face ease, his jaw softens and his shoulders drop as he takes in a deep breath. "We'll have a large pepperoni and two Cokes," Trent orders, without asking me.

"It'll be out in a moment," the waiter says, then walks away.

There's an uncomfortable quiet between the two of us. I don't know what to say. He got angry at that waiter for no reason, and then ordered for me. Lucky he did order, because I have no idea what I'd like.

"Are you angry with me?" he finally breaks the stony silence.

I shake my head. I want to ask why he said what he did, but I opt to remain quiet and not say anything.

"He was looking at you," Trent answers my unasked question. "And I don't like it."

"I'm sorry," I instantly reply.

"Don't worry about it, let's just eat our pizza and enjoy the movie." I nod and look at Trent. He's visibly calmed and now he looks like the cute boy I met at the bus stop on the way home.

"What movie are we going to watch?" I ask, trying to make conversation to take his mind off the waiter looking at me. I know we talked about a movie, hopefully he has an idea what's playing, because I don't.

"It's a new comedy. I saw the preview for it and it looks really funny. Is that okay with you?" He reaches over and lays his hand out for me to lay my palm in his hand. Slowly I lift my hand and put it in his. "This feels nice," he adds with a smile.

"It does?" I ask, chancing a look up at Trent from beneath my lashes.

"It feels nice to me. I like holding your hand. Don't you like it?"

The same waiter comes back and sets down two tall glasses with Coke in them. I sip mine through a straw and the bubbly, fizzy drink feels funny on my tongue. I giggle when I take a bigger sip and Trent looks at me with his head slightly tilted.

"It tickles," I say, as I sip some more of the soda.

He scrunches his eyebrows together and asks, "You've never had a soda before?"

"I think I have. I can't remember. It tastes funny. But it tickles."

"It tickles?" he asks with his own big smile. I nod and take another sip. "Don't have too much; it'll make you feel sick." He strokes his thumb up and down the back of my hand.

It's different. Not the feel of the drink, my taste buds are used to it now. But the fact there's someone who's saying things to me and making me feel like more than just the stupid, ugly person I am.

"It feels nice to me. I like holding your hand. Do you like it?" Trent asks sweetly.

A smile bursts from him, uncontrollably erupting. I can feel the foreign riot of emotions dancing inside of me. "Yeah I do," I quietly say.

Suddenly, my heart begins to race and I feel a patch of heat settle over my cheeks. Trent's brown eyes smile at me as the warmth from his touch reaches a part of me I never knew existed. There's a heat inside my body, an emotion I have never felt.

"Your pepperoni pizza," the waiter says as he sets a large round tray in front of us, then places two plates down.

"Wow," I say as I take in the large pie. It's huge. I don't recall the last time I saw so much food on a table. Well, not where I was welcomed to have any.

"It's really yummy, here." Trent picks up a slice and places it on my plate.

The smell alone is beyond intoxicating. I can't wait to try it. I lift it, and the excess cheese drips onto my hand. The heat burns my fingertips, but I just can't wait to taste it.

My stomach makes a small rumbling sound just as I take a bite, and I pray no one heard just how hungry I am.

"It's good, right?" Trent asks through a mouthful of food.

"Mmmm, it really is." I take another bite and really savor the flavors of the pie.

I can't believe I end up eating three whole slices. I don't think I've ever eaten so much. My pants feel really tight around my stomach, and I think I need to undo my button. "Ready for dessert?" Trent asks.

"Dessert? I don't think I can fit anything more in my tummy."

Trent laughs and lifts his glass to have a sip of his Coke. "Okay, no dessert. But, you have to have some popcorn at the movies."

I smile. *I can't wait to try it.*

"Ready to go?" Trent asks as he stands.

"Yes, thank you." I stand and Trent links his fingers through mine. We make our way over to the cash register where the waiter who served us is waiting for us.

"How was your meal?" he asks me.

"You don't talk to her, you ask me," Trent half shouts, pulling me behind him as he steps in front of me.

"How was your meal?" The waiter asks Trent in a sarcastic tone.

"Watch your damn mouth. I'm a paying customer, and if you're not nice to me and my girl, I'll have you fired."

His girl? I'm not his girl. I'm just Lily. Stupid, ugly Lily.

"That'll be twenty-five dollars," the waiter says, though now his tone sounds bored and dismissive.

Trent takes his wallet out and I see he gives him the exact amount. "I would've given you a tip, but you eye-fucked the wrong girl." He turns, and almost pushes me out the door.

"Whatever, man," I hear the pizza-shop worker say to our retrieving backs.

"Bastard. I should go in there and teach him a lesson." Trent's fingers squeeze my hand, tightening to the point of pain.

"Let's just go to the movies and enjoy our night," I encourage him, taking a step toward the cinemas, trying to pull him away.

"Yeah, alright." He nods his head, but looks back over his shoulder toward the pizza place.

We walk hand in hand toward the theater and I can sense Trent calming down. He loosens his grip on my hand and his steps become slower.

"Thank you for inviting me out," I say.

"I like you, Lily. I think you're real pretty, really nice, and easy to talk to." I smile, because I haven't said much. "Here we are," Trent says, holding the door open for me to enter before he does.

We go up the escalators to get our tickets, and Trent also gets two sodas and a huge tub of popcorn. When we get into the movie and find our seats, Trent lifts the arm rest separating us and throws his hand over the back of my chair.

I smile to myself, because for the first time ever, I actually feel wanted.

The movie was fun and I ate way too much popcorn and drank my soda. As Trent and I leave, a realization quickly washes over me.

"Are you okay?" Trent asks as we get off the bus and head in the direction of my home.

I simply nod, but Trent can tell something's not right because he keeps quiet and every few minutes he turns to look at me.

"I can tell you're not okay. What is it? Maybe I can help."

"It's nothing, really." I don't want to tell him about my Dad, how I live, or that I'm going home to darkness and an empty house. I don't want to tell him how the moment I step inside the house I'm filled with dread because my surroundings are as hopeless as how my soul feels. "But, you can drop me off here, I'll be fine. There's no need to walk me all the way home."

"It's after dark, this isn't really the best neighborhood and I'd feel better knowing you got home okay."

"There's nothing wrong with my neighborhood," I protest angrily.

"I'm not saying it's bad, it's just not great."

"Honestly, I'm fine. I've lived here all my life, and nothing's ever happened."

Trent lets go of my hand, tilting his head to the side and lifting his eyebrows. The look makes me laugh. "I'm not taking no for an answer," he says, giving me a cute look.

Slumping my shoulders, I know he's not going to let this go until he's walked me home. "Okay," I finally relent. I mean, what bad could come from it?

As we walk home, Trent and I talk about the movie and I tell him what I really liked about it. It was an experience in itself, being in an unlit room with all those other people. As we round the corner on my street and get closer to home, I see Dad's car is in the driveway.

Damn, he's not supposed to be home tonight! Why is he home?

My legs suddenly become leaden and I find it difficult to take those steps toward my house. My heartbeat accelerates and I can feel sweat beading on my forehead.

No, no, no. Please be asleep. Please be asleep.

"Are you okay? You're shaking," Trent says, as he squeezes my hand in his.

I simply nod, but keep my eyes glued to screen door of my house. When Trent and I are two houses away, Dad opens the front door and steps out on the small porch. He looks down the street, then up straight in my direction.

At first he looks past me and away, he then runs his hand over his face and through his hair. Within seconds he whips his head back to me, finally registering that I'm walking home with a boy. Instantly I let go of Trent's hand and hang my head down.

"What the hell is going on?" Trent whispers to me, trying not to draw attention to me.

"Nothing, please go," I respond in a frantic, pleading way.

"Like hell, Lily. Tell me what's going on?"

"Where have you been?" Dad yells at me.

"Just go," I whisper to Trent. Wrapping my arms around my body, I take off toward home, leaving Trent and not looking behind me.

"Lily," he calls, but I ignore him.

I get home, climb the first creaky step and Dad's blocking my path inside. "Imagine my surprise when I get home, and a certain ugly little bitch isn't here," he says, but his tone is slightly slurred. I know he's been drinking, which means I know what I'm in for.

"Sorry," I mumble with my head lowered, not daring to look into his angry eyes.

"Get inside," he spits as he puts his hands on his hips. I still don't dare look at him, but I can see his movements from the corner of my vision. His stance alone tells me he's angry and his words just confirm it.

I'm in for it now.

CHAPTER 4

SCHOOL TODAY HAS DRAGGED ON. It seems like the hours haven't moved at all. Every time I look at the clock it seems like it's stuck on five past two. It doesn't move.

I look down at my math book, look up and it's five past two. Mr. Daniels, my math teacher explains an entire problem, how to break it down and how to work it out, and when I look at the clock, it still says five past two.

Why is the hand not moving? Why is time standing still?

I tap my pencil on my book, and look out the window. The rays of the sun are reaching my desk, and the chatter of other students melts into white noise. I really can't wait until I see Trent today.

All weekend all I could think about was Trent. What he was doing, if he was thinking about me and mostly, I was hoping. Praying he didn't think I was ugly and stupid, because of the way I left him.

Finally I hear the last bell for the day, and I walk as fast as I can to the bus. Sitting at the front, I try and blend in, so no one notices me. No one ever does, but there have been times when the pretty girls, who dress nicely, look at me and snicker among themselves.

The bus fills at a steady pace, and it feels like I've been sitting here for three hours just waiting for the bus driver to leave. Of course, it's only been a few minutes.

As the bus pulls out onto the road, something funny happens to me. I get butterflies flapping their wings crazily in my tummy. And I can feel a smile bloom and widen as the bus halts at every stop, bringing me closer to mine.

My tummy back flips, knowing in a few minutes I'll see Trent. I stand and wait by the door as the bus begins to slow, cruising into the stop.

As the bus rolls to a stop, I see Trent standing under the shelter. He has his school bag on his shoulder, and his arms crossed in front of his chest. His light brown hair is flapping against the wind and he looks like he's waiting for me. Well, I *hope* he's waiting for me.

"Hi," he says when he sees me get off the bus. "How was school?"

"It was kind of boring today, I really wasn't paying attention to anything." I look down and smile as we begin to walk toward my house.

"Why is that?" Trent teases as he nudges me with his shoulder.

"I just had a really good time at the movies, and I was kind of hoping you did, too."

"I did, I had a great time." I smile. "Here, let me." Trent takes my backpack and continues walking. "There's something I'm concerned about though." *Oh crap.* "What is it with you and your dad? The moment you saw him, all the color drained from your face and I knew something wasn't right."

I shrug my shoulders and avoid his intense stare. "Nothing really."

Trent stops walking and grabs me by my upper arm. "Does he touch you?" he asks, his tone angry and his eyes wild with fury. "Does he fucking touch you?" His voice heats with pure rage.

"No," I answer, though it's not entirely the truth. But I know what Trent is asking, and Dad has never touched me sexually.

"Don't fucking lie to me, Lily. If he's tried to…"

"No, he hasn't," I interrupt before he can say those disgusting words. "It's not like that," I add, stopping any thoughts of Dad doing *that* to me.

"Then what is it? Tell me so I can understand what it is you're going through."

"You can't understand, no one can. It's just how things are."

"I can help you, Lily. If it's bad, I can help."

"You can help me? No one can help me. Seriously, it's okay. Don't worry about it." I shake my head and continue to walk toward my house.

"Look," Trent exhales and jogs to catch up to me. "Here, take this." He thrusts a phone into my hand. "My number is programmed into it, and if you ever need me, just call."

I stop walking and look at the tiny phone in my hand. "I wouldn't even know how to begin to use this," I say looking at it, and then back at Trent. "Thank you for the gesture." I hand the phone back.

"No way am I taking it back. Here's the charger and the phone number is written on the back of it." I turn it over to see a phone number scribbled on the back. "It's easy to use, here." He takes it, and shows me what I need to do to call him. "I got that number for you, so only you and I have it. No one else. And don't give it to anyone either."

"Okay," I say as I slide the phone into my pocket. Trent puts the charger in my bag.

"Whenever you need me, you just call me. You probably don't trust me enough to tell me what it is that goes on in your home, but one day, and soon, I hope you'll tell me."

I keep my eyes down and keep walking. "Thank you. If I need you, I'll call."

"Great. Now Wednesday nights I train for the hockey team, and I'd really like you to come and watch."

"You would?"

"Yeah, well yeah…"

I smile as we round the corner to my street. "I'll see if I can, but I can't make any promises."

"That's cool." Trent goes quiet and he walks me to the front of my house. Dad's car isn't here, so I know I'm safe for a while. "Um, this is my house."

"Ahhh, um… Um, can I kiss you, Lily?" Trent asks shyly.

I feel my face turn bright red, heat immediately going to my cheeks. No one has ever kissed me before. Never. I've never even had a kiss from Mom or Dad. I don't have grandparents or aunties or uncles. So I've never experienced anything like a kiss. And now, a boy wants to kiss me.

"Um," I say, not really sure I want him to kiss me.

"Just on the cheek, nowhere else."

I count to ten in my head, just letting the nervousness settle before I nod my head. On the cheek is okay, but I'm nowhere near ready to have a kiss on the lips. That's too much. And I don't want him to think I'm like some of those girls at school. I hear what they're up to, and how many boys they do things with. I'm not like them, I'm different.

Trent steps closer, and instinctually I take a counter step back.

"I won't hurt you, Lily," he says as his right hand rubs up and down my left arm.

"It's okay." I sort of tell myself.

Trent steps closer, and this time I stay still, not moving. I close my eyes and just wait until I can feel his mouth on my cheek. His touch is incredibly soft, a tiny warm breath spreads against my flushed skin. His lips stay connected to my blazing cheek for no longer than it takes the human heart to beat.

"Thank you," he mumbles near my ear. I let out a sigh, and take a deep breath in. "It wasn't *that* bad, was it?" he asks and chuckles.

"No, it was nice."

He holds my hand for a minute before handing over my school bag. "I'll see you tomorrow, after school?" he asks.

"Of course," I say as I take a step closer to my house. Trent stays on the sidewalk and watches me as I go to the door.

"See you tomorrow, beautiful Lily," he calls after me.

I smile and go inside to start on my homework, but what I'll really be doing is thinking about that amazing kiss and hoping next time, I may be strong enough to kiss Trent on the lips.

Lying on my bed, I let my eyes drift shut. A stark, cold silence has fallen over every inch of the house. I turn on my bed and look through the worn curtains. The dark outside is broken by the soft beams of the shimmering moon.

With my hands tucked under my head, and my knees brought up to my abdomen I simply watch the night. My eyes get heavier, and my mind floats towards happiness. To a place where I'm pretty, I'm smart and I can move through every day without suffocation and dread.

I'm woken by the slam of the front door and Dad yelling in a slur, "You better be in your room you fucking ugly, dumb bitch."

"Whoooo's herrrreee?" I hear a high-pitched woman's voice. Her speech is as garbled as Dad's and I know they're both drunk.

Dad's never brought anyone else home, and just the mere thought of someone other than Dad here terrifies me.

"No one. A stupid, ugly loser who stays with me. Wish she'd fuck off."

The woman giggles. "Come on, Stanley. Don't worry about her, let's go to your roooom," she drunkenly says.

"Where are you, bitch?" Dad yells louder.

I bring the blanket up and hide beneath it. I know it's stupid, it's not going to save me, but I can't make a run for the closet in the hallway, he'll see me. Maybe if I remain quiet, if I don't say anything, he'll just forget about me.

"Where the fuck are you?" he shouts even louder.

"I'm here," I say in the quietest voice I can. Hoping he hears me and that's enough to leave me alone.

My heart is beating with such fury I can hear it in my ears. My body begins to shake and I feel a heavy lump of terror sitting in the pit of my stomach. *Please Dad, just leave me alone.* But I know tonight is different.

"Get out here!"

Silently, I stand from my bed. My legs are wobbly and now the cold inside my room is also inside me. Slowly I tiptoe out to where Dad and his companion are. Dad's sitting in his chair and the woman is on her knees in front of him.

Dad turns to look at me. His face is demonic, his eyes are full of wrath.

"See this?" he says as he laces his fingers through the brunette woman's hair. "This is the only thing you'll ever be good for. Better start doing it soon and making some money, because you're one dumb and ugly bitch." He bucks his hips up, and I instantly feel the bile rise to the back of my throat.

Turning, I go back to my room because I don't want to see him doing that to the woman.

As I slide under the covers, I hear his heavy footsteps coming toward my room. "Get up!" he yells as he bolts into my room.

I bring the blanket over my head, and pray. Pray to God to finally end me right now and stop me breathing. I can't take it anymore. This can't be what I was born for. This isn't what life is supposed to be. Is it?

"You fucking little slut, you'll come and watch so you know what you have to do." The blanket gets ripped away from my head and Dad grabs onto my hair, dragging me out of bed. "It should've been you who died. It's all your fucking fault," he screams, as he keeps dragging me toward the family room.

"You're hurting me, please stop," I cry as I clutch onto his hand, trying to use my feet to push along so the pain isn't as intense.

"You stupid bitch. You don't deserve to fucking live. They do, but not you." He slams me against the wall.

"Dad, please stop," I beg. The way Dad thumped me against the wall made my head hit it hard.

"Look at what you did." He points at the wall and I turn to see a small hole.

"I'm sorry, I'm so sorry," I plead, hoping he's not going to keep hitting me.

"You will be." His belt is already unbuckled, and he rips it out of the loops holding it in place on his pants.

I cower and cover my face in defense. The first strike is excruciatingly painful. He hits with so much force I can feel the skin on my arms burning. The second strike is worse than the first. He hits on the same spot and I try to curl myself further into a small ball. The third, and fourth strikes are fueled by nothing more than utter hate.

"Please," I cry through the heavy tears. I'm gulping for breath and wish for this to be over. To finally just end.

After what feels like an eternity, the hitting finally ends. Carefully I lower my arms from around my head and try to peep out to see where Dad is and what he's doing.

The woman with him is now standing beside him, her eyebrows knit together as she stares at me. Dad's looking down at me, his top lip curled into a snarl.

"She didn't do nothin'," says the woman.

"Shut up," Dad replies, while still looking at me.

He wipes the back of his hand over his forehead, his evil eyes still glued to me. Dad spits on the floor and he straightens his back. "You've made a fucking mess. You're bleeding," he says as flicks his chin at me.

Through the thick tears I try and focus on the welts on my arms and legs. Some are cut and are bleeding, a few are just a trickle, but a few have quite a bit of blood seeping out of them.

"I'm so-sorry," I stutter through the heavy breathing.

"You will be." He takes a step toward me, rears his hand back making a fist.

It seems like an eternity. My face feels on fire as the punches continue. *Please God, take my life.*

Suddenly, I feel nothing. No pain, no pressure and no sadness. Just a beautiful veil of black that falls over me. I begin to float and find sanctuary in the peace I've finally been blessed with.

Is this how death feels? I like it here.

CHAPTER 5

WHEN I TRY AND OPEN my eyes, they hurt. I can barely open them without pressure pounding away in my head. I blink a few times, trying to focus and to see where I am.

I'm lying in my family room, exactly where I was when Dad started laying into me.

There's a heavy buzzing in my ears, a massive thump squeezing the inside of my head. Blinking, I manage to focus on the hole in the wall and slowly drag my eyes from it.

From somewhere close to me, I can hear a predatory grunting. The sound of constant and fevered desperation. There's also a female who's moaning in rhythm to the grunting.

"You feel so good, Stanley," she says, in drawn out gasps.

Trying to be as quiet as I can, I move to my hands and knees, attempting to find my balance. The thrusting continues, and I can hear the vulgar sound of my father having sex with the woman he brought home.

Shaking and unsteady I manage to drag my body toward my room. The sounds coming from the family room are not letting up as they continue their sex-fest.

"You really need to use that pussy of yours, make yourself some money, you ugly piece of shit," Dad pants as he keeps propelling his cock into the woman.

"Leave her alone," says the woman. "Just keep your eyes focused on me." I turn to look at them as I drag my broken and bruised body through the opening to my bedroom. The woman looks at me, and in that one moment, that one single atom in time she sees me.

Her eyes connect with mine, and she notices me. Her eyebrows slightly draw together and she winks at me. She turns her head, brings her arm up to put her hand on the side of Dad's face, essentially blocking his view of me.

"Don't look at her, she's a retard. She deserves everything she gets," he says before smashing his mouth down on hers.

I keep crawling, and hide in the closet. The journey to get there has been nothing short of excruciatingly painful, each movement filled with pain that shoots straight through to my bones. Every breath causes a severe ache so deep, I don't think I'll ever be able to breathe normally again.

Remembering the phone Trent gave me, I feel for it inside my jacket where I hid it and finally grab it. My hands are shaking so badly I can't manage to turn it on. I'm not even sure I'll be able to dial it, even if I can power it up.

I keep blinking, trying to calm my shaking down so my bloodied hands will work. My heart's pounding starts to ease and my pulse slows until my body is back to almost normal.

Turning the phone on, I look down at the backlight and keep my eyes focused on the small cell. The rusty smell of blood fills my nose, and I wipe at it, trying to get that smell away. The rich crimson clings to me, my hands are covered and small droplets are falling to my jeans.

Struggling to remember what Trent showed me, I finally dial his number.

"Lily," he answers virtually right away.

"I need help," I say in a thick, gravelly voice.

"Where are you?" I hear a beep and a car engine starting.

"I'm in my closet. I don't feel so good. I think I'm going to be sick." My stomach contracts. The tightening is twisting in my tummy and vomit rises rapidly to the back of my throat. It sits like an orange lodged in my neck, not moving in any direction.

"Are you sick?" he asks in a gentler voice.

"Dad, he…" I can feel the vomit moving slowly. It wants to come up but it's stalled, not ready to be expelled yet. "He…he… hit." And the bile pushes through, and soils my clothes. "Sorry, I'm so sorry," I begin to cry. I don't want Trent mad with me, too.

"Lily!" he screams into the phone as my stomach continues to churn and eject the very little thing in there. "Hold on, Lily. I'll be there in a few minutes."

The soft cloak of black is returning. Not as fast as it was before, but just like a curtain closing on the final act at the theatre, it begins to fall. "I don't feel…" And once again, the peaceful black sings to me. A love song filled with rare beauty, of peace, and something I've never experienced before. Love.

"Lily. Lily. Where are you?" It's not Dad's voice, it sounds sweeter. Someone who's calling me not to hurt me, but to help me. "LILY!" Such a desperate plea to find me.

"Here," I try to yell. But my voice is tiny, the sound barely whispering past my lips.

The darkness is desperate to drag me under again. It's clawing its way through my veins, desperate to strangle whatever fight I have in me.

But I'm only seventeen, and I don't want to live in fear anymore. I may not deserve something better, I may never find it, but I can't keep living blanketed under hate.

"Here," I yell, finding a strength in me I don't think I've ever had. "I'm here, Trent."

"Sweetheart, what the hell happened?" Trent says as he falls to the floor and caresses my face. He strokes my hair and moves it off my face.

"D-d-dad," I manage to whimper. "He, he, h-hit me," I say through my strained breath.

"Come on, you're coming with me. Where's your suitcase, so I can pack your clothes?" He stands from where he was kneeling beside me and looks around my room. "Jesus, Lily how the hell do you live like this?"

I'm completely horrified and embarrassed about where I live. My bare room is a physical representation of my life. So empty and devoid of anything that could make me human, anything allowing me to identify with people. Anything that could make me a person and let me find my own personality.

"I don't have much," I say through the tears threatening to break through.

"You don't need anything, just take my hand and come with me," he says, as he turns and offers me his hand.

This is my choice, possibly my last chance to get out of here alive and finally be able to breathe freely, without fear. I hesitantly lift my hand and slowly place it into Trent's warm palm. He leans down, winds his arm around my waist and lifts me.

"Ahhh," I cry in pain.

"Where does it hurt?" He eases me up and stands beside me, supporting my body weight.

"My legs and arms hurt." I look at Trent and his eyebrows are knit together as he studies my features. His brown eyes dart all over my face, taking in everything Dad's done. "Lily," he says, then sighs in a way I think he's disgusted with me.

"I'm sorry." I try and fix my hair so he can't see any part of my face, but I wince in pain as I lift my arm to move my hair.

"Don't," he says, as he walks us out of my room.

I look in the family room, Dad and the woman aren't here, but the smell of sex is thick in the air. My eyes go directly to the hole in the wall, and instantly vomit rises and threatens to erupt. "Please, get me out of here."

Trent looks at me and nods his head. No more words need to be said. He's seen the worst of me, the darkest shadow I live under and the extremes of my daily nightmare.

He takes most of my weight as he leads me outside. The night is dark and silent. The cold touches me right down to my bones, horror filling every part of my mind. Or maybe it's not horror that's consuming me. Maybe it's something else.

The taste of freedom.

I'm finally going to leave the house I've been chained to all my life. My one safety-net had never really been safe. Not once have I ever felt anything but hate and resentment toward me while living here. Never have I been able to breathe in clean air and feel it travel through me, caress and embrace me. I've never felt welcome or had a sense of belonging.

"Watch your head, Lily," Trent says as he helps me into his car.

I sit back in the passenger seat and look at the house I've lived in all my life. No sign of life comes from it. The little grass on the front lawn is brown and dead. The faded blue weatherboard on the house looks like it's about to fall down. If you drove past my house, you'd swear squatters had taken up residence, not a family.

Trent starts the car and backs out of the driveway. As he slowly leaves, a part of me finally manages to breathe.

"Are you okay?" Trent asks.

I simply nod and smile at him, before turning my head and watch the house that sucked my soul, slowly disappear from my view.

Trent rests his hand on my thigh and squeezes softly bringing my attention back to him. "It'll be alright, Lily, I'll look after you."

A lump of uncertainty forms and sits in my throat, a cloud of questions hangs over my head. But I also feel the weight of the world gradually lifting off my shoulders as Trent gets further away from my father's house.

The ride to Trent's house is silent. Other than the occasional tightening of his hand on my thigh, nothing much is said. I simply sit, stunned I'll never go back there again, but relieved maybe I'll find safety.

Fifteen minutes after leaving, Trent pulls onto a street lined with lush, green lawns. The moonlight only hints at the true intensity of the colors, and I can't wait to see it tomorrow when the sun rises. The houses are fairly close together, but all well cared for. A few proudly fly the American flag from their porches.

It's peaceful here, serene. I already love it.

"We're here," Trent says as he pulls into the driveway of a beautiful white home, meticulously cared for. "Come on. Mom and Dad are waiting." He gets out and rounds the car, opening my door and helping me out.

Winding my arm around his neck, I let Trent lead me inside.

My legs are aching, and my entire body protests in pain. My head thumps with each step I take, and all I want to do is lie down and let today's events disappear.

"Mom, Dad," Trent calls.

I hear footsteps upstairs, and a lady wearing a dressing gown comes down the wooden stairs, followed closely by an older version of Trent. The man has thick salt-and-pepper hair, and a stern scowl on his face.

"Welcome, Lily," his mom says as she comes to hug me.

I don't even know what to call her. "Thank you, ma'am," I say, but flinch from the pain in my leg.

"You can call me, Mrs. Hackly," she says and puts an arm around my shoulder. "Come on, dear, let's get you cleaned up." She begins to lead me toward the back of their house, and suddenly I'm adrift. Have I woken in an alternate universe? One with people who don't tell me how ugly and stupid I am?

I look behind me, trying to search out Trent. "Mom, will look after you," he says, as she continues to lead me down the hallway.

"Why did you bring her here?" I hear Trent's dad ask.

"I couldn't leave her there. Can't you see that?" Trent whispers, though I can still hear.

"Now, why don't you tell me about yourself, Lily? Do you have family?" Mrs. Hackly asks. I'm sure it's to stop me trying to listen to Trent and his dad's conversation.

"No, ma'am. It's just me and my dad. But after tonight, I'm not sure I can go back there."

She leads me into the bathroom, and sits me down on the closed toilet lid. "Let's have a look." She stands back and looks at me, bringing her hand up to glide over her face. Her long, brown hair is up in a perfect ponytail, and it strikes me as odd that so late in the night, her hair is flawless. "I think I have something here to help you with your wounds, but you'll need to take your clothes off, okay?" she asks as she takes a cautious step toward me.

"Um." I don't know what to say. She's offering to help me, something no one's ever done before. "Okay."

She takes another step closer to me, and I notice her face has make-up on it. Everything I've heard about and seen on girls in school. Eyeliner, eyeshadow, foundation and even a light lipstick. I can't help but stare at her and wonder why she'd be almost perfect and ready to go out as if she's on call to go somewhere.

Mrs. Hackly helps me up, and assists me in stripping my worn clothes off. "I have some clothes here that will fit you. Once I dress these wounds, I'll get them for you." She smiles at me, and it's so soft and caring. "It's alright, Lily, I won't hurt you," she says to me.

For a fleeting second, the fact that she didn't say '*we* won't hurt you' plays on my mind. My suspicious and overly wary mind is telling me something's not right. Why would she not say 'we' but only say 'I'?

As I stand, stripped of my clothes, Mrs. Hackly brings out a large plastic container taking up the entire bottom of the vanity unit in the bathroom. She props it up near the sink and opens the lid. Peering over I see it's sectioned out with every type of bandage, ointment, and medical aid that could fit inside it.

She takes out an ointment and some bandages and places them on the small counter space available. She turns to look at me, her eyes regarding me, taking every part of me in. "The gash above your eye looks the worst, but the cuts on your arm and your leg aren't too far behind that one. I can fix them here, no need to go to the hospital. They tend to ask all sorts of questions, and you don't want them knowing what happened, do you?" she asks with so much sympathy in her tone.

I shake my head, wrap my arms over my chest and look down. I don't want them asking questions, because they'll only think I'm stupid for staying there and not leaving. But really, where was I supposed to go? I have no one. Not a living soul who would take me and care for me…until now.

Mrs. Hackly goes about cleaning and dressing my wounds. With nothing more than her soft humming and kind words, she cares for me. When she finishes tending to my wounds she stands back and smiles, pleased with herself. "Now, I have a t-shirt and sweatpants you can wear. I'll talk to Mr. Hackly and see what we can do about getting you some new clothes tomorrow."

"I have some second-hand clothes I got from the charity shop back at…" I pause and point toward the door. *Back where? Home? Hell? What do I call it?*

"That's alright, dear. We'll see what we can do, okay?" She smiles sweetly to me.

I nod my head and look down at the tiled floor again. The cold of the tiles is snaking its way through my body. An icy chill grips every part of me and I shiver. I feel goosebumps quickly forming on my skin.

Mrs. Hackly sees me shiver and runs her hands up and down my arms. "I'll get you those clothes. I won't be long." And with that she leaves and softly closes the door behind her.

I'm left naked in the bathroom waiting for her to return. I look around the pristine room and notice how everything sparkles because it's so incredibly clean. There are three hand towels and they're in alignment, one not hanging lower than the other two. The labels of the shampoo and conditioner in the shower all face outwards. Everything is beyond picture-perfect.

The door opens and Mrs. Hackly comes back into the room carrying a gray, long-sleeved t-shirt and black sweatpants. "Here you go, Lily. Why don't get you changed and come out. I'll be waiting outside the door."

"Thank you," I respond immediately. The moment the door closes, I get dressed.

When I get to the door and open it, Mrs. Hackly is standing outside, eagerly waiting. "You already look better. Come, I'll make you something to drink and eat."

"As in real food?" I ask, not really thinking before the words tumble out.

"Of course. We have left over pot roast and how about a glass of warm milk?"

"Fresh milk?" I sound like I'm salivating, and truthfully, I am.

She walks us into the kitchen where Trent and Mr. Hackly are standing at the counter, talking. The moment we enter, their conversation ceases and Trent comes over to stand beside me. "Are you okay?"

"Yes, thank you," I reply and look away from the intense stare of Mr. Hackly.

"Here, sit down, Lily. Mom, get her a drink," Trent says as he pulls a chair out for me.

"Yes, son," she says, as she gets the milk out of the fridge and proceeds to pour some into a mug and heats it in the microwave.

I sit in the seat Trent has pulled out for me, and he sits beside me. But the room is eerily quiet, like we're all waiting for something to happen. My heart pounds in my chest and I can feel three sets of eyes on me, but one is the hardest, and most intense.

"Tell me about yourself, Lily," Mr. Hackly's harsh tone rips across my skin like a hot knife cutting through butter.

"Um, I'm Lily and um, I'm seventeen. I um..." Nerves overtake me and I burst into tears.

"Dad," Trent says as he rubs a hand along my back. "We talked about this, just leave her alone for now."

I look up at the fire burning in Mr. Hackly's eyes. "We did talk about it. And Trent has already told us what he knows about your father and your..." he pauses, but tilts his head to indicate the bruising and bandage on my face. "But, if you're going to be living here, then I'll need to know what it is you've had to deal with," he says. "Not tonight, because I can see how upset you are, but by the weekend."

Mrs. Hackly returns with a cup of warm milk for me, and a bowl of pot roast, gravy, and vegetables. The food smells fantastic and so appetizing. I can't even remember the last time I had anything homemade.

She stands on the other side of the table, and waits. For what, I'm not sure. Maybe to see if I like the food, maybe to see if I need anything. I've never experienced anything like this before.

"You can sleep in the guest room downstairs, next to the bathroom. Lina, sit," Mr. Hackly says.

"Thank you, sir," I say, offering the only thing I have, a kind word to show my appreciation.

Mr. Hackly and Trent talk quietly between them. Mrs. Hackly silently listens and I eat the most delicious thing I've ever tasted. The two men talk about me, making plans for me and even discuss taking me to the mall to buy me new clothes.

In this moment a fleeting thought passes by me. I've seen healthy family dynamics at school and on the street with loving families, but I've never really understood them. I've always been a spectator with my nose pressed against the glass, desperately attempting to climb through. Now though, I think it may be my turn for a family.

CHAPTER 6

I'VE BEEN LIVING WITH TRENT and his parents for ten days now and I've even been back to school for a few days. I went back when I could cover the bruises and I wore large sunglasses I borrowed from Trent's mom. No one noticed; no one asked. I'm still trying to understand exactly where I fit in. It took two days before Mr. Hackly sat me down and asked me about my home life with Dad. He simply sat and listened and nodded his head. Not once did he meet my eyes, and not once did he say anything negative. As a matter of fact, once I finished telling him about my life, his lips drew up in the smallest of smiles and he thanked me for trusting him enough to tell him.

But it's not really trust. I figured I owed him an explanation, seeing as he was kind enough to open his home to me and allowed me to stay.

I've also noticed how Trent's mom doesn't really say much. She sits at the dinner table after Mr. Hackly and Trent have been seated, she doesn't start her dinner until Mr. Hackly picks his fork up. She's always the last one to go to bed, and the first one up every morning. I've had ten days of full breakfasts and hot dinners.

In the mornings, Mr. Hackly comes into the kitchen dressed in his suit, takes the coffee cup Mrs. Hackly holds out for him, sits at the head of the table, and eats his breakfast. When he's through, he gets up and leaves. Trent and I walk to the bus stop and get on our busses for school.

But for some reason, although the Hackly family looks normal, there's still something just not quite right. The relationship between Mr. Hackly, Trent, and his mom seems a bit off.

Trent and I have grown closer, which is surprising because I never thought I'd open up to anyone. Trent often tells me how beautiful I am. When Mr. Hackly is in the room with us, I often catch him looking at me. His stare is obvious, and he makes no attempt to look away from me. It shouldn't make me feel uncomfortable, because he's never said or done anything inappropriate. But for some reason, I just feel yucky when I notice him staring.

"We're coming up to the end of the school year. How do you feel, Miss Valedictorian? I'm really proud of you, Lily. Even Dad said how impressed he is with your 3.9 GPA, especially with everything that's happened."

I walk along, hand in hand with Trent and just take in the rays of the glorious sun. Summer will be here before I know it, and it means the end of school. "Yeah, I'm happy with it. Doesn't mean much though, with me not being able to go to college."

"If you had the chance to go, and do anything you want, what would you do?" Trent asks as he swings our joined hands and brings them up to kiss my knuckles.

I look at him and smile, happy in this moment. "I'd like to teach English a the high school level. But that's just wishful thinking. I know we only have a few weeks left of school and I'll need to find a job. I can't expect your mom and dad to support me."

"What about a scholarship?" Principal Murphy told me I should get someone interested in giving me a scholarship, but we're nearing the end of school and I've heard nothing – which means no one noticed me.

It's not a bad thing, not being noticed. Sometimes it's better that way. It's hard to explain to people why I don't talk much, or why I keep my eyes on the ground. I'm getting better, but I'm not sure I'll ever really be normal.

I shake my head at Trent, silently telling him there have been no offers.

"I find that really hard to believe. I got offered a partial scholarship and my GPA was 3.5, so I don't know why you weren't offered at least a partial one."

"I don't know what to tell you." I shrug my shoulders and lower my eyes as we keep walking toward the bus stop.

We reach it with a few minutes to spare, and Trent hugs me. It's the first time he's been so publicly affectionate with me, and I find it strange. I wiggle around in his embrace, feeling self-conscious. Maybe people are staring and thinking, 'What's that cute guy doing with such an ugly, stupid girl?'

"Hey, where did you go?" Trent asks as he smooths my hair down with his big hand. "I lost you and I don't want that to happen." He leans in and kisses my nose.

"I was just thinking." I look down at the new sport shoes Mrs. Hackly bought for me, and back up into Trent's eyes.

Trent takes a deep breath in, looks to his left and sees the bus coming. "Your bus is here. I'll see you this afternoon. I'll be waiting right here," he says, as he kisses my cheek and lets go of my hand.

I get on the bus and sit at the front at one of the window seats. As the bus pulls away, I look back to Trent who raises his hand and waves to me.

"Lily Anderson to the principal's office. Lily Anderson to the principal's office," comes over the loudspeaker while I'm in my English class.

Mrs. Richards looks up from the desk and says, "Lily, you can pack your desk and go."

Silently, I pack my bag and leave the classroom, making my way to the office.

When I get there, I sit and wait for the office staff to tell Mr. Murphy I'm here. I'm not sure why I'm being summoned. I haven't done anything wrong.

"Lily," Mr. Murphy says as he comes out of his office and looms over me. "Come into my office." He leads me in and I sit down, waiting for him to tell me whatever it is he has to say. "You're almost finished with high school. What are your plans for the summer?"

"I need to get a job, but I'm not qualified for anything. So I'll see if I can get a job at the supermarket."

"That's admirable, to save some money before you head to college?"

He links his fingers together, like he's praying and leans his arms on the chipped and old desk.

"I'm not going to college," I say as I purse my lips together, not really wanting to say why.

"Why? A mind like yours shouldn't be wasted in a supermarket. Don't get me wrong, I'm impressed you want to get a job instead of hanging with your friends at the beach the entire summer, but you can't just get a job and stay there. A supermarket is not for you. You need to be in college, studying something that will make a difference."

I look down at my shoes. I can't really tell him why I can't go. He'll think I'm stupid.

"Lily?" he questions. When I look up, his bushy gray eyebrows are drawn in tight, and he's looking at me with a lot of concern. "Why can't you go? Is it money?"

I nod my head, and look down again.

"What about the scholarships that have been offered to you? Berkley, Brown, University of Pennsylvania, even Princeton. They all want you, full scholarships."

I look up again, and Mr. Murphy is smiling at me, clearly telling me this is not some kind of joke. "No, Sir. No one has approached me. I've had no interviews, no letters, nothing. You must have me mistaken for someone else." *I'm stupid. It can't be me.*

"I see," he says leaning back in his chair and moving his hands so they're on his lap. "Well then, we have a problem." He moves again, opens his drawer to the right and takes out a stack of papers. "You see, Lily, when the first one contacted me and wanted to know why you hadn't replied I thought maybe one of the offers didn't make it to you. Then two days later, another university called to say you hadn't replied. Then a third, and a fourth."

What does that even mean? Some of the top universities of America want me? Is that even right? I look over my shoulder outside the door, then turn to look over my other shoulder. I just want to make sure no one is going to jump out from behind a potted plant and yell "Gotcha!" putting the joke on me.

"I thought it was really odd that all these colleges want you, and you had not even been courteous enough to reply. But the more they called me, the more I thought, this is not like you." I look at Mr. Murphy, not sure what to say. "You never received any offers, did you, Lily?"

Damn, damn, damn. "No, Sir," I finally say after a few seconds of quiet. My Dad must have thrown them away.

"I didn't think so. I've spoken to every one of them and convinced them to give you until the end of the week to make a decision."

"That's tomorrow," I say, as I look up into the kind and gentle eyes of Mr. Murphy.

"Yes, it is. But these four universities are offering you full scholarships." He taps on the small pile. "These here are offering you partial scholarships." He taps on a second, bigger pile. "In this pile, there's one of the top universities in America." He indicates the ones offering full scholarships. "And in this pile, there's a university that's furthest away from here, in case distance away is a factor." His tone drops, and in that one sentence, I know Mr. Murphy knows.

He may not understand everything, but he's most likely picked up on something.

"Thank you, Sir," I say as I feel my eyes begin to water.

"You should have come to me, Lily. Whatever is happening at home, whatever it is, I could've helped."

"Yes, Sir," I say, simply to placate him so he doesn't feel any responsibility for how my dad has treated me.

But in truth, how could anyone have helped me with the hell-hole that was my home?

"Take these and look at them. Come into my office first thing in the morning, and we'll make the phone call together," he says as he stands, offering me the pile of full scholarships. I eye the other pile, but I know without a full scholarship I won't be able to go to university.

I tuck them into the new bag Mrs. Hackly bought me, and I walk out of Mr. Murphy's office.

For the first time in as long as I can remember, I can breathe. I can take a step toward tomorrow and know tonight won't be filled with words of hate.

"Hey, sweetheart. How was your day?" Trent greets me at the bus stop.

"Good. Actually, really good," I enthusiastically answer.

Trent wraps his arms around me and gives me a kiss on my cheek. "Really good, huh? Tell me about it." We start walking toward his home.

"I got offered full scholarships to four universities. Actually, I got offered more, but these four are *full* scholarships."

"What? That's fantastic. Wait…" he stops talking, going perfectly quiet as we keep walking home. "You're not leaving me, Lily," his tone changes and he sounds angry. "Unless one of those universities is the same as the one I'm going to, you're not allowed to go." He sounds angry with me.

"Not allowed to go? What do you mean?" I ask.

Trent lets go of my hand and walks away from me. He stops a few feet away, and puts his hands on his hips. *He's really angry with me.* "You're not going if I'm not with you, end of fucking story, Lily."

"What?" I still don't know what I've done wrong.

"I'm not going to have you running around sucking another guy's cock when you should be with me."

Wait…what did he say? "I've never done *that*," I say as I take a step closer to him. He counters with one step back and my eyes go to his hands. I see them closed into fists and my heart beats faster.

I take a cautious step back, completely aware of how Trent's body is reacting. This is how Dad would get before the insults would start, sometimes followed by his fists.

"Just don't think you're ever going to leave me," he says, his tone somewhat calmer. "I'll never let you go, Lily." He relaxes his hands and he takes a step toward me.

I take another step back, frightened he may hurt me.

"Don't move away from me. I promise, I won't hurt you. I like you too much to hurt you," he whispers as he takes another step toward me, closing the gap. "I'm sorry if I scared you, it's just that I need you close to me, do you understand? I need to keep you safe, so I know no one can hurt you."

When we get home, Mrs. Hackly is folding the washing. "Hello. Need some help?" I ask as she's folding someone's dark shorts.

"No, dear. How about I make you kids something to eat? You must be hungry?" She finishes folding the shorts, puts them in a pile, and goes into the kitchen before Trent or I can say anything to her.

"Hey. Let's go to my room and have a look at which university you're going to go to."

"Your mom is getting us food ready."

"Don't worry about that, we'll eat at dinner, let's go." He starts tugging me up the stairs.

"Let me tell your mom, so she doesn't waste her time."

"Don't worry about her, she'll figure it out."

"Trent, please," I beg, looking up at him.

He takes a deep breath, rolls his eyes and gives me a half nod. "Hurry up," he instructs, in a grumpy voice.

I run into the kitchen just to let Mrs. Hackly know Trent and I are upstairs in his room, looking over university applications. She slumps her shoulders slightly and nods, looking at me from what she was doing with a slight sad smile.

"Come on," Trent yells.

"Are you okay?" I ask as I take a step toward her.

"I'm fine, dear. Go ahead. I've got to finish folding the laundry and get started on dinner." She smiles again, but the warmth doesn't reach her eyes.

I simply nod and go back to Trent who's waiting for me on the staircase.

When we reach his room, he closes the door and sits on his bed. "Lily, I want to ask you something."

"What is it?" I sit on the floor near the bed and take the university offers out of my bag.

"Will you be my girlfriend?"

I stop doing what I'm doing and look up at him. "What do you mean?" I ask.

"I want you to be my girlfriend. As in going steady. Is that okay?"

I'm not really sure what to say. Having a boyfriend isn't something I ever thought would happen. I mean, I'm not pretty, and I don't have nice clothes or nice…anything. *Why would he want to be my boyfriend when there's a ton of pretty girls out there?* "Um," I say unsure on how to reply.

"What's wrong?" He slides off the bed and kneels beside me. His hands cup either side of my face and he looks me straight in the eyes. "You're so beautiful, Lily. You have to know that. And if you say yes to being my girlfriend, I promise I'll look after you and never let you go. You mean too much to me to let anything happen to you."

I can't hold the intense stare his eyes are giving me. "Okay," I finally answer. I'm not exactly sure what being someone's girlfriend means, but I'm positive Trent will tell me.

"Thank you," he says. Trent moves his head, and kisses me. First on my right cheek, then my left. But he doesn't move his face away from me, instead I watch his chest going up and down rapidly. His breath is shallow and I notice a bulge in his pants. "Thank you," he whispers. Trent leans in further and softly kisses my mouth. With a small movement he sweeps his tongue over my lips and gently probes to open my mouth.

His kiss becomes fevered. Trent moves his body closer to me. He slides his hands from my cheeks, down my arms and to my waist.

He lifts me to sit on him, and I can feel his erection pressing into me. "Trent," I sigh. *I can't give him sex. It's not what I want. It's way too early for that.* But Trent continues to kiss me, his body engulfing mine. "Trent, please," I beg as I push on his chest.

"You're my girlfriend now, Lily. This is what we do to show each other how much we love one another."

Love? Love? What? "Trent." I use more strength to push him away, but he's much stronger than me. "Please, I'm not ready."

"Come on. I love you. Don't you love me?" He keeps kissing me, his mouth moving away from my mouth down my neck. He's sucking, licking and nibbling on the exposed skin. His left hand leaves my hip, and he starts to fondle my breast.

"Trent, please," I say. But it comes out more like I'm begging him with a whine. "Don't."

He stops kissing me, and pushes me off him. I fall backward and look at Trent, who's already up and standing in front of me. "Fine," he says with a fierce fire. He takes a step back and sits on his bed. Picking up my university offers he looks at the names of the three and tosses two on the floor beside my feet. "This is the one I'm going to, so this is the one you're going to." He holds it up showing me the name of the university. "You better go help Mom with dinner, I heard her calling you." He stands, turns his back to me and goes to the far side of the room.

"Are you angry with me?" I ask as I stand to my feet and take a step toward him.

"No."

"Then why are you so short with me?"

"You're a prick tease, Lily. You flutter your eyes, and kiss me, begging me to take you. Then, when I want to fuck you, you back away."

What? "When did I do that?"

"Just now. But don't worry about it. Just go help Mom."

I stand by the door and continue looking at him. *Is that what I did? Did I indicate I wanted sex?* I lower my eyes to the floor, not really sure how I did that.

"Just go," he says again, but still hasn't turned to look at me.

"I don't want you mad with me. I'm sorry, I didn't know that's what I was doing," I beg, as I take a few steps toward where he's standing.

"Whatever," he spits, his back to me. "Just go."

"I can't go knowing you're angry with me." I reach him and put my hand on his back.

Trent turns to look at me and my eyes are immediately drawn to the bulge in his pants. "Yeah, this is what you did and now you just want to leave. I've now gotta go to the bathroom and jack off, all while you're down stairs probably laughing and thinking how funny it is to give me a hard-on and walk out."

"I'm not like that. I don't know why you're saying that." Tears begin to cloud my eyes, and I feel so terrible for him.

"You're my girlfriend, Lily. If you're not gonna let me fuck you, the least you can do is jack me off or suck me." I stand looking at Trent. "It's only a blowjob. All the girls are doing it. Hell, my friends are all having sex with their girlfriends. You owe me at least a blowjob."

I don't know what to do. I don't want to do that, but what if he gets madder with me for not doing it. I don't even know how to do what it is he wants. "I'm not sure," I finally say, as I look away from him.

"Just get on your knees and I'll do the rest." He stands in front of me, stroking himself through his jeans. His erection is really big and I don't want to do this, but he said all the girls are doing even more to their boyfriends.

I slowly sink to my knees, and Trent takes his penis out of his pants. I feel tears burn in my eyes. I don't want to do this, but if I don't, he'll be angry at me. I close my eyes tight.

"Open your mouth, sweetheart."

I open my mouth, and do what Trent wants me to do.

CHAPTER 7

IT'S BEEN THREE DAYS SINCE I did what Trent wanted, and he's had me do it again every day since. I don't like doing it, but I hate it when Trent gets angry at me. Last night he said I must be stupid if I don't do it, because all the smart girls are doing it.

"Good morning, dear," Mrs. Hackly says as I come into the kitchen.

"Good morning, ma'am. Can I help you with breakfast?" I always ask and she always says no. Sometimes I lay awake at night and still hear her doing things around the house. I often want to ask her if she needs help, but she always says no.

"No, breakfast is ready. Sit, and I'll bring it to you."

I have an overwhelming urge to hug her. She's the first woman who has ever acted like a mother figure to me. I wrap my arms around her and cuddle her. But Mrs. Hackly lets out a cry, like I've squeezed her too tight and she's in pain.

"I'm sorry," I say, immediately unwrapping my arms and stepping back to look at where I've hurt her.

"Oh no, it's not you, dear. Last night as I was putting Mr. Hackly's laundry away, I backed into the door handle and it hit me here on the ribs," she says as she quickly puts the plate of pancakes down on the table.

"Are you okay?" I ask, concerned I've hurt her further.

"Yes." She smiles at me, though her eyes say something else. Or maybe, they aren't saying anything. Maybe they're just devoid of any kind of emotion. Mrs. Hackly looks flustered and slightly awkward. "How about on the weekend you can help me cook for the barbeque?" She says, as she goes over to the sink to stack the dishwasher.

"I don't really know how to cook; but if you're willing to teach me, I'd love to learn."

"I'm more than happy to teach you." She looks over her shoulder at me and smiles again.

Trent comes into the kitchen, followed by Mr. Hackly. "Good morning," I say to both of them. Trent comes around and leans down to kiss me deeply. This is the first morning he's been so passionate with me in front of his parents. I pull away, not really wanting his parents to see.

Because if they see him kissing me like this, maybe they'll guess what else we've done.

"Babe," Trent says as he sits beside me and puts his hand on my thigh. "Hope you slept okay. I know I did," he says and winks at me. Trent looks over my shoulder to his dad, and I turn to see his dad smirking at him.

I feel so disgusting. Like a dirty, used girl. I can tell by his dad's reaction, Trent told him what I did. I'm so humiliated and embarrassed. Lowering my head, I look at my plate and wish the world could crack open and swallow me whole.

"Did Mom tell you, there's a family barbeque on Saturday?" Trent asks, as he squeezes my thigh. I nod my head, too afraid to say anything in case I crack and begin to cry. "You alright, babe?"

Silently, I nod again.

"You okay, Lily?" Mrs. Hackly asks.

"Leave her be," Mr. Hackly barks at her, and in my peripheral vision I see her take a step back and continue stacking the dishwasher.

"Here, babe. You have to eat. Get your strength up." Trent puts a pancake on my plate, but his tone was almost comical.

"Thank you," I respond, still too embarrassed by the entire situation.

"Trent told me you want to get a job," Mr. Hackly says. I look to him and he's happily eating his pancakes.

"Yes, Sir. I'd like a job until Trent and I go to college. Save some money so I'll have it in case I need anything."

"That's a mighty fine idea, Lily. I can set up an interview with the grocery store. I know the manager there, she's a nice woman," he says as he lifts his eyebrows at me.

"Thank you, I'd appreciate it."

"Good, consider it done." He keeps eating, and when he stands to leave, Mrs. Hackly quickly takes his plate.

"Have a good day," he announces to all of us as he leaves. "I won't be home for dinner."

I turn to look at Mrs. Hackly, and I notice her shoulders drop just marginally. "Okay," she says without questioning him.

Trent and I finish, and I go to brush my teeth. When I'm through, I meet Trent by the front door so we can walk to the bus stop together.

"Is there an occasion for the barbeque?" I ask Trent as he walks beside me, holding my hand.

"It's Uncle John's birthday. Every year we go to their place for lunch. Mom usually cooks a few dishes, and we just have a good day. He's got a pool so we spend the day in it and just chill."

"I don't know how to swim."

"You'll be helping the women in the kitchen."

"I will?"

"Yeah, that's what the women do, and then we all eat, and the women go in and clean the kitchen and get dessert ready."

"Oh," I say. It sounds so backward, like things were in the 1950s. *But what would I know? I've never been around functioning families before. Maybe this is normal.* "You once said your dad came from a big family. How big is it?"

"Dad has four brothers, and two sisters. But we only talk to Uncle John and Uncle Martin. Dad fought with everyone else, so we don't talk to them."

"And your mom?"

"She doesn't talk to any of her family, I don't know why."

"Does she have any friends?"

Trent laughs. A big belly laugh. "No way. She's got no time for friends."

We keep walking, hand in hand toward the bus stop. This morning's humiliation is really prominent in my mind. "Trent, can I ask you something?"

"Yeah."

"Why did you embarrass me this morning?"

"Embarrass you? How?"

Heat is rising through my body as I become mortified by Trent outing me like he did at breakfast. "You know, by saying what you said at breakfast?"

"My dad knows," he says casually.

"What?" I whisper. "Please don't say that. I'm so embarrassed."

"He asked me if I'd had sex with you, told me to wear a rubber so I don't get you pregnant. I told him you're too frigid for that. He said now you're my girlfriend and I should just take what's mine."

"What?" I mumble. Now I'm completely horrified.

"Well, you are my girlfriend now, and like I said, all the other girls are doing it. Some of them are even letting their boyfriends put their cocks in their asses. I haven't asked you to do that yet, and I think I've been fairly patient with you. But if you don't give it to me soon, I might just have to go to someone else to get it."

"But..." I don't say anything else, because I don't understand.

"You know I love you, Lily, but I really can't wait forever before you decide to give up your virginity." He stops walking and pulls me to a stop too. "You are a virgin, right?" he angrily asks.

"Yeah, I am."

"Good, because if you weren't, I'd have to kick you out and dump your ass." He leans in and kisses me on the cheek then starts walking again.

"Oh, um... okay."

The bus approaches just as we reach the bus stop. Trent gives me a kiss then whispers in my ear, "I can't wait until my cock is deep inside you."

I pull away and get on the bus, not really saying anything. Truthfully, I feel disgusted by the entire situation. If Trent goes to another girl to get what he needs, maybe he'll dump me. *And I'm not pretty enough, or smart enough to be able to cope on my own.* My dad told me I better learn how to suck a man's penis, because I'll never be good at anything else.

Maybe he was right.

My phone has been buzzing in my pocket all through English. But Mrs. Richards has a rule in her class, if you're on your phone, you lose it. Up until recently, I never had to worry about that. But since Trent gave me the phone, he's always sending me messages. And sometimes he gets angry if I don't answer them right away.

It has not stopped vibrating against my leg and I know it must be Trent. I don't want him angry with me, so I ask to go to the bathroom.

When I get out of the classroom, I look at the screen and see I have twenty missed calls from both Trent, and Trent's dad. When Trent moved me in, Mr. Hackly put his number in the phone and said I can call him if I need anything.

The phone starts ringing again and this time it's Mr. Hackly. "Hello," I answer it quietly.

"When I, or my son, call you, I expect you to answer it promptly. Understand?"

"Yes, sir, but I'm in class."

"I don't care. I got you an interview at the grocery store straight after school this afternoon. The manager's name is Stacey, and she'll be waiting for you at four. Do you need a lift getting there? I can come get you," he says into the phone.

The hairs on my arms stand and I involuntarily scrunch my nose. "I'm okay, thank you. There's a bus that will get me there."

"You know which store, right? I can come get you," he instantly says.

A shudder of ice rips up my spine. The sooner I can get some money together, the better. I'm not ungrateful, truly I'm not. I just think it would better if I found a studio apartment on my own. "Thank you, but I'm okay." I tuck some hair behind my ear as it limply falls over my face.

"Make sure you look presentable. She's a good friend of mine and I told her you're a good kid. Don't disappoint me, Lily."

"No, Sir. I won't."

He hangs up without saying another word and I walk back into my

English class.

At lunch, I sit at a table on my own, and I eat the sandwich Mrs. Hackly has prepared for me. As I'm looking over my math homework, Audrey, one of the popular girls, comes and stands in front of me. "Hey," she says to get my attention. I look up from my math homework and smile at her. "Are you going out with Trent Hackly?" she asks. There are four of them standing together in their designer clothes, with their perfect hair, flawless make-up and incredibly low vocabulary.

"Yeah," I say as my gaze flows among the four girls.

Trisha and Candy laugh, while Audrey quickly sends them a dangerous scowl. The fourth is holding in a laugh, though her face betrays her. "He's going out with *you?*" she asks condescendingly. She looks down her nose at me and sneers.

"Yeah," I say again, but my voice is so small.

"Must be good a lay," Audrey snorts to the other three girls as she turns her back and walks away.

What a nasty person. But what does she mean by that? I know I'm not pretty, and I don't look anything like those girls, but what does she mean?

I quietly sit and eat my lunch, but I'm distracted by Audrey and her words. Ordinarily, she's not a nice person. She's horrible, a bully. And one day it'll come back and bite her on the butt, but her words have cut straight through me.

All these years I've been invisible – a shadow, simply walking behind everyone else. No one knew me. And I liked it that way, because it meant no one got close to me. If I had no emotional connections to anyone, they couldn't ask me questions. They couldn't see who I was. I was just the girl everyone ignored.

But now I have someone's attention. And I don't want it. I don't want the looks, the laughs, the pointing, or the stares that come with hormonal teenage girls who are naturally nasty.

"Hi, I'm Lily Anderson and I'm here to see the store manager, Stacey," I say to one of the girls working the front counter at the supermarket.

The girl looks at me with a smile and says, "I'll call her down." Her name badge reads 'Shayne' and she seems really friendly. And beautiful. Her hair is long and a rich mahogany, and she has the biggest, brownest eyes I've ever seen.

"Thank you," I say as I step back and adjust my school bag on my shoulder.

Shayne calls Stacey then looks over at me. "You here for an interview?"

she asks.

"Yeah, I am."

She looks over her shoulder then whispers, "She likes hard-working people." Then she winks at me.

I smile at her, feeling comfortable already. Strange, because I don't feel comfortable around anyone. Except for Mrs. Hackly, I like her. Even Trent doesn't let me fully relax. Something about him niggles away at me.

"You must be Lily Anderson. Chris has told me a lot about you," says a striking blonde woman as she walks toward me and stands beside me.

"Pleased to meet you, ma'am." I hold my hand out to her, she takes it in hers and shakes.

"Come upstairs and we'll have a chat." She turns and quickly starts walking away. My eyes are instantly glued to her sexy, hour-glass figure. Her strides are filled with such confidence and strength. It makes me envious to see those qualities in a woman. "This way," she says, as she leads me up a narrow staircase.

At the top on the right, she opens a door and steps inside before closing it and sitting behind an ordinary looking white desk. I sneak a look around the room and see how everything is in its place. Nothing out of order. Her desk is immaculately clean, with papers stacked neatly, and all pens in a container pointing down.

"Tell me about yourself, Lily. Chris says you're living with them?" Her cheeks pink just slightly, and when she says the word *them*, it's almost like she's spitting the word out in disgust.

"I'm seventeen, and I'm about to graduate high school as the valedictorian, with a 3.9 GPA. I've been living with Mr. and Mrs. Hackly for almost three weeks."

"Mr. Hackly," she pauses and clears her throat, "told me you came from an abusive household."

Instantly I feel myself cringe and retreat in total humiliation. Why would he say that? Why would he tell someone about that? How many others has he told? I feel like the butt of all jokes. "Um," I mumble, trying to catch my breath.

My head spins around and I can't help the tears that leak from my eyes as I try and hold them in.

"Don't cry. I just need to know you'll work hard for me." Stacey looks at me, and her eyes, though pretty, are very cold.

"I will, ma'am," I manage to say through a strangled and painful sob.

"Yes, I think you will. Summer is nearly here, and I'm going to need extra cashiers. You have the job if you want it. I trust Chris when he says you're a good kid." She stands, comes beside me and leans on her desk.

"Here." She reaches around to some papers which were on her desk. "Fill these out, bring them back on Saturday, and once I've got you a uniform, I'll have you trained and ready to go."

I look up at her, I'm sure I'm a mess with tears clinging to my cheek and my eyes red, but I smile. "Thank you," I say.

"Tell Chris I'm still waiting for that lobster he promised me. You can tell him tonight while you're having dinner."

"Yes, ma'am," I say as I stand and take my backpack.

As I walk out of the office, I thank Stacey again and promise I'll do my best for her. I tuck the papers in my backpack and walk downstairs past Shayne. "Hey," she says. I stop by her counter. "Did you get the job?"

"Yeah, I did."

She smiles at me. "That's excellent. I'm Shayne, and I think you and I are going to be great friends," she cheerfully says.

"I'm Lily, and I really hope so."

A friend. A real life friend. Someone I can just be myself around. I hope she'll be my friend. I really need someone.

CHAPTER 8

"UNCLE MARTIN, THIS IS MY girlfriend Lily. This is my uncle, Martin," Trent says as he introduces me.

"Hello," I say as I extend my hand to the balding, middle-aged man standing in front of me. He doesn't look anything like Mr. Hackly. He's short, with not much hair, a big belly and when he smiles, half his teeth are rotten.

"What's this, little lady? Where I come from we're all family and this is how we greet each other," he jovially says as he steps into my personal space, wraps his arms around me and hugs me tightly while he lifts me clearly off the ground.

He puts me down and chuckles. "Pleased to meet you, Sir," I say, breathless from the bear-hug.

"Sir? You can call me Uncle Martin or just plain old Marty. And you." He looks at Trent, "You're way too old to be calling me Uncle, you can call me Marty." I smile at Marty, because he's nice.

"Come on, I need to introduce you to Uncle John," Trent says, as Marty goes back to flipping the burgers on the barbeque.

We walk toward a gentleman sitting near the pool. He's nursing a beer as he watches some kids in the pool. He looks almost exactly like Mr. Hackly, but older with gray hair.

"Uncle John, I'd like you to meet my girlfriend, Lily."

He stands from where he was sitting, and his intense green eyes go directly to me. Automatically, I feel uncomfortable. He trails his eyes down from my face to my breasts, then further down. A violent, intense knot forms in my stomach as I take his offered hand and shake it.

"You're Lily?" he asks. The question sounds wrong. Almost like he was expecting someone beautiful and he's shocked by just how ugly I am.

"Yes, Sir," I answer.

"She sure is pretty, Trent," he says to Trent while leering at me.

"She is," Trent answers as he puts his arm around me and pulls me into him. "Go inside and help Mom with the food."

I force a smile at Trent's uncle and turn to go inside, but I hear him say, "Fucked her yet?" I speed up and leave because he just creeps me out to the point I don't want to be anywhere near him.

When I go into the kitchen I see Mrs. Hackly working, and two other women sitting at the table, laughing and drinking a clear liquid in a tall glass. From the way they're looking at Trent's mom, and how they're acting, I doubt the liquid is water.

"Ma'am, do you need help?" I ask, as I step inside and stand beside her at the kitchen counter.

"Yes. Thank you, dear. Can you peel these potatoes?" She asks, as she dumps a bag full in the sink.

"Sure thing." I pick the peeler up and start peeling them, and I can hear the two women at the table whispering and giggling like schoolgirls.

"Who's this, Lina?" one of the women asks in a condescending tone.

Mrs. Hackly stops chopping the salad, gives me a sideways look that I interpret as 'sorry about them', then plasters a fake smile on her face. "This is Trent's girlfriend. Her name's Lily," she says in a saccharine voice.

"Come here, girl," the older woman tells me, as I turn around to smile at them. I dry my hands on the tea-towel beside me and move toward the older one who is holding her hand out to me.

I reach her and take her hand in mine, "Pleased to meet you, ma'am," I say as nicely as I can.

She looks so old, with heavy wrinkles around her mouth and eyes. She's got a thick crown of coarse gray roots that need to be dyed, then straw-like dark hair that comes to just above her shoulder. "You're not very pretty," she says to me.

I lift an eyebrow at her and hold in a chuckle. "Frankly ma'am, you're not the first person to say that to me." *Pot calling the kettle black.*

"I'm Terri and this is Laura. You can call me Mrs. Terri, and you can call her Mrs. Laura," she says, pointing to the skinnier and younger woman sitting beside her.

"I'm just Laura. Don't listen to a word the old bat's saying to you. I'm married to Marty and Terri is married to John."

I smile at her, and feel somewhat more at ease. "I better get back to the potatoes."

"Soooo," Terri draws out in a huff of a breath. "You're going out with Trent, are you?"

I see Mrs. Hackly's shoulders tense and she takes in a deep breath. "Yes, ma'am," I answer.

"Really? And you think a good-looking boy like him will be happy with a girl like you?"

"Terri," Laura hisses, "stop it, leave the girl alone."

"Really Laura, Trent is a handsome boy. He can have anyone he wants, and he probably already has. So why would he choose someone as plain as her?"

"Stop being such a bitch."

"Lina, are you happy with the girl?" Terri says as if I'm an infected, disease-ridden animal.

"Lily is a very nice girl," Mrs. Hackly replies in my defense.

Terri mumbles, but doesn't say anything else to me.

Mrs. Hackly and I spend the rest of the time in the kitchen cooking. I should say, Mrs. Hackly is cooking, and I'm doing whatever she says.

When all the food has been prepared, we take everything outside on the back porch and call everyone for lunch.

Trent instantly is beside me, and wraps his arm around my waist. He pulls me into his side, as he chats with his dad.

Mrs. Hackly waits for everyone to be seated before she sits opposite me. I have Trent on one side, and John on the other. The conversation is mostly among the brothers, the kids and Terri. I notice Mrs. Hackly, Laura, and I are all pretty quiet, not saying much.

As the conversation continues, I also pick up on Marty's reaction to things. He seems slightly slower, with a lot of the jokes the other two brothers tell going over his head, as if he's not understanding them.

"Like some more potato salad?" Trent asks.

When I turn my head to look at him on my right, a hand grabs my left thigh and squeezes it. Automatically I jump back and swing around to look at John. He moves his hand, but not before he chuckles at me.

"You okay?" Trent asks.

"I'm fine, I just need to go to the bathroom," I say as I push my chair back and leave the table quickly.

"Are you okay, dear?" I hear Mrs. Hackly ask me in a concerned tone. I turn and look at her over my shoulder, feigning a smile.

The moment I'm inside the double glass doors, I run to the bathroom and lock myself inside. I feel sick, like I'm going to throw up. I remember the moment his leer made me feel ill, and now the thought of his hand squeezing my thigh sends terrifying shivers throughout my entire body. There's a rock in the pit of my stomach, but it's hurtling up my throat at such speed I doubt I'll be able to make it to the basin.

As soon as I vomit, my nerves calm. I breathe deeply in through my nose and out my mouth enough to let the wave of nausea pass. "What was that?" I ask myself as I look in the mirror. My eyes are all bloodshot and my face is splotchy and red.

Standing at the basin, I let the cool water run and splash it on my face. I stand looking at my ugly reflection in the mirror and finally feel strong enough to go back out to the barbeque. I'm not sure if I should tell Trent or if I should just keep it to myself. Telling him will cause a rift if he tells his dad, but not to tell him is dishonest.

I take a few more deep breaths and open the door. The second I unlock it and push down on the handle, it's forced open and John barrels in, pushing me back into the bathroom. His lunge is so powerful I stumble back and fall on my bottom.

He quietly closes the door and locks it. I scoot back until I feel the cold wall through my t-shirt. "You're such a good girl, waiting for me," he says as he stalks toward me.

"Please, don't," I beg as I brace myself for what's about to happen.

"Shhh, no need to say anything, sugar. I'll take care of you." He unzips his jeans and begins to push them down over his hips. He grabs me by the shoulders and easily lifts me. "Now, be a good little girl and pull your shorts down."

This makes me feel sick. My heart is beating so quickly in my chest, and that nauseous feeling has returned, but even worse. "No," I cry as his hands grope at my body. "No!" I shout louder.

"You're feisty. I like a woman when she fights back. It's sexy." He leans in and licks my neck as his hands keep fondling my breasts.

With all my might, I push him away and run for the door, unlocking it and bolting out to the table where everyone is eating and enjoying their lunch.

I sit beside Trent, and he immediately sees me shaking. "What's wrong?" he asks as he puts his fork down and wraps me in his arms.

Breathing through the lump in my throat, I try and form a sentence. But there's no words molding into anything comprehensible.

"She fell and it frightened her. I was there to help her up," says John as he confidently strolls back to his seat and sits beside me. I move my chair over closer to Trent and further away from John. "Lucky I was there, actually, she could've gone through that glass coffee table. Now that would've been ugly, wouldn't it, sugar?" he says. But his tone is giving me a warning. To shut up and not say anything or next time, I'll be hurt.

As I sit beside Trent, in his arms, shaking, I can't say anything.

"Thank God you were there," Trent says to John as his hand rubs up and down my back. "Isn't that right, Lily?" He kisses me on the forehead. I can't do anything. I can't agree and I can't say a word. Not now, not with everyone here. "Poor thing, she really is spooked." He kisses me again on the forehead.

I stay cocooned in Trent's arms, not wanting to look at John. But I can feel his evil eyes boring into me, drilling through my back.

"Aren't you hungry, sugar?" John asks. Just his mere words sends another shiver up my back.

I shake my head, and try to move even closer to Trent. "You have to eat," Trent says. I can barely form a sentence let alone consider eating. But I have to put on the appearance everything is okay. Because if I don't, then everyone will know. I'm good at not letting anyone in.

John's already convinced everyone he saved me, when he's the one I needed saving from. I move my chair out so I'm far away from the table's edge, this way if John tries grabbing me again, Trent can see it for himself. Picking up my fork, I push the food around, but take small bites. The food is sitting high up in my stomach, ready to make a quick reappearance if John touches me again.

When lunch is done, Mrs. Hackly stands and begins to gather all the used plates. I stand with her, and decide to stick close by to her. This way, John can't come near me.

We take the plates into the kitchen. Everyone else stays outside talking and laughing. I scrape the wasted food into the trash can and shake my head. A few weeks ago I would've pleaded to have food like this. And now, I couldn't eat what was on my plate because of what happened with John. I'm so ashamed I let it go to waste, I'm no better than people who disregard others who are starving.

"He touched you, didn't he?" Mrs. Hackly whispers.

Every hair stands to attention all down my arms and on the back of my neck. Ice runs through my veins, touching the furthest extremities of my body. Slowly I turn my head to look at her. She's rinsing the dishes in the sink and her head is lowered. I can see tears slowly rolling down her cheek and drip one by one into the dirty dishwater.

"How did you know?" I ask as I struggle to keep my voice steady. Her tears intensify and she looks at me. The look itself screams a thousand words. Telling me the entire horrific chapter in her life that she's desperately trying to not let anyone see. "Oh my God," I whisper as I put a plate down and go to give her a hug.

Mrs. Hackly shakes her head at me and says through her tears, "Don't, please."

I step back and give her space. Picking up the plate I silently continue to scrape the wasted food. Laura comes in a few moments later and stops by the door. I can see her looking and assessing us. "Are you okay, Lina? Did Lily upset you?"

"No, dear. I'm alright. Just thinking how quickly my boy's growing up," she says, quickly recovering from the truth.

This makes me think, how many more things does she recover so quickly from? How many more questions does she avert by lying? Has she done that to me?

"I'll bring in the rest of the things. Do you need a hand for dessert?"

"Lily and I have it covered, thank you."

Laura makes a few trips bringing everything in, while Mrs. Hackly and I continue to silently work. The only words are her instructing me what to do. When we finish, we take the desserts out, and I notice John's left the table and is in the pool. I take a steadying breath, relieved he's nowhere near me or Trent's mom.

"The water's beautiful, who's coming in?" he shouts from the pool.

I feel myself shudder as I try not look at him. "Did you bring your swimsuit?" Trent asks me as he stands from the table.

"It's in my bag, but I'm not feeling well. I might just sit this one out."

"Okay." Trent leans down, kisses me and then he runs toward the pool.

"How 'bout you, sugar, you coming in?" John asks me.

It terrifies me that he wants me in there with him. He scares me. "She's not feeling well. She's sitting this one out." Trent explains.

"Come inside, dear, out of the sun. I'll make you something cool to drink," Mrs. Hackly says, before John can say anything. She's caught on to what he wants to do, and she's helping me. And more than likely, helping herself, too.

Mrs. Hackly comes around and as I stand, she links her arm through mine. She gives me a small wink, and I'm fairly certain, that winks means two things. First, *I won't let him near you*; and second, *you're saving me, too*.

We go inside and I sit at the kitchen table. "I understand," she says as she makes me a cool drink. "Trust me, I understand."

As we sit in the kitchen, we're talking but not saying anything important. The day wears on, and soon it's time for us to go. I make sure Trent is beside me when I say goodbye to John, and the moment I'm out of there, I take a deep breath.

"Are you feeling better?" Trent asks and Mr. Hackly turns to look at me.

"She better not be pregnant," Mr. Hackly says from the driver's seat of the car.

"What?" I quietly whimper. *Pregnant?* I don't ever want children. This world isn't made for kids. It's too cruel to subject a child to it.

"We're not having sex yet, Dad. But when we do, I'll wear a rubber."

I'm humiliated. Totally embarrassed. "Better still, take her to the doctor and get her on birth control," Mr. Hackly says to Trent.

I can feel my face burning, and I feel like crying. The conversation goes on around me as if I don't exist. "I'll use a condom, dad," Trent says again.

"Problem is son, girls like her get knocked up 'cause they're onto a good thing with people like us."

I turn my head away, looking out the window, completely and utterly mortified. In all my years with Dad, the way he spoke to me, the way he was, I was always prepared for him. Regardless of his mood swings, of what he'd say or do, I was always on guard.

But Mr. Hackly is talking about me as if I'm trash. Nothing more than a thorn in his side, *another mouth to feed*. It makes me feel beyond small. I can't even hide this from Trent, because he's in the car as his dad continues to belittle and reduce me to something even more worthless than I already feel.

"Okay, Dad," Trent says as he puts a hand on my thigh and squeezes it. "Tomorrow I'll take her to the doctor."

"I have my first shift at the store tomorrow." I took the paperwork in before we left for the barbeque, and Stacey told me to come in tomorrow so she can have one of the others train me on the register.

"See, son? Girls like her will always find an excuse."

The tears are streaming down my face. I feel like jumping out of the car and just ending it. This humiliation has to stop. I'm not sure I can continue a life like this.

"She has to work, Dad. I'll take her after work."

"Hmm, she'll probably just make another excuse," Trent's dad says.

"I'll pick her up and take her. Cut it out," Trent says back to his dad. "You okay?" he whispers to me. I don't turn to look at Trent, instead I stare at the nondescript scenery we're passing and focus on keeping my sobs silent.

The rest of the car ride is quiet. No one says a word. How can anything be said? Mr. Hackly's made it clear what he thinks of me, and I'm really not in a position to say anything to him. I should be grateful someone's feeding me and caring for me. But if you call how Trent's dad is treating me caring, then I suppose I really should look to move out.

And that's what I'll do, the moment I can.

By the time we get home, it's nearly dusk. I go to my room, get my pajamas and go for a shower. When I get out, everyone is in the family room with the TV on, but it doesn't seem like anyone is watching it. A wave of pure ice floats through the room, and suddenly I feel like a stranger. An unwanted guest as the six eyes stare at me. "Goodnight," I say and quickly turn away.

I run to my room, close the door and cover myself under the blanket. This is my fortress, my safe place, where no one can touch me.

I lay awake and listen to the sounds. Muffled talking, Trent's dad raises his voice, and Trent yells back. This continues for what feels like hours, but I look at the clock, and the angry red numbers tell me it's been less than half an hour. I hear footsteps, and hold my breath. But the footsteps go upstairs. There's louder talking, and now I know it's only Trent and his dad left downstairs. Then no sound. No words, no footsteps, nothing.

I take a desperate breath and wait. I'm not sure what exactly I'm waiting for, but something's bound to happen. I can feel it. There's tension, and it all revolves around me.

Suddenly the door flings open, and I whimper as the door handle hits the wall.

"What did you do, Lily?" Trent angrily asks. "What the hell did you do?"

"Nothing! I didn't do anything," I plead. I'm not sure why I'm pleading. Maybe to make him believe me? I don't know.

"Uncle John said you kissed him."

"What? No!" I shout. "No, it wasn't like that. I didn't do anything. He came into the bathroom and started feeling me up."

"He said you told him you want to fuck him."

"No, I don't. I don't want to have sex. I certainly don't want *him*. He scares me."

"He told Dad you'd say that."

"It's true."

"Then why didn't you tell me when it happened?"

"I don't know. I didn't think you'd believe me and I didn't think it was right to tell you seeing as we were together with everyone else. I didn't want to start trouble."

"I don't know what to believe, Lily." Trent runs a hand through his hair and paces in my bedroom. "I just don't fucking know."

"He put his hand on my thigh, and that's when I ran to the bathroom because it scared me. Then he was waiting for me outside the bathroom, and he pushed on the door as I opened it and he…" I stop talking, and downcast my eyes.

"That's not what he said."

"That's how it happened. I'm sorry for not telling you, but…"

"There's no damn 'but' in this equation. If you had told me what happened then, I'd believe you. But seeing as you're telling me now after Uncle John told Dad, well now I'm fucking angry."

The damn tears quickly form in my eyes, and I'm absolutely dumbfounded by his words. *He doesn't believe me.* "Sorry," I say as loudly as I can, but the tightness in my throat isn't allowing the sound to come out in anything but strangled noises.

"Not good enough!" he yells and turns around to leave the room. Before he does, he puts his fist through the drywall, and I jump back at the raw explosion of anger. Trent leaves, slamming the door behind him.

I can hear his angry, heavy steps as he stomps upstairs. I lay awake, huddled beneath the warmth and security of my blanket, just listening to the dead night air.

The house is completely silent. Nothing can be heard, not a sound. It's stark and cold, and completely isolated.

I turn to watch the blinking lights of the alarm clock beside the bed. I can't say 'my' alarm clock or 'my' bed. This can all be ripped away from me in the blink of an eye. I'm under no illusion I even own the clothes I'm sleeping in. Everything was paid for by the Hackly's. Everything. Every morsel of food, every thread. They own everything.

My eyes begin to drift shut as sleep slowly pulls me toward her. Maybe if I wake tomorrow, I'll find this was just a bad dream. Maybe my life is just a bad dream. A constant nightmare I'm just waiting to wake up from.

The black of slumber has claimed me, and I'm finally dragged into oblivion.

BANG.

I jump out of bed, quickly checking the room I'm sleeping in, but nothing seems out of place. My heart's racing in my chest and my breathing is rapid and short. I stay still, listening for the noise that woke me. But I hear nothing.

Letting out a huge gust of air, I get back in bed. The clock beside me is relentless, the time continuing to flash. It's only been an hour since I fell asleep.

Lying in bed, I let the native sounds carry me forward again to sleep. I don't let the bang worry me, because Mr. Hackly or Trent would have come to check it out if it was something serious.

It was probably a bat flying into the side of the house. It can't be anything else. Right. *Right?*

CHAPTER 9

SUNDAY MORNING WAS INCREDIBLY STRANGE in the Hackly home. I didn't see Mrs. Hackly at all before I left for work, and Mr. Hackly and Trent were cold toward me.

"You ready?" Trent asked, as he grabbed the keys from the hallway table and stood at the door. It was my cue to hurry up. Mr. Hackly didn't even look at up at me from his tablet as he read the news.

The ride to work was just as icy as the Hackly home. Trent tapped his thumbs on the steering wheel to a song that wasn't even playing.

I didn't bother asking him if he was okay, because I already knew the answer. A lifetime with an alcoholic parent had taught me to never ask a question I already knew the answer to. As a matter of self-preservation, I shouldn't say much anyway.

Trent dropped me off at the grocery store, and told me in a no-nonsense way, "You're going to give me sex tonight, and I'm taking you to the doctor after work to make sure you don't become pregnant." It wasn't really a question; he wasn't asking. He was telling.

Shayne's been teaching me what I need to do at work, and now it's just before my break. Stacey put me on a register on my own, with Shayne on the one behind me so I can ask her questions if I need help. As the customers come through with their full shopping carts, I mindlessly scan each item. But all I can think about is tonight. It's inevitable I'll give him sex, I know that. But I was hoping it would happen when I was more ready.

I hear someone ask me a question, and it brings me back to the present, and not what's going to happen tonight. "Sorry?" I say to the old lady who's standing in front of me with her few groceries.

"I said you're a very pretty girl," she says, and smiles warmly at me.

"Thank you," I respond with a wan smile. Though deep down inside, I know she must be talking about Shayne. Shayne is beautiful. And so bubbly and outgoing. How can anyone not say she's pretty?

The old lady looks at my badge and squints to read it. "Oh, you're training are you?" she asks as she adjusts the glasses perched on the bridge of her nose.

"Yes, ma'am I am. This is my first day." I scan one of the last products on the conveyor belt.

"Your first day?" She shrills, then adds, "My goodness, you'll be running this place before you know it." She smiles again to me.

For the first time in a long time, I feel something other than judgement. A complete stranger, a random elderly lady, isn't looking at me like I'm trash. Her words are meant to give me strength and confidence, and I know these words, although they would be inconsequential to many, will live with me a lifetime.

"Thank you," I say, feeling my face brighten and my lips turn up in a genuine smile. I scan her last items, she pays for them and I wish her a fantastic day. She'll never know the impact of the kindness she's shown me, with just that one simple sentence.

I begin to scan the next customer's items and Luke, the manager of the cashiers, comes over and tells me to turn my light off. Shayne and I finish at the same time and I step away from the register, about to go to the staff room.

"Hey, come out and grab some lunch with me," she says happily.

Damn, I didn't bring anything with me, and I don't have any money. "I'm not very hungry," I respond, though truthfully my stomach is growling, though thankfully, not loud enough for her to hear. But it's enough to remind me I want food.

"My shout, come on, let's go. We only have half an hour." Shayne links our arms together and starts to lead the way outside. Next to the grocery store is a deli and we walk in there. "They make the best pastrami on rye. You like pastrami, right?"

I can confidently say yes, because Mrs. Hackly has made it for me. "I do, especially with mustard."

"Two pastrami's on rye, both with mustard. I'll have a bottle of water and…" Shayne turns to me and motions just with her eyes what beverage I'd like.

"Water too, please."

The lady serves us, and Shayne pays for our lunches. She goes out the door first, and walks down the street to a small park that has three tables and a set of swings. One of the tables is occupied by a mom who's watching her daughter on the swing set.

"So, tell me about yourself," Shayne says as she sits, unwraps her sandwich and takes a bite.

"Not really much to tell. I'm seventeen and about to graduate high school. How about you?"

"Me? Well, I'm kind of stuck in this town. But I want to be an actress. I just need to save enough money to buy my ticket out of here. Been at the store for two years and I keep saving, but…" She shrugs and takes another bite.

"But what?"

"It's hard to save anything on just under eight bucks an hour. I live on my own, and we have to pay our own medical insurance. It's hard you know. I'm hoping one day I'll be promoted and they can at least pay for my medical insurance."

"Why do you live on your own?" I bite into my delicious sandwich.

"Mom split, and Dad died. Mom found herself a new guy who didn't want a kid hanging around, so last year she told me I had two months to move out. I live in a garage that's been converted to an apartment. The rent is cheap, and the people are real nice. They have a little girl and sometimes they ask me to babysit. When I do, they give me a break on my rent. But you know, it's just hard."

I like Shayne. She's not telling me her story for me to pity her. In fact I think she's really level-headed about it. "This is my first job," I say trying to swing the conversation.

"Yeah, really? You're doing really good," she says. I'm dying to correct her English, but it's not really my place to say anything to her. "What are you going to do with your first paycheck? Go out and party?" She does this little dance in her seat. It makes me laugh.

"What was that?" I tease as I eat my lunch.

"What? This?" She does the same wiggle but more exaggerated. We both laugh at her silly, innocent ways. "But really, what are you going to do? Not that you can drink, but you can have fun with your friends."

This changes the mood of the conversation. I put my sandwich down and grab my water, trying to restore that barrier up between us. "I just really want to buy a book." I drink my water.

"A book? How old are you?" her tone changes and she's being sarcastic with me.

"Yes, I know it's probably really weird, but I had a favorite book and recently it was destroyed, and I want another copy. It's not even a book; it's a play."

Shayne looks at me strangely. "No, really, are you an eighty-year-old woman in disguise? I'm being punked, right?" She looks around her like she's searching for something. It makes me laugh again. "Where are the cameras, grandma?" She stands and looks around.

"Hi, Shayne," a guy says as he walks past.

"Hey, Liam. Am I being punked?" she asks the guy.

"Not that I know of." He keeps walking after he winks at her.

"Seriously? A play?" She sits down but her eyes don't move off the guy who walked past.

"Yes, a play. And you can stop making fun of me for it."

"What's the play?"

"It's called, *The Crucible*."

"Oh yeah?" Shayne sounds interested, like she's heard of it.

"Do you know it?" I ask hopeful we can share a love of the written word.

"Nah, is it like a romance? I don't read much. I mean I can read, just I don't." She shrugs her shoulders.

"It's a play by Arthur Miller."

"Oh, right." She looks lost in the conversation.

"He wrote *Death of a Salesman*." She nods her head, though her face says she has no idea. "He was once married to Marilyn Monroe."

"Really?" Her eyes perk up now, she's heard a familiar name.

"Yeah, really. Anyway, that's what I want. Another copy of *The Crucible*."

"This town is small if you haven't noticed already. Maybe you'll need to order it from the book shop. Anyway, where are you from?"

"Just a couple of suburbs over, but now I've moved here."

"With your parents?" she asks innocently, as she drinks the last of her water.

"No, not quite. My um, my boyfriend and his parents."

She puts her water bottle down and her eyebrows fly up. "Wooooo," she teases. "You have a boyfriend. Is he cute?"

"Yeah, he is," I say, though don't say anything else.

"Shit, Lily. We gotta go. Our break's almost over."

We both stand and start walking back to the store, and just as we reach it, I see Mr. Hackly's car parked outside with Trent leaning against the car. "I'll meet you inside," I tell Shayne and jog over to Trent. "Hey," I say.

"Where the fuck were you?" he asks and grabs the top of my arm and pulls me toward him.

"Shayne took me out for lunch."

"Who the hell is this Shayne guy?"

"No, it's not like that. Shayne's the girl who I was walking back with. We went to the deli and then to the park around the corner to eat."

"Yeah right, Lily. Like a girl has a name like Shayne. Shayne's a damn guy's name. I don't fucking believe you." He squeezes his fingers tighter around the top of my arm.

"Ow. You're hurting me," I say as I look at his hand, then back into his angry brown eyes. His face is livid, he looks so mad with me. "Come inside, I'll introduce you to her." He lets out a ragged breath, and his eyes hold on to his fury, his rage clearly consuming him. And this now scares me, because he's reminding me of how Dad was. "Please don't be angry with me," I say trying to calm him.

His grip lessens slightly, as I cuddle into him and lay my head on his shoulder. "Okay, introduce me," he says in a calmer tone.

"Thank you." I stretch my neck up and kiss him on the lips. "Thank you," I repeat.

"Just introduce me," he says sourly. We walk hand in hand into the store, and Shayne is already working.

"Hurry up, Lily," she says, as she looks over her shoulder toward the rear of the store.

I quickly get in and check my register, and do every step Shayne has showed me up to now. "Shayne, this is Trent, Trent this is Shayne."

"Nice to meet you," she joyfully says. "Sorry, but we're busy. Maybe we'll hang out one time after work or something."

"Yeah, that's a good idea," Trent says. Then he turns to me and kisses me chastely on the lips. "I'll pick you up at five. Bye, baby. I love you." He doesn't leave though. He stands and waits for me to say something to him.

"Thank you." I start to scan my first customer's groceries. But Trent still doesn't leave. "I'll be ready by five."

"That's it?" he challenges as he looks over to Shayne then back to me. "I love you," he says again.

He wants me to say it back to him. I don't know what love is. It's never been given to me, and I'm not sure if I've ever given it to anyone. I like Trent. When he doesn't get angry with me, he's nice. He can be fun, caring, and protective. But love? I don't know what it is. Maybe I do love him, maybe this is what it feels like.

I smile at him as I keep scanning the lady's groceries. "I love you," I say for the first time in my life. But, I feel nothing. They're just words, just like any other in the English spoken language. Maybe that's all they are. Just words.

Trent smiles and winks at me. "Bye, babe. Nice to meet you, Shayne." He waltzes out of the store.

"He's really cute," says the lady I'm serving. "Nice eyes." I smile at her, and continue with my work.

Finally, about half an hour before I finish, there's a break in the customers and Shayne taps me on the shoulder. "Your boyfriend is super cute."

"He is," I agree with her.

"Love how he waited for you to tell him you love him."

"Yeah." I turn away to avoid her questions. She's nice, really nice, but I don't want to talk about Trent and how cute or anything else she may think of him.

"You up to anything tonight?" she sweetly asks.

"I'm not sure." I lie. I really don't want to tell her what Trent wants from me, and what I'll have to give him. "Customer," I whisper. But deep down I'm thankful I have to work because I want to avoid her questions.

She may think these are all harmless things she wants to know, and to most people, they are. But they aren't to me. I don't want to talk about them. It's no one's business.

The rest of my shift goes by fast. Shayne shows me how to close out my cash drawer at the end of the day and everything else I need to do as I finish work. I'm ready to leave when Stacey calls me into her office.

"How was your day?" she asks as she sits behind her desk and watches me stand beside the door.

"Good. Shayne showed me how to do a lot of things."

"I saw. You were working the register on your own, and only needed Shayne's help a handful of times. She showed you how to close your shift and what to do. I'm impressed."

I smile and feel so proud of myself. "Thank you, ma'am." *Someone's proud of me.* She said she's impressed with me. I'm so ecstatic over her words.

"What time do you finish school?"

"I finish just after three every day. And I only have two weeks left before I graduate."

"Good, I need a girl on the register Wednesday, Thursday and Friday from four until eight. And you can work Saturday from eight in the morning, and Sunday from midday."

"Oh I um…" I have to check with Trent and make sure he's okay with it.

"If there's a problem I'll call Chris and let him know I need you."

"No, ma'am. I'll work around it."

"And once school's done, I'll be able to give you more work."

"Thank you," I say and stand waiting for her next instructions.

"You did well, Lily. I'll see you Wednesday." She lowers her head and continues working. I gather this is her way of telling me to go.

I leave and quietly shut her door, going downstairs and out the front. Shayne's already gone and I wait for Trent out front. I take my phone out of my bag that I collected from the staff room, and I check the time. He's running a few minutes late, but I don't want to leave in case he comes and doesn't find me here.

Another minute passes and Trent comes around the corner in his dad's car. He stops and I get in. "You ready?" he asks. I nod my head, although having sex with him is still something I'm not ready to do.

We drive a couple of blocks down and he parks in the doctor's parking lot. We go in, and I stand behind Trent and let him do all the talking.

We sit in the waiting room and I begin to fidget in my chair. "Trent," I say as I squeeze his hand which is in mine.

"Yeah."

"I'm nervous."

"Don't be." I wait for more, but instead he takes his phone out and begins doing something on it. This is terrifying. I'm waiting beside my boyfriend to be called in by an unknown doctor so I can be put on contraception. I don't even want to have sex. All I want to do is read and get lost in a book, not what Trent wants me to do.

"Trent, I'm really scared. I'm not sure I'm ready to have sex yet," I say in a small whisper, because I don't want the entire waiting room to hear, although, there are only three people in here including the receptionist.

"There's nothing to be scared of. And as far as sex is concerned…" He leans over and kisses me softly on the cheek. It's a beautiful and innocent kiss. "You're seventeen. It's time you had sex." He leans back, and looks down at his phone.

My shoulders slump. It feels like it doesn't even matter what I say, he's going to take what he wants.

"Lily Anderson," a male doctor calls. Trent stands and leads me into the small office.

The next half hour is spent in the doctor's examining room. After numerous questions, all of which Trent answers, I was given an injection in my bottom. It was explained to me, and the doctor gave us some pamphlets too. I switched off listening after a few moments, because regardless of how I felt, it was going to happen.

In the car on the way home, Trent has his hand resting on my thigh. "Doctor Simmons has been a good family friend for years."

"Okay," I say. I already could tell there was a deeper connection to just patient/doctor.

"He's one of Dad's good friends."

"Okay." I turn my head and look out the window.

"But we still need for me to wear a condom. I don't want a kid yet, and until the injection kicks in I'll make sure I don't knock you up."

"Okay." I purse my lips together as I look up at the darkening sky. I look at the sky. Dusk is so beautiful. Majestic and serene, I wish I could get lost in it.

As we near Trent's home, he swerves the car. I look out the front and hold on to my seat belt. I'm expecting to see another car coming toward us, but Trent's sped up and is swerving toward a dog trotting along the road. "Trent! Watch out," I yell as he almost hits the dog.

Trent starts laughing and corrects the car, missing the dog by no more than a couple of feet. "I'm just having some fun," he says, and continues laughing.

I'm horrified, and so disgusted he swerved to hit the dog. It was cruel and unnecessary.

My heart starts to calm and when we reach the house, I get out and go inside. Trent's right behind me. "I'll see if your mom needs help with dinner." I go into the kitchen to find Mrs. Hackly standing near the stove, making something. "Hi, need help?" I offer.

"I'm fine, dear." She turns and looks at me, and I see her lip is fat and has split.

"Mrs. Hackly, what happened?" I rush over to her, but I'm unsure on what I can do to help her.

"Oh this." She touches her lip and smiles at me. "Last night I fell out of bed. Hit my face on the corner of my bedside table. Stupid really. Who falls out of bed? Obviously, me. Just a silly woman." She turns the meat on the stove top and turns back to preparing the vegetables.

But I know, there's more to it. I know bruises like that, I've experienced them before. "You can tell me," I hint in a soft voice.

"Nothing to tell, dear. Nothing to tell. A foolish old lady falling out of bed. That's all."

I have to respect her words and trust she's telling me the truth, or maybe it's her version of it. "Okay." I look over what's cooking, "What's for dinner?"

"Ribs, mashed potatoes, and asparagus. I don't need any help here, you can go spend some time with Trent."

Automatically I feel my breath drain as I leave the kitchen. I don't want to spend time with him, because I don't want to have sex with him. I leave the kitchen, and Mr. Hackly walks past me. "Did you see the doctor?"

"Yes, Sir."

"You're covered?"

I feel my face turn red, "Yes, Sir."

"Good." He keeps walking away from me.

"Lily, come upstairs," Trent calls me. Here goes. As slowly as I can drag my legs I walk up the stairs and go into his room. Leaving the door open I walk over to where he's sitting on the bed. "Close the door," he instructs me.

I turn and close the door, and lock it. As much as I don't want to have sex with him, I'd be even more humiliated if his mom or dad walked in. "Is your mom okay? She has a fat lip."

"She fell. She'll be fine. Come sit here." He pats the bed beside him. I sit down and wait. He leans into me, and starts to kiss me, his hands all over me. That's normal for him, to feel my breasts and he's putting his hands inside my panties and touching me. "After dinner, you need to have a shower so you can wash the smell off you, because tonight I'm coming into your room and we're having sex." He continues kissing me.

"Okay?" Although he's asking, it's more rhetorical.

We keep kissing, doing what Trent wants to do until his mom calls us for dinner.

When we get downstairs, he smacks my bottom and tells me to hurry up with dinner. When I sit, I try and take as long as I can, but Trent keeps eyeing me and mouthing the words 'hurry up'. No one really talks tonight, Mrs. Hackly asks how my first day of work was, but I noticed she wasn't really listening when I responded. So I opted to remain quiet, and just eat my dinner.

"May I be excused?" I ask once I'm done. Mr. Hackly nods, and I leave to have a shower. I take as long as I can in there, not wanting to get out of the bathroom.

Once I delay it as long as I can, I put my pajamas on and go into my room, where Trent is lying on my bed, with just his boxers on. "Hey, babe. You took your time. Wanted to make sure you were extra clean for me, right? Come here." He sits up in bed and puts his feet on the floor. My heart's beating so fast it feels like it's growing wings and is about to take off. My hands are sweating and I'm shaking from nerves.

Trent stands and removes my clothes, leaving me completely naked in front of him. I move my hands so they're covering my body, but he gently takes them and lowers them beside my body. "I'm nervous," I whisper. What I want to say is, *please don't do this, please wait*, but he's already made it clear, *he's going to take what he wants.*

"You're really pretty, Lily. But next time, you have to shave this bush." He points to my vagina.

I'm now humiliated *and* nervous. "Okay," I murmur.

"Lie on the bed and open your legs." I lay on the bed, and open my legs.

CHAPTER 10

I'VE BEEN LIVING AT TRENT'S house for nearly four months now, and in three weeks we'll be leaving to go to university together.

I've been working at the store every possible opportunity I get. I'm so proud that in the thirteen weeks I've worked here, I've managed to save a little over two thousand dollars. I even managed to buy another copy of my beloved book.

Trent has sex with me whenever he wants. The first night he did it twice to me, and it hurt. But he said it's supposed to hurt, that's how he knows how much I love him. I don't like it, I don't enjoy it, but if I lay there and let him do whatever he wants, he finishes quite quickly and then goes back to his room.

He also told me when I'm on my break at work, I need to call him and tell him when it starts, and again when I go back to work. He says he doesn't want to be worried about me. I guess that's pretty sweet.

Shayne and I have become good friends. She's still trying to plan a night out with me, Trent, and herself, but that hasn't worked out yet. It's nearing my break and today Shayne and I are going to the park to have lunch.

"Hey," I say over my shoulder, as the new customer loads up the conveyor belt. "I'm buying lunch."

"No way, girl. You have college to save for, I'm buying."

"I still owe you from the first time."

"You don't owe me nothing." I really want to tell her it's 'you don't owe me anything', but she once told me she feels dumb when she talks to me. And I'm the last person in the world who wants her to feel anything other than what she is – a beautiful person and an amazing friend. "Five minutes, and I've got something to tell you," she whispers.

Five minutes seem to go on forever, but our break finally comes and Shayne and I start walking out. "Hang on, I just need to call Trent."

"Okay." She walks ahead into the deli.

I dial Trent's number and it goes to voicemail. "Hey, it's me. Shayne and I are just going on our break. We're going to the park. I'll call you just before my shift starts again." I hang up, putting the phone back in my pocket and jogging into the deli.

"I ordered for you. You're usual. Pastrami on rye with extra mustard. I'm getting a soda, do you want one?"

"Just water, thanks."

Delores, the older lady behind the counter smiles at me. "Hi there, Lily. You getting excited? You'll be going to college soon and leaving this place behind."

"I'll never leave it behind, I'm just migrating for the season," I say, she laughs. Delores has been so kind, and she always gives me extra pastrami, telling me I'm too skinny. Trent recently told me I'm starting to put on weight and he doesn't want to be known as the guy with the fat girlfriend. When I'm at home, he dishes up my dinner, and I just eat that. But Delores always gives me extra food.

"You're a good girl, Lily. You'll make it far."

"And she's super smart," Shayne pipes up.

"Thank you," I reply, but I know they're just trying to be nice, nothing more.

Shayne grabs our lunches and goes to hand over the money to pay for both, but I beat her to it and pay with my money. It makes me feel so proud I can do that. I got that money through working hard for it, and it's mine to spend. A huge sense of achievement and accomplishment washes over me. It's something so trivial to most, because they haven't had to eat rotten fruit, or go days without anything more than water and maybe someone else's discarded leftovers. To them this is so small. To me, it's a massive confidence booster that I, Lily Anderson, *can* do it.

"Guess what I heard?" Shayne says once we're out of the deli.

"What?"

"I heard Stacey talking on the phone and saying if he doesn't leave his wife, she's going to tell everyone they're having an affair."

My very first reaction is to say, "Who was she talking to?" But the moment the words left my mouth, I immediately backtracked. "You know, never mind. It really has nothing to do with me. I don't want to know."

"Doesn't matter anyway, she was on her cell talking to whoever."

"I told you, I don't want to know."

"You're funny." She laughs and runs ahead to our table at the park. It's nearing the end of the summer and the temperature has begun to cool slightly during the days. "Come on," Shayne happily encourages me to hurry up. "Come on." From a distance she looks so happy and carefree. But the real Shayne has a story to tell, just like everyone else in the world.

"I'm here already." I sit at the table and unwrap my extra plump sandwich.

"So, we have to go out before you go to college and forget all about me." She bites into her lunch.

"How can I forget about you? You're really the only friend I've ever had. Unless you can count Delores and the ladies at the thrift shop I used to go to."

"What?" Shayne looks up at me, her eyes bursting with wonder.

I've never really told her about my past, it's embarrassing and beyond humiliating. "I used to go to this thrift shop sometimes. The ladies there were really nice."

"Why?" Her question isn't said with judgment, but with genuine interest.

"I kinda came from a pretty bad home."

"What? You? But you're the nicest, most normal, prettiest, and smartest person I know. I don't believe it."

I chuckle at her. "Trust me, I'm none of that." I take another bite and chew while thinking about what Shayne must see.

I'm a clown, standing in this circus called life, just trying to step forward from the back of the line and be more than just everyone's joke.

"That's bullshit, Lily. You're the hardest worker I know, taking every shift offered to you. You're super smart, and real, real pretty." Her face softens as she describes how she sees me.

"Thank you." *But I don't believe you.*

"Tell me about why you'd go to the thrift shop."

I take a deep breath, smile and look down, avoiding Shayne's beautiful eyes. "Because I didn't have any warm clothes to wear, and one day I went in there and the ladies helped me. They even fed me sometimes. I didn't go too often, because I didn't want them to think of me as a burden."

I hear her gasp, but I don't dare look at her. "You were homeless?"

Shaking my head, I keep looking down at initials which have been etched into the table. There's a love heart and 'D.D 4 A.L' has been carved in the middle. "No, I wasn't. But I was alone most of my life. Now, I'm not."

"Far out, Lily. I don't know what to say. I want to hug you."

"Don't, please. I don't want you to think badly of me."

"I don't. It makes me love you more as a person." I look up and she's smiling at me. "You're my best friend, and I love you so much. But now I want so much more for you. If any of us is going to make something of herself, it's you. You got so much smarts girl, you can be anyone and go anywhere."

"Thank you. Anyway, enough about my past. Let's talk about you."

Shayne keeps looking at me and she looks like she wants to say more. She opens her mouth to say something, but closes it, several times. "You only have a couple of weeks, we really need to organize a night out." Thankfully she changed the subject without intruding any further on my upbringing.

"I'll ask Trent. But you know how it's been, with me working so much, any spare time I get I've been spending it with him."

"I know, but come on, Lily. I may never see you again."

"Don't be silly. I'll be back on every break. And besides, I go where Trent goes. But I've been thinking, I want to get my permit. Learn to drive."

"Yeah, go for it! That's great."

"Hey, Shayne," Liam says, as he walks toward us.

Shayne's face goes a pale pink as she looks at him. "Hey," she says. I've come to learn she has a big crush on him. And I think he's crushing on her too. He always seems to be walking past the park whenever we're out here, and at first he'd walk past with just a hello, but now he stays and has a chat with her. I feel slightly uncomfortable, because to me it's really obvious how much they like each other.

"Liam, Shayne and I were just saying we need to organize a night out. Why don't you come with us? It won't be awkward for Shayne that way, because my boyfriend Trent will be with us." I see Shayne's face go a bright red. Crimson is more an accurate term. I don't want to embarrass her, but they've been dancing around each other since the first day I started, and probably before that.

"Yeah." He turns to me smiling, "I like that idea. I'd love to go."

"Love to fucking go where?" Trent's deep voice says from somewhere behind me. I turn to see Trent charging toward us. Anger rolling off him, waves of fury so clear on his face. "I said where are you taking my girl, fucker?" He lands a punch in Liam's face.

"Trent!" I scream and try to pull him back. But Trent brings his fist back, and lays into him again. This time knocking Liam back on the ground. "Trent!" I scream again and lunge at him to pull him off Liam. Trent turns, and in his fit of absolute fury, slaps me hard across my face.

I stumble back barely able to keep my balance. The slap itself stings across my cheek, but the shock of it has thrown me off balance.

"Oh my God, Lily," Trent says as he gets up off Liam and rushes over to me. "I'm so sorry. I didn't know what I was doing, please forgive me. I'm sorry."

"He and Shayne like each other, I was trying to get the four of us to go out together." I clutch the side of my face as Trent tries to console me, holding me close to his chest.

"I'm so sorry, baby. So sorry." He kisses the top of my head. "But it looked like he was hitting on you, and you were just letting it happen."

"I wasn't, I promise."

"Okay, I know that now. But next time, don't talk to men the way you were talking to him. You were leaning in toward him, you looked like you were hanging on every word he was saying."

I was? I thought I was just sitting normally, talking normally. "I'm sorry, I'll make sure I'm more aware of that."

"That's okay. Just don't do it again, alright?" he says as his hands travel up and down my back and he leans in to rest his chin on the top of my head.

"Shayne and I need to get back to work. Will you think about us going out with Liam?"

"I'll consider it." He moves me away and kisses my cheek, which feels like it's on fire. He then goes over to Liam, offers him his hand and apologizes. I'm so glad he recognizes he was in the wrong and is saying he's sorry.

"We gotta go," Shayne says, and side-steps Trent. Her eyes keep focus on him as she's coming toward me.

"I'll pick you up after work," Trent says and stays back to talk to Liam.

"What the hell just happened?" Shayne whispers while we walk quickly toward the store.

"He thought Liam was trying to hit on me, that's all."

"Did you see how he flew at Liam? He went crazy."

"I know, but I was leading Liam on, too. The way I was flirting with him."

"What? Are you serious? You weren't leading him on or flirting with him!"

"Yeah, I was. Trent said he got mad because he thought Liam was flirting, and the way I was sitting and listening to Liam, made him think I was into him."

"Lily?" Shayne stops walking and turns so we're facing each other. "I was right there. You were *not* doing that. If I thought you were I would've said something. But you weren't flirting with him any more than he was flirting with you."

"I just have to watch myself, because it upset Trent. That's why he hit him, because of me."

Shayne draws her eyebrows in together and shakes her head. "It's not my business Lily, but you better be careful of Trent. What he did back there? That's not right. Not right at all." She points toward the park where Trent punched Liam. "And, he hit you."

"That was an accident, he didn't mean to. He said he was sorry."

"You're a good person. I don't want to see you hurt."

I smile at her, because I know she wants what's best for me, but I do need to watch how I interact with people, too. "Okay." I take a deep breath, "Come on, let's go back to work before Stacey docks our pay."

CHAPTER 11

TRENT STANDS FROM THE BED and puts his jeans on. He's been really quiet lately, and I'm not sure what's happening. Maybe it's because we leave for college in five days, maybe it's because I've been working a lot at the store. I've been picking up as many shifts as I can, and I haven't been able to spend much time with him.

"Hey, I've got an idea," I say, trying to break the tension in the room.

"What? We just had sex, what else do you want?"

I didn't want to have sex; it's always him who instigates it. "Um, I was thinking maybe I can get my permit and you can teach me to drive. What do you think?"

He's putting his t-shirt back on and once it's over his head, he comes and sits beside me on the bed. "Why do you need to learn to drive? I take you wherever you need."

"What if you can't take me one day because you're not with me?"

"Where would I be, Lily? You're everything to me. If you and I ever broke up, life wouldn't be worth living."

"I'm not saying anything about breaking up, just…you know…what if you're out and I need to go somewhere?"

"Where would you need to go without me?"

"I'd like to get a job when we move. And what if you're in class and I need to get to work?"

"Our apartment is really close to campus, and the bus comes right outside our door. If you need to go to work you can go by bus. Or you can find a job close to the apartment and walk. You've put on some weight around your hips, and it doesn't look like the dieting is working, so maybe walking will do you good." He leans in and kisses the tip of my nose. "Go take a shower. You smell like a well-used whore, and unless we're going out somewhere, I don't like you smelling like that around my parents."

"Okay," I say as I dress in an oversized t-shirt and slip some yoga pants on. He's right, I do smell like him, and I don't like *anyone* knowing that Trent and I are having sex, let alone his mom. I'm so embarrassed when Trent talks to his dad so openly about what I do with him. But I suppose, this is what a normal family does. They talk candidly about everything, with no secrets.

Once I've showered, I get dressed and go out to find where Mrs. Hackly is. She hasn't changed much since I've moved in, and Mr. Hackly tends to ignore me, only saying things in passing to me. He's cordial, but there's never really any conversation.

"Stacey called, said there's a shift available if you want it," Mr. Hackly says.

"Yeah that'll be good. Thank you, I'll ask Trent if he can take me."

"I'll take you, I have a few things to get from there," Mr. Hackly replies.

"Thank you," I answer, and go to find Trent to tell him I'll be working.

He's up in his room, he's lying on his bed talking in a hushed voice on the phone. "Yeah, I'll see you later," he says louder when he sees me walk in the room. "Hey, babe. You alright?"

"Stacey called, said there's a shift available. Is it okay if I go?"

Trent jumps off the bed quite enthusiastically. "Yeah, of course. Good idea. I'll call Jason back and let him know I'll go out tonight then. If you want to get ready I'll take you in."

"Your dad said he can take me."

"Even better. Have a good night at work, text me what time you're finishing and I'll be there to pick you up," he says as he leads me out of his room and closes the door, before I can say anything.

I go downstairs to my room, put on my uniform and go find Mr. Hackly. "I'm ready, sir," I say, once I find him in the family room on his tablet.

"Go wait in the car, I'll be there in a moment."

"I'll just ask Mrs. Hackly if there's anything she needs, then I'll go wait in the car." I haven't seen her today, I heard her in the kitchen and when I went to see if she needed help, she was already gone.

"She's laying down; she has a headache. You can go to the car." He takes his phone out of his pocket and thumbs through it.

"Yes, sir." I take myself outside and wait in the car until Mr. Hackly comes. I'm not left waiting long, but when he gets in the car he's wearing cologne. "Thank you for taking me."

"That's fine, Lily." The rest of the ride is quiet. Mr. Hackly barely speaks to me as it is, so it's no surprise when he puts the music on and doesn't look once at me.

When we get to the store, I jump out, thank Mr. Hackly again and go put my bag away. But first I need to find Stacey and ask her what time I'm finishing, so I can let Trent know. I go up to her office and she's not there, I go down on the floor and ask the girls working, but no one's seen her. I've been here for ten minutes already and I can't find her, so I decide to duck to the ladies room before my shift starts and I'll ask Stacey when I'm on my break.

I go into the bathroom and pull my pants down to sit on the toilet when I hear murmuring. The sound is very familiar. Someone's having sex in the cubicle at the end of the stall. Gross. I quickly finish and pull my pants up when I hear Stacey say, "Shhh, someone's in here."

The response from the other person is, "Then you best be fucking quiet, whore." And the voice is one I know all too well. He brought me here.

I don't even wash my hands, I just flush the toilet and run as fast as I can, fleeing what I just heard. I duck into the men's room to wash my hands in there. No one else is in here, so I put my ear to the door and wait until I can't hear anything.

Creaking the door open, I look down the hall and notice it's completely isolated. I run down to the front and ask what register I'm going to be on. As soon as I'm ready, my conveyor belt is already laden with a customer's groceries and another two are waiting in line.

The shift is going by quickly, but my head is swimming with what I heard in the bathroom. I have to keep this to myself until I speak to Trent, because I don't know what to do. The queue at my register is three deep, and all the other registers are the same. Tonight's really busy and it doesn't seem to ease up. But Mr. Hackly's gruff voice as he was having sex just won't leave my mind.

"You okay there, Lily?" I look up to see Mr. Hackly standing in front of me. I startle at his presence and I can't help but look down, embarrassed and unsure of where to look.

"Yes, Sir," I say as I scan the items he has. Milk, bread, coffee cream, deodorant, and a few other things.

"You look like you've seen a ghost."

"No, Sir. We're just busy tonight."

"I see," he says as he looks around at the other busy registers. "As long as you're alright, Lily."

"Yes, Sir." I finish scanning the last item and say, "That'll be forty-eight dollars and six cents, sir." Mr. Hackly takes a fifty out of his wallet and hands it to me. But instead of passing it over, he grips my hand tightly in his, squeezing. "Sir?" I look at him and silently plead to let my hand go. What he's doing is aggressive, almost like he's warning me.

"I'll see you when you get back to *my* home, Lily. Keep the change." He picks his bag up and walks out of the store not once looking at me. This time, he's saying he can kick me out in a heartbeat.

What do I do?

Sometimes it's better to stay with the devil you know, instead of risking it all on the devil you don't know. *Isn't it?*

But I'm really confused about what to do. If I tell Trent, he'll tell Mr.

Hackly and then I might get in trouble. *What do I do?*

Just before my break, Stacey comes out to the floor and I get her attention to come talk to me. I have to pretend I don't know what happened in the bathroom, but I'm not sure I can look her in the eyes either.

"What do you need?" she asks curtly.

"What time will I finish, so I can let Trent know?"

"At midnight."

"Thank you," I say, and continue on with my work.

But Stacey doesn't leave. She waits until I finish serving the customer I'm on, then she comes behind the register to stand beside me. "Do you like working here, Lily?" she asks, her voice very low.

"Yes, ma'am." I start to scan the next set of groceries, and Stacey stays beside me.

"Good. Would you like a job here when you return for vacation?"

"Very much, ma'am."

"Then remember I have the power to give you work, or toss your ugly ass out." She, like Mr. Hackly, is warning me.

"Yes, ma'am," I say as I keep my head down and avoid looking at her. I don't want to meet her eyes, because I don't want her to know it was me in the bathroom while they….well, while they had sex. "I understand." I keep working, waiting for her overwhelmingly aggressive presence to leave.

"Good then. We won't have a problem." Out of the corner of my eye I see her leave. Her heels clack against the concrete flooring, and I can hear the sound get smaller and smaller.

When I finish with the last of my customers before my break, I close off my register and go to the staff room to get my purse and to call Trent. I walk out and go toward the deli so I can get something to eat while I dial Trent's number.

"Shhh, it's *herrrrr*," I hear a woman slur in the background.

"Hey, babe. How's work?" Trent says, but he sounds intoxicated, too.

"Good. Um, I finish at midnight."

"Yeeeeeaaaaahh, about that, babe. You'll have to catch a bus home." I hear some people laughing in the background. "Achuly, you best walk 'cause you're looking real fat. I feeeeeeeeel like I'm fucking a piiiig." There's a huge uproar of laughter from whoever he's with.

"It'll be midnight, Trent. I don't want to walk back on my own. I'll get a cab."

"Noooo you fucking won't. I'm not letting you spend myyyyyy money on cabs. You can walk, you faaaaat coooow." Then there's mooing noises in the background.

"Um, okay. I'll walk. Bye, Trent." I won't walk, it's too late for me to walk back on my own. I don't hear anything from Trent before I hang up. I go into the deli and one of the young men who works here is serving, and there's another man who's standing in front of me waiting to be served.

I stand and wait, and think about how I'm going to get home. "Usual, Max?" the guy serving asks the gentleman, who's now moved to the serving counter.

"Y-y-yes, p-p-please," he says with a stutter.

I can't see his face, but he's tall and dressed in jeans and a t-shirt. "Working late tonight are you?"

"Y-yep. Anoth-another nigh-night at the ho-ho-hospital."

"Hope it's not too busy for you."

The guy chuckles and says, "Wh-when isn't it bu-busy?"

"Yeah." He looks down at the roll he's making 'Max' then looks back up to him. "Juice, too?"

"Y-yes, p-please." I notice his stutter is fairly bad, but the more the guy talks to him, the more at ease he gets and the more the stutter lessens.

"Here you go. Have a good night, Max."

Max pays and takes his food. As he's about to walk out, a young lady goes to push the door to come in. Max opens the door, and stands to the side to let her enter first. "Ma'am," he says and tips his chin. He looks over to me, and I'm speechless and breathless. He's beautiful. Like one of those perfect statues from ancient times. I can't help but keep looking at him as he holds the door open for the young woman. He winks at me, then turns back to her.

I watch as she enters, smiles at him and comes to stand behind me.

I've never seen that happen before. A gentleman. A real life gentleman.

"How can I help you?" the guy calls to me, breaking the spell I'm under watching Max walk away.

"Um…" I lose my words for a fleeting second, "Can I have a salad please?" I turn to look out the front window, but Max is gone. Like a dream, a beautiful fantasy, he's left as if he were never real to begin with.

With my dinner of a salad, I hope soon this extra weight will drop off me. I don't want to be fat and ugly anymore. I can't help being unattractive, but being fat I can certainly do something about. I take my dinner back to the staff breakroom and sit in it on my own, picking at the green leaves.

Before my break, I was overwhelmed remembering the sounds while I was in the bathroom, now though, all I can think about is the man I saw in the deli. Such a simple gesture, holding the door open for someone else. It's playing on my mind, and I can't let it go. One day, I hope to be treated the same way.

I check the time and see I've got to get back on the register. I have four more hours left of the night before I can go home.

The four hours fly by and before I know it, it's the end of my shift. I close my register out and go get my bag. Taking my phone out, I figure I'll try Trent once more in case he can pick me up. The phone rings out and goes to voicemail. I try once again, and the second call goes to voicemail, too. I sling my bag over my shoulder, and walk out through the front of the store. As I walk out the front door, I see Liam parking his car and coming toward the store. "Hey," he says as he stops to talk to me.

"You're in here late, what's going on?"

"Shayne wants candy. So being the good boyfriend I am, I volunteered to bring her some." Liam and Shayne found their groove last week, and since then they've been together virtually every spare moment. She's still trying to organize the four of us to go out, but Trent hasn't said we can go yet.

I smile at Liam; he really is a good guy. "That's really nice of you."

"What are you doing out so late? Did you finish a shift?"

"Yeah, there was one on offer so I took it. I need all the cash I can get before I go to college."

"Aren't you going on a full scholarship?"

"I am, but I still need money for back-up."

"Yeah, you're right. Hey, are you going home?"

"Yeah I am. I can't get in touch with Trent, so I'm just going to walk."

His eyes fly wide open. "Are you crazy? You can't walk home on your own, not this late. Just give me five so I can get Shayne's candy and I'll drive you."

"No, it's okay. I could do with the exercise. I've put on so much weight lately, and I really need to get rid of it."

Liam goes to take a step toward the store, but instead he stops and turns to look at me. "What? You think you're fat?"

I nod my head and tap my hips and thighs. "See, hefty hips and thunder thighs." That's what Trent said I have.

"You can't be serious, Lily. You'd be lucky to be a hundred pounds, fully clothed and soaking wet. And you're what five foot seven? No way are you fat."

"Close. I'm five foot six, and ninety-five pounds. I've put on ten pounds. It's so obvious, look at my thighs. Worst of all are my hips."

Liam looks at me with an unbelieving look, "Really?"

"Yes, look." I hit my thighs again and watch them jiggle.

"Lily, if anything, you're underweight. You should eat more, not less. And besides, it's not safe to walk home alone in the dark."

"What? You must need glasses, because I'm a fat cow."

Liam shakes his head and rolls his eyes. "Whatever, but I'm not letting you walk home, anything can happen to a pretty girl like you." Now I know Liam's just being nice. "I'll be back in a minute. Don't start walking home." He points to me as he walks backward into the store. "I'm serious, I'll only be a few minutes."

I smile at him, "Okay, I'll wait." I go and sit on a bench which is a few feet away and wait for Liam to come back out. When he does, he's hold a shopping bag and he's swinging it. He looks so young and carefree, and really at twenty, he is.

"I got her a selection of things so she can't complain. Not that she would." I stand as he approaches me. "Come on, I'll take you home."

"Thanks," I say, because really I didn't want to walk home in the dark, but I also didn't want to inconvenience Liam either.

"Your chariot, milady," he teases as he opens my door. It makes me laugh, because Liam's kind of a goof.

Once we're in the car, he turns the music off and asks, "You excited about college?"

"Yeah I am. I'm looking forward to it."

"What will you be doing?"

"I want to be an English teacher, so I'll be studying to become one."

"Really?"

"Yeah, why?" I look at him and he's got a smirk on his face.

"With how smart Shayne says you are, I'm amazed you're not going to be more. Like a doctor or a lawyer or something fancy like that."

"What? I'm not smart enough to do anything like that, and besides, English is my favorite thing in the world. Books and reading. I figure seeing as I can't write a book, I may as well learn how to teach it to kids." Liam chuckles and shakes his head. "What? Turn here." I point to the right.

"You really underestimate yourself, Lily. Shayne said you were always second guessing yourself and I didn't believe her. Now, I see what she means. You're gorgeous and smart, don't let anyone else tell you anything different. But mostly, don't let yourself try to talk *you* out of how smart you are."

His statement leaves a heaviness in the car, and I almost want to jump out and go the rest of the way on foot. I feel under the spotlight, as if all eyes are on me. Watching to see what I'm going to say or do. "Yeah, okay," I say, desperately trying to find something to say to break the dense energy swirling around. "Turn left up there." Although I'm giving him directions to the Hackly residence, I still feel the weight sitting on my chest.

When we get to the Hackly's, Liam pulls up in front. "Thank you for the ride," I say as I get out of the car.

"Anytime. See ya," he responds happily.

Maybe I'm reading too much into what he said, or maybe he's just trying to save me from any further embarrassment. I close the door to his car and walk up the driveway to the front door.

I go into my room, change into my pajamas and lie down. Grabbing my copy of *The Crucible*, I start reading it again. But the words seem all jumbled on the page. Not that I can't read them, more like everything that's happened tonight is trying to force its way to the front of my mind.

Trying to focus I'm consumed, absolutely eaten away by the man in the deli, Max. The way he winked at me, it was as if he noticed me. Saw past the ugly exterior, and the broken interior. From a distance he didn't see the damage, he just saw a girl.

As I slip into unconsciousness, I dream of a time when I was a little girl. Mom, Dad, me and a little blond boy playing in the park. Happiness wrapping around us, laughter touching us to the very core.

"Who the fuck brought you home?" I startle awake to Trent jumping on my chest as he sits on me and open-handedly smacks me across the face. The smell of alcohol is so coarse and dense that it overtakes me.

"What?" I struggle against his entire weight on me.

"Dad said a guy brought you home, who the hell is it?"

"Liam brought me home. He offered to drive me. It was late, Trent. I swear nothing happened."

"You stupid bitch, what do you take me for?" He slaps me again and this time I cringe as his hand descends onto my cheek.

"I swear, nothing happened. He brought me home, that's it. Nothing else."

Trent goes to hit me again, but this time I close my eyes and cover my face. "Nothing happened?" he half slurs.

"Nothing at all. He was getting candy for Shayne and saw me walking out. That's all. Nothing else."

"Oh, baby." He collapses on top of me and starts kissing me. "You make me so mad sometimes. I'm sorry, baby, but next time just walk like I said for you to, okay? If you just did what I told you to do, then I wouldn't have been angry."

He's hugging me, and through the overwhelming alcohol smell, I can also smell a rose-like perfume. It's strong, like he's sprayed cologne on, but what man sprays a floral scent on his skin? "Sorry," I say, knowing I probably should've just walked home.

"It's okay. I love you. You just make me crazy with how much I love you. I just want you safe, and I can't stand the thought of another man having his hands on you." He kisses my cheek where he hit me. "I'm sorry.

I didn't mean to hit you."

"I'll be okay."

"Move over, I'm going to sleep here tonight. I need to be close to you."
I know what that means. He wants to have sex with me.

"I'm tired, Trent."

"I'll be quick, then you can go to sleep."

I take a deep breath and close my eyes hoping the next few minutes will
be over quickly.

CHAPTER 12

"GET DRESSED, WE'RE GOING OUT" Trent says as he comes into my room.

"Where are we going?" I ask as I close *The Crucible* and leave it laying on the bed.

"We've officially graduated and I'm taking my girl out for dinner."

I smile at Trent and get a warm tingle throughout my body. He wants to take me out. "I bought a new dress. It's the first nice dress I've ever owned," I say enthusiastically.

"Did you? I don't remember you asking me if you could spend any money," he says as he flops down on my bed, and pushes my book to the floor.

"I didn't realize I had to ask you," I declare.

"You do now, next time just ask. Okay, babe?"

"Um…" Why should I ask how I spend the money I work hard for? It's my money, if I want to buy something pretty for myself, then why can't I?

"It's still your money, babe, but you don't want to spend it on something then regret it because you can't buy a textbook you may need. I know you have a scholarship and all, but what if you need it?"

I can see the reason in that. "That makes sense, but it's not like I've been spending my money on anything. I tried talking to your dad about paying him board, but he wouldn't hear of it."

"Of course he wouldn't, because he knows we're in love and I'll do anything for you. Anyway, you have an hour to get ready. Show me this dress you bought, without my permission." He smiles at me.

I go to the closet and take my dress out. It's dark green, with thin straps and it's fitted all the way to my knee with a small side split. "Do you like it?"

"Huh? Well that's a bit shorter than I thought it would be. But I'm sure it'll look good on you. Go have a shower and get ready. I want you to leave your hair down, it looks better than those ponytails you always put it up in for work."

"Okay, I can do that."

I take my clothes and toiletries to the bathroom, jump in the shower and wash. When I get out, I quickly towel dry my hair and blow dry it straight.

My hair is still mousy, and doesn't really have a lot of body or a pleasing color, but tonight it looks really good.

I'm feeling really good about myself. I've applied a little bit of make-up, not that I know how to do it properly. I go into my room, put on my dress and step into some flat shoes Mrs. Hackly bought me when I first moved here.

I walk out and go to the family room, where Trent is sitting with his mom and dad. "There she is," Mr. Hackly says and Trent looks up from his phone.

"Shit, Lily." I smile because Trent can't take his eyes off me. He's looking me up and down. "You look good." I beam with pride.

"You look beautiful, dear," Mrs. Hackly says, as she stands to come over and kiss my cheek.

"Thank you," I say to both of them. Mr. Hackly doesn't say anything. He just continues to look at me.

"You ready to go?" Trent asks. I nod and step toward the door. "Are you bringing a purse?"

"I didn't know I was going to need it. I'll go get it." I go back into my room and grab my purse to bring it with us. I don't have a bag other than my back-pack I used to take to school and work.

We walk out to the car, and Trent can't keep his eyes off me. "You look good enough to eat, Lily." He drags his hand down and rests it on top of my bottom.

"Thank you," I say, happy that I look good for Trent.

"You're gonna love the restaurant I booked. It's real nice. It's The White Swan. You know which one that is don't you?"

"You're taking me to The White Swan?" I sound giddy and excited. "Thank you, thank you, thank you. Shayne said Liam took her there and she loved it. She said the shrimp was the best thing she's ever tasted. Maybe I'll try it," I eagerly say.

"The sky's the limit tonight, babe. Whatever you want, you can get. And don't worry about it going to your hips because tomorrow you can wake up and go for a run."

"A run? I'm working tomorrow. I'll be at work all day."

"You don't want to keep looking like a pig do you? You'll have to start exercising so you lose that huge ass of yours." I look down at my legs and suck in my stomach. "But tonight, don't worry about your weight."

"Okay," I say, but I sound disheartened, because truthfully I am.

We arrive at the restaurant and all the patrons look so beautiful and elegant. I feel out of place here because now I know my bottom looks really big, which means I look fat in comparison to all the women here. I stand behind Trent and discretely pull my dress down so it's covering me and hopefully people won't look at my big butt.

"Sir, ma'am, I'll show you to your table," the maître'd says, as he leads us through the busy restaurant. The lights are dim and there's a lot of chatter happening as we walk past the tables. People are elegant and stunningly dressed in lovely gowns and suits.

We reach a table and I see Audrey and Jason sitting at the table the maître'd has lead us to. They're sitting close together and Jason has his arm around the back of Audrey's chair.

"Trent," I whisper as I hold onto his arm.

"What?"

"What are they doing here?"

"They're joining us."

"Audrey doesn't like me. Why would you invite her?" I whisper trying not to drag attention to myself.

"Get over it, Lily. They're my friends, and I want them here." He goes and sits down, and I'm left red-faced in front of them and the maître'd. He pulls my chair out for me, pretending not to have been witness to the very embarrassing exchange.

I sit between Trent and Jason and listen to the conversation they're having. They're loud and embarrassing, talking about their school.

"How does it feel coming out at the top of the class?" Audrey asks. Her delivery is somewhat bitchy.

"It's okay," I say as I pick my water glass up and have a drink. The waiter comes and takes our orders and brings us all our drinks. The three of them are having a great conversation, it easily flows for them and they keep excluding me by talking about the times they have together.

Jason is Trent's best friend, and Jason is also dating Audrey. I stand to go to the bathroom, excusing myself from the table, but none of the three are paying any attention to me.

I go to the bathroom and stand looking at myself in the powder room mirror. The door swings open, and in comes Audrey in all her absolute perfection. She has beautiful, silken, black hair and the most amazing green eyes I've ever seen. She may not be ugly on the outside like me, but she's ugly on the inside, where it counts most.

"You look good, Lily. Amazing really, well amazing for a river rat," she spits at me as she comes to stand behind me, holding my gaze in the mirror.

"You look beautiful, too," I say trying to ignore her horribly spiteful remark.

She moves in closer and I get a hint of her floral perfume as she moves my hair to the side, exposing my neck to her. "You know," she whispers, her mouth dangerously close to my skin. "The other night while you were working." She sweeps her mouth down on my neck and slightly kisses me. "Jason, Trent and I had a really good night." She pushes her breast into my back. "So good, I couldn't walk the next day." She steps back and smiles at me, then turns and goes into one of the cubicles.

Slumping my shoulders, I wash my hands as quickly as possible and go back to the table. When I return I notice Trent's moved closer to where Audrey's chair is. I sit down and let the last few moments fully register.

Trent is cheating on me with Audrey, and not only that, he shared her with his best friend. How sick is that? All while I was at work.

"You alright, babe?" Trent asks, but doesn't bother waiting for my reply before turning back to Jason and talking to him.

"Did you have sex with her?" I ask not caring who can hear me and who can't.

"What? Who?" He quickly turns his head back to me and sits forward.

"Audrey. Did you have sex with her while we've been dating?"

"What? No!" he shrieks. "I swear, baby, I haven't touched her. Never." He looks at me and holds my gaze. I can feel myself getting angrier.

Audrey comes back, sits down and both Trent and Jason glare at her. "What?" she says and looks straight at me. "I don't know what she said to you, but I didn't touch her."

"No, you kissed my neck and told me you slept with both Trent and Jason together." I feel like I'm finally able to say something and stick up for myself.

"You lying, bitch. Why would I say anything like that? I'm not even interested in Trent like that."

Our food arrives and everyone goes quiet as it's placed in front of us. But suddenly, I'm not feeling hungry. The server leaves and Audrey, with a smug look, starts eating. Jason does too, and sneaks a look over to Trent who smirks and continues to eat.

Why do I feel like I'm at the butt of their joke? As if they all know a secret and I'm not allowed to know? It catapults me back to school, as if it were years in the past but in fact it was as recently as two weeks ago. I'm the uncool kid walking with her lunch tray, and the mean girls trip me and laugh when the spaghetti lands on my head.

The meal is eaten in complete silence. I can't hear anyone talking, and it feels as if the entire eating area is waiting to see who is going to break first.

Once the meal has been eaten, Audrey looks at me and crosses her arms in front of her chest. "You think I had sex with your man? Let me tell you something, Lily. I could have anyone I want, and *if* I wanted him, I'd take him."

"Audrey," Jason warns her in a low, hushed tone.

"Just don't lie to me," I say as I look among the three of them.

Trent's face changes color. He turns pink, then red from the fury he's attempting to conceal. I can tell he's mad, and so he should be. Audrey is saying things to me, and about me, which are offensive.

"I can't believe this shit, and I can't believe you," she says as she stands and gets her bag. "Jason, take me home."

Jason stands and throws his napkin on the table. "Nice one, Lily," he says and goes after Audrey.

I put my elbows on the table and bury my face in my hands. The entire restaurant is looking, I can feel every set of eyes on me, and I'm beyond humiliated.

"You know what, Lily?" Trent says. I peek out from behind my hands and find him standing beside me. "You've disgraced me in front of my best friend and his girl. I really can't believe the fuss you've created. You can walk home. I'm going out tonight. How dare you embarrass me in front of my friends!" He walks out of the restaurant.

I'm left sitting on my own, on a night that was supposed to have been about us. Instead, I'm mortified *and* alone. I get up and walk toward the front door.

"Mademoiselle," the maître'd calls to me as I'm about to walk out the door.

"Yes, sir." I turn back to him.

He walks over to me and gently puts his hand on the small of my back. He leans down and whispers, "They are not nice people. You shouldn't be around them."

"Thank you," I sigh. His words are the kindest I've heard for a while.

"But I am sorry, they left you with the check." He winces at his own words.

"Of course they did. My apologies. I'll pay it." I follow him to the register and he gives me the bill. My eyes almost fall out of my head when I see none of them have paid. The bill is well over three hundred dollars, and I'm grateful I have that in cash.

"Thank you," he says nicely.

I turn and leave, not only humiliated but also poorer, with over three hundred dollars gone from what I was saving for college. I have no phone, because I left it back in my room, choosing to only bring my purse. And I have no idea how I'm going to get back so late.

I walk down the street and sit on a bench as a few people walk past me, looking me up and down. I'm not wearing a jacket, and the night air has got a crisp chill to it. I look up at the sky and notice the many stars twinkling brightly against the dark backdrop.

"You know, you've been fairly cruel to me," I say to God, or whoever may be listening to me. "I've heard the expression that you don't give out more than a person can handle, but don't you think you've given me enough?" The beautiful bright lights glimmer as if my words have not been absorbed. "Can you go easy on me? Please?"

"Who are you talking to, sugar?" An old man sits beside me on the bench seat. I take in his appearance and come to the conclusion he's homeless.

"No one, sir." I shrug, "Or maybe someone. I'm really not sure."

He looks up to the sky and looks back to me. "Do you know how I know He's listening?" He points up to the sky to indicate God.

"No, sir. How?"

"I ask Him not to let it rain on nights I can't find shelter. Tonight, I'm going to the park down the street, because I have nowhere to lay my head." He smiles at me, exposing his rotting teeth.

A homeless man, completely without anything, has hope. And I'm the one who's feeling sorry for myself. Maybe I'm not noticing what I need to. Maybe my own self-pity is erecting barriers to just how fortunate I am.

I have a boyfriend who loves me, and he said he didn't cheat on me. His family has kindly taken me in because he loves me. I have a job to come back to. Clothes, food, and shelter. I really don't have anything to complain about at all.

"Have you eaten tonight?" I ask him as he sits still looking at the stars.

"I haven't eaten since yesterday," his gruff voice says as he continues his star watching.

"Stay here, please." I get up and walk back to the restaurant.

I've been fed by the ladies at the thrift shop when I was hungry, so I can't see why I shouldn't feed a man in need. I order some food to go, and wait for ten minutes until it's ready to go. The maître'd asks me why I'm still here. When I tell him I'm not sure how I'm going to get back to the Hackly's house, he offers for me to use the phone.

When I take the homeless man food, he looks at me. I can tell he's almost too proud to accept it. "Please, take it," I say as I force it into his hands. "I was once hungry, and I had kindness shown to me, now I'd like to offer you the same."

"Thank you. Thank you," he repeats as he looks down at his holey shoes. "I'll be on my way now. You stay safe. And just remember…" I look at him and he points up to the sky, "It may seem like He's not listening, but the messages always find their way to His desk." He smiles again, and walks away.

I watch as he walks toward the park he pointed out, and I walk back to the restaurant.

I dial Shayne's number. "Hello," she says sounding quite cheery.

"Shayne, it's Lily."

"Hey, girl. Where are you?"

"I've got to be quick. Can you come pick me up please? I'm at The White Swan restaurant."

"What? Why are you there?"

"I'll explain when you get here. And there's one more thing, can I stay with you tonight too, please?" My voice cracks, and I'm about to break down in tears.

"Of course you can. Liam's here, we'll come and get you right away. We'll get there as soon as we can."

"Thank you," I say. She hangs up and I thank the maître'd.

"You may want to wait at the bar, just so you are not sitting outside on your own." He smiles and goes to the dining room. Although he's kind enough to allow me to stay in here, I don't want the eyes and whispers associated with people feeling sorry for me. I go outside and walk down the road to the bench.

Sitting alone, I come to realize that's exactly what I am. Alone. I'm not sure why Trent is with me, because clearly he doesn't care for me or he would not have let Audrey get away with what she said. He would have believed me. Instead he left me, and stuck me with the check to go and hang out with someone who's happy to cause me problems.

"Hey, need a lift?" I look up to see Shayne in the passenger side, smiling at me.

I go and get in the back and Liam says, "You're looking really pretty tonight, Lily."

Shayne adds, "Yeah, you look hot, girl."

"Thank you," I say and take a deep breath.

"What happened?" Shayne asks, and the mood instantly sinks under the heaviness I feel inside me.

"Trent said he was taking me to dinner to celebrate, and Audrey and Jason were there. Anyway, when I went to the bathroom, Audrey followed me in and told me she'd had sex with Trent. When I asked Trent, he got angry and basically the three of them up and left. Stuck me with their food bill and left me there with no way to get home."

"What a prick," Liam says under his breath, though still loud enough for me to hear him.

"I don't know why you put up with him," Shayne says. "After he attacked Liam for no reason, I knew something was off about him."

"I'm leaving him," I say with so much confidence.

"What?" Shayne swings around in her seat to look at me. "You can stay with me. I know you leave for college next week, but stay with me until then and in the meantime you can try and get a dorm room on campus. Stay with me."

I smile at her, and know I really have nowhere else to go. "Do you have anything to pick up from their house? I can take you now if you want?" Liam asks.

"There's only one thing I want, and I can buy it again. Just take me back to your place. Can I borrow a t-shirt to wear to bed, please? Although, I'm way fatter than you are, so I hope it'll fit."

"Do you hear what you're saying, Lily? You are not fat. And while I'm on the subject, just so we're clear, you're attractive and super smart. So wherever you heard that bullshit, you can just ignore it. You. Are. Gorgeous," Shayne tells me.

"She's right, you are," Liam pipes up to add.

I smile at them both. They really are good people. "Thank you." I look out the window and focus on the darkness of the night.

Liam and Shayne talk between themselves, and occasionally add me into the conversation, but my silence tells them I'm not really in the mood to talk.

When we reach Shayne's studio, Liam gives her a kiss and asks us if we want him to stay. Shayne whispers, "Girl time, Liam. Lily and I need to talk. She needs to make a plan and not have a testosterone-filled guy hanging around."

"Okay, sweetheart. I'll come back in the morning. Any problems, just call me." He kisses her on the lips, as I look away, giving them privacy. "See ya, Lily."

"Bye, and thank you for coming to pick me up."

"You're welcome." He gets back into his car and leaves.

"You okay?" Shayne asks as she rattles around in her handbag for her keys.

"I'll be okay. I just need to work out what I'm going to do. We're both going to the same university, so avoiding him will be impossible. But if I can use your computer, I can see if I can get a dorm room this late. If not, I don't know what I'll do. Maybe I can find a room for rent somewhere, but I'll need to find a job, too."

"We'll do it in the morning. How about for now," she stops talking and kicks the bottom of the front door which is stuck. "For now," she continues, "we eat the triple chocolate ice cream in my freezer and just talk about what's going on."

"Sounds like a perfect plan," I say, resigned to the fact that tonight, I'm going to have to tell Shayne everything.

We go inside and she shows me around her small, tidy loft. It's cute and cozy and I can see why she likes it here.

"So," she says as she gets two spoons out of her cutlery drawer and the ice cream tub out of the freezer.

"So." I sit on the small sofa under the only large window in her room.

"It's not my business, Lily. Really it's not. But behind your beautiful green eyes, you hide so many secrets. And I'm sure I'm not going to want to know, but in a way I think it would be better for you to tell someone." She comes and sits beside me, and offers me a spoon. "I'm ready when you are." She dips the spoon in the untouched ice cream and grabs a big spoonful.

"It's kind of…" I avert my eyes and look past her not at her. I don't want her to see everything I've gone through. I'm not scared she'll judge me, but that she'll feel sorry for me. That's more abhorrent to me than judgement.

"Take your time, I've got all night." She smiles and jiggles her eye brows trying to soften the intense and heavy mood encompassing us.

"I don't remember a good time in my life." I start but stop when Shayne reaches her hand out to touch me. "Please, don't. Just let me tell you."

The next three hours is spent telling Shayne my life story. Every part of it, leaving nothing out. As I finish telling her about my life I look at the ice cream, and other than the first spoonful she took, the rest has turned into thick chocolate milk. She's not touched it, and nor have I.

"My God," she says still holding the container of mush. "My God," she says again. Her face is blank, she's showing no expression at all. "My God," she says for a third time.

"There's been some good parts, like meeting you and Liam. You especially. You're so strong and positive, and I really strive to be that myself."

"You're seventeen."

"Eighteen tomorrow," I correct her.

"What? Your birthday is tomorrow, and you haven't told anyone?"

I shrug my shoulders. "No one ever asked and besides that, I've never had a reason to make a big deal out of it."

"That's because you've been broken down, Lily. You've been stomped on your entire life."

"There were good times, I'm sure of it. I sometimes dream of when I was little and we'd be at the park. Mom, Dad, me and a little boy."

"Do you have a brother?

"No. It's always been just me." I take the ice cream container from her hands. "I'm sorry you wasted your ice cream, I'll buy you a new one."

"You will not. It's just ice cream," she scowls at me. I smile again because this is just how Shayne is. She's kind and beautiful and compassionate. Why I was worried about telling her, I have no idea.

"Thank you for listening."

"Tomorrow I'll help you find a job. Hey, I've got an idea, why don't you ask Stacey if she can set up an interview for you at one of the sister stores close to your college? I'm sure she can do that for you. She likes you 'cause she keeps calling you in for any available shifts."

"I can ask." But seeing as she thinks I know about her and Mr. Hackly, I doubt she's going to do anything for me. And considering I'm leaving Trent, I'm sure Mr. Hackly will tell her not to help me.

"Alright, well how about I get you something to wear and you can go have a shower and go to sleep."

I look around her room and other than the loveseat we're sitting on, there's her double bed and a small kitchenette with a table and two chairs. "Um, are you sure I can sleep here?" I question.

"Yeah, don't get too excited. We'll have to share the bed." She stands and goes to a chest of drawers, opening it and throwing me some sleep shorts. "Oh, and I like to spoon, so if you wake in a few hours and my arms are all over you, pretend it didn't happen." She chuckles to herself, and her infectious laugh makes me snicker too.

"Got it, you did not spoon me." I teasingly salute her.

She throws the t-shirt at me, and then gets me a towel. Shayne shows me to the bathroom and leaves me alone. I get in the hot shower and just let the crap of today wash away.

Tomorrow before work, I'll call the university and see if there are any dorm rooms available. Hopefully I'll be able to get to work early and speak to Stacey.

There's an uneasy feeling bubbling away in my stomach. The hot water streaming down on my body doesn't do anything to lift the tension in my shoulders. My mind is spinning and I can't seem to just switch off.

A storm is brewing. I've known darkness in the past, but this feeling of imminent disaster, of doom, seems right on my doorstep. If I open the door, what will I find?

CHAPTER 13

"CAN I BORROW A UNIFORM? I only have a couple shifts left, and everything of mine is back at Trent's place," I say to Shayne in the morning.

"Yeah, that's cool." She stretches in bed and rubs her eyes. "Do you want Liam to give you a lift in? Or the bus comes down the road."

"It's fine, I'll take the bus. Hey, thank you for last night."

She rubs her eyes again and then looks at me. "You're welcome."

I sit on the bed beside her, where I was sleeping last night. "I've never had a friend before, Shayne. I was always scared to let anyone in. And it's taken me eighteen years, but I think I've found my best friend."

"Oh my God, it's you're birthday today! We have to go out tonight. I'm taking you to dinner."

"No need, I've never had anything done for me, so really I don't need anything now." I turn away so she can't see my embarrassment.

"No one *needs* to have anything for their birthday. It's a day to celebrate your birth."

"There's nothing really to celebrate. So can we miss it? Please?"

Shayne sits up in bed and runs her hand through her long, dark hair. "I tell you what, we can skip going out, but here are my conditions."

"You have conditions?" I chuckle, now not ashamed but amused.

"Yes. You have to stay here until you leave for college and I have to order pizza tonight and have cake. Just me and you."

An easiness floods me, because I'm so relieved she's dropped the whole 'going out' thing tonight. "I can do that."

"It's settled. After work tonight, pizza and cake. And just so you know, my cake will taste terrible, but you have to pretend you love it and eat it."

"No one's ever made a cake for me before." And with just that one sentence, the mood shifts again and the room is filled with heaviness. "Sorry," I whisper because I brought Shayne's happiness down.

"Hey." She gets up off the bed and goes to her drawers. "Here, a uniform." She hands me the folded shirt and pants.

I take it and go into the bathroom to change. The pants are slightly big and the shirt too long, but they'll have to do considering I only have a couple of shifts left before I leave for college.

When I come out, Shayne is up and making coffee. But I forgo it and tell her I want to get into work to speak with Stacey.

Taking the bus to work I feel a weight sitting firmly in the pit of my stomach. I only need to get through the next few days, then I'm off to college. And it's a huge place, so I'm hoping I won't have to see Trent. The apartment his parents rented for us is not on campus. If I can get a dorm room, other than going to work, I won't need to leave campus. And seeing as I know the location of the apartment, I'll get work on the opposite side of town and then the chance of seeing him will be small.

Walking in to work, I see Stacey's already here and standing to the side of one of the registers talking to one of the other girls. I hang back, giving them both privacy until they've finished talking. Stacey turns to walk away and she looks at me and indicates with her head to follow her.

"Stacey, can I talk to you for a moment?" I ask.

"Up in my office, Lily. Not down here." The way she says it, I feel like I've done something wrong.

Walking behind her, I go over the last few days here in my head. I try to replay all my interactions with the customers; if I was rude to anyone, or if I said something to anyone who could've taken it as rude.

She goes into her office and sits down behind her desk and says, "Close the door."

A shudder of cold washes over me, as if she's going to pink slip me. "Have I done something wrong?" I ask, the tension in my body bursting through in the way I ask.

"What? No, you've done nothing wrong at all. But I did get a call from Chris, and then I got a call from Trent."

"I didn't do anything," I automatically respond.

"No you didn't. Both of them are very upset that you didn't go home last night. They seem to think you've broken it off with Trent."

"It's something I need to discuss with Trent." It's not her business, and nor will I talk to her about it.

"You do realize I'm a very good friend of Chris and if he calls me unhappy, then I try and make him happy. Not to mention, his son, your boyfriend has called here in a total panic because he believes you've left him. This is my store, and if they call me, then yes, it's something you can discuss with me. From what Chris and Trent told me, you were rude and accused Trent of cheating on you."

"What?" I feel my shoulders slump that Trent would even say something to my boss. "It's not how it happened."

"Then sit down, and tell me so we can work through it and you can stop this childish behavior and return to your boyfriend."

I sit on the chair and knit my hands together. "I'm not going back. And

I wanted to talk to you and ask you if you can recommend me to a store near the college for a job."

"You're not going back? Why would I recommend a brat who likes to create problems? And don't think I don't know about the night you tried to come on to Shayne's boyfriend and had him drive you home."

"What? I don't know who's telling you these things but again, that's not how it happened."

"Then you better tell me what happened last night and hurry up because your shift starts in a few moments. The longer you take, the less you'll get paid because it's eating into your hours. And if I'm satisfied with what you tell me, only then will I recommend you to the store." She sits back and crosses her arms in front of her.

I've got no choice, I have to tell her because if I don't then not only do I lose out on my hours here, but she won't refer me to the store near campus.

When I finish telling Stacey what happened, she simply shifts in her seat before considering what to say. "So you're saying all this happened because you believed her over your boyfriend?"

"He stuck up for her."

"*Your* boyfriend, who *you* live with and brings *you* to work, and protects *you* and I hear even gave *you* a phone. The same guy?" She emphasizes the words, looking at me as if I'm not getting her point.

"He was angry I even said anything. What am I supposed to do? Sit there and let her say things to me and not ask about them?"

"He's your boyfriend. He's the man in the relationship and you should stick by him, no matter what."

That's such archaic thinking, especially considering he's not in the right. "That's not fair. She bombarded me, saying she's had sex with my boyfriend, and then the three of them left me with the bill to pay, and made a scene so it humiliated me."

"You deserve to be humiliated, because you're in the wrong. Think about it, Lily. Really think about it. Why would Trent want you around if all he's going to do is cheat on you?" When she puts it like that, it makes sense. "And why would he go to that trouble of protecting you and looking after you if all he's going to do is screw around?" Her point is valid.

I dart my eyes away from hers, and focus on a lone paper clip on her desk. "I didn't think of it that way."

"Not to mention actually go to the trouble of organizing a date to start with, at The White Swan no less. A beautiful restaurant where the dishes are some of the best in the state. It may have turned to shit, but do you think it's fair to blame him over miscommunication? And not only that, but over something someone else said, over which he has no control? That's not the type of girl you are, Lily."

She's right, I'm not. Trent really didn't do anything wrong. I shouldn't punish him because Audrey is horrible. She's not his responsibility. "You're right," I admit, finally able to see clearly how I reacted.

"Just talk to him, not right now, after your shift finishes."

"Yeah, okay, I think that's a good idea." I stand and smile to her. "Can you see if you can please refer me to the store near campus? Or even see if they have any positions vacant?"

"Sure, I'll do it and let you know on your last shift."

"Thank you." I turn to walk out and go start work.

"Oh, Lily. Some of the girls want to surprise you and take you out on Friday night for your last shift. Maybe it's a good idea if you let Trent know. He may want to come with you."

"Thanks, Stacey, I will."

I leave her office and go down to start my shift. Clinton, one of the shift supervisors, tells me what register I'm on, and I go to start my ten-hour shift.

The first five hours drag on, and I can't wait until I go on my break so I can get something to eat. I missed out on breakfast this morning because I wanted to get here early to speak with Stacey, and now I'm starving.

As I finish with the last customer, I see a guy in a brown uniform and cap walk in carrying a large bunch of lilies. They look beautiful and I can't help but think, that possibly they're for me. But that would be stupid, because if anything I'm to blame for what happened last night, because as Stacey pointed out, I overreacted and caused the problem. So if anything, I should be the one sending Trent flowers and begging him for forgiveness. Stupid really. Why *would* he send me anything?

"Lily Anderson?" The guy in the brown uniform asks me.

"Yes," I say, looking at him suspiciously.

"These are for you. Enjoy your day," he cheerfully tells me, hands me the huge bouquet of flowers, then walks out.

"Wait, what?" I call after him, but he's already out the door.

"Aren't they beautiful? Who are they from?" my customer asks.

"I'm not sure." Maybe they're from Shayne, and this is her birthday present to me.

"Open the card," the lady encourages me.

"But your groceries?"

"They'll still be here in a few moments. I want to see that lovely smile grow even wider when you read the card." She's an elderly lady, and I think the fact there's someone around her who's happy, makes her happy.

"Thank you, ma'am." I stop working, only for a moment and open the card.

My Darling Lily,

Please forgive me for being an idiot. I love you and I don't want to lose you. I promise I'll do better because I never want you to leave.

I love you with my entire heart,

Trent x

PS: Happy birthday, baby.

"Who are they from?" she asks again, as tears well up in my eyes. *He's so sweet, I did something wrong, and he's sending me flowers.*

"They're from my boyfriend," I answer her and read the card again before sliding it between the flowers and continuing with her groceries.

"You're a very lucky girl. Because they really are beautiful." She smiles at me again.

"Thank you, ma'am." I finish with her groceries, close down my register for my break and take my flowers toward the staff break room.

"Lily," I hear from behind me. I turn around and see Trent's dressed beautifully. He's wearing a suit, and his hair is nicely done.

"I got your flowers," I say, as I look down at them. "They're gorgeous, thank you."

He walks toward me with such confidence and strength. "I know why I've been going crazy. And I'm so sorry, but I'm here to make it right, and it starts right now." He drops to one knee, in the middle of the candy isle. "Lily Anderson, I love you. I've been going crazy since last night. I tried to understand what happened, and it was like a light bulb moment brightened up my whole room when I figured out what was wrong. I'm wrong. I'm wrong because I'm scared of losing the best thing that's ever happened to me. We don't have to get married right away, but please say yes to being my wife?" He takes a small black box out of his coat pocket and flips it open.

I can't help but smile at the tiny diamond ring he's presenting me. I'm not laughing at the size of the rock, but at the fact that he's done the best he can with the money he has.

Looking around, people are gathering and the women are all 'ooohing' and 'ahhhing' and pointing at how Trent's wearing his heart on his sleeve,

"Trent," I say as I step closer to him.

"Please, Lily. Please forgive me. I'll try harder; I'll change; I'll do anything you want me to. I love you so much it hurts. Last night was the worst night of my life, because you weren't with me. I love you so much." He's still on one knee and I can't bring myself to say anything to him. "We can go to college together as a real couple. One who can plan their wedding and be totally in love."

I smile at his request. He really is cute. "Yes," I whisper, finally happy I'm getting my very own family, and someone who loves me so intensely.

The onlookers erupt in cheers, and Trent stands and rushes over to me, places the ring on my finger then he swoops me up in his arms and spins us around. His mouth takes mine, and he continues to kiss me as he spins me. The lilies are now being held by a lady who was standing beside me.

"Thank you, babe. Thank you. I'm taking you out tonight to celebrate, just you and me."

"I can't," I say as he stops spinning us and places me on my feet. He knits his eyebrows together and tilts his head to the side. "I made plans with Shayne. We're getting pizza and she's making me a cake. No one's ever made me a birthday cake before." I gleam. I'm so happy.

"Okay, babe. Whatever you want. We can go out tomorrow. But, can I take you and pick you up? I just want to spend every minute I can with you."

He's so sweet, and I can tell he has changed toward me. "Thank you, I'd love that." I kiss him again.

"Come one, babe. I'm going to take you to get something to eat. Do you want me to take the flowers home with me?" He holds his hands out for the bouquet.

"Thank you, yes. But I have to go back and get my purse." I go to walk to the where my bag is.

"No you don't; the least I can do is pay, considering I left you to pay for last night. I'm so sorry about all of that." He leads me out toward his car, and just his attitude is lighter than what it's ever been before.

"Thank you, Trent. For letting me go out tonight, and for buying me lunch."

He puts the flowers in the back of the car, and he snakes his hand around my waist. "Anything for you." He kisses me on my nose and walks us over toward the deli I love. "Hang on, you didn't tell me what you think of your ring?" He smiles as he moves his hand to entwine our fingers and then bring my hand up to his mouth to kiss my fingers.

"I love it, it's perfect." I look down and admire the cute, little clear stone.

Today is going to be fantastic. I can't wait to tell Shayne tonight.

"Trent brought you over?" Shayne says with raised eyebrows, as she looks out the door toward Trent.

"Yeah, he did. So much has happened today." I step inside and she shuts the door.

"Clearly. Tell me, how was your day?"

We both go into her apartment, and we flop down opposite each other on the loveseat. "It was unbelievable. It really couldn't have gone any better." I look at Shayne, and her face is screaming a thousand words. I can tell she's not impressed, not one little bit. The scowl on her face, the way her lips have thinned out and her eyes look like they're judging me. "Please don't, Shayne. You mean so much to me. And I don't want you to be upset with me."

"I'm not upset with you. I just don't think he's the best person for you."

"He's changed. He was so different. He let me come here even though he wanted to take me out for dinner to celebrate."

"Celebrate your birthday?" She twines her hair around her fingers.

"That and this." I show her my ring. But her face doesn't change into the happiness I was hoping it would. "Oh," I sigh. "You're not happy for me?"

"I am, really I am. But how can you say yes so quickly after how he treated you?"

"I told you, he's changed."

"You're telling me he changed overnight? He left you to pay the restaurant bill, he walked out on you, but less than twenty-four hours later, he's changed? You can't really believe that?" She looks at me with her eyebrows raised, clearly disbelieving his change of heart.

"I'm not stupid, Shayne. I know how people can be, but he's genuine and I can see he's changed."

"Either that, or he's saying all the right things." She rolls her eyes and looks away.

"Look, I don't want to fight with you. I was going to ask you if you'd be in my wedding party. You're my absolute best friend in the whole world, and I want you and Trent to get along. You are the two most important people in my world."

She looks back to me smiling. Her shoulders relax and I can see all the anger leaving her body. "I love you, girl. I'll do anything for you. Just promise me one thing. Just one."

"What?" I lean in to hug her.

"Start keeping a journal. You've had so much shit thrown at you already, and I think keeping a journal might help you cope with everything that has happened to you up to now."

The request is reasonable, and she's right. Writing can be therapeutic. I know I love the English language and although I may not be an author, I can still write my feelings down. "Yeah, okay. That sounds good, I can do that." I hug her tighter. "Hey did you know the girls at work are throwing me a going away party?"

"Who do you think organized it?" She winks at me. "Friday night, girl, get dressed really pretty. Go buy a new dress and some killer hot heels. We're going dancing and having some fun."

"I'm underage, I can't get in anywhere like the place you're describing."

"Keep your panties on, we're not doing anything illegal. There's a club that opens its door to under twenty-ones up until eleven at night, then they kick everyone out and it's strictly over twenty-one. Half the girls coming are underage, so this way whoever is over twenty-one and wants to stay can, and the rest will need to go."

"This is going to be so much fun. I can't wait. I'm going dress shopping," I squeal happily.

"I'm coming with you, I don't have to work until tomorrow afternoon."

The rest of the night is spent talking, eating and just having the best time ever. For the first time in forever, I'm so happy. I'm lucky to have a caring fiancé, the best best-friend in the world. Life is looking good. Really, really good.

CHAPTER 14

"I CAN STAY HOME AND look after you," I say to Trent who's looking slightly ill. He's coming down with a cold, and he's been in bed.

"Don't be silly. Go out with your friends, they've been organizing this for a while. I'll take you and I'll pick you up. You said the club changes over to over twenty-one at eleven, right?"

"Yeah," I say, as I get my outfit ready for tonight.

"I'll be there by ten-thirty and I'll wait for you."

"I can ask Liam to give me a lift home. You don't have to come out if you're not well." I place my new high heels beside the bedroom door.

Trent's lying on my bed with his arms beneath his head as he's watching me. "No, I'll come pick you up. I want to be there for my girl."

How sweet. I hang my dress on the back of the door handle, and go sit on the bed with Trent. He sits up and drags me so I'm lying across his chest. He kisses my forehead and runs his hands gently up and down my back. "Thank you, Trent. You really have changed." I lay my head on his chest and he keeps drawing circles on my back.

"I told you, babe. I don't want to lose you. Just promise me you'll behave tonight." He kisses the top of my head.

"My heart belongs to you, and no one else." I close my eyes and revel in one of the sweetest moments in my life. Pure perfection. We're lying together, melting into one, and I just can't believe how lucky I am to actually have found Trent. *Or maybe he found me.*

"Come on, you need to get ready or you're going to be late," he says as he gives my bottom a light, playful smack. I stand, grab my dress and my new panties and bra I bought and I'm about to go to the bathroom to change. "Where are you going?"

"To the bathroom."

"No you don't. I've seen you naked heaps, babe. No need to go to the bathroom to change. Do it here, I wanna watch my hot fiancé change." He smirks at me, and I see the look of desire in his eyes.

"Okay," I say, as I take my t-shirt off and take my yoga pants off. His eyes keep a close watch on me. And I slide my bra off, and my panties and pull on my new sexy red ones.

"Damn," he says and sits up in bed. I put my new red bra on and do up the back. "Double damn." He smirks at me, and I can almost see him salivating. "You really are hot."

"Thank you," I answer him. And just by him saying that, I already feel so much more confident, and even kind of sexy. Though compared to Shayne, and the other girls coming, I'm nothing to look at. I slide my new black dress on and my new black shoes. "Do you like?" I say as I spin in front of him.

He knits his eyebrows together and purses his lips into a thin, irritated line. Immediately my confidence deflates, I look down at my dress and run my hands over my stomach smoothing the material down. "Hmmm," he huffs and scratches the gruff on his chin.

"What? Don't I look nice?"

"You kind of look like a hooker. I don't want people thinking my fiancé is there to be paid for sex."

"What?" I look down again, shocked that's how I look. "I thought it looked nice. Shayne said the dress suits me. She wouldn't lie to me."

"Neither would I. But if you want to go out and have people thinking you're a whore, well…" He shrugs his shoulders. "It's your decision, but I don't want that for you. I love you too much." He stands and comes over to me. "Like I said, your decision." He kisses me on the cheek and opens the door. "We have to go in fifteen minutes." He leaves and closes the door behind him.

I don't want to give anyone the impression I'm a prostitute, and I'd be mortified if someone did try to pay me or ask me how much for *those* services. I take my dress off, and put it back in the shopping bag it came in. I'll give it to Shayne; she said she liked it. I get a pair of jeans and a white blouse and put them on instead. I can still wear my new shoes.

When I'm ready I tuck some money in my pocket and go to find Trent. He's standing by the front door, with the keys to his dad's car in his hands. "There you go. You look like a very respectable eighteen-year-old woman. Come on, babe." He holds his hand out to link our fingers together.

The drive over to the club is short, and Trent and I talk about when we're going to leave to head to college. We're both packed and ready to go, and we'll be leaving in a four days with classes starting early next week for both of us.

"Have a good night, babe. I'll be back by ten-thirty, but don't come out until you're ready. I'll just wait." He kisses me again. "Love you," he adds, as I'm about to walk away.

"Love you, too."

I go in and find Shayne and a couple of the other girls. Liam's here and they're all having a great time. The night flies by, we're dancing and talking and just really having a good night.

"Hey," Shayne says as she sips a pink drink with a little umbrella in it. "Why aren't you wearing your new dress?" she asks as she dances in her seat to the heavy beat of the bass.

"Oh yeah, I forgot, I'm going to give it to you if you want it."

"What? Why?" she shouts over the music.

"I put it on, and I looked at myself. It didn't suit me." I don't want to tell her I look cheap in it, because I actually think it'll suit her so much better than me. The dress is just not for me.

"What? You looked super-hot in it. Seriously, smoking hot."

"Who looks smoking hot?" Liam says as he approaches us, sits and puts his arm around Shayne. "I gotta check her out." He looks around the club.

Shayne playfully smacks Liam in the arm, and he leans over and kisses her shoulder. "You're a dork." I smile at their carefree, easy relationship. "I was saying Lily looked really hot in this dress she got yesterday, but she said she didn't like it, so she's giving it to me."

"Didn't you try it on before you bought it?" Liam asks.

"Yeah, but when I put it on tonight, I just didn't like it."

"So I score a new dress thanks to my best friend, Lily." Shayne points to me. "But, it might be tight around my boobs seeing as mine *are* bigger than yours." She points to her breasts than to mine.

"Hot," Liam says making a stupid face.

"Hey. Let's go dance," Penelope, one of the girls says as she bounces over to our table.

I pull my phone out and notice it's quarter to eleven, so I may as well get another dance in before I leave to meet Trent.

Shayne and Liam follow, and they're dancing really close together, his hands all over her. I'm dancing in the circle with Penelope, Jasmine and a few of the other girls when I feel someone put their hands on my hips.

I turn to see some guy grinding up against me. "Hey, hot stuff," he says as he continues to dance.

I sidestep him, breaking his contact on my hips and continue dancing. But he does it again. "Hey, don't," I yell over the music.

"We're just dancing, not screwing," he shouts back.

"I don't want your hands on me." I move to be on the opposite side and keep dancing with the girls. He disappears and I just close my eyes and feel the music. But then I feel his hands on me again. I whip around and see he's just about to kiss me. But before his lips come anywhere near me, he's dragged away.

"Keep your hands off her," Trent yells and punches the guy.

"Trent," I scream as I try to stop the continuous blows he's landing.

"Trent," I yell again and grab onto his fist as he rears his hand back.

His head whips around to look at me and he angrily spits, "Don't, Lily. I saw the whole damn thing."

The moment he looks back, two huge bouncers have him up and are hauling him out. There's two more who've grabbed the guy who had his hands on me and are dragging him out, too.

I look around and see Shayne. She's looking shocked as she watches both the guys being dragged out of the club. "Bye," I mouth to her as I go to leave.

As I walk away, she runs after me, throws her arms around me and whispers, "Be careful." Just as am I about to ask her who I should be careful of, she's gone.

When I reach outside, Trent is already pacing and completely irrational. "What the hell was that, Lily? I saw everything."

"Then you saw how I told him to take his hands off me? And did you see how I moved away?"

"I saw you look at him like you wanted him to kiss you."

"No I didn't. I was going to tell him to leave me alone, again. But you grabbed him and…you know the rest."

Trent turns and walks toward his dad's car. "Are you coming?" he shouts over his shoulder to me.

I run to catch up to him, and link my arm in his. "I wasn't to blame, really. I didn't do anything."

He takes a few breaths and calms down, "Yeah I know. I just saw his hands on you and I lost it. Isn't it lucky you changed? Because if you had worn that dress, God only knows how many others would've had their hands all over you."

"I know, I'm sorry." I lean in and kiss him. "Thank you for coming to get me."

"It's alright, babe."

When we reach the car, he opens my door and waits until I'm in. Then he comes around and gets in the driver's side. "Will you teach me to drive?" I ask as I watch him pull out onto the street.

"Not this again, Lily. You don't need to learn how to drive. I'll take you anywhere you need to go. You know that." In a comforting gesture, he squeezes my thigh.

"I know, but I'd like to be independent, too. I mean, what if something happens and we can't be together."

I can see his mouth turn down in a frown. "That's just ridiculous. We'll always be together. In life and in death."

In life and in death? What exactly does that mean?

As it turns out, I don't have to wait too long to discover what he means.

November 13th 2009

Dear Diary,

It's been just over a year since we got married. Trent wanted to marry me right away, but we managed to wait until just before my nineteenth birthday. This last year has been, for the lack of a better word, difficult. We celebrated our first year anniversary the way we spend every night.

I go to class during the day, as does Trent, then after class I go to work and Trent comes home. Some nights I manage to get more than four hours sleep, but since Trent's taken over our finances, he says I need to work more because we need the money. He's got a job too, but he only works two days a week. He says school is stressing him out, so he can't work more.

Seeing as this is my very first diary entry, I may as well tell you, Shayne and I don't speak much anymore. She said Trent was trying to control me and he was coming between us. She also said when I leave him, I should come find her. She was bridesmaid at our wedding, and after that night she barely talked to me again. Trent says it's because she's jealous Liam hasn't married her yet. I don't know, maybe it is. It hurt at first, but now I've been so busy with school, work and being a wife, I don't really have too much time to notice she's gone. Does that make me a bad friend? There are times, like when I got the top marks in my last three papers for English Lit I wanted to tell her, but she wasn't around.

Trent says he wants a baby, but I'm nowhere near ready for a child. And really, I wouldn't have any idea what to do with one.

Trent's dad came over last week, but Mrs. Hackly wasn't feeling well, so she stayed behind. I found a recipe on line and made it. Mr. Hackly told me it tasted like cat food, and Trent laughed and told him I was still learning. I liked it. But maybe I liked it because I know what it's like to have nothing.

It was my twentieth birthday yesterday, and Trent bought me a box of chocolates, saying we don't have extra money to go out.

The apartment is small, but it'll do for now. I really can't work anymore to try and get us anything nicer, because school takes up so much of my time.

Trent says he wants to change what he's doing. He doesn't want to be an accountant anymore. He wants to be a doctor. I support him, of course. He should follow his dreams.

Anyway, I have to go. I've picked up an extra shift at the supermarket and I need to get ready. I think having a diary is good idea, it'll let me keep track of everything in my life.

Bye diary.

PS. How funny that I'm talking to you like you're a real life person.

October 8th 2010

Dear Diary,

It's been so crazy lately. I can't believe I haven't been able to write in you for a while. My twenty-first birthday is next month and life couldn't get any busier, even if I wanted it to.

Okay, so over the last month. I don't know even where to start. Trent went out one night, came home completely drunk from one of those frat parties and tried having sex with me. When I told him he stunk like beer and vomit, he backhanded me and told me it's my job as his wife to give him sex whenever he wants. I managed to get free of him and lock myself in our bathroom. I was so shocked by what he did, all I could do was cry. He tried beating the door down, but he passed out and fell asleep across the threshold of the door. I was too scared to leave the bathroom, so I slept in there. The next day I heard him leave and when he finally returned, he had bought me the most beautiful bracelet he could find. He told me it was from a pawn shop because we don't have a lot of money, and he told me a thousand times how sorry he was for hitting me. I felt bad I was scared of him, and he's right, I do have to give him sex whenever he wants. "Men have needs," he said. Of course they do, and it was stupid of me not to realize.

They've given me a promotion at the supermarket. I'm now a shift supervisor, which means I get more money. I'm not sure how much is in our account, because Trent looks after all the bills, but he says we scrape by from paycheck to paycheck.

I'm also doing really well at school. One of my lecturers is impressed with me and says I really should try and become a professor in English. He thinks I'm smart enough to teach at the university level, but of course, I think he's just being nice.

Trent changed his major and is now in his first year of becoming a doctor. He's got so many years left. He quit his job, saying he just couldn't handle all the stress of both med school and work. He said me learning how to be an English teacher is so much easier, it only made sense I'd keep working and he'd concentrate on his studies. I fly through my studies. His career is so much more important than anything I'll ever do.

I heard from Shayne, too. She and Liam are still together, and they got engaged. But they're saving so they can go to Italy and Greece. She said they want to travel before they settle down. I miss her, but if I want a career as an English teacher, some things need to be sacrificed. That's what Trent says, and I can totally understand. I don't even have time to make friends from any of my classes. If I'm not at work, I'm at school. If I'm not at work or school, I'm here studying.

See ya next time diary.

Bye.

October 7th 2011

Dear Diary

Oh my god. What has happened to my life? I'm twenty-two next month and I'm pregnant. SQUEEEEEE. Can you believe it, diary? I'm pregnant!

I've had to stop school, because Trent said I can't put too much pressure on the baby by working, and going to school. So we decided I'll stop school but keep working until I have the baby, and Trent will continue medical school.

He got one of his exam results back and he didn't do too well. He passed, but only just. He told me it's because I was too busy working and couldn't help him study. That night he was so angry, he lost control of his temper and he hit me. Actually, he punched me. I was so embarrassed because I got this big bruise around my eye. I had to tell everyone I sleep-walked into the door. But it's okay now, because I've put school on hold until after the baby.

Trent says I need to work extra hours because once the baby is here, I'll need to have some time off. He also thinks it'll be a good idea if his mom looks after the baby so I can go back to work. I'm not sure I like that idea. Last time Mr. and Mrs. Hackly were here, she looked like she'd lost so much weight. She was also wearing long sleeves and it was so hot here. I'm not sure what's going on, I just hope she's okay.

Well, the baby will be here in seven short months. I just hope once the baby is born Trent calms down some. He's pushed me a couple of times, but only when he's stressed. I really should know when not to say anything and just do what he asks. I'm getting better at reading his moods. It did hurt my feelings when he said I was ugly and no one would want me. But then he apologized and said he didn't mean it, but I shouldn't wear sweats around the house.

Anyway, today's entry is short, even though I still have more to say. I have to go get ready for work. Midnight shift. Yuck. But the money is really good. And if Trent says we need the money, then we must need it. He's going to a party while I work. He says he doesn't like spending time on his own, and his friends keep him company.

Bye Diary.

PS: Isn't it still funny, that after three years, and only a few entries, I feel like I'm talking to you like you're a real person.

Bye.

December 24th 2012

Hi,

Just hi. I hate this. I've spent the day crying. Trent tells me to get up and stop acting like a twenty-three year old child. I lost another baby yesterday. This is my third miscarriage, and every time it just gets harder and harder.

I think the last time was from the punch in the stomach Trent gave me. He said he didn't mean it, and if I just listened to him, he wouldn't act so crazy. I was home late from work yesterday. It wasn't my fault, the bus was running late, and I didn't get home until fifteen minutes after Trent was expecting me. I walked in the door, and he was standing there with his belt in his hand and steam coming out of his ears. Not literally steam, but boy was he mad.

Whenever he has the belt out, I know I haven't tried hard enough for him, and I've made him mad. He's been really good, but last night I was late from work and he was angry. So I had to take it like a big girl. This morning I woke and the bed was covered in blood. I knew it was going to happen because when he hit my stomach, I started to hurt straight away. I'm so stupid, why didn't I just run home? Why didn't I do everything I could to be home? I just can't believe how stupid I am.

When Trent woke this morning, he saw the blood and was just so good. He drew me a bath, changed the sheets and took care of me. He loves me so much. He tells me every time. It's my fault these things happen. I just have to try harder.

Anyway, Trent said I'm allowed to stay home from work today, so I'm just lying in bed. Trent said he had to go out, and he'll be back later. I don't think he's gone to get my Christmas present, because when I was putting his clothes away I found a little black box with the most beautiful diamond necklace. Although I feel terrible and have been crying, I kind of can't wait until tomorrow morning. We're going to Trent's mom and dad's house; it should be good.

Bye.

May 6th 2013

Diary,

I just read my last entry, which was just before Christmas. I know it's been months. I'm sorry, but so many things have happened. That beautiful necklace ended up not being for me. I'm not sure who it was for. I opened the present Trent got me, and it was an electric toothbrush. He said my breath stinks, and maybe it's the toothbrush I've been using. I told him I saw it in his drawer and he lost it with me. He told me I was a nosey bitch and he hit me. This was bad, this one. He hit me so hard I ended up falling and knocking myself unconscious. He took me to the hospital, and told them I fell down and that's how I lost consciousness. When I woke, he told me that's what happened and I mustn't remember. At first I believed him, but then I started remembering small things and when I was finally released and got home I asked him. He told me I hit my head hard, and must be misremembering it. But I know what he did.

Anyway, he hasn't hit me that bad again. A push here and there, and if dinner's not on the table when he's home by five-thirty, then I get a slap, too. I definitely deserve those ones, because he's said what time it has to be on the table, and I try and be a good wife and do what he asks me.

It's just because I'm stupid that I keep making these silly mistakes _ that's what Trent says.

He's under so much pressure at school, and he's not keeping up with the work. Sometimes I do his assignments, and those ones he does really well on.

Work is crazy, they've promoted me again. And they were so good to me when I lost the babies. About the miscarriages, I'm happy to report I haven't had any more, because I haven't gotten pregnant again. I don't think I can go through another miscarriage. It'll hurt too much. It's not the physical pain I'm worried about, but I don't think my heart will be able to cope. I barely made it last year when I lost the last baby.

I got a postcard from Shayne recently. It just said 'We hope you're keeping well and it had a picture of the Coliseum on it. I cried when I got it. I'm so happy for her and Liam, they're living their dream and having a great time. I just hope when they get married I'll be invited. Even if I'm not, I'll sneak in and stay right at the back so they don't see me, and I'll watch them exchange vows on their perfect day. I do hope they want me there though.

I have to go, Trent is due home soon and I need to make dinner. If it's not on the table at five-thirty, well you and I know whatever he does to me could've been avoided if I just do as he asks.

See ya.

September 29th 2014

Diary,

"If you ever leave me, I'll find you and kill you. Then I'll kill myself because life without you isn't worth living." Trent said that to me, then he told me, "It's only because I love you so much."

Damn...

I've got to go. He's back early and I haven't made the bed yet. He likes it when everything is tidy.

November 24th 2014

I can't even start this entry by saying 'dear diary', really I can't. Yesterday I got back from the hospital. I did something so stupid, I really only have myself to blame for Trent hitting me.

Why, and I repeat why, would I have asked him if he's seeing someone else? I was doing the laundry and there was lipstick marks on one of his shirts. He lost his temper at me. He said it was probably me fucking around and that I'm accusing him to distract from the truth. I yelled at him. Why would I do that? I'm so stupid, I just can't believe how dumb I am.

I deserve what I got. He's my husband. He wouldn't cheat on me. He twisted my arm around behind my back and broke it. It was an accident, I know it was, because when he dropped me off at the hospital he said it was an accident and he didn't mean to hurt me – he just lost his temper because I said something to upset him.

The doctors didn't have to operate because they said the fracture didn't require surgery, just a cast. Trent said he couldn't stay with me, because he was helping a friend get ready for a party. He told me I could do it on my own, and he also said to tell the doctors and nurses I was running and tripped. I said what he told me to say. They didn't believe me, but I insisted and convinced them.

One of the nurses came in on the sly and tried to talk me into saying Trent beats me. But he doesn't. Because he's not a bad person, he just wants things done in a certain way, and I get punished if they aren't done how he likes them. I make him angry, and it's then when he hits me. See it's my fault, not his. And this hospital visit, well this one was an accident. But I told her, I'm just a silly woman who's clumsy. She believed me after that.

While I was resting, after they had put a cast on my arm, a nice-looking man wheeling the food trolley came in to deliver a tray to the bed beside me. He looked really familiar, but I couldn't place him. But I know I knew him. He offered me something to eat, but

I didn't feel hungry. I tried to remember who he was, and when I closed my eyes to rest, I remembered where I saw him before. He was the man at the deli that one time. His stutter was unforgettable. Remember, the man who held the door open for that girl who was coming in? I think his name was Max. I remember how he was really nice to that girl, and I remember his stutter, too.

Anyway, I'm going to try extra hard from now on. Trent always tells me how much of a disappointment I am to him. So now I'm going to try and make him proud of me. He also told me I look like a fat piece of meat. So I'll be starting my diet tonight. I need to get down to eighty pounds. God, I'm so fat.

Bye diary.

Ps: I can't wait to be the best wife in the world for Trent. He deserves the best. He loves me so much.

CHAPTER 15

Present

IT'S MY TWENTY-FIFTH BIRTHDAY today and I'm spending it alone in the hospital.

Curling up on my side I can't help but let the tears fall. Losing the baby this time was hard. The hardest one yet. Maybe because I was just under half-way there at sixteen weeks, or maybe because I was hoping this time it would be different.

"How are you, Mrs. Hackly?" an older nurse asks as she comes through the door.

All I can do is cry. The heaviness inside me doesn't ever lighten. I can't look at her; I can't even make eye contact. The hurt rolls through me, the absolute abyss of misery overtaking every part of me.

"Have you eaten today?" She asks as she walks around the side of the bed, and gently smooths my hair away from my face. I'm a complete mess, worse than a tragedy.

Trent dropped me off at the hospital after I woke with blood-soaked sheets. I don't know why I miscarried this baby. Maybe I shouldn't call it a baby. If I just say a fetus then it seems more impersonal, like it was nothing more than a mere heavy period.

The day before yesterday I did the stupidest thing ever. I just won't learn and I don't know why I keep pushing Trent's buttons and making him mad. I had an extra bowl of soup at dinner without even asking him if he wanted it.

He's on his residency at the hospital two counties over and his hours have been crazy. He comes home and tells me to give him quiet, I try but sometimes I might sneeze or cough and that sets him off.

"You know, if a child is what you really want, you should try again," she offers as she continues to pet my hair and stroke my back.

I look up at her and give her a weak smile. She's being kind to me, saying beautiful things, but I know it's only her job to pretend to care. "Thank you," I respond. Then I curl further into myself and don't want to hear anything else she has to say.

"You have to eat something, gain your strength back so you can go home and try again." I simply nod. What she doesn't know is Trent told me I'm not allowed to eat anything, because it's too expensive and we can't afford it.

"I'm okay," I whisper. "Not hungry," I add. I'm not famished, I have no desire to eat anything. All I want to do is stay curled in this spot until the day they release me.

"You're skin and bone, sugar. There's nothing to you. You need to eat something."

"Not hungry." She must be delusional if she thinks I'm skinny, they weighed me when I came in and I'm eighty-three pounds.

"You had a dilation and curettage, you need your strength to get through this. An operation like that is only minor, but your body needs to heal and it can't heal if you don't eat." Her voice is so sweet and gentle. She's really trying her best, but what she doesn't understand is I'm not allowed to eat.

"I'm fine, thank you," I say and close my eyes. This will give her the very clear indication I don't want her here any longer.

"If you don't eat, the doctors may not allow you to leave," her voice holds a slightly harsher tone.

But I ignore her. She stands beside the bed, and right now I want her to leave. I don't need pity. I don't need the sadness in her eyes, because I have enough of that sloshing through me to last a lifetime.

"I'll send one of the aides in with something for you to eat," she says in a quieter voice. She knows I can hear her, I'm simply choosing to ignore her because it's easier.

The door opens and closes and I'm left alone. Not totally of course. There's a woman in the bed beside me and she's been chatting since the moment I was wheeled in. She got the idea once I turned my back and didn't respond.

"You okay?" she asks me. "I know how tough losing a baby can be. I've lost three, and now I can't get pregnant." Her voice is wispy, as if she's talking to herself then to me. "My husband says we can try again, but I don't think I'm ready. It's just too much pressure."

I open my eyes and blink the fat tears away. They cling to my eye lashes for a split second, before they fall and wet the pillow beneath my head. I try and draw in a deep breath, but all I seem to attract is more hurt.

Shutting my eyes, I want her to stop. I want the world to just freeze and never move again. I don't want to be here, but I don't want to go back to our apartment either. I'm not sure I can face Trent. He'll see the hurt in me and I'll see the immense disappointment in him.

Thankfully, it's not long before the woman in the other bed stops talking. And now I'm left to my own thoughts. Maybe it's better when her voice is constantly chatting, because for those moments I'm not consumed by my own self-hatred. I don't know. I don't know anything anymore. *Why am I even breathing? What's the point to my life?*

The door creaks open, and I hear the tell-tale sound of the food cart being wheeled in.

"La-ladies," says a confident deep voice, despite his stutter. There's a serene tone to it, like a beautiful, calming chime. "I-I-I br-brought y-y-your d-d-dinner," he stutters, though his voice is still strong and peaceful.

I turn to look at him, and immediately his eyes focus on me. My tears have eased, but not stopped. He gently brings his eyebrows together and slightly turns up one side of his mouth. I sit up in bed and focus on him.

He's still as beautiful as I remember him from all those years ago. His face still holds the mystery and beauty of an expertly-crafted statue of ancient Roman times. His hair is thick and dark, and beside his dark, captivating eyes there are small lines.

"You-you haven't or-ordered anything," he gently says to me.

I'm completely spellbound by him. It's not a lustful attraction toward him, more like he's a beam of high-intensity light shining down and its brightness holds me captive.

He's older than me, maybe by ten years, maybe less. He has broad shoulders I can't help but pay attention to, and his eyes are hauntingly perfect. "Are-are you hungry?" he asks me again.

"I've ordered," the woman on the bed beside me pipes up and says.

"Y-yes, I-I have y-yours here." He pulls out a tray and takes it over to her side table and wheels it up to her. I watch their exchange, she smiles and her cheeks turn a slight pink.

"Thank you," she replies.

Fluently he replies, "You're welcome." As if he doesn't have a stutter. "For you?" He smiles at me, and his warmth travels the entire length of my body. My arms erupt into goosebumps, and the hair on the back of my neck rises in anticipation of his next words.

"No, nothing for me, thank you," I respond, but I want to keep him here and pamper myself with the sound of his smooth drawl.

"Y-you have to e-eat." He stands tall and looks at me.

I look over to the woman sitting on the bed beside me and actually notice her. She's possibly slightly older than me, with wiry dark hair and blackened circles beneath her eyes. I look back at him then back to the woman. "I'm not allowed," I whisper, hoping the words are loud enough for him to hear, but not her.

He stands still for a few seconds. Maybe he's trying to decipher the words I said and in what context I meant them. He takes the few steps over to the separating curtain and draws it closed between the beds. The way he's quietly done it is not scary or intimidating to me. It's like he's protecting me, not allowing another to see the broken part of me.

"A-are you h-hungry?" he asks as he sits in the chair beside the bed. I don't say anything to him, I just wrap my arms around my chest and find a sudden chill touching me. It's not cold in the room, but he's unnerved me in a way I've never experienced before.

"I think so," I answer honestly, as I continue to look into his almost black gaze.

He looks at me, and his stare travels to my left hand where he sees my thin wedding ring on my finger. "The d-doctors n-need you to eat before they dis-discharge you," he whispers as he sits forward and rest his elbows on his thighs and looks down at the floor.

I look behind me, but the curtain is masking my view of the lady in the bed beside me. "I'm not allowed," I softly sigh, almost like it's a guarded secret only a few highly trained operatives have the privilege of knowing.

He looks up at me, and in that one intense second, in that simple and plain exchange, I see it. His eyes hold pity for me. They're so consumed with tenderness and warmth, but I know he's looking at me with disgust and trying to mask it, so I feel something other than the useless, ugly girl I am.

"Please, don't," I mutter in the smallest of voices. "I've never been one who enjoys sympathy." I look down to the blanket and move my hand to pick at a loose thread. He doesn't say a word. He just keeps his eyes on me, watching me, seeing something no one has ever noticed before. My hurt. My pain. My imperfection.

I've lived a life of hiding. Hiding behind the exterior others see, hiding inside myself, just being one in a universe filled with many. But the way he regards me, tells me he's seeing something I never want the world to know.

"Please," I whisper again, trying with all my might to raise each and every one of my walls.

The seconds draw out, time has stopped. I fidget because his stare is uncomfortable. He sees through me, as if I'm made of a thin, exquisite piece of paper originating in the fourteenth century. His focus penetrates directly through to my soul. "Please." A teardrop escapes and it reminds me just how stupid I am. Why would he be concerned for me? Why would he even bother? He sees a dumb, ugly girl who's nothing but damaged and alone.

"M-my name is M-M-Max, p-pl-pleased to meet you." He waits for me to tell him my name.

"Lily," I answer him, though I know the moment he leaves, he'll have forgotten me as quickly as he would seeing the first fall leaf drift from the tree, baring its soul as it awaits winter.

Max doesn't extend his hand to me. He doesn't do anything else except stand and walk over to his food trolley. Why would he? I'm less than nothing. He takes a tray out, brings it over to me and places it on my bare table.

I look up to him and tilt my head to the side. "I'm not allowed to eat," I say in a quiet voice. He gives me the most sincere and gentlest smile before turning to walk away. "Max." He stills the moment his name flickers past my lips.

He turns back and winks at me before he says with perfect pronunciation, "What food?" With that he leaves, taking his food trolley out and going on to the next room.

I'm left gazing at the door.

I once thought he was a true gentleman, someone who saw a woman and knew how to treat her.

But now I'm convinced he's something much more. Now I know he's an angel.

CHAPTER 16

I'M BACK AT WORK TODAY. Trent told me I was allowed to stay home and recover for three days after I left the hospital, and I did. But I think he wanted me to do two of his assignments which were due, because the first morning before he left for his residency he woke me and told me he'd leave work on the kitchen table and to make sure it's done by the time he got home.

It was a difficult assignment and I'm not even sure if I got it right, but he said he was happy with it when he got home. The next day, he left another. This was easier, but considering I don't understand much of medicine, he said I did well and he should pass. He also told me if he failed, it'll be my fault. He said it in that low voice, which tells me it'll be in my best interest for him to pass.

The store has been crazy. I've got three cashiers off and it's Thanksgiving in a few days, so it's been extra busy.

"Excuse me, ma'am, could you show me where the cranberry jelly is please?" one elderly gentleman asks me.

"This way, sir." I take him to the aisle well-stocked with cranberry sauce.

"Thank you," he says, as he tips his bowler hat to me.

I smile at him, and go back toward the cashiers to see how they're coping.

"Excuse me, canned pumpkin?" a young girl asks me. She looks worried and stressed. "I forgot to get the pumpkin for my pie, and Mom told me to make sure I get to the store and get some before you sell out." She lets out a long, drawn-out sigh and runs her hand through her light brown hair. "I'm so stupid," she resigns.

"No you're not. Everyone forgets things from time to time. And I'm sure we've got extra." I smile warmly as I lead her to the aisle.

"Thank you, you're a lifesaver," she says, as she juggles four cans of mashed pumpkin.

"You're welcome." I step away and go to check the cashiers and their need for change when I get a tap on the shoulder. I turn and come face to face with the dark, captivating eyes I saw in the hospital. "Max," I cry. I feel my face burn with embarrassment as I look around me trying to see if anyone knows where I know him from. Of course my mind is aware that's a completely ridiculous notion, but there's a small part in my brain which screams in my ear, telling me everyone knows.

"H-how are y-you?" he stutters as he stands tall before me. I notice just how tall he really is. I need to look up, to see his stellar, dark eyes.

I fist a hand through my thinning hair and pull a few strands out. It's something I've been doing when I get nervous, especially just before Trent is due to come home. "I'm good." I steady the wave of fear cascading through me.

"Y-you're look-looking really good. Much be-better than wh-when I saw you l-last."

I feel the corners of my mouth tug up in a smile, and I can't help but beam at his words. "Thank you, Max," I say nervously shifting from one leg to the other.

"I-it's okay, y-your secret is s-safe with me." He winks at me again. He's done that before, and although I find it peculiar, I also like it.

"Um…" I look to him and feel my bashfulness overtake the sane and logical part of my brain. "Do you need help with anything?" I stop for a moment as a thought strikes me. "How did you find me?" Suddenly I feel exposed, because he's somehow stalked me to here.

"I-I live near here. J-just down the road. B-but I don't like this st-store, it's always t-too busy." He chuckles at his own words, and I smile.

"Hang on, when did you move here?" Suddenly, I remember the first time I saw him was back where I was living with Trent and his parents. Now we're hours away and I find myself standing in front of the one man I actually think of as a gentleman.

"I be-beg your par-pardon?" he questions in a somewhat agitated state.

"I'm sorry, I should explain," I say, then continue to tell him how I once saw him at the deli beside my old work.

"I-I thought you might h-have followed me," he jokes, then laughs.

"I'm sorry, I must have come across as a stalker. Trust me, I'm not." I look down, knowing for a moment that a miserable feeling of humiliation is pending. He's going to tell me he'd never look at such a fat, ugly, stupid person so there's no need to stalk him.

"I-I wouldn't m-mind someone as b-b-b-beautiful as you s-st-stalking me." He chuckles again and I laugh with him. But I only laugh because he's being gracious in not shaming me. Clearly, he's just saying those words to be kind, nothing more.

"Can I help you find anything?" I say, changing the subject. Not some silly 'let's feel sorry for the stupid, ugly girl' conversation. No one in the world can think I'm anything special. Only Trent loves me. He always tells me how much he loves me, especially after he's been angry at me.

"N-no, ju-just saw you and I thought I'd say h-hi." He smiles at me, and then adds, "Hi."

I feel like an idiot, foolishly thinking he may need anything from me. "Lily," my boss and the second in charge, Dale, calls me.

"I have to go. Nice seeing you, Max."

"Y-you too, Lily." He turns and walks toward the back of the store and I go to Dale who's standing beside the staffroom door.

"Dale, we're getting slammed today," I say when I reach him.

"We are, and it'll be busier tomorrow seeing as it's the day before Thanksgiving. Have you checked staff and made sure we have enough on?"

"I have. Gone over it a few times, and I'll be here in case we need an extra set of hands, too."

"Great. Um...on a personal note, how are you feeling?"

Automatically the humiliation returns. "I'm really good. Couldn't be better."

"Excellent! If you need anything, let me know." He leaves and returns to his office and I go back out on the floor.

The rest of my shift passes in a blur, and before I know it, it's after five-thirty, which means Trent will already be waiting at home for his dinner. I grab my bag and my cardigan and run out the front doors toward the bus stop. I know he's going to be angry and I'm going to have to make it up to him.

The bus seems to be going slower than usual in every sense of the word. The weather's changed drastically and the nights are getting colder and longer. The moment I get off at my stop I run as fast as I can to get home.

I put the key in the door, and the door flies open. Trent scowls at me. The anger in his eyes tells me to not say a word. The way his chest heaves, angrily pumping air into his lungs, is an absolute guarantee of my silence.

"You're fucking late and I'm hungry. Where were you? Are you having an affair?"

"No, Trent." I profusely shake my head. "Work was busy. It's two days before Thanksgiving and everyone is coming in."

"Liar," he yells at me and gives me a backhanded slap. I fall toward the left and tumble into the entry wall. He hits my ear making a high pitched ringing sound through my head. "Where the hell were you? Were you with another man? Who the hell is he?"

"No, really no. I was at work. And the bus was slow. Please, Trent. I only love you."

"You're lying to me!" He pulls me up like a rag doll by my shoulders and slams my back into the wall I fell into. "Who the hell is he, Lily? I'm going to kill him for touching what's mine, then I'm going to kill you for lying to me." His face is beet red and as he screams in my face, small thin strands of spittle fly out of his mouth. I can smell the distinct sweet aroma of whisky on his breath.

"Call Dale, he'll tell you. We've been busy, really busy. It was like last year, remember?" He pushes me against the wall and steps back putting some space between us. He turns his back to me, and runs his hands through his hair before bringing them to wash over his face. Trent then goes and sits on our old sofa. "You make me crazy, Lily. Damn crazy."

"I'm so sorry. I should have messaged you or called you. I didn't think. I just wanted to get home so I can make your dinner. It just completely escaped me. I'm really sorry."

"You could've just avoided me getting angry if you would've called. It *is* your fault, it's all your fault." He pauses and picks the remote up to the TV. "Make me some dinner, I've had to wait for you to get your fat ass home and I'm starving."

"I'll do it right now." I go to the kitchen and start making dinner. It takes just over half an hour but I have his steak and his sides. "Dinner's ready," I call from the kitchen as I finish setting the table and place his meal down.

Trent strolls in and sits at the head of the table. He looks at the food and raises his eyebrows at it. Clearly, he's not happy with his steak and sides. "What's this crap?" he asks as he sits back in his chair and crosses his arms in front of his chest.

"Steak with the sides you like." I put my plate down and come to sit beside him.

"It looks like shit. I wouldn't even serve this to my dog, if we had one. You expect me to eat this?" he asks as his beastly eyes drill into me.

I look down at my smaller portion and look at everything on my plate. The meat looks succulent, the sides all are exactly how Trent likes them. I look back to Trent and silently question what he's saying. "I'm sorry," I mumble as I feel tears beginning to fill my eyes.

"You're gonna cry now? Just like a baby. I say it looks like shit and you're gonna cry. It's not like it took you long to make it. God, Lily, you're so ungrateful. I'm working my ass off so I can give you everything, and you repay me by making the worst dinner I've ever laid eyes on." He shakes his head and leans forward to grip the edge of the table. I look and see his knuckles changing color and I can't help but let the salt water escape from my eyes. Tears cling to my cheeks and silently slide down to drip into my plate.

"I'm sorry," I say again while looking down at my food.

"Jesus, you're so useless. I can't believe how much of a disappointment you've turned out to be. You're not even a good lay; you never have been."

Out of the corner of my eye, I see him stand. I'm looking up at him, begging him wordlessly to stay and to eat dinner with me. He picks the plate up and flings it toward the sink. "I'm not eating that trash. I'm going out. I'll be back later."

Trent leaves the small kitchen table and goes into our room. I'm left sitting alone, feeling like a complete failure. If I can't make my husband happy with something as simple as dinner, there's no way I'll ever make him proud of me.

He comes back a few minutes later, dressed in nice pants and a shirt, and smelling of the new cologne he bought for himself. "I'll be back later. Clean this shit up, Lily. In my briefcase in the bedroom there's an assignment you have to do. It's due next week, but I want at least half of it done by the time I get home."

Looking up at him, my cheeks wet from the free falling tears, I simply nod and whisper, "Okay."

"Doesn't really look like you'll have time to eat. You really are lucky you have me, because if you didn't, I'd hate to think how much fatter you'd be. I mean, God, look at you. What do you weigh? Like a hundred and thirty pounds? You're so lucky I love you."

"They told me at the hospital I was under weight," I say through quiet sobs.

"Yeah I bet it was a nurse who said it to you. They're so stupid over there. Nurses say all types of crap. I can tell you, as a doctor you're definitely over weight."

"You're not a doctor yet," I let slip. Then realize what I said and clasp a hand to my mouth.

Trent stands still for a moment, and then comes to stand beside me. He towers over me, his frame hovering so close I can feel the heat rolling off him. "What. Did. You. Say?" he asks slowly. The anger is gripping him, making my heart pound at dangerously rapid speeds in my chest.

"I'm sorry," I choke through a strained sob. I can barely breathe as the fingers of dread tighten more around my windpipe, making me choke on my sorrow and fear.

"You should be. You're damn lucky I keep you around. No one will ever want you, Lily. You're useless and ugly. Just remember that." He finally moves, taking a step back. I tightly close my eyes and brace myself for whatever is about to happen.

But as my ragged breath finally begins to ease, I hear the click of the front door and know he's gone. I open my eyes and take a look toward the door. He's definitely gone. I pick at the carrot on my plate, pushing the contents around, not really hungry enough to eat any of it. Standing, I take my plate and empty it in the bin, then clean the mess where Trent threw his dinner.

It takes me just over half an hour to clean the kitchen and to get all traces of mashed potato off the blinds and the microwave where it splattered. I go into our room and go to his briefcase, opening it and getting the top papers out.

I go back into the kitchen and look over his assignment. This is going to take me a while to do, and I think I'll have to spend Thanksgiving on it. But I'm more than okay with that, because we're due to go to Trent's uncle's house. John.

He creeps me out. Every time we're anywhere he is, he's always trying to corner me and touch me. Most times I've managed to escape him, sometimes he's gotten his tongue into my mouth. I hate it; I hate him. I tried telling Trent a few times, and he just says I overreact and his uncle wouldn't do that. He says his aunt Terri is so much more attractive than me, and why would John stoop as low as to try anything on me? But either way, I'm relieved I'll have to stay here to finish his assignment.

The hours pass and I'm immersed in Trent's assignment. The words jumble and begin to become unfocused, and although I'm not near half-done, I still need to sleep. In four and half hours I've got to be up for work. Tomorrow is the day before Thanksgiving and I know the floor will be absolutely chaotic.

As my eyes keep drooping closed, I get up and shuffle into the bathroom to have a quick shower. Then I get dressed in my warm pajamas and curl into bed.

Sleep is my friend and luckily it takes me off to a place of beauty and serenity.

"Do you want a sandwich, Little Lily?" Mommy asks, as we sit on the green picnic blanket.

"Not yet, Mommy. I want to wait for Daddy and Wade to come back." I sit on Mommy's lap and she plays with my hair.

"Look at your hair. It's so long, I think we need to cut it."

"NO!" I shout at Mommy and shake my head. "I don't want my hair cut. Please, Mommy. No."

"Wiwi, Wiwi," Wade calls as he runs toward me with his arms out, ready to hug me.

"Slow down. You'll fall and hurt yourself," Daddy scolds Wade.

There is a heaviness on top of me and I open my eyes to see Trent, naked and pulling my pajama pants down. His breath reeks of cheap beer and it makes my stomach roil with nausea.

"Trent," I say as he pushes into me.

"Shut up." He does what he usually does, then gets off me. He lays on his back and instantly he says, "Go clean yourself up. You smell like a common street walker."

I silently stand and go to the bathroom, and clean myself. When I finish, I go back to bed and lay down. Trent is already snoring heavily beside me. Visions of that dream keep swirling around in my head. Whenever I've dreamt of that little boy, he's never had a name before. He's always had the same face. The same blond, floppy hair and the same sweet voice. But he's never had a name.

If I close my eyes, maybe I'll find out more about that little boy. Of maybe I'll find the happiness he's feeling. Maybe tonight is the night I'll close my eyes and never have to open them again.

CHAPTER 17

"LILY," OCEAN, THE CASHIER ON register eight calls me.

"What's wrong?" I ask as I walk over to her.

"I'm not feeling well." She has dark circles under her eyes, and although she's looking pale, I can see sweat beading on her forehead. She's shivering, most likely from an onset of a fever. "I think I need to go home."

I look down her conveyor belt and it's full with three people waiting. "As soon as this customer is done, close your register and I'll take over. Do you want me to call your mom or dad to come get you?"

"Yes, please. Here." She hands me a phone from her pocket and I raise my eyebrows to her. "I usually leave it in my bag, but I was feeling off when I got here. Sorry, Lily, I won't do it again."

The policy is no cell phones while the staff are working. I've had to confiscate a few, but generally the staff follow the rule.

"What's the number? And what's your mom's name?"

"It's under favorites and 'mom', and her name is Melanie," she says, scanning the customer's groceries.

I press 'mom' and listen as it connects then start ringing. "Hi, sweetie, you feeling better?" her mother answers.

"Hi Melanie, this is Lily Hackly, Ocean's supervisor at work."

"Oh my God!" she shrills loudly into the phone. "Is she okay? Oh my God." I get a tingle up my spine. Her protective maternal nature is beautiful, and something I've never known or experienced.

"Ocean's not well. She looks like she's burning up and she's too sick to be here. Could you come and pick her up, please?"

"I'm on my way. Is she okay? Is she hurting? Does she need me to bring her anything?" She's flustered and in a panic.

"Melanie, she's okay. She's just finishing with her current customer, and I'll send her to the staffroom to wait for you," I say in a calm and soothing voice. "Text Ocean when you arrive and I'll walk her out."

She breathes a relieved sigh, and I hear her take a deep breath. "Thank you so much for calling me, I'll be there in a few minutes."

She hangs up at the same time Ocean finishes with her customer. She quickly closes off her register and I call over the store's PA system for the supervisor of non-perishables to come to the register.

Carl comes over as I'm scanning and I get him to sign in and take over while I go with Ocean to wait in the staffroom for her mom.

She huddles in the corner and brings her knees up to her chest. "Can I tell you something, Lily?" she asks me.

"You can tell me anything." I sweep my hand across her forehead and notice how rapidly her temperature is rising.

"From the very first time I worked here, I thought just how beautiful you are. I think you have the prettiest eyes I've ever seen." She balances her chin on her knees and she smiles at me. "Sorry," she adds.

"How old are you, Ocean?"

"I'll be eighteen next year." I smile at her and she returns me a weak smile. "You are really pretty though."

"Thank you." Poor child, she must be delirious if she thinks that.

Her phone vibrates in her hand and she looks down at it. "Mom's here." She stands on shaky legs and I notice now she's shaking even more than before.

"Come on, Ocean. I'll help you out." I put my arm around her shoulder and help her out to the front of the store. Her mom's waiting for us and comes directly to us when she sees us.

"Thank you so much," she says as she wraps her arms around Ocean and takes over what I was doing.

"You're welcome. Take care, Ocean. I'll see you next week for your shift."

"Thanks, Lily," Ocean says over her shoulder to me.

I watch as Melanie takes Ocean and carefully, lovingly helps settle her into the car. She gets in the driver's side and leaves. I go over to where Carl has been working the register, and he's getting slammed with people. Today is one of the busiest days of the year and it's all hands on deck, even the store manager, Chase, would need to come down if we weren't coping. "Close off after you've served that gentleman." I point to the last man, and Carl turns his light off.

I go to one of the few registers that has no one on, sign in, check the float and start working the register. We're one person down since Ocean's left and the wave of people is relentless.

The hours melt into each other, and before I realize it my stomach is protesting, needing food. I look up at the clock above the door and see I have half an hour before it's my break time. I've been consistently looking around the floor and analyzing what's needed. Although we're extremely busy, it's running smoothly.

"Oh my God!" I hear the distinct voice of my once best friend and look up to see her standing in my line.

I can feel my mouth fall open as I look at her in disbelief. I've not heard from Shayne in years, and she's still as beautiful as she was the last time I saw her. "Shayne," I say but it comes out like a high-pitched squeal. "You're still beautiful," I blurt.

"She certainly is," says the older gentleman who I'm serving. He turns to her, and innocently winks.

"Thank you." She grins toward him. "Look at you. I thought you'd be finished with your degree and working in some exclusive high school somewhere," she says. I feel my face drop immediately, and I look down at the groceries I'm bagging. "You *have* finished, haven't you?"

"Um," I don't say anything more because I'm coming to the end of the older gentleman's items. "That'll be sixty-seven dollars even, please." The gentlemen pays, wishes both Shayne and me a happy Thanksgiving, and leaves. "How are you?" I say, changing direction of the conversation.

"Absolutely fantastic. Liam and I got married and we moved to the other side of town. His dad bought a tire store and offered Liam a job on the floor, and me one in the office. We couldn't say no. It's just too good an opportunity."

I scan her few items and bag them. "I'm so happy for you," I say with sincerity.

"Hey, what time do you get off? We can grab a bite to eat, what do you think?" she asks eagerly.

I look up to her eyes and it instantly transports me back to the carefree and happy days we shared. But I suddenly realize I have only enough money for the bus. Trent gives me the exact amount I need on a daily basis. And sometimes when he's forgotten, I have to walk the twenty-five minutes either way. I'm completely embarrassed that I have to say 'sorry but my husband doesn't give me money for food' so I give Shayne another excuse. "I really wish I could, but I forgot my purse at home and I only have enough money for the bus trip home. I'm sorry, maybe next time." If there's ever a next time, I'll have to think of another excuse.

"I'm not going to let you forgetting your purse at home stop us from having lunch. My treat. I have so much to tell you, and I'm sure there's so many fantastic things you've done, too. What time is your break?"

"I really can't." Even as I speak the words, I know they aren't convincing. Because I'm jumping out of my skin that she's here. I want nothing more than to run around the counter, throw my arms around her and squeeze her.

"This is going to happen, Lily. I'm not taking no for an answer." She puts her hand on her hip, snaps the fingers of her other hand and shows me her usual 'Shayne sass'.

I smile at her, and suddenly the darkness has lifted from inside me. The everyday gloom that blankets me and doesn't let go, vanishes as if it was never there to begin with. "I've missed you," I shamelessly announce.

"Me too, Lily." She goes quiet and scrunches her mouth in a way which tells me she's thinking. "So, I'm not taking no for an answer. I'm taking you for lunch. What time is your break?" she persistently asks again.

"In a few minutes." I look up at the clock and add, "Actually, in ten minutes."

"Great!" she loudly shouts, then claps a hand to her smiling mouth. "Oops," she cheerfully adds as she looks around her.

"You've not changed, not one little bit."

"Why would I change?" She shrugs her shoulders. "Anyway, I'll put these groceries in my car and I'll wait for you outside. It's cold though, so don't leave me waiting too long." She pays for her groceries and takes her bags.

I finish up with the next three customers, close off my register and go grab my coat. I take my phone out of my bag and see the dozen messages from Trent. His usual questions of 'what time will you be home?' and 'I want chicken for dinner' and even 'don't forget you have my assignment to do'. But the last one is something he does frequently. And this one I'm eternally grateful for, because it means I get a chance to breathe and not be on edge worrying about what he might say or do. It says 'working late, don't make me dinner, eating out with the boys.' I answer all the messages he's sent me and avoid telling him about Shayne, because I know he won't be happy.

Putting my coat on, I slip my phone in my pocket and head outside. It's so cold out. I think we're in for a snowy winter. Shayne is waiting outside, shifting from foot to foot to try and keep warm. "I'm so cold," she says as she throws her arms around me and gives me a kiss on the cheek. "Girl, what the hell's happened? There's nothing to you. You're even skinnier then you were all those years ago." She grabs onto my shoulders and steps back as her eyes travel the length of my body.

Suddenly I feel on display and completely self-conscious. "Skinny? I'm not skinny. I'm fat."

She scrunches her nose at me and bares her teeth in a 'what the hell' look. "Do you own a mirror? Seriously, girl. I'm fattening you up. Come on," she says as she links our arms and walks down past the grocery store. "Is that café down the road good?"

"I've heard good things about it."

Shayne falters in her steps and turns to look at me. "What do you mean you've 'heard good things'? It's literally less than a hundred and fifty yards from where you work. How can you never have been in there?"

Embarrassment and shame overtake me. How can I tell her I never have any spare money? Trent controls all the finances and gives me what I need to get to and from work. I have to take my own food to work. And if I forget, I need to go without. But I can't tell Shayne that, she won't understand. Trent is just looking out for our finances. He tells me he's doing it so we can save enough money to buy a home. "Um, I've just never…you know." I shrug my shoulders.

We reach the door of the café and Shayne opens it, steps through and goes to sit at one of the unoccupied booths. "Lily," she starts saying as she takes her gloves off and unwraps her scarf. "What is going on with you?"

"Nothing," I say immediately defensive. "Why?" I respond a little calmer.

"How long have you worked next door?"

"A while. About six years."

"And you've never eaten here? How's that possible?"

"I just haven't been interested in it." I look down to avoid her eyes, because she's always been so perceptive of me and what I'm feeling.

The quiet between us breaks the minute a young waitress comes to our table and offers us the menus.

"Everything looks so good," Shayne says dropping the subject of why I haven't been in here. "What are you getting? I'm really hungry I think I'll get a burger, fries and maybe a chocolate shake."

"A shake, in this weather?" I look at her.

"Hmmm." She scrunches her mouth. "You have a point. Maybe I'll get a hot chocolate with marshmallows."

"That sounds so good. But I think I had better get a soup, or maybe a salad."

"Why? If you want a burger, get a burger." She lays the menu flat and looks up at me. I can feel her eyes boring into me, burning with questions she wants to ask but maybe doesn't want the answers to.

"I'll just get the soup and some water." I keep pretending I'm looking at the menu.

Within a few seconds the waitress approaches. "Hi, what can I get you two ladies?" she asks as she flips open a small order pad and grabs the pen behind her ear.

"Um," I start, but Shayne cuts in.

"We'll have two burgers, medium, with fries, and two hot chocolates. Extra marshmallows in the hot chocolates, please." Shayne picks up both the menus and quickly gives them to the waitress. She does it in a way that leaves me speechless and before I can say anything the waitress is gone.

"Why did you do that?" I whisper.

"Because you want to eat it and I think you may have been embarrassed to admit it, so I just ordered it. Now if you keep complaining, I'll make sure I order you a slice of cake, too." She lifts her eyebrows at me, and a devious little smirk appears on her lips.

"Nope," I say shaking my head.

"Nope what?"

"Nope, you haven't changed one little bit. Never change, Shayne. I love you just the way you are."

"I won't. Now tell me about everything that's been happening with you. Did you finish college?"

"No, I had to leave. It didn't work out."

"What's that mean? You had to leave and it didn't work out? You had a full scholarship. You're the smartest person I've even known, there's no way you flunked out. So…what happened?"

"You know, Trent and I got married then I got pregnant, and we decided it was best if I left school and Trent concentrated on his career."

"Wait up. You've got a child?" She half jumps out of her seat over to me.

"No, I lost the baby," I say softly.

"Oh, I'm sorry, Lily. Really sorry."

Again there's a tense cocoon of awkward quiet that embraces us until the waitress brings over our hot chocolates. "It just wasn't meant to be; it's okay. I couldn't care for a baby anyway. I wouldn't know what to do."

"You'd have Trent's mom to help."

I look away, avoiding her again. "Yeah," I answer half-heartedly. "Anyway, Trent's doing well in medical school. Well, he's doing his residency now and although there's a lot of stress for him, he's enjoying it."

"Good," Shayne says and sits back on the bench seat. "Why didn't you finish school, Lily?" She picks her hot chocolate up and sips on it.

"Trent's career is so much more important than mine. We made the decision that I'd work and he'd go through medical school."

"So then when he's a doctor, you'll go back to school and finish?"

"Um. We haven't talked about that. I'm happy at the grocery store. They've promoted me a few times."

Shayne squints her eyes at me, and nervously I push my fingers through my hair. "All you've ever wanted to do was read and teach, why can't you do it once he's a doctor? They earn really good money, maybe not initially, but a couple of years into him being a doctor, you can go back to school."

"I don't know. I'll have to see what Trent wants to do."

Shayne straightens in her seat and her face takes on a questioning look. "What do you mean by that, Lily? I know you're married and you have to discuss things with your husband, but you're also fifty percent in your marriage. Your voice on what you want should be considered too."

"Oh, it is," I say too eagerly. "He's looking after our finances because he says we need to save to buy a house. And he says him being a doctor is much more important than me being a teacher. He's looking out for both of us."

"Do you see how much is in your bank account? Do you know what's happening with the finances?"

"Trent says I don't need to know."

"For God's sake, listen to yourself. It's been seven years, Lily. Seven damn years since I've seen you, and I don't recognize the person you've become. Physically or mentally. The Lily I knew was battling demons from her past, but now I think she's living with the biggest demon of them all."

"That's not true. Trent loves me."

"Trent's not the one I'm talking about. I'm talking about what's up here." She leans over and taps her finger to my temple. "You're battling yourself. You've got no sense of self-worth whatsoever. You're literally just a shadow of the girl I once knew."

Shayne's trying to tell me something I already know. I've led a life where I was shown and told consistently how worthless and useless I am. It wasn't gradually introduced to me once I was married to a beast masquerading as a man. No, my worthlessness was ingrained into me before I reached the age of ten. While my mind was still forming and growing, I was shown and told many times how stupid I am, how ugly I am, how useless I am, how no one will ever love me.

I've got someone in my life who sometimes tells me he loves me, and I'm sure he's the absolute best I can do. I'm not worth anything. I never have been. If I died tomorrow, there'd be no one to mourn for me, or to lay on my grave because they're going to miss me. Miss my smile, miss me just being near them. No one will ever grieve me, because I'm worthless.

"I'm trying," I say in a small voice.

"What exactly are you trying? Do you even read *The Crucible* anymore?" She remembered. I can't believe Shayne remembered. I look up at her and I can feel I have tears pooling in my eyes. "You thought I forgot, didn't you? I haven't. I remember the day you got it from the bookstore, the glazed look in your eyes as if you'd been told you'd won millions of dollars. You breezed through work for a week, on the happiest of highs because you had something important to you."

The tears can't be contained any longer, now they're falling and I'm desperately trying to wipe them away so I don't look like such a crybaby.

"I'm sorry; don't be mad with me," I get out through heaving sobs.

"I'm not mad with you." Shayne stands and comes to sit beside me. "I love you, Lily. I hate how we haven't been able to stay in touch. All I want is what's best for my friend. You see, she's been through so much shit in her life, she should be able to live a happy adulthood. That's all I want for her…for you." She hugs me, and draws me into her warm, loving frame. "I've wanted to get in contact with you every single day, but I lost the paper you gave me with your address. Liam kept telling me to look you up on social media, or to call you. And when I did try calling you, your number was no longer connected. Liam even went past Trent's parents' place, and his dad swore at him and told him if he ever came back, he'd shoot him. So I tried, and I saw someone near the window, but they wouldn't answer the door."

"You went there looking for me?" *Someone cares about me?*

"Yes, and then I found the address you had given me. I sent you a couple of letters, but I never got anything in return, so I thought you'd moved." *I never got any mail, only that one postcard from Italy.*

"We haven't, we're still in the same apartment. Trent says we can't afford to move."

Shayne sighs and slightly slumps, and she pulls me in for another tight hug. "Why don't we just put this behind us, and be happy that we've found each other again?" She moves to the opposite side of the booth again and smiles at me.

The waitress brings over two huge plates and carefully puts them down in front of us. "Can I get you two ladies anything else?" she asks.

"No, thank you," I answer her then turn to look at one of the biggest meals I've ever seen in my life. "There's no way I can eat all this and not be sick."

Shayne's already started in on her burger, shoveling in fries between mouthfuls. She's got mustard all over her mouth and she looks like a kid. I chuckle at her and her sauce-smeared face. "What?" she says with cheeks puffy with burger and fries. "I wuve ood." I burst into laughter, because I seriously have no idea what she's attempting to say. She chews and then swallows, picks up her napkin and wipes her face. "What? There's nothing wrong with me. I love my food." She's so savage I can't help but burst into laughter.

I'm so glad the mood has shifted and isn't as somber.

We sit, eat, and talk. Before I know it, I need to get back to work. "I have to go," I say. But my voice is sad and sudden gloom overtakes me, a feeling of dread because I don't ever want to lose contact with Shayne again.

"Here, take my number," she says, as she roots around in her bag for a pen. "Aha," she proudly announces and pulls a pen out. She writes her number on the back on a napkin and gives it to me. "Now, yours." She looks at me eagerly and waits.

I rattle off my number as she enters it into her phone and we both stand to leave. As soon as I get home, I'll write hers in my diary, just to make sure I have it and can never lose it.

We walk over to the cashier, and I feel completely mortified by the fact Shayne is buying my lunch. "We were that table," Shayne says as she turns to indicate the booth we were sitting at.

"Oh, your check was taken care of," the cheery young girl says.

Ice chills my blood, the hair on the arms instantly rise and I feel like I'm about to lose what I've eaten. Trent knows and he paid the bill, it's his way of saying I'm in so much trouble. My heart is beating so fast, and I feel a tightness across my chest. *Damn it, damn it, damn it.*

"What? Who paid?" Shayne asks, but I already know the answer. I'm in for it tonight. He's going to be so mad at me. He's going to accuse me of stealing from his wallet, and he's going to punish me.

"He didn't say his name," the girl replies. Her answer is even more frightening. Trent wants me to worry, and to anticipate what I'm going to cop when I get home. "But I gotta say, he was kinda cute." Oh my God, Trent's going to kill me. Not figuratively speaking, but actually kill me. "I could tell he was nervous, because he stuttered when he was talking to me."

Wait.

Trent doesn't know?

"How nice of him to pay for us. I wonder who he is, it would be nice to say thank you," Shayne says. She pops a twenty in the tip jar, and winks at the girl.

And I'm left standing beside her, suddenly not nervous anymore. The giant rock tumbling around in my tummy disappears, and the barrage of explosive panic completely settles.

"He was sitting over there, in that corner, on his own. And he got up, looked over toward you two ladies and smiled. He then handed me a fifty, paid for himself and your check, and told me to keep the change. Really nice-looking guy, too." She slightly blushes.

"Wow," I say, taken aback by someone else's generosity.

"Yeah, wow. And cool," Shayne adds. "Come on, you've got to get back to work." She goes to the door and I retreat the few steps back to the waitress.

"Did you say he stuttered?"

"Yeah, he did."

I walk out of the café trying to understand why someone would do something so charitable and not want anything in return.

"How cool, never had someone buy my lunch before. Drinks, yeah, all the time when I go to clubs, but never a whole meal. Not like that." She throws her thumb over her shoulder to indicate the café.

"Me either," I reply honestly.

"Okay, well, you need to get to work and I have a husband who's due home in two hours. Call me, Lily. And don't wait to call me, call me tomorrow." She hugs me, "I love you." She kisses my cheek then whispers, "Pretty cool about lunch. Wish I knew who it was though."

I hug her back and promise to call her.

For the rest of the night at work, I'm in a daze. A man, a mostly perfect stranger, paid for my meal.

But he's not completely unknown.

He's Max.

CHAPTER 18

"Wake up!" Trent yells, then I feel something wet hit on my face. "Wake up!"

I sit up in bed and my face and some of my hair is drenched from the water Trent just threw on me. "I'm awake." I wipe my face and get out of bed.

"We need to leave, the drive is going to be hectic."

I look over at my alarm to see the time, and see it's minutes before four in the morning. "I'm getting up now, Trent."

"Get changed, and get my clothes ready while I go make myself a coffee." He walks out of our bedroom and I hear him rattling around in the kitchen.

Going into the bathroom, I do my morning routine, and get changed. I get Trent's clothes ready, and when I finish I go out to our tiny kitchen. Trent's sitting at the head of the table stirring his coffee.

"Come here, babe," he says grabbing me around the waist and sitting me on his lap. He pulls the sleeve of my sweater up and starts drawing circles on my bare skin. "Your skin is pretty." He leans in to nuzzle my neck. "Really pretty." He nips at the skin and then sucks it into his mouth. This is the most affection he's shown me in a long time. I can't remember the last time he's been so attentive toward me. Closing my eyes, I relax into his frame and enjoy the small amount of attention he's lavishing on me.

Suddenly, there's a burning sensation on my arm, where Trent had pushed my sleeve up. He starts laughing against my throat and I try to move my arm away. Screaming, I open my eyes and try harder to yank my arm away. But Trent is holding my arm down with one of his big paws, and has the spoon from his coffee cup pressing into my skin.

"Trent!" I yell, but I'm still mindful we have neighbors in the apartment complex we're living in. "You're hurting me, please stop," I beg.

Trent's laugh is so evil, it's soul-consuming, as if he's reaching inside me and killing the small amount of life left in me. Like a plant, finally dying as it fades away from a lack of sun or water. He's killing one of the last parts of me.

"Trent." I finally break down and cry. The pain has gone, I can no longer feel the heat of the spoon, all I can feel is nothing.

"That was funny." He lets go of me, and pushes me off his leg. I fall back on my bottom and look to see the angry, red welt on my arm. "Should've seen your face, one of the funniest things I've ever seen. You were wriggling around, and crying. Honestly, babe, I haven't seen anything funnier." He stands and goes toward the bedroom.

I keep looking at the wound, and I know it'll need medical attention. "Trent, I'm hurting."

"You'll be fine, babe. It's just a scratch. Put it under cold water," he loudly says from the bedroom. "Then if you really can't cope with that small scratch, put some ointment on it."

I stand from where I was pushed to the ground, and run the wound under water. Then I go to the medicine cabinet and take out a small tube of ointment, rubbing it onto my wound.

"Trent, I don't think I should come today. I've still got that paper of yours to finish." I'm trying to stay here so I don't have to go anywhere near John. "I really want it perfect for you." I nurse my wound, and where he had pushed the spoon onto my arm, there's an ugly, red mark. The skin around it is irritated and flaming hot. Just as hot as the blood is below my sensitive skin.

"No, babe, you gotta come. What kind of wife doesn't want to come to her husband's family Thanksgiving? There's a long drive ahead of us, and you know how long drives make me. Hurry up so we can get on the road."

My shoulders slump in resignation, and I get my handbag, not like there's anything of importance in it. Just a small packet of tissues, and my purse which never holds more than my bus money, but I decide to leave it behind because there's nothing I need.

By the time we leave, it's near five am. The entire time we're driving, Trent is silent with me. My burn is stinging, but I try and keep the pain inside so he doesn't tell me I'm a baby for complaining.

When we're about half hour from John's place, a call comes through on the car's Bluetooth. Trent looks at the number displayed and smiles. He then gets his phone and answers it, taking the call off the speaker.

"I can't talk now, I'm driving," he says. He listens for a few seconds and smiles. "Yeah, but I can't now." He keeps listening and nods his head. "Tonight, when I drop *her* off." He emphasizes 'her' and I know he's talking about me. "Okay," he whispers in a soft voice and steals a quick side-ways glance at me.

I tune out from this point, I close my eyes and hope the next half hour is spent in as much silence as the first few hours.

"Mommy, can I have an ice cream?" Wade asks Mommy as we can both hear the ice cream truck's bells come toward our home.

"No. It'll spoil dinner."

"I want an ice cream!" he shouts and stamps his foot. *"I want an ice cream!"* he yells again.

"I said no, Wade."

"Hey, Lily, wake up," Trent says and hits my leg.

Opening my eyes I see we're at John's house, and I look over to Trent, who's getting out of the car. I get out and walk to the front door, behind Trent. "I should've made a pumpkin pie," I whisper to Trent.

He knocks on the door, and John opens it. He's holding a drink in his hand and his beady eyes go directly to me. He looks me over as if I'm a piece of meat he's been wanting to try. He brings the drink up to his lips and steps aside to let us in.

"Look at you two. I haven't seen you in a long time." Trent walks ahead of me, and when I enter John grabs my bottom and squeezes it.

I turn my head to look at him, frowning at him. "Don't," I say in a quiet voice.

He licks his lips and then flutters his tongue at me. It's disgusting, he's revolting and I just don't want to be anywhere near him.

When we go into the back room, which is set up as an indoor entertainment area, Mr. and Mrs. Hackly are both already here.

"How are you, dear?" Lina says and gives me a hug. "You're way too skinny. You need to put on weight." She wraps her arms around me and squeezes me.

"Trent thinks I'm too fat."

"Oh, well, then…" She pauses then whispers in her lowest voice, "please eat more." She steps back, and kisses me on the cheeks. "You're my only daughter-in-law and I want to make sure you're okay."

"I'm fine," I answer her with a smile. I get a good look at her and see the dark circles under her eyes and her face looks haggard and sunken. "Are you okay?" I ask, concerned there's something going on with her.

She smiles and brings me in for another hug. "I'll be fine, dear. I'll be fine." She carefully places her arm around my shoulders and she walks us further into the entertainment area.

"Hello, Mr. Hackly," I say as I walk past him.

"Lily," he barely stops talking with Terri to acknowledge me.

Quietly, I sit beside Lina and say hello to anyone who looks my way. Martin is always the happy brother, and he's not here yet. I welcome having him around because then I don't feel under so much scrutiny from John's lecherous, watchful eyes.

His gaze is always so sleazy and makes me feel very uncomfortable. He glares at me, as if he wants to consume me and rip me apart. "How are you, sweet Lily?" John asks when he comes into the room.

"Fine, thank you," I answer coldly. I feel my shoulders stiffen and my body breaks out in goosebumps, and not the good kind.

"Tell me something, Trent?" John says, interrupting the conversation Trent and his dad are having.

"What would you like to know?" Trent asks.

"Whiskey, it's good for you," John says as he hands Trent a glass a quarter filled. "My question to you is, does Lily taste as sweet as I think she would?" he chuckles, then looks at me. Trent laughs it off, and goes back to talking to his dad. I suddenly feel like I'm going to vomit. What a horrible and poor excuse for a man. "Just joking, darlin'," he says to me as I try to shrink into the chair.

I can't stand this man. He's so disgusting, with his inappropriate sexual remarks and the way his beady eyes always follow me around.

"Tell me, dear. Are you going to give me a grandbaby one day soon?" Lina asks in an almost hushed tone.

I look away from her begging, brown eyes. I don't want to tell her about all the miscarriages, or the cause of them either. She looks frail and only marginally like the woman I met all those years ago. If I tell her, it will make her cry and I don't want that. Instead, I lie. "We're not ready yet."

"You can't wait too long, I'd like a happy home filled with love and grandbabies before my time on this earth is over." Lina looks away and sighs. It seems as if the statement she's just made has more meaning than she's willing to share.

"Are you sure you're okay?" I rub my hand up and down her back. The moment my hand moves toward the bottom of her back, she winces and propels forward on her seat. "Tell me, Lina. Please tell me," I beg her as I move my hand away at lightning speed in case I'm causing her pain.

"There's nothing to tell." She gives me a weak smile, and flicks her eyes over to where Mr. Hackly is sitting. "Nothing at all. Everything's perfect. Well, it would be, if we had a baby in the family." The joy in her words is contradicted by the sadness and heaviness in her eyes.

"Lily, can you come help me in the kitchen?"

I visibly shudder because the words are spoken from the one person who makes me ill. An electric bolt of fear tears through me and I can't help but shake at the thought of being alone with John.

"I'm not feeling well, John. Lily's just sitting with me, to make sure I'm okay," Lina says as she squeezes my thigh.

"Thank you," I whisper so low I'm sure Lina didn't hear me. But she does, because she gives me the smallest of nods, telling me she understands.

"As we were saying, tell me about how the baby-making plans are going."

"Lily, I really need some help," John yells out and comes to the entertainment area door.

"I'm sorry, I tried," Lina says in a soft and hushed voice.

"She's lazy like this at home, too. I told her to make a pumpkin pie but she couldn't be bothered. She said she didn't have time. Like the little job I let her have takes up so much of her time," Trent always mocks me and my work. I hate when he speaks so badly about me, but I also know if I say anything, he will get even more vicious and nasty. Sometimes, it's best to just shut up and not fight back. "Get up, Lily. Go help in the kitchen."

Standing, the fear of going into that kitchen has hit my knees and they're almost buckling as I slowly start moving. Terri's sitting beside Trent and Mr. Hackly, and other than looking me up and down when I walked in, she hasn't even acknowledged me. But now, she's got a smug look plastered on her face. It's as if she knows I'm about to be mauled by a ravenous lion who's been starved and prodded with nails on a stick, just before being let loose to chase down its prey.

With my stomach in complete knots, I walk into the kitchen, where John is leaning against the counter with his arms crossed in front of his chest. "You need help?" I weakly ask. I'm terrified of this entire situation. Everyone is less than a few feet away and I know he's going to try something, I can feel the cold snap of the stale air as I still when I reach the door way.

"The turkey needs basting." He eyes the oven and then looks back to me. He's standing directly in front of the oven, which means when I bend to get it out, he's going to be looking at my bottom.

"Perhaps I can chop some vegetables while you do that," I offer, hoping he'll accept my alternative. But I know why he's summoned me here, and it's not to help him in the kitchen.

"Get the turkey, Lily." He uncrosses his arms, and leans them against the counter.

I look around the kitchen for towels or gloves to slide the hot tray out of the oven. He starts chuckling, but the sound is forced and pretentious. I look over to him, and he has two tea-towels, one in each hand.

"May I have them, please?"

He lifts an eyebrow and smirks at me. "Sure, come and get them," he says in a suggestive, yet disgusting manner. I slowly walk over, and when I get close to him, I hold my hand out to him. "Closer," his voice has turned husky as his leer has become more revolting. I take another step, and he quickly darts an arm out around my waist and smashes me to his body.

"Please, don't," I beg as panic has now overtaken all my senses.

"I love it when sluts like you beg for me." He licks the side of my face. I whimper and try to break free of his hold, but he's stronger than me, and is keeping me firmly pinned against his body and his despicable erection. "I can't wait until I get to taste that sweet spot of yours. I'm going to make you hurt, then I'm going to make you bleed."

Bile rises to my mouth, and his words scare the life out of me. I'm hit with 'fight or flight' and I automatically scream and bring my knee up to connect with his groin. He lets me go as he doubles over in pain, but just as quickly as he buckles, he straightens and lunges toward me.

Grabbing me by the throat, he rears his arm above his opposite shoulder and back-hands me. I scream in pain as his strong hand makes contact with the side of my face, and he strikes again on the opposite side. "Bitch," he screams at me.

In this one moment, all the air in my lungs painfully expels. My chest is heaving fire, and I can't drag any oxygen into my lungs.

"What the hell is going on here?" I hear Trent yell.

John lets go of me, and I scuttle over behind Trent. He puts a protective arm out, a barrier between John and me. "He…he…" I desperately try to gasp for air. I bend at the waist and grab onto my knees, attempting to steady myself so I don't lose consciousness and faint.

"Little bitch attacked me," John says calmly as he grasps his groin. "She kneed me in the cock for no reason."

"That's not true," I yell. "He grabbed me and told me he was going to make me hurt and bleed." Wheezing, I'm still trying to calm my frightened body down. "He grabbed me." I try to stay hidden from the beast.

"Lying, bitch. I invite you into my home, and this is how you repay me?"

"You're sadistic and cruel. I didn't touch you until you grabbed me and wouldn't let me go."

"Why are you lying, Lily? Why? You've been flirting with me from the day you met me."

"You do flirt with him," Trent says as he turns to look at me.

"No I don't. I don't even like him. He disgusts me," I scream.

"You'll be respectful to John, Lily. You're in his house, and you're a damn guest. Do not embarrass me," Trent warns.

I can't believe this, now I'm expected to thank him for almost assaulting me. "No." I stand tall. "I will not respect him. Nor will I let this go. He grabbed me!"

It's then Trent does what he always does. He hits me, reigniting the pain from where John slapped me. "You ungrateful, bitch." Trent wraps his hand around my upper arm and starts dragging me out to the entertainment area, where everyone is standing, gawking at us.

Terri has a look of mischief on her face, mixed with contempt, as if she's smugly enjoying the way Trent's handling me.

"Wait, before you go," Lina protests, and runs up to me. She hugs me tightly, and whispers, "I'm sorry you were ever introduced to these monsters." She grips me tight, not wanting to let me go.

Trent pulls me away from her, and she's standing, looking like a shell. A broken woman, saddened by the loss of something which once was her most precious gift.

Trent drags me out to the car, he pushes me into the passenger side and then gets into the driver's side. "I can't believe the scene you've made back there. You're a damn embarrassment." He reverses out of the driveway and takes off like a madman possessed, driving well above the speed limit. "I swear to God, Lily. I've had just about enough of your bullshit. I've had it, you hear me?" He grabs my arm and squeezes it with as much force as he can.

Silently I cry and look out at the blurry scenery passing the window.

"Jesus, Lily. I thought I told you not to throw yourself at John. Why is it, every time you two are together, you're always flirting with him?" Trent goes quiet, and I'm not sure he wants an answer. "For God's sake, tell me why!" he yells at me and slaps my leg.

"I've never liked him," I reply meekly. "I told you he scares me, and today he said he wanted to…"

"Stop lying. You sound like a hopeless slut. Someone who knows she's been caught in a lie and is desperately trying to get out of it. He said you threw yourself at him."

"I didn't." I look to Trent who's so angry his face is red with fury.

"I'm supposed to believe some common whore who probably slept with, who knows how many before I came along. My dad and John were right about you, I should get you fixed, because a bitch in heat will always bring home strays. I'm going to be a doctor, Lily. I can't be worried about what my wife is doing when I'm working hard at the hospital."

"I'm not a slut! I've never been with anyone except you."

His right hand tightens slowly into a fist. His nostrils are expanding and retracting as his eyes are wide with rage. "What the hell did you just say?" His voice is incredibly low and contained. And that terrifies me even more than his actions. "I said, what the hell did you say?" He repeats himself, even deadlier and more eerie.

My skin crawls from the savage and gruesome tone of his voice. I want to open the door and jump out of the car, regardless of the fact he's travelling at speeds well above the limit. "I'm not a slut, Trent. You know this because I hadn't been with anyone else before you. And I've certainly never been with anyone else while we've been married."

"What's that remark supposed to mean, Lily? Do you think I'm cheating on you?"

I shrug my shoulders and turn to look away from him. Somewhere, deep inside I suspect he is, but I also know girls like me don't deserve anything more than what he's given me.

"You ungrateful, selfish, bitch," he says. I keep my head turned away from him, because I know he'll only get angrier with me if he sees the tears falling.

The drive is taking forever, and I'm starting to struggle with the tension filling the car.

Many times I catch Trent fisting his hand, then relaxing it moments later. I remain quiet, knowing any words from me will only ignite the dry kindling surrounding us and create an intolerable situation.

When we finally get back to the apartment, Trent pulls up out in front. I unbuckle my seat belt and get out. "Here," he says as he hands me the key to the front door.

"What's this?" I ask looking at his outstretched hand.

"I'm going out, I won't be back until tomorrow."

"What?" I ask, perplexed by the situation.

"I need time away from you, Lily. If I stay here tonight, I'm scared I may hurt you, or even worse, kill you. Don't wait up for me."

"But I don't have any money to get to work in the morning."

"You need to lose a few pounds. You'd better walk." He takes off and leaves me standing, stunned at him.

Walking up the stairs to the apartment, I open the door and take a deep breath. It's Thanksgiving and I'm alone, stuck in an apartment that brings me no happiness or joy. Once, there were days when I smiled. Now, those days are gone.

As I sit on the small sofa, I take my shoes off and notice my right shoe has a hole in the sole. These are the only shoes I have, so they serve all purposes including work. Trent says we can't afford new things, and I can only have the basics, wearing them out before I can get them replaced.

Picking up my phone, I send Trent a message.

> My shoe has a hole in the sole. Could you drop off some money so I can go buy another pair before I go to work tomorrow please?

I wait for Trent's reply. I can see he's read it, but he's not responding. I turn the TV on and flick through the channels, but nothing catches my interest. I wish I still had my copy of *The Crucible*, it was always something I could get lost in, becoming totally immersed in the characters and living in their lives. But Trent threw it out one day, saying it was taking up too much of my time. Standing, I go into the tiny bathroom and draw a bath, deciding maybe it can relax me.

As the water runs I go into our bedroom and strip, and as I finish the ping of a text message comes through.

> Line it with cardboard. When the other shoe gets a hole, I'll find the money to buy you another pair of shoes.

He wants me to walk to work tomorrow – and it's bound to rain – with a hole in my shoes. I reply with:

> It's going to rain tomorrow. My feet will be soaked by the time I get to work.

Virtually instantly he says:

> Then you best take an extra pair of socks with you. No is no. I'm turning my phone off now. Don't bother me again.

I put the phone down, and take myself to the only comfort I have. I sink into the bath and let the warm water embrace me. Relaxing into the bath I begin to wonder about so many things. Here I am twenty-five years old, and I have no identity. I don't know who I am, or even what I'm supposed to be doing. I have no love. No love for life, or Trent, or even myself. Is this God's way of proving to me I'm worthless?

I keep mulling over the day's events. They are like a cyclonic storm whirling all around me, as I stand in the eye of it and watch life drag me further under the constant, heartless doom that haunts me. Is my destiny only to exist and never live? What kind of legacy can a girl who *never was,* leave behind? Never was pretty, never was smart, never was anything?

I never was meant to live. This isn't a question. This I know absolutely.

What's the point of breathing?

CHAPTER 19

I CUT FIVE CARDBOARD STRIPS that will fit into my shoe. This way I have spares in case the heavens open up and my foot becomes drenched. I've also packed an extra pair of socks so if my feet become saturated, I won't end up catching a cold.

Trent will be even angrier if I get sick and can't go to work. I have some vacation I can take, but I know he wants me to save that for when he's sick and needs looking after. Me getting sick isn't an option.

The walk to work takes me just over forty-five minutes, and when I get there, I change the strip in the bottom of my shoe and my socks. I still have half an hour before I'm due to start and I do something I've never done before. I get the courage to go to the Bank of America, where my pay is direct-deposited, and see if we have the funds to withdraw fifty dollars to buy a pair of shoes.

The moisture that got into my shoe from the walk to work has caused my foot to rub on the inside of my shoe and has given me a blister on my little toe. I'll risk the wrath Trent is surely going to explode into once he learns I've taken money out of the account, because I need a new pair of shoes. I'll go in on my break, and see if I can buy something appropriate I can wear to work, and everywhere else.

I have to be mindful not to be greedy and spend too much money, because Trent says I can't frivolously spend. If he does get angry at me, I'll tell him I'll walk to work for two weeks, which covers the fifty dollars I'll withdraw for the shoes.

I take the little ID I do have and walk down to the bank. Waiting second in line, I get called quickly to the teller.

"Hi, I'd like to withdraw fifty dollars please. I have my account number, and here's my ID," I say sliding over what I have.

She types in the number I give her and she chats with me about how busy her Thanksgiving was, and did I have a nice time. I lie, of course, and put up the exterior everyone expects. "Did you say you wanted to withdraw fifty thousand? Because that will take me some time to get organized," she says with a gentle smile.

"Fifty thousand?" I ask. "Goodness, I wish there was that much in there." I smile.

She peers at me from on top of her glasses which are perched on the tip of her nose and she tilts her head to the side. "There's more than that, Mrs. Hackly. Here you go. This is your account balance." She swings the computer screen around so I can see the balance, and there's in excess of eighty thousand dollars in the account.

"I'm sorry, ma'am, I think you're showing me someone else's account," I swiftly say, blocking my eyes so I'm not intruding on anyone's personal information.

"No, it's yours," she happily confirms.

"Oh my God," I gasp and look around me in the bank. Suddenly I feel like everyone in the bank is looking at me. Watching me to see what I'm going to do. "I'll just withdraw fifty dollars. No wait, make it fifty-five please." I'm not walking home, now I have bus money too.

She gives me the fifty-five dollars and I ask for two copies of proof of what's in the bank. I'll keep one in my drawer at work, in a sealed envelope because it'll be my own secret proof I've actually got money. At one point in my life I, Lily Hackly, who used to eat half rotten fruit and bury the foul part before her dad found out, now have been able to amass over eighty thousand dollars, all thanks to Trent's precise budgeting. I know that half this money is his because we're married, but I'm also smart enough to know that money has been from all the years I've been working, because Trent's never really had a job until now, his first year residency.

For the first time in my life, I skip, just like a child, to one of the small shoe stores and search for shoes to the value of fifty dollars. When I find a pair which look nice and fit me, I nervously, but excitedly hand over the fifty dollars. I've never spent so much money on myself. Trent bought the last pair of shoes and they cost forty dollars, he absolutely cringed handing over his card to pay for them saying I had to look after them because he didn't have the money to buy any more for me.

The rest of my shift at work I keep peeking at the slip that proudly displays all our money. Now I know why Trent keeps such a tight rein on our finances. I truly understand. He's building a better future for us. The smile on my face is having a positive effect on everyone I'm coming in contact with today.

"You're happy," Dale, my supervisor, says when I walk past him.

"I am," I cheerfully answer. "It's a great day."

"So it seems, Lily. Keep up the great mood and while I'm at it, keep up the great job you're doing on the floor, too."

His words of appreciation make me smile even broader and I now also have the best and most carefree happiness chirping away inside me.

My shift ends, and I catch the bus home. The entire way I keep smiling at the shoes I bought, stealing small looks to admire and appreciate them. I want to shout to all the people on the bus how I bought these shoes with my very own money. This seems like nothing to most people and I'm sure, they all have more than one pair of shoes. But to me, I've never in my life bought something with my very own money. Not something so insignificant, though completely important as shoes.

The bus trip ends, and I walk, with my new shoes, to the apartment. I go in, and get to work preparing Trent's absolute favorite dinner. I want to show him my appreciation for everything he's been doing for us. Because now I understand just why he's been so controlling with our finances, I know why he's always saying I need to work more and we can't afford to buy me new clothes and shoes.

Once dinner is in the oven, I go into the bathroom and have a quick shower, washing my hair and scrubbing myself. I quickly dry off, and style my hair exactly the way Trent's told me he likes it. Given, it's been a long time since he told me he liked it a certain way, but I remember when he'd run his hands through my hair and say he liked it left out. I cover the bruise on my cheek with cover-up, just like I did this morning before I got to work, and when I got to work. The bruise isn't big, but I didn't want anyone to ask either.

I dress in a tight, black dress Trent bought me at a yard sale, and I look myself over in the mirror. I can't wait until he's home. I'm going to lavish him with kisses and anything else he wants.

Checking the time, I know Trent will be home soon, he hasn't messaged me to tell me he's not coming home, and I haven't talked to him since he dropped me off yesterday. I flutter around the apartment, cleaning and making sure everything is put away and in its place. I fluff the odd mismatched cushions on the sofa, and tidy up all of Trent's clothes. I hang his suit jacket up and smooth it down, ensuring it falls nicely on the hanger. Trent has said it's important he have nice clothes because being a doctor means you need to present yourself in the best possible manner. And whenever I've had to see the doctor, he's always dressed nicely, so I agree with Trent. Trent said the only way to make an impression is if he bought the nicest suit, which turned out to be Armani. And really, he's so right about impressions.

The timer to the oven beeps, and I glide, still on cloud nine, over to the oven and check dinner. It's almost ready and should be done by the time Trent comes through the door. I dress the table with the prettiest table cloth I have, and I have time to cut love hearts out of a page from my journal. I cut out a few love hearts, and scatter them on the table near Trent's position at the head of the table.

I can't wait until he gets home.

Just as I finish putting the scissors away, back in the third drawer in the kitchen, I hear the key go into the lock. I fly across the room, the biggest and warmest smile for my husband, to welcome him home.

The door opens, and I jump into Trent's arms, peppering kisses all over his face. "Get off me," he says as he pushes me away. "Jesus, Lily, I just got home, give me a few minutes to wind down." He drops his bag beside the door and walks in, taking his tie off. He's not in the clothes from yesterday, but that's understandable, because he told me he keeps clothes at the hospital in case he needs to sleep there.

"Sorry, Trent," I say as I pick up the tie he dropped on the floor.

"Get me a drink."

I go over and get his whisky, preparing it exactly how he likes it. Two fingers of whisky and three ice cubes. When I turn around, he's sitting at his usual spot at the table looking at the love hearts. "Here you go," I cheerfully hand him his drink.

Trent picks up one of the hearts, looks at it, frowns and tosses it aside. "What's this shit?" he asks, as he pointedly looks toward the hearts.

"I'm just really happy," I answer as I try and move toward him to sit on his lap.

"What's got you finally behaving like a damn wife should instead of acting like a bitch?"

"You. I'm just so happy, and now I understand what you go through. I just want to make you happy, that's all." I bend to take dinner out of the oven. "Dinner's done, I'll just serve yours up."

"What I go through? What's that supposed to mean?"

"Well…" I start saying. "Don't be mad, but I went and bought a pair of shoes today."

"You did what?" he slams the glass on the table and it makes me jump back, dropping the knife in my hand onto the tray of food I've prepared.

"I had to, but I'll walk to work for the next two weeks to pay for the money I took from the bank for the shoes," I say as quickly as I can in one breath.

"You what? You went to the bank?" He stands with so much force and anger, his chair falls backward on the floor, and his thighs move the table forward. "You went to the damn bank?" he asks again.

His tone scares me, my body temperature drops to what feels like freezing and every hair on my body trembles with fear. "I got new shoes." I point to my new shoes, resting just inside the family room.

His eyes widen and he tightens his jaw. His nostrils are flaring and his lips snarl at me. "Go get them," he eventually mutters through his closed jaw.

I go into the family room and pick the shoes up, bringing them over to Trent. I extend my arm and hold the shoes out to him. "Here you go," I whisper.

The look on his face is filled with so much anger. "Get the scissors," he instructs in the same low, grim voice.

I walk over to the drawer and get the scissors and walk back to him. "Here."

He shakes his head at me. I'm not sure what he's saying, and he's not actually verbalizing it. I look down at the scissors, then back to him. I count in my head, because I'm still so unsure of what he wants. The tension in the room rises, the knot in my stomach is desperately tying itself tighter and tighter again. My throat begins to constrict and I'm having difficulty trying to breathe.

"Cut them up," he says looking between the shoes and the scissors.

My heart breaks into tiny pieces as I realize the severity of his words. "What?" I whisper. "But they're new, and I don't have other shoes."

He takes a step toward me, and I counter by taking one away. Trent pushes me with both hands, with much force I stumble back into the fridge. The door handle jabs me in the back. "Cut them up," he repeats in the same deadly, low monotone.

"But I'll walk to work for two weeks to pay them off. I don't want to cut them."

He grabs a fistful of the hair on top of my head and slams my head back into the door of the freezer. "Cut them!" He screams no more than a hair's breadth from my face. Spittle flies out of his mouth, and lands on my face.

"But..." *Smash.* He hits my head once again against the door.

"This will teach you to meddle in my business. It's *my* money, not yours, you no-good piece of trash." Tears are rolling down my face, my head is splitting from where he's slammed it against the hard fridge door. "That money is *mine*, not yours."

"But I've been working for it," I stupidly challenge. I realize belatedly I should have kept my mouth shut.

"It's *mine* you stupid piece of shit. *Mine*, not yours. *I* control it, *I* control everything. And *I* control *you*." He lets go of my head, and punches me over and over again. Some of them land on my face, and when I try to shield myself with my arms, he punches my stomach. "You bitch!" he roars.

"Help!" I yell. But the apartment next to us has been vacant for some time, and it's still early so most people wouldn't be home yet from work.

"Shut up!" *Bang.* I keep crying and trying to scream. "I said shut the fuck up." *Punch.*

Please God, please let me die. He stops hitting me and I try to blink through the hot tears to see what's happening. But the beating doesn't stop. He wraps his hands around my throat and begins to squeeze.

"You stupid bitch, you make me so angry. You shouldn't have gone to the bank. It's all your fault."

As I struggle to breathe, my eyes try to focus on the last thing I'll ever see.

But all that's in front of me is Satan. His eyes are wide and blood-shot from the burning hate that must be pulsating through his body. His face is red from his intense fury, and his hands have a death grip around my throat.

And now I understand my fate and I know my future. You can try to change the devil, but he'll always remain evil.

"Kill me, please," I beg.

I close my eyes and give my life over to the beast.

CHAPTER 20

"YOU CAN'T BE IN HERE, Max. She's resting."

"B-but how can she r-rest wh-when there's p-p-people coming in and out? Sh-she-she n-needs a pr-pri-private room."

"You know we don't have the room."

"I-I-I d-don't c-c-care," Max angrily responds. "I-I'll p-pay for it. P-p-put her in a pr-private r-room."

"Max, you can't do that."

"It's m-my m-money. I-I'll do wh-what I w-want."

Sleep.

"Mommy, Mommy, can Wiwi and me go pway in the back yard?"

"Wade, you need to have a bath. Daddy will be home soon, and it's getting dark. No playing outside, you need to go get your pajamas ready. Off you go." Mommy taps Wade on the bottom and turns to look at me. "You too, missy. Go get ready for a bath."

I stand and just look at Mommy. She's so pretty. She has the brightest eyes I've ever seen in my whole life. Her hair is just like running honey. You know when you drip honey from high above and watch it as it falls on the bread? That's what Mommy's hair looks like. Her smile is always so bright. I love Mommy so much.

Why can I hear people but I can't respond? I've heard the nurses talking about me like I'm not here. Is this heaven? Am I dead? Did Trent kill me? Am I waiting to open my eyes and see God in front of me?

"I'm sorry, Lily," Trent says. His hand takes mine, and he squeezes it. "I don't know what came over me," he whispers. I try to open my eyes, but they're so heavy. "Please, babe, wake up. Please don't die."

I'm struggling against the suction of whatever this is keeping me buried and under a heavy veil. I can hear everyone, but I seem to drop off and drift into dreams. Or maybe memories, I don't know. I don't ever remember happiness, so they're more than likely dreams. But I like these dreams, they make me happy. They let me forget all about what I've been through, the tests I've been thrown into, the situations I've had to endure.

"Lily, I swear I'll change. I'll stop the cheating. I'll be a good husband. I'll never hit you again, or do anything bad. Please, babe, please wake up."

I'm sucked back into a beautiful dream. I'm in a field of tall wildflowers that sway slightly from the warm breeze gently caressing my sun-kissed skin. I'm skipping through the flowers, and skimming the palm of my hand along the top of the blossoms. The sun is beaming down on me, her happy rays engulfing me in her warmth. Pointing my face up toward the sky, I let her embrace me. It feels natural and raw, like a mother's kiss on the nose when you stumble and scrape your knee.

"I kn-know what he d-does to you, L-Lily." A sense of calm blankets me as I feel the warmth of a hand over mine. "It's n-not r-right," he pauses, then adds, "Wh-what he does. N-no m-man should r-raise his hand to a w-woman. He n-needs help. I-I knew when I saw y-you in the hospital, I c-could tell he h-hurts you."

I want to scream at Max to stop, to tell him I don't want to hear what he has to say, but I can't open my mouth, I can't find my voice.

"D-do you kn-know what he said h-happened to y-you?" *No, stop, please just stop.* "H-he said he c-came home from w-work and the door had b-been k-kicked in. H-he said he found you like this."

What? Trent said he found me like this? He did this to me, no one else.

"H-he said y-your h-house had been r-r-ransacked be-before he got home. He said y-you were in the k-kitchen, laying on the floor," his voice drops to an almost inaudible level. "I hate what he did to you." His last sentence is said in perfect speech, with no stutter. "I-I know h-he did this, L-Lily. D-don't let him g-get away with it."

A perfect silence falls over me. I can't hear anything, not a single word. Maybe, I've finally given up and I'm in heaven. But if I'm in heaven that would mean God actually exists. And if he is real, why have I lived a life of pain? Why have I...

"My m-mom was ab-ab-abused by my step-stepdad. When he'd b-b-beat her to the p-point she'd be un-unconscious, he'd start in on me. I-I kn-know what he d-d-does to you, b-because it used to h-happen to my m-mom and me." He tightens his grip on my hand and I hear something in his voice. It's not pity; it's not shame. It goes beyond those emotions. "I-I wish I c-could have st-stopped him b-before h-he k-k-k..." Max pauses, his voice cracks and I hear him intake a deep breath. "Before he killed her." He lets go of my hand and sobs. I imagine his head falling into his hands as he cries.

If I could open my eyes and move to embrace him, I would. I want to comfort him and tell him it wasn't his fault. I can imagine him sitting beside me, weeping just like he'd probably cry when his stepfather would lay into his mom while he sat in the corner and watched such violent acts happening to the one he loved most.

A long time passes and I begin to fight the darkness. The isolation of not being able to communicate is something I don't want anymore.

"Max, you need to go home. This isn't right," a soft female voice gently says to him.

"Sh-she's b-been like this f-for thr-three days. S-someone has to b-be here incase sh-she wakes."

"You're a good man, Max Sterling. But you can't stay here. She needs to rest and so do you."

I want to scream at her and tell her to leave. Max has been talking to me, telling me his pain, and it may very well be exactly what he needs. And furthermore, what I need.

"H-her h-husband hasn't b-been to s-see her s-since the f-first day. H-has h-he called?"

"You know I can't answer that question. It's privileged and confidential. But let me just say, Mrs. Hackly has had very few phone calls enquiring on her well-being. So few that if I didn't know better, I'd think she had no family."

"B-bastard," Max mumbles.

"What was that?"

"N-nothing. I-I'll go in a wh-while."

"Okay, Max. As far as I know, you're going home."

"Th-thank you."

I hear soft footsteps, then a door close. I'm not sure how much later, I hear a chair being scraped along the floor.

"Babe, you know you're really starting to piss me off. You need to wake up, you gotta come home and make my dinner." I cringe, I'm not even sure how that's possible, but it feels like my skin is crawling. "I told you I'd stop screwing around on you, why can't you just damn well wake up. God, Lily, you're such a selfish bitch. It's always about you, you never think of me and what I need."

Sleep.

"I-it's because of h-him I st-stutter," Max says. "I-I used to w-wet the b-bed until h-he l-left f-for jail and I w-went to live with my d-dad. M-my d-dad was pretty cool, I could never un-understand why my m-mom and d-dad couldn't be t-together. Of course, I was o-only a y-young boy then." He goes silent, and I want to know what he's thinking. I'm desperate to open my eyes and gauge him by how he's carrying himself. I suspect he's sitting beside me, focusing on a spot on the wall or floor, staring at it as he thinks about what his childhood was like. "It took me years to realize they'd never work," he says. I'm not even sure he's talking to me anymore, it sounds like he's speaking to himself.

Sleep.

"How's she doing today, Max?" a female voice asks.

"Sh-she's got some color in her ch-cheeks. I-I think any t-time n-now, she'll wake."

"I think you may be right."

Sleep.

CHAPTER 21

OPENING MY EYES I KEEP blinking until I can focus on something, anything. I look over to my left and see Trent sitting on a chair, texting on his phone. "What happened?" I murmur to him.

He closes the cover to his phone, and puts it on the spare chair beside him. "Babe, oh thank God you're alright," he says as he stands and leans over me, moving some stray hair off my forehead. "I was so scared, I thought something happened to you." He kisses my forehead and then my cheeks. "You don't look that hot, Lily. Lucky I love you."

"Love me?" I question. "If you loved me, you wouldn't have beaten me."

"You don't know what you're talking about. I didn't do this to you," he says. His face is indifferent and cold, but his eyes beastly and knowing.

"You beat me, Trent because I bought shoes with money I took out of the bank. The bank where *my* money goes," I challenge.

"They must've done a number on you, because you're being delusional, babe. I've never hit you, ever. And if I did, which I didn't, I'm sure that smart mouth is what made you deserving of a slap or two." He pulls the blanket around me and tucks it into the side.

I watch him, I notice just how he's treating me. Without even flinching he's lying through his teeth. "I can't do this anymore, Trent," I whisper as I continue to watch him.

"Do what?"

"I can't live like this anymore. It's not right."

"You don't know what you're talking about." He disregards me again. "I'll get them to discharge you and when we get home, it'll all be different, and much better."

"Have you had a change of heart? You said you'd stop cheating on me."

He looks at me, and takes a step back sinking into the uncomfortable looking plastic chair. "I don't cheat on you," he says as he watches my response. "God, Lily, why do you say things like that? Do you want me to get mad?"

I feel myself draw my eyebrows together and I think back to what I heard. "How long have I been here?" I ask changing conversation, in case

I really did just dream everything.

"You were beaten fairly badly. You were unconscious for just over seventy-six hours. I came home and found you slumped on the floor." He shakes his head and runs his hand over his face, then through his hair. "I thought you were dead," he whispers. "It's damn lucky I'm a doctor and I checked you out, but damn, you scared the shit out of me."

He's so convincing, maybe I just dreamt it all happened. Maybe my mind has pushed something like Trent beating me and choking me to an extreme where it's created that memory and blocked out the truth. "You didn't do this?" I ask.

"You think I could do this to you? Babe, I love you, no way could I ever go to this extreme."

"Mrs. Hackly, you're awake," says a young pretty nurse as she comes in the door and her eyes widen when she sees me awake. "Hi, Trent." She smiles at Trent and her cheeks pink in color. Quickly she averts her eyes and looks back to me. "How do you feel?"

"I'm thirsty," I say as I feel the dry parchment in my throat. "I think I'm okay."

She smiles at me, but it's just a plastic smile. Something she shows everyone because she has to. She checks my vital signs, and says she'll call in the doctor on duty.

"What actually happened, Trent?" I ask when the perky nurse leaves.

"Jesus, Lily. Do I have to repeat myself? Just listen will you? I came home, the door was kicked in and you were lying in the kitchen. I checked you out and called an ambulance. That's what happened." He links his hands together and cracks his knuckles. "That's it. Nothing else."

I completely relax, and just let his words wash over me. "I'm tired, Trent. I'm going to close my eyes for a minute."

"All you've been doing is sleeping. If the doctor okays it, I'm taking you home tonight."

I look over to him and he's back on his phone, typing away. "Did you call work, tell them what happened?"

"Yeah, babe. Of course. Dale said to get better."

"Thank you," I say and close my eyes.

What the hell happened? Why does the beating I thought he gave me feel so real? Did I really just imagine him placing his hands around my throat and choking me? Have I manifested the entire thing and made my husband out to be a predator, an abuser? The serene black gives me an escape, and I grab onto it with both hands and let the darkness claim me.

"Y-you said she w-woke?"

"She did, Max, earlier today."

I open my eyes and see a different nurse standing beside my bed and Max, who's just come through the door. I look at her, then him and smile.

"Y-you're a-awake," he says as he takes a step toward my bed.

"I am." Something courses through my body. I can't describe it, or even identify it because I don't know what it is. It feels like excitement mixed with anxiety. "What are you doing here?" I ask him.

"I-I sh-should go," he responds as he turns around and is just about to open the door.

"No, please don't." My own words surprise me. I don't know why I'm asking him to stay, or even why he's here to begin with.

Max stands in the far corner, and watches as the nurse checks me over. She leaves quite quickly and tells me she'll let the doctor know I'm awake again.

"Y-you l-look b-better than you d-did a few days a-ago," Max says nervously, as he continues to stand in the corner furthest away from me.

"Please, don't stand over there." I move my hand to indicate the chair beside the bed. Slowly he moves toward it, his movements are so meticulous and calculated he takes a good minute before he reaches the chair. "You sat with me, didn't you?"

He looks at me, his intense brown eyes have the most alluring flecks of green to them. They're unlike anything I've ever seen before. They are fierce, and protective. "I did," he answers with perfect pronunciation. "I had to," he adds.

'Had to'? What does that even mean? "I don't understand."

"O-one d-day you will."

My heart jumps and my body prickles with a flush of adrenalin. "I don't understand," I say again.

Max smiles and leans forward on the chair. He places his elbows on his knees and links his hands together, dropping his chin to rest on them. "H-how are you f-feeling?" His voice is pure gold. I don't hear his stutter, just the deep, throaty tone.

"I can't explain it, Max, really I can't. Why am I feeling so comfortable around you? I should be freaking out, and shutting down just from your presence. But...I'm not." I slowly sit up in bed. Max's eyes intensely watch as I maneuver so I'm sitting. Suddenly I realize how hideous I must look after being in bed for days, not being able to wash or even brush my hair. I can feel the bruising on my face from where I was beaten by whoever broke in.

"Y-you should n-never be frightened b-by me." Max smiles. My shoulders relax and any confused and unsure feelings I may have had all disintegrate, like ash being carried by a small breeze. His relaxed behavior makes me even more comfortable around him.

A moment later, the door opens and a doctor comes in with the nurse who was just here. Max stands to leave. "Don't go," I foolishly say to him. These feelings of complete ease are uncommon and foreign to me. I don't understand why I'm calm. It doesn't make any sense, but I like it.

"I-I'll go and g-get a c-c-coffee. B-but I'll re-return," he says as he steps outside.

"How are you feeling, Mrs. Hackly?" The doctor asks as he begins his examination of me.

"I'm okay, just tender and sore."

"You're very lucky your husband came home when he did. The wound on the back of your head was extensive. You needed stitches, twenty-one to be exact, they're dissolvable stitches and should fall out on their own within another week or so."

We continue talking and he tells to me the police are going to want to talk to me when I'm feeling up for it. My spirits sink at the thought of having to talk to the police. At first I thought it was Trent who did this to me, but he's convinced me it was a break-in and my memory of the situation is hazy. Because of this, I don't want to talk to the police and give them muddled information.

The doctor decides I'm not well enough to speak to the police and tells me he'll tell them to come back tomorrow. He's given me the all-clear to eat and says if my reactions and vital signs are healthy, then I'll be able to go home tomorrow.

A few moments after he leaves, Max comes back into the room and stands by the door. I think he's waiting for an invitation to come sit beside me. "Max, would you like a seat?"

"Thank you," he says with a smile, and he moves to sit beside me. "So h-how are you f-f-feeling?"

I touch the back of my head where my hair has been shaved and I wince when my fingers run across the bandage over the stitches. "I'm tender and sore, but I'll live. I'm a tough cookie." I weakly smile. "It's just lucky my husband came home when he did."

"L-l-lucky? Y-you call that lucky?" He points to my head. "L-lucky he d-didn't k-kill y-you," he says through a tight, clenched jaw.

"What? Trent didn't do this, someone broke into our house and did this to me."

Max's eyebrows fly up in question, and his top lips snarls in the smallest of ways. "I-is th-that what he t-told you?" I nod my head. "A-and y-you believe h-him?"

"He's my husband. Why wouldn't I believe him?" Although I know something's not right. I can feel the uncertainty of the entire situation deep inside me.

"O-okay, y-you believe him," he says as he shrugs his shoulders. "E-everyone used to b-believe my m-mom, too."

"Your mom?" I question.

"My m-mom w-was b-beaten b-by my st-st-stepf-father, until he k-killed her."

Wait. This feels like déjà vu. My mind is swirling as I sit up in bed, waiting for Max to say more. I want to ask him what happened to his mom, but I know it's insensitive of me to do so.

"Um." I look around the room trying to focus on something else. I notice I'm in a private room, and again something's not adding up. "Why am I in a private room?" I look around once more before turning and having my eyes land on an inquisitive Max.

"You r-really d-don't know?"

"Know what?"

"It d-doesn't m-m-matter then."

We again sit in silence. The room is quiet, but my mind isn't. It's screaming at me that certain things just aren't adding up. It's like I'm fighting my way out of a dark forest and I have no light to guide me. I decide to just let that go, because eventually the answers will come to me. "Can I ask you a question, without sounding rude?"

Max smiles and I see his tall frame relax. "N-nothing you say c-could ever be r-rude."

I try and formulate the question as tactfully as I can. "Why is your stutter sometimes more prominent than other times?"

A corner of his mouth rises, and he blinks slowly as he brings both his hands up and rests them on his head. "The m-more comfortable I am w-with someone, the l-less I st-st-stut-stutter."

This of course leads me to my next question, "Are you nervous around me?"

This question has him chuckling. "Y-you make m-me most n-nervous."

"Hmmm," I answer as I carelessly run my hand through my hair. The moment my fingers touch the bandage where the slash is, I wince in pain.

"Are you alright?" he asks as he protectively leaps up and leans toward me.

I lower my hand and gaze at Max. His caring nature is confusing to me. "I'm okay," I say as I watch him settle back into his seat. "Why do I make you nervous?"

"Y-you r-remind me of my m-mom." I feel myself scrunch my nose at his response, and it must be quite obvious because he hastily adds, "I mean the way sh-she w-was around *him*," he says, emphasizing 'him'. He gets lost for a moment, perhaps talking about his mom and what she went through is still difficult and traumatizing. I can only imagine what a battered woman would go through, let alone the son who witnessed it. "I-I h-have to go," Max announces as he abruptly stands and heads toward the door.

"Did I do something wrong?" I ask, shaken and concerned I've made him feel as if he has to flee.

He stops before he puts his hand on the handle. Turning to look at me he says in a low, soothing tone, "No, Lily. You could never do anything wrong." His words are perfect. Max leaves without waiting for a response from me.

What's going on? Why does it feel like he's walked out and is never going to return? Why does the thought of his absence make my stomach knot in uneasiness?

Before I even realize, the door opens again and a burly lady comes through, carrying a food tray. "Here you go, darling," she says, as she places it on the table beside me without even looking at me.

"Thank you," I answer and wonder who ordered what for me.

She leaves quietly and I take the plastic cover off the plate and start to eat the bland hospital food. As I'm picking at it, the door opens again and Trent waltzes in. "You're awake. Good. Spoke to the doctor on shift, and I swear, the guy is an idiot. Where he studied, I have no idea." He rolls his eyes and sits in the chair Max was in. "Anyway, don't eat too much. You don't want to end up like a fat pig." He pointedly looks at my half-eaten plate of food and then takes his phone out of his pocket.

I slow my eating and place the fork on the plate. "What did the doctor say?"

"He said if you eat and keep it all down, I'll be able to bring you home tomorrow."

"Well that's good."

Trent dials someone, and holds a finger up to me as he starts talking into his phone. "Hi, it's me." He listens for a few seconds. "Yeah, I can't. Maybe on the weekend." He listens again. "Okay, bye."

"Who was that?" I ask.

"Someone from work wants me to help 'em move. No big deal, I said I couldn't."

"Who's 'them'?"

"You don't know them, so don't worry about it. Anyway, you'll come home tomorrow, just don't freak out because of the blood in the kitchen."

"Didn't you clean it up?"

"I'm not a fucking cleaner, Lily. These hands are precious. I'm going to be a surgeon one day. Speaking of which, you still have that assignment to do. Do you want me to go get the work and you can do in here tonight?" he asks me in the most serious of tones.

"I can't do your work for you, Trent. You need to do it, so you learn."

Trent's jaw tightens and he stands from his chair. "I gotta go, babe. I'll be back tomorrow to pick you up."

"Wait," I call to him as he disappears out the door. "Where are you going?" I ask no one, because he's already gone.

I sit in my room, my cold, isolated room, feeling more alone and lonely than I've ever felt before.

The only thing to keep me wondering is the fact Max has been here. A plethora of thoughts whiz around in my mind. But the biggest one, and the one I can't seem to find an answer to is…*why?*

CHAPTER 22

"YOU READY TO GO HOME, babe?" Trent asks as he walks ahead of me carrying the small bag he brought me, which contains a change of clothes and clean underwear.

Once I'm in the car and we're heading toward home, I relay to Trent what the police said when they stopped in this morning. "They asked me if I remember anything from the attack."

"What did you say?" he asks. And I notice he decreases the speed of the car.

"I told them the truth; I told them I can't remember."

"Come on, Lily. I told you what happened. You should've just told them what I said."

"I won't lie to them, Trent. I can't remember what happened." I shake my head in disbelief at myself.

"You should just believe me. It's how I said. Anyway…" he pauses talking and takes three deep breaths. "Anyway, what are you cooking for dinner? I've had to live on take-out and I'm ready for a home-cooked meal."

"I'm not well enough to cook yet. Can't we just get pizza? And besides, I need to rest, the doctor said so and I have to go back next week to see him."

"He's an idiot, I already told you that. I'll look after you, it's the least I can do since I am your husband."

I turn in my seat to face him. There's something which has been playing on my mind, and it's always there, trying to push forward. And left lingering, it's manifesting into more. "Trent," I start saying.

"Yeah."

"How do you feel?" I ask, hoping he understands what I'm asking.

"Good. Why?"

"I mean, how do you feel about the situation? You said you came home and found me in the kitchen. Did you panic or were you worried?"

"Oh babe, you're really going to ask me such lame questions? I don't feel anything, as soon as I saw you and I checked out your vitals, I knew you were going to be fine."

"Is that the reason you were barely at the hospital?"

"These questions are bullshit, Lily. I have work, you know that. Just because you got a small cut on your head, my work doesn't stop. For God's sake, Lily! You can be so selfish sometimes." He looks coldly out the window. "Christ," he mumbles to himself.

I do what I always do, I remain quiet for the rest of the trip back to the apartment.

Trent parks in our allocated spot and gets out. He takes the steps two at a time until he reaches our apartment. "Hurry up," he yells out. "Don't forget your bag."

I go to the trunk of the car and take my bag out, then go up the steps to our small apartment, where the door is opened and Trent's already inside watching TV. I look at the door, and see it's been replaced and try to think back to the day of my attack.

Looking down at my feet, I notice new sandals Trent must have bought for me to wear home and absent mindedly, I look around the room. Again, something's not quite right but I can't quite place what it is that's wrong.

"Babe, get me a soda," Trent says, as he flips through the channels of the TV.

I drop my bag beside the door and close it, locking it and double checking I've locked it. My mind is spinning and I can't help but think *if there was a break in, why aren't I frightened to be back here? And what did they take? It's just not adding up.*

Walking over to the fridge, I stand in front of it and see the dent in the freezer door. There's dried blood splattered on it, and suddenly a snippet of what happened pops into my mind. *Shoes.* Something happened with shoes.

I go into our bedroom, get my diary from my hiding spot and flick through the minimal entries, but there's nothing about shoes in it.

My mind is hazy, like a jigsaw puzzle with all the pieces spread across the floor. I can see all the pieces, but they're not in order. I need to sift through them and put them together creating a perfect picture.

"Get me my drink," Trent hollers.

I tuck my diary into the back pocket of my jeans and pull my sweater down over it, because I need to read it properly to see if there's anything in there to give me the vital clue to help me piece the puzzle together.

I go back to the fridge and open the door, bending to get a soda from the bottom shelf. As I squat to get the drink, I see a tiny love heart cut out of paper on the floor.

Picking the heart up, I carry it, along with the soda, over to Trent. "What's that?" Trent asks, as I hand him his drink.

"I'm not sure," I say, as I turn the love heart over in my hand.

Trent peers over the top of my hand, his eyes widen and he snatches the heart right out of my hand.

At Trent's reaction to the heart, memories of everything that happened on the day I was beaten flood me. "IT WAS YOU!" I scream as I back away from him. My body's trembling from fear and my heart races as I remember every single moment, every blow of Trent trying to kill me. I feel as if I'm being pounded by tsunami waves of shock, fiercely trying to submerge me and keep me under.

"It was an accident," Trent yells at me as he stands and takes a step toward me. His hands curl into fists and his face is turning red.

"Don't touch me." My back touches the door, and I turn the handle to make my escape.

Trent's entire frame changes. He straightens his shoulders, his mouth turns up into a snide, evil smirk and his eyes narrow at me. Every hair on my body stands to attention, and goosebumps suddenly rise, as my body recognizes evil.

"And where the hell do you think you're going to go? You're the stupidest, fucking ugliest person I've ever known, Lily. You have no friends, I made sure I separated you from the one you did have. You have no family, and you have nowhere to go. And let me tell you something else, you now have no job, either. I told that Dale prick, the one who's always trying to give you confidence and boost you up, I told him you've been stealing money from there for years. I convinced him not to press charges against you, but you know what that means, *babe*?" I shake my head, unable to comprehend what he's saying. "It means I fucking *own* you." He steps closer to me and grabs my upper arm and squeezes, reminding me I'm his, silently telling me he can do whatever he wants with me.

It's this moment, this one situation, when I finally realize if I stay, the next time I won't go to the hospital, it will be to the county morgue instead.

No more.

"Let me go," I say as I grind my teeth together. "You have no more power over me."

Trent throws his head back and laughs as he tightens his grip further on my arm. "You stupid girl," he huffs as he lowers his voice and brings his face so his nose is almost touching mine.

"No more, Trent. I'm going to walk out this door and you're never going to come anywhere near me again." I straighten my back and square my shoulders.

Trent's features flinch, a small tremor beneath his right eye as he considers my words and his lip curls up in disgust. "I can take your life, Lily and no one will ever know or care."

"I've been keeping a diary." I won't tell him it's on me or he'll take it and then he'll kill me. "It's in my locker at work. You may have gotten me fired, but if they open my locker, they'll find it."

"You're bluffing. You're not smart enough to do something so devious."

"Are you really going to risk everything over whether or not I have a diary?"

"You stupid bitch. I *will* get you."

"Then do it now, because if I walk out that door and you come after me, I'll tell the police what you did to me." I shrug out of the grip he has on me. Of course, with his size he can easily overpower me, but the worry etched deep on his face is enough to tell me he's considering the severity of my words. "Kill me now Trent, or let me go."

Trent takes a step back, his shoulders slumping slightly forward. "You walk out this door, and you'll never come back again." I turn the latch on the door, unlocking it. "I swear to God, you leave and we're over."

"Your future as a doctor is now in my hands. Just leave me alone. Don't ever come near me again."

I open the door. "Don't you fucking go!" he orders me. I step through the door and turn to look at him over my shoulder. "Get your God damned stupid, ugly ass back here." He points to the spot in front of him. "NOW!" he shouts.

I walk out.

Down the steps.

And I start toward…I don't know what. But it's got to be better than this.

I hear Trent scream, "Lily!"

I'm not anyone's punching bag anymore.

CHAPTER 23

I WALK INTO THE STORE with nothing but the clothes on my back, and the sandals on my feet. And most important, my freedom.

Shivering, I head toward the back where I know Dale will be. I try my code to open the door, but it's not working. I head to the front and find Vivian, the shift supervisor. "Vivian, is Dale here?" I ask as her eyes land on me and take in my appearance.

"Oh my God, Lily, are you okay?" she asks.

I can feel my teeth chattering from the freezing cold. "I'm cold," I answer, as I try and wrap my arms around my body. It's about thirteen degrees outside and all I'm wearing is jeans, sandals, and a light sweater. "Is Dale here?"

"Here you go." Vivian grabs her jacket from behind the counter, and slings it over my shoulders. "I'll call Dale down." She picks up the phone, and turns her back to me talking quietly into it. A few seconds pass, and she turns to me and says, "He's coming down."

"Thank y-you," I stutter from the cold. Now I've stopped walking, the cold has hit me, and hit me hard.

"Lily," Dale says from behind me. "Jesus. Come upstairs." He waits for me to go first, and he follows. When we get to the door, he puts his code in, and I go up the stairs to his office. He comes in, closes the door and grabs his coat from the coat stand, and throws it over Vivian's jacket. He then goes back to the coat stand to get his scarf, wrapping it around my neck. "What the hell is going on?" he finally asks when he sits at his desk. "Sit," he offers, as he gestures toward a chair.

I take my diary out from my waist band, and place it on his desk as I sit. I breathe in deeply and try to regulate my body to get warm. "S-sorry. I'm r-really cold."

"I'll make you a hot cup of coffee. Just wait." Suddenly he leaps up, and runs toward the staff room. He's so fast I don't even have time to tell him I don't like coffee. But if it's hot, and it'll warm me up, then I'm going to accept it.

A few minutes pass, and he brings in two coffees. "Thank you," I say, as he places one in front of me. I wrap both my hands around the coffee, and the cup is so warm, it stings against my frozen digits. But my hands warm quickly, and I no longer find it uncomfortable. "Thank you for agreeing to see me," I say, once I've sipped some of the coffee.

Dale's eyes have stayed on me. He's regarding me closely and evaluating my appearance. "What's been happening with you, Lily? I have to say, when Trent called me and told me someone broke into your apartment and you'd been hurt, I was shocked. But the biggest shock was when he said you've been stealing money from here. I terminated you and thought you'd never show your face around here again."

I half smile, more at the irony than the actual act. Trent wanted me isolated from everyone, and he was successful at convincing a man I've worked alongside for years I was a thief. "I've never stolen anything, from anyone," I begin to say.

"I don't understand. The Lily I know would never do those things he said you'd done, but he was very convincing. I couldn't risk having you here and impacting the store any further. Not you, per se, but more what trouble Trent could stir up. I'm still conflicted and trying to gather my thoughts on what's going on. But I'm willing to hear you out, and your story about what exactly has gone on." He takes a sip of his coffee. The one thing about Dale, he's always been fair in the way he conducts himself.

Dale is an older gentleman, maybe in his late fifties, but incredibly patient and the fairest person I know. His hair is thinning and he's quite round and cuddly. He always speaks so highly about his wife and two older daughters. And everyone, including myself, has a lot of respect for him.

"Did Trent tell you I was in the hospital?"

Dale's eyes widen and he presses his lips together. "No, he didn't. Why were you in the hospital?" he asks.

"I was beaten," I say in the smallest of voices. I don't say it with conviction or anger. I simply say it with no feeling. Because the only feeling I can show, and I'm trying to hold onto it, is embarrassment.

"What?" he says in a whisper. "Beaten? What happened?" He's trying to remain impassive, but the way his jaw has tightened and his eyes have darkened, I can tell he must be thinking I deserved it.

"By…" My gosh, this is hard to say. "By…" I start again, trying to say Trent's name, but I can't. The humiliation coursing through me is preventing me from saying his name. "By…" I burst into tears. I can't handle this. I'm not strong enough to tell him, I can't be…anything.

I'm so weak, so stupid for even trying to make a change in my life. I'm nothing; I'm of no significance to anyone. I'm a waste of air and shouldn't be alive.

"I'm sorry. I should go," I say through the thick, strangled sobs. I stand to my feet and so does Dale.

"You're not going anywhere, Lily. You'll sit down and tell me what the hell is going on." He rounds the table and engulfs me in a hug. It's the first time in years when I've needed human contact, I've gotten it. He doesn't suffocate me or drown me in his body, he's just holding onto me, offering comfort.

I bawl into his chest, my arms tighten around him and I'm left a mess. "I'm sorry," I keep repeating into Dale's chest. My sobs eventually dwindle into small hiccups and I finally calm down.

"Tell me what's been happening," he probes gently. He's still holding me. It's not sexual or sleazy, it's like a father would hold his daughter when she cries because her first love has broken her heart. He's a gentleman, and a truly beautiful soul. "It's okay, Lily. In my office, here at work, it's safe. No one can hurt you here." His tone is low and soothing, and I know he means the words he's speaking.

I let go of my shame, and open my mouth. No, that's not right, I'm not letting go of my shame, I'm still holding onto that, but I'm risking the consequences by telling Dale what's been happening. I unwrap my arms from Dale, and step back, giving us some space and room. I look up into his aging eyes, and notice for the first time the wrinkles and dark bags under them. "It's okay," he says again and leans back against his desk.

"Trent beat me."

Dale's eyes widen and he contorts his mouth, clearly chewing on the inside of his cheek. His hands tighten around the desk and his chest puffs out. "Tell me what happened, Lily."

I spend the next half hour telling him about the most recent incident which landed me in the hospital, including what happened when we got home a few hours ago. Dale's been sitting on the edge of his desk, not moving or saying anything. But his face gives everything away, the way his left eye flinches, and his arms strain below his button-up shirt is enough for me to see the anger building up inside of him.

"Please don't be mad with me," I say when his jaw tightens and his face morphs into anger.

"With you? Christ, Lily, I'm nowhere near angry with you. I'm mad at myself for being duped by such a heathen and manipulator."

"You're not mad with me?" I ask, surprised.

"No." He takes a deep breath and asks, "Where will you be staying?"

"I was going to ask if I could use the phone, so I can call my friend Shayne."

"Of course, and if he can't accommodate you, I have a guest room you'll be comfortable in."

I smile at his offer of hospitality, and truthfully, I'm somewhat shocked he'd be willing to accept me into his home. "Shayne's a girl, and my best friend from years ago. You don't have to put yourself out. I'm sure there is a shelter close by I could stay in if Shayne can't help."

"You're not staying at a shelter. End of story. Now, when you left, you left like this?" he asks as he gestures toward my body.

"Just me and my diary, nothing else."

"I'll organize another uniform for you, and here, take my credit card and go buy some warm clothes." He takes his wallet out, and offers me his card. But I don't take it.

"No need, I just need to go to the bank. He'd been controlling our finances, and we have over eighty thousand in the bank. I just need some ID to go and get some money out. But I don't have any, I've left everything back at the apartment."

"I'd have some here on file from when you first came to work. I can give it to you and take you to the bank if you like?" he offers.

"Yes, please. I need some shoes, and clothes."

Dale gets up, "I'll go to the file room, and see what I have for you. But please, use the phone and call your friend." He leaves me in his office.

Damn it, I don't have Shayne's number, it's in my bag back at the apartment. I pick my diary up and start flicking through it, trying to think of how I can get in contact with Shayne. I remember I wrote it in my diary when she gave it to me. I thumb through the pages until I find it.

Picking up Dale's phone, I nervously punch in the numbers and wait until it starts ringing. My heart's leapt up into my throat, and my anxiety is making me tremble with fear and uncertainty.

"Hello," Liam answers.

"Hi, um, Liam."

"Yeah, who's this?"

'It's me, Lily."

"Holy shit. What the hell? Oh my God. SHAYNE!" he yells.

I move the phone away from my ear when he screams for Shayne. I put the phone back and hear Liam telling Shayne I'm on the phone.

"Lily, how are you? Are you okay?" she says without even taking a breath. I burst into tears again, I'm so ashamed I have to stoop to calling Shayne for help. "Oh my God, where are you, Lily? I'm coming to get you."

I can't seem to make the tears stop, but through the uncontrollable sobs, I finally manage to say, "I'm at work, up in the boss's office."

"Stay there until I come get you. Liam and I are on our way." She hangs up before I can say anything else.

Moments later, Dale comes back into his office holding a folder. "Here, I have some of your personal information so you can use it to go to the bank. I'll come with you, if you like," he offers.

"Shayne and her husband, Liam are coming here to pick me up. I'll go with them."

"Anything you want, Lily. Now, about work."

"Do I still have a job?"

"Well, actually…no."

I huff and let my shoulders slump. "Okay."

"Not downstairs, but Candice, the CEO's personal assistant is leaving next Friday, and I know Peter hasn't replaced her yet. He told me to keep an eye out, and I think you'll be perfect for the role."

"But I don't know what to do."

"Don't worry about that for now, take the rest of the week off. Call me or come in and see me on Friday and we'll talk about it then. But for now, just don't even worry about work. You'll always have a job here."

"Thank you, Dale."

We sit and chat, and I can tell Dale's trying to drag my mind away from my marital situation. He's telling me about the guest room he has, and how his daughters would love having me around.

Although he's being generous, Trent is first and foremost in my mind. I'm frightened of him and his capabilities, and I'm struggling with even asking Shayne for help, let alone asking Dale to put himself, his wife, and his daughters in harm's way.

Trent will try to kill me. There's no doubt in my mind he has the ability and the sadistic nature to do so. As my mind swims with fear of Trent, Dale gets a phone call from downstairs saying two people are waiting for me.

"Thank you for everything," I say as I stand.

Dale comes out from behind his desk, and blankets me in another hug. "Whatever I can do to help you, you let me know."

"Thank you for everything." I leave his office and go downstairs to Shayne and Liam.

Shayne opens her arms the moment she takes in my appearance and I fly into them. "You've left him, haven't you?" she whispers. I nod my head, confirming her question. "Come on, let's get you home."

"I have to go to the bank first."

She lets go of my shoulders and looks at me. "Bank?"

"I'll explain everything in the car, I just need to go to the bank."

"Okay, we'll come with you."

We link our fingers together, and walk down toward the Bank of America. Liam's four steps behind us, giving us space. When we walk in, Liam sits at one of the chairs lining the wall, and Shayne stands beside me in line.

When I get called, I give the teller all my information and tell her I'd like to withdraw some money. It's only fair I take what I think belongs to me, so I'll take forty thousand, and leave the other half for Trent.

"How much would you like?" the pretty, young teller asks me.

"What's the balance?"

"Here you go." She turns the monitor and shows me the account balance. Three thousand and fifty-eight dollars and ninety-two cents.

"What?!" I half scream, completely floored by the lack of funds.

"Is there a problem?" she asks looking worriedly between me and the screen.

"There's supposed to be over eighty thousand dollars in there."

"I see there's been some recent activity on the account. Let me have a look." She hits some keys and then says, "Here you go. There was a check cut to a car dealership, um, let me see which dealership, for fifty-five thousand." She taps away. "This is the BMW dealership downtown."

I turn to Shayne, shaking my head. "He bought a car."

"And there was another check cut to another dealership, here." She taps again, bringing up the details. "This one is to Toyota for twenty thousand dollars."

"He bought two cars, not just one, with *my* damn money," I say to Shayne. Shayne's not saying anything, just shaking her head. I turn back to the teller and say, "I'll withdraw everything in that account and have my name taken off it."

"I'll have to get a manager to do that," she says. "I'll be back in a moment." She locks her window, and leaves Shayne and myself standing their dumbfounded and speechless.

"This is unbelievable," I say as I look around the bank about to cry again. *Can this day get any worse?*

An older man, who's soft around the center with no hair on his head comes and introduces himself. He leads me to a private office, and we sit for fifteen minutes taking my name off that account and opening another in just my name. When we're done, I walk out with just over three thousand dollars in my new bank account and the clothes on my back. I go back into work, and quickly speak to Dale, giving him my new bank details then leave with Shayne and Liam.

I'm going to start my life over again.

CHAPTER 24

"Hey, I made hot chocolates," Shayne says, as she comes into the guest room and sits on the bed I've been occupying for the last three days. "Why don't you come have some with us?"

I look over at the clock and see just how late it is. "It's nearly eleven; I just want to sleep," I say as I turn over in the bed. I went into work and spoke with Dale and Peter, and they both agreed I'm too valuable to the company to be on the floor. I've been given a pay raise of five thousand a year, and the position of Peter's personal assistant. Peter told me he'd review my performance in six months, and will adjust my pay accordingly.

"Too bad. This is the first time in, I don't know how many years, I have my best friend back," she says as she pushes on my body. "I'm not going to waste the opportunity."

I smile because Shayne is, if nothing else, tenacious. "Okay, get me my...I mean *your* slippers." I point to the bottom of the bed.

She chuckles, gets up and throws them at my head. "Here's *your* slippers." She's laughing, and I can't help but laugh, too. "Now, get your butt out of bed, or I'll sit on your head and fart." Again, she makes me laugh, and she leaves the room, laughing too.

I get up and walk out to their kitchen. Liam is sitting on one of the stools sipping his hot chocolate, and Shayne sits and picks her mug up too. "Why does this feel like an intervention?" I ask as I sit and look into my mug. "If it is, then I think I should at least get a couple of marshmallows in my mug."

"Oh good idea, and tomorrow night, we're having s'mores. Can you get the fire pit going?" she asks Liam.

"Yeah I should be able to, unless it snows."

"It hasn't snowed yet, so it probably won't tomorrow night either."

Liam goes to the cupboard and gets the marshmallows, putting them down in front of us. I pick two up and pop them into my hot chocolate.

"You know we love you, right?" Shayne starts saying.

It's never good when someone starts the conversation off with a statement like that, then adds, 'right?' on the end of it. "Yeah," I say, drawing out the word. "But...?" I include, "there's always a 'but'."

"Well, Liam and I have been talking…"

"No, sweetheart, you've been talking and I've been listening," Liam butts in.

"Yes, that too." Shayne pokes her tongue out Liam playfully. "*Liam* and I have been talking," she emphasizes his name. "And we think you should go back to the university. You always wanted to become an English teacher. Now I think you should do it."

"It's all her, not me, I had nothing to do with this," Liam says throwing his hands up in mock surrender.

"It's okay. It's a great idea. But I can't. I need to work, and my scholarship became void once I dropped out."

"You can work part time at the supermarket, and maybe do some proofreading to supplement your wages and take a course or two," Shayne excitedly says, as she bounces in her seat.

"You've put a lot of thought into this," I say, watching her enthusiasm as she beams toward me.

"Oh my God, have I! I think you can do it, Lily. Really, I think you can. You're the smartest person I know. And even though it'll mean you'll be super busy, if there's anyone who can do it, it's you." She takes a deep breath and smiles at me. "I know you can do it." She points at herself. "He knows you can do it." She points to Liam, and Liam's nodding with a goofy smile on his face. "And *you* know you can do it." She points to me. "You've lived your entire life in hell. Now, it's time to move to heaven." She smiles at me.

I can't help but feel the tears prickling behind my eyes. "I wouldn't know where to start," I say. "I've never proofread anything in my life. How am I supposed to do something like that? I wouldn't even know where to find anyone to ask them if I could work on their book."

"Well…" Shayne starts saying, jumping up and down in her seat again. "One of the girls who works for us has written a romance book and she's looking for a second pair of eyes. I could always ask her. I'm sure she'll say yes."

This is overwhelming to me. I've never considered doing anything like this before. "Um, I suppose I can give it a try," I say, shrugging my shoulders. "But what if I suck?"

"You won't suck. You'll be great."

"What if she hates what I do?"

"Then she can find someone else to double-check it."

"What if I cost her sales because I'm really no good?"

Liam chuckles and I look over to him. "You have to have faith in yourself, Lily. Really, you do. What's the worst that can happen? You'll do it, she won't like what you do, and you'll part ways. No hard feelings."

"I suppose I can try."

"Yay." Shayne claps her hands together. "I'll tell her in the morning, she'll be so excited."

"I've been thinking about something, too." I look down at my hot chocolate and avoid both Shayne's and Liam's eyes. "I've been thinking it might be a good idea to start seeing a psychologist, maybe they can help me deal with all these feeling I'm having."

"This is the best night ever!" Shayne shrieks, as she leaps out of her chair and hugs me tightly. "You're so strong, Lily. I know it, I can feel it in my bones, you're going to be the best proofreader around. You mark my words, you're going to be fantastic. And when you find a psychologist, you're going to be even stronger still."

"Thank you," I say, though I do have my reservations. As we sip our hot chocolate, Shayne and Liam are making sweet eyes at each and suddenly I feel as if I'm intruding in their own personal time. I finish drinking and take my mug over to the sink, rinsing it out. "Can I borrow your laptop, please? I want to do some research on proofreading and what it entails."

"Sure thing, buttercup," Liam says as he winks at Shayne. A silent flirtation happens between the two, and I know I'm definitely overstaying my welcome out here in the kitchen. Liam gets up and goes to get their laptop and I hug Shayne and give her a kiss on the cheek. "It's in your room, Lily," Liam says, as he walks to stand beside his wife.

"Goodnight, guys. And…" I look down, staring at the pink slippers on my feet. "Thank you for everything."

"You're welcome," Shayne happily cheers. I hear a clap and I turn to see Shayne jumping with the biggest, most beautiful grin on her face. "I might put some music on," I say.

"Good idea, 'cause we're gonna have wild monkey sex," Liam says playfully.

"Liam!" Shayne scolds him.

"What? We are." I chuckle then I hear him whisper; actually more like beg, "Please?"

I go into the guest room, close the door and sit on the bed. The laptop is already open and the search engine is on the screen. First, I look into proofreading, and what exactly a proofreader does. I peruse many sites, and it becomes apparent to me, proofreaders check spelling, grammar, word repetition and punctuation. Some do more but when I go into the 'more' they do, it begins to cross over into copy editing, content editing and line editing. All things I'd need to study if I was to be successful.

Once I've exhausted myself looking into proofreaders and what they do,

I look for psychologists, specifically someone who specializes in domestic violence. The moment I type in the words 'domestic violence psychologist' it all becomes very real. The enormity of the situation hits me like a ton of bricks. A massive heaviness sits on my chest, I start to breathe very shallowly, desperately trying to suck air into my lungs.

My hands are shaking, and I can't seem to get a grip on myself. Sweat beads on the back of my neck, and despite the cold weather outside, I'm boiling and trembling with anxiety and nervousness. My vision is blurring and I can't seem to make my blood cool and my pulse settle.

Taking a few deep breaths, I'm finally calm enough to logically try and work through whatever the hell just happened. I close the laptop for a few moments, turn on the radio and find a station which is playing soothing music, and just lay on the bed and close my eyes.

When my body is completely calm, and I feel all the tension disappear. I sit up in bed and turn to the laptop again. The search page has a list of psychologists who are located near work. Some work with children, others with trauma victims. As I scour the pages, trying to find someone, I come across a name of a doctor whose introduction reads, 'Specializing in women who have suffered domestic abuse.' The listing itself is simple, and on the third page of the search engine. I click on the link, and see a picture of her. Her name is Dr. Katherine Scott, and it says she's the only one in her practice. For some unknown reason, her picture and her page tell me she's the person who can help me. I open up my email, copy her email address and type out an email to her.

I sit and look at the words I've typed, and delete them. I write something different, a shorter introduction, and again I delete it. It takes me over an hour of writing and deleting before I glare at the words I finally do write: "I need help." The words are brutal, but also simple and to the point. I get up off the bed, and I pace back and forth in my room, stopping to stare at the three little words which have the potential to change my life. *This is stupid, Lily. You're an idiot.*

Going into the guest bathroom, I brush my teeth, and just to be sure, I brush them again. When I go back into my room, I look at the words and hope I've magically written something else. Something more profound, maybe something which will make Katherine want to help me.

I sit on the bed, close the laptop and continue listening to some music. All the while the words haunt me, and keep me coming back to what I've written.

Do it, Lily. Take control.

Opening the laptop, I see the words I've typed. They mock me, sitting there teasing me, silently saying I don't need help, I'm strong enough to get past this on my own. Dad and Trent's constant belittling creeps back in. *"You're so stupid,"* they'd say. *"You're so ugly."* The taunts were always there. *"No one will ever want you."*

The mouse cursor continues to hover over the 'send' button. I want to send it, but what if she just laughs at me and says I really don't have problems? What if she dismisses me? What if she's right, and I can handle this on my own? *"You're the dumbest person I know."* Trent and Dad's words whirl around in my mind. I feel like screaming as loud as I can, and pulling my hair out in frustration.

As the turbulence spins in my head, a moment of absolute clarity occurs right as I'm feeling the most lost and vulnerable. The music changes track and for only a few seconds there's no sound at all coming from the radio. The anguished torment roiling in my mind, becomes silent. Not a single sound can be heard. Not from the radio, not from the laptop, not even in my mind.

And it's then I realize this is one of the most important moments in my life.

I may fall, I may stumble, I may even ask for help. But I am *not* weak. I *am* the strongest I've ever been.

CHAPTER 25

IT'S MY FIRST DAY IN my new role at work and Peter hasn't left his desk the entire day. Candace is on her last week, and she's been showing me everything I need to do in order to keep up with him. Peter also oversees another five stores in the district, but works out of this office. He's barely spoken to me, but Candace assured me, this is just how he is.

He came out a few times or buzzed through what he needed, and Candace stepped me through everything, giving me a complete run down on what happens on a Monday. I've been taking avid notes, because she also did say every day there's something else that needs doing.

By the time lunch comes around, I'm starving, but I also need to go get myself a new cell phone. I forgo sitting at the café for lunch, and head straight to the convenience store four blocks down to get a pre-paid phone.

I grab a coat I've borrowed from Shayne, and start toward the store. It's cold outside, and I make a mental note I need to go buy a coat. Liam took me to Target on Saturday and I bought some clothes, but Shayne insisted she had a spare coat and not to buy one because the prices are so high, and to wait for end of the season when they're on sale.

As I walk past the small café near work, I look in and see Max sitting at the counter drinking from a mug. I stop myself from going to get a phone, and instead find myself walking into the café.

I go and sit two seats over from him, and wait, like a cheetah, until he looks at me. I'm smiling to myself, because he's picked up his mug and sipped from it twice, and he's still not looked over to me. The young waitress who served Shayne and me last time comes over to me. "How can I help you?" she asks.

"What's your soup of the day?" I ask as I keep looking straight at her. But out of the corner of my eye, I see Max turn his head to look at me, and his face breaks into a large smile.

"Today we have two. We have tomato and chicken noodle," she says and smiles.

"Hmmm," I grumble as I consider which one to have. "I'll have a hot chocolate, with extra marshmallows and I'll think about which soup to have."

"I'll be back in a moment."

I'm smiling, because I can see Max looking over to me and he's trying to hold in his smile. "I h-hear the t-t-tomato soup is the b-best," he says as he slightly leans in toward me.

"Really?" I turn to look at him and feign surprise he's sitting beside me. "Max," I say and smile.

"Y-you saw me f-from the w-window."

"What? I did not," I tease.

"I-I know y-you d-did, because I s-saw you s-stop walking." He winks at me, and turns back in his seat, all cocky he caught me.

"That's not fair. You weren't supposed to know."

"I-I can p-pretend. Look." He faces forward, looks to the opposite side then slowly turns his head to face me. His eyes light up and he smiles at me. "Lily, s-so n-nice to see you," he teases, pretending to have seen me for the first time.

"Cheeky," I add. The waitress brings over my hot chocolate and puts it in front of me. "I'll have the tomato soup please, I hear it's excellent."

"It's our most popular. One tomato soup, coming right up," she says and goes to enter my order into their computer system.

"You're not working today?" I ask Max as I wait for my food. I stand and take off my coat, gloves and scarf.

"N-not until l-later. Are y-you on y-your l-lunch break?" he asks as he takes in my uniform.

"I am. I was actually going to forgo lunch and go get a new cell phone, but I saw you and thought I'd come in."

"A n-new c-cell phone? Wh-what h-happened to your old one?"

I look away, avoiding his intense green specked, brown eyes. "Um," I mumble, not really wanting to say anything to him.

"Wh-what is it?" he asks in a concerned and deep voice.

I look around the café, making sure no one can hear me, and then I whisper, "I left Trent. I walked out and left everything behind."

Max's eyes light up and he kind of moves away, as he mouths, "Wow." The waitress comes over and places a bowl of tomato soup in front Max. "Th-thank you," he says to her. But he doesn't pick up his spoon and start eating, instead he sits quietly and stares at it. "Y-you l-left him?" he asks as he continues to look at his bowl.

I just nod and don't say anything. It seems like hours pass, but of course it's only a few moments before Max goes to say something, but the waitress places a bowl of tomato soup in front of me. "Here you go, enjoy," she chirps happily and leaves.

Max picks his spoon up and stirs the soup before turning to face me.

"You re-really left?" He eats some soup waiting for my response.

"I did." I hold my breath and wait for his reply. But he continues to eat, obviously considering what I said to him. "Are you mad?" I ask when the silence becomes unbearable.

"Am I m-mad?" He looks at me and places his left elbow on the counter and has two fingers tapping his chin. "Am I mad?" he asks again, this time I know it's rhetorical. "I'm the f-furthest th-thing from m-mad." He watches for my reaction. I'm not sure what to think or even say, so I just eat my soup in silence. "I'm a-actually r-really p-p-proud of you. It t-takes a lot of st-strength to leave."

"Thank you," I quietly respond. "But I don't feel strong today. I may have a few days ago, but today I'm feeling vulnerable and somewhat stupid for trying to make it on my own."

"There's n-no reason to feel like that." His stutter fades to almost nothing. "F-finding the st-strength to leave is the most c-courageous thing an abuse survivor can ever do." He eats the last of his soup. "My m-mom tried leaving, but sh-she kept coming back to him. It w-was hard for her b-because she h-had me. Sh-she thought it was better to st-stay with him, then f-force us to be ho-ho-homeless. Th-the last time she tried leaving, was the l-last breath she t-took."

"Oh my gosh," I say as I sip on the last of my soup. *How does someone deal with such intensity, and survive it?*

"It took me y-years b-before I was able to t-talk about it. I had a therapist wh-who helped me once I went to live with my d-dad. I used to wet the bed, too," he says.

"You told me about what your stepfather did when I was sleeping. I heard every word you said, Max."

He breathes in deeply, avoiding me and I can tell he's trying to gather his thoughts. "You heard it?"

"Every word. But when I woke, Trent convinced me otherwise by saying he didn't say what he did. I figured out he was lying and its then I realized you had been there for me more than my own husband."

"I w-was."

"It's okay, Max. I know why. It's because you see your mom in me, and you didn't want me to suffer the same way she did."

Max turns his head to look at me. "Yeah, that's it." He stands to his feet, and puts his coat on. "Are you d-done?" he asks. Why do I feel like suddenly the conversation is going in whatever way he wants it to? As if he's purposely changing it.

"I am."

Max takes my borrowed coat from the empty seat between us, and holds it out for me to put on. The waitress comes over and gives us our checks,

Max scoops mine up and hands the waitress a twenty. "Is th-that enough?" he asks her without looking at the bills.

"Sure is, wait up for your change."

"K-keep it," he answers, as he leads us out the door.

"Thank you," she calls toward Max.

We get outside and the cold air smacks right into me, winding me from the warmth inside the café. "You didn't have to buy my lunch. Thank you though, I do appreciate it."

"You're welcome."

"I'm sorry, Max, I have to go. I was trying to go get a phone, and I just don't have time now. I need to get back to work."

"Y-you have to get a ph-phone. Especially considering y-your circumstances."

I hop from foot to foot, trying to warm myself in this blazing cold air. "I'll go tomorrow. I promise."

"Okay. Y-you best get back to work," he says to me.

"Okay. Well…thank you for lunch. I suppose I'll see you around."

"T-take care, Lily." Max turns and leaves, and I hurry back to work. As I go upstairs, I find Candace at her desk and she gives me another task to do. She shows me a report which needs to be printed, and I write it in my notepad so I know what I need to do next Monday when Candace is no longer around.

The day flies by, Dale comes up and stands in front of the desk I'm sharing with Candace. "Can I borrow Lily for about ten minutes?" he asks Candace.

It's toward the end of my work day, and Candace wants to duck out to get a coffee. "That's fine, I'll be back in about ten minutes," she says, as she takes her purse out of the bottom drawer and goes downstairs.

"How are you doing, Lily?" Dale asks, as he comes to sit where Candace was.

"I'm good. Working through it all, one day at a time."

"Have you had any problems with Trent?"

I shake my head. "No, I've heard not a peep out of him. Nothing at all. Maybe he's moved on." I shrug my shoulders and add, "I don't know."

"Look, I think it's a good idea if you take my number, and Peter's, and if he does contact you, let us know. We need to protect our staff, and him lurking around here won't be allowed."

"I doubt he'll do anything to jeopardize his career as a doctor." I shake my head. Trent really wouldn't go that far, would he?

"It's better to have people on board rather than not." He stands and walks around the front of the desk, toward the door. "We don't tolerate violence regardless who it's against. We're anti-bullying, and definitely anti-violence." He turns back, gets a piece of paper and a pen and scribbles his number down. "Don't be afraid to use it, no matter what time of the day or night. I've written my cell number, and my home number." He hands me the paper and smiles.

"Thank you, Dale." Dale leaves, and moments later Candace comes in holding a cup in one hand and a wrapped present in the other.

"Vivian said this was dropped off for you," she says and gives me the box.

My heart leaps into my throat, and I quickly unwrap it, afraid of what sick thing Trent's giving me. There's nothing he can do that will surprise me. I rip the paper off the box and inside is a pre-paid cell phone. There's an envelope under the paper and I open it.

A PHONE IS IMPORTANT, AND YOU NEED ONE. I'VE ALSO GIVEN YOU MY NUMBER. IF YOU EVER WANT TO CALL ME, YOU CAN.

~ MAX

I smile at the gift, and make a mental note to call Max and tell him I'll reimburse him for the phone.

"You got a gift?" Candace asks, as she takes a sip from her Styrofoam cup.

"He was just kind enough to get me a phone because I didn't have time," I say as I tuck the small box into my hand bag along with Dale's number.

"Well, kiddo, you did really well today. Tuesdays are busier, and I also have to go over end-of-month things with you, too. So, try to come in early."

"I will. Thank you for teaching me and being so patient."

Candace stands, and heads toward Peter's office. "I've just got a few things to talk to Peter about, but you can go, and just make sure you're here at eight."

"Thanks again." I slip on Shayne's coat, sling my bag over my shoulder and get ready to go downstairs.

When I leave work I start to head over to the bus stop, but Shayne pulls up. "Get in, good lookin'," she calls once she puts her window down.

"Hey, I was just going to catch the bus home." I get in and put my seat belt on.

"No need. I just went in and grabbed some things for dinner. I'm making pasta."

"Yum, I'm starving."

"Good, you can cook it then." She chuckles, and I can't help but laugh at her sarcastic sense of humor. "Actually, guess what I have for you?"

"What?"

"You know that girl who works for us? I have a USB drive with her manuscript on it. She said can you get it back to her by the end of next week?"

Wow, that was quick. "I can try."

"Great. Remind me when we get home to give it to you."

"Speaking of home, I'd like to pay you board until I can find my own place."

"Not gonna happen. Liam and I already discussed this, and we both decided you're not gonna pay us a single dollar."

I sigh deeply, because it feels as if I'm taking advantage of their generosity. "I have to pay you something."

"No can do, sister."

"Look," I start saying. I may as well be open and honest with her. But Shayne interrupts what I want to say, "Would you take money off me if the roles were reversed?"

Damn it, she's using the 'role reversal' trick to prove her point to me. "Before I answer your question, I'm just going to say this. I don't want to come into your home and feel like I'm using you, and although you don't see it like that, I will feel like I'm not pulling my weight. So please, let me pay you something or at the very least pay for the food. Something, anything for me to hold on to the small amount of self-worth I have."

Shayne does a funny squirmy thing with her mouth, and I know she understands why I want to contribute. "I'll talk to Liam."

"And to answer your question, no I'd be exactly like you and not take your money. But once you'd explained how important it is to you to pay your way, then yes, I would."

"You, Lily Anderson, can damn well manipulate me so easily." I smile and look out the window. "I take it back, you can't cook tonight. If you're gonna make us take money, I'm punishing you with my cooking."

I chuckle, and so does Shayne. Her cooking is amazing. Every meal I've eaten with them has been some of the best food I've ever had.

"Deal," I agree. "Guess what happened today?"

"What?"

"You remember that Max guy? I was telling you about him the other day."

"Oh yeah, he paid for our lunch at the small restaurant just down from where you work."

"Yeah, him. I had lunch with him today."

"Lily," Shayne says with an exasperated sigh. "Do you think it's a smart idea to go from Trent to someone else so quickly?"

"What? No, it's nothing like that. We just had lunch, nothing else."

"Did he ask you for your number? Or out on a date?" she asks in a 'told you so' tone.

"No."

"No? Are you just saying that?"

"No, not at all. Actually, I was on my way to buy a phone, and I saw him in that café so I went in. We just sat and talked while we had our lunch. I told him I had to get back to work and ran out of time to buy a cell phone. A couple of hours later, there was a package waiting for me and he had bought me a pre-paid phone."

"Man, Lily, he's probably done something to it to track you, or some crazy weird ass stalker thing like that."

"It's still in the plastic."

"Hmmm," she huffs as she looks out the window driving toward home. "Really?" she snarls disbelievingly.

"Yeah, I'll show you when we get home." I tap my bag, indicating the phone is inside.

"That's pretty cool then."

"He wrote a note too, giving me his number and saying I can call him if I need anything."

"Girl, don't go jumping into anything."

Jesus, the last thing I want is a relationship. "I won't." I look outside the passenger window. "I have so many things to work through, Shayne. The biggest thing is to figure out who I am."

When we get home, Shayne hands me the USB drive of her friend's book, and yells out to Liam to set up the laptop in my room. I'm going to have to buy a computer if I'll be proofreading. I won't be able to always use Shayne's and Liam's, and proofreading at work is out of the question.

I plug the USB drive in and open the manuscript. The title of the book is *Love Is Perfection.* I begin to read the prologue and before I know it, the story has sucked me right in.

"Hey, you coming for dinner?" Shayne pops her head into my room and asks.

"Yeah, I'm reading Michaela's book. I'll just finish this chapter and come out. Start without me, I'm not sure how long this chapter is."

"Okay, don't be too long, or it'll get cold." She knits her eyebrows at me, and scrunches her nose up. "Did you hear what I said?"

"I was looking right at you. Of course I heard," I say jokingly.

"Good. See you in a few." Shayne closes the door and I go back to the book.

The book is completely intriguing, about a girl who was left by her biological parents at a young age to her aunt. The aunt turned out to be a madam in a high-priced sex club. The girl grew to become a woman who was taught sex is power, and with the power of sex you have a bargaining tool. I just can't seem to stop reading it, but I know my dinner will be getting cold so I have to stop and go eat.

I quickly get up and go out to the kitchen, but all the lights are turned off and there's a note on the kitchen counter. It reads, 'Knew you'd have your nose stuck in the book all night. Your dinner is in the fridge, just pop it in the microwave. Love you. X.'

I smile as I read the note, and go to the fridge to get my dinner. I can't believe it's almost eleven at night, and all I want to do is inhale my dinner and go back to the story. But I need to be in at work by no later than eight and there's no way I can function well on so little sleep.

I quickly eat my dinner, put the bowl in the dishwasher, and go back to read just one more chapter. When I start reading again, I'm sucked back into the world of the characters Michaela's written. I get to the end of that chapter, and I can't help but want to read one more. But my eyes are tired, and I'm yawning. *Go to sleep.*

Finally, at one in the morning, I close the laptop with thirty-five pages left to read, and I slide down into bed. My eyes shut and I dream. I dream of a time when a little blond-haired boy and I play in a field of wildflowers. Our mom and dad sit cuddled together, watching over their most precious creations. Me and my brother.

CHAPTER 26

WHEN THE ALARM WENT OFF this morning, it was the first time I can remember that I didn't want to get out of bed or go to work. All I wanted to do was stay in my warm bed and read Michaela's book. But, of course, I got up and got dressed and was ready in time for Shayne and Liam to drop me off. I even had time to activate my new phone.

Both have insisted they take me to and pick me up from work. But I can't be their responsibility. I need to learn how to drive and buy a car for myself.

At eleven-thirty, Dale comes into the office and stands in front of the desk I'm sharing with Candace. "Lily, can I take you to lunch today?" he asks.

"Thank you, that would be great. I'll be ready to go in about half an hour. I can come and find you if you like."

"I'll be on the floor, so just come downstairs." He turns and leaves and I wait for the half hour until lunch.

"Oh shit, Lily. What's that about?" Candace asks as she points toward the door Dale just walked out of.

"Nothing." I shrug.

"What did you do wrong?"

Suddenly my hands sweat and my heart beats frantically against my chest, what if he's taking me to lunch to tell me they made a mistake and I'm not really suited to the position? Can they really tell just after one day? Oh my gosh, now I'm so nervous. I'm beginning to feel sick in the tummy, like I'm going to throw up. If they pink slip me, I'll have nowhere to go and I won't be able to earn a living.

Crap, crap, crap.

The half-hour flies by, and before I know it Candace tells me it's time to go find Dale. With a lot of tension coursing through my body, I take my bag, put on my coat and go downstairs to find him.

He's talking with one of the floor managers, and looking over some paperwork. He sees me and smiles, holding up one finger indicating he'll be a few moments. My stomach tumbles around nervously waiting. Bile slowly creeps up to sit in the base of my throat as I walk toward the front entry to wait for Dale.

"You ready?" he asks as he comes to stand beside me.

I look up to his tall frame and stand with my shoulders slightly slumped. "Are you going to fire me?" I blurt and quickly bring my hand to my mouth. "I'm so sorry, I don't know why I just blabbed that. I'm so sorry."

Dale laughs a huge belly roar, so loud some of the shoppers are turning to see what all the noise is. "Come on, let me buy you lunch. And no, we're not going to fire you."

I breathe out a huge expulsion of air, relieved I still have my job. *Oh crap, what if Trent is trying to create trouble with them and they want me to deal with him? Crap, crap, crap.*

Dale's talking as we walk down toward the café, but I can't pay attention to what he's saying. All I can think about is what problems Trent might be stirring up, and what Dale's going to say to me.

"Here you go, ladies first." Dale opens the door and waits for me to go in first. "How about we get the table in the furthest corner?"

Oh my God. What has Trent done? If Dale wants a table in the furthest corner, then I'm definitely in trouble. "Okay," I answer, though what I really want to do is let the earth open up and swallow me. My own personal sink hole.

"Here." Dale pulls out my chair and waits until I'm seated before he sits opposite me. "So I do have a reason I've asked you to lunch, and a reason as to why I wanted to sit at a table where we'd get the fewest interruptions." He looks around, and I do too, following his line of sight.

"We certainly are isolated," I say as I pick the menu up and start perusing it.

"They make the best hamburgers. I already know what I'm getting. Don't tell Betsy, she'll kick my butt. If she asks, I had a salad with extra salad crap." He chuckles, and I can't help but join in on the chuckle, too.

"Your secret's safe with me." I wink at Dale.

"Hi there, what can I get you today?" the waitress asks. She's the same girl who was here yesterday, and she looks at me and smiles then does a double look at Dale, obviously remembering I was here yesterday with Max.

"I'll have a burger, with a side of onion rings and a Coke. Not diet, the full-strength good stuff." Dale leans over and whispers to me, "Don't tell Betsy."

I tap my nose and wink again. "Shhh," I confirm by putting my finger to my lips. "Have you got chicken noodle soup?"

"We do."

"I'll have chicken noodle and a hot chocolate with…"

"Extra marshmallows. I remember. I'll be back in a moment." She smiles and takes our menus, turns and leaves.

"So, Lily, the reason I brought you here is because I talked to Peter about your situation." I shudder when he says that. "I had to talk to him, and tell him what happened with you and your husband, in case there's going to be a problem at work."

"Considering he got me fired, I'm hoping he doesn't find out I have my job back and cause any problems for me, especially at work."

"He may, and if he does involve work, then you need to come to Peter or myself."

"Thank you."

"There's something I've been wondering about you. And it's something Peter brought up too, when we had a meeting about you." My cheeks pink, and I feel like a fool. "Don't be embarrassed, Lily. Trent had me convinced you were stealing money. That's what manipulators do. They convince everyone around them they're saints, when in actual fact, they're nothing but evil."

"Yeah, logically I know your words are right, but..."

"There really isn't a 'but' to the situation. The guy isn't good at all. Down to his soul, he's rotten."

"Here are your drinks, folks," the waitress announces and puts down our beverages. First mine, then Dale's.

"Thank you," Dale says on behalf of both of us.

"Your food won't be too long." She turns and goes to serve a customer sitting at the counter.

"As I was saying, Peter and I were talking and there's something we both noticed about you. And with your permission, I'd like to ask you." He sips on his Coke.

"Please, ask away."

"You catch the bus here and home?"

"Yes, I do. But my friend Shayne and her husband have taken it on themselves to drive me to work and pick me up. They don't want me catching the bus home, for the obvious reason." *I mean Trent, without actually saying his name.*

"Are you too frightened to learn to drive?"

"Oh my gosh, no! I've wanted to learn how to drive since I was old enough, but Trent said he'd take me anywhere I needed to go, and I didn't need a license. I asked so many times, but he just kept saying no, so I stopped asking." I pick my mug of hot chocolate up and sip on it, focusing on it rather than the intensely sympathetic look Dale is giving me. "Please," I whisper. "I don't want your sympathy."

"I'd have to be made of steel if I didn't respond to what's happened to you. I may be a man, and I may be old enough to be your father, but I still have a heart. And I'm sure what you've told me, is probably only the tip of the iceberg."

I nod my head, not saying anything because I'm not sure if Trent or my Dad was the worst out of the two. I don't know, and it's not something I want to spend time thinking about, either.

"Back to why I brought you here."

"Okay. Why did you bring me here?"

"Peter and I have decided if you want to get driving lessons, we'll pay for them. We'll also lend you the money, without interest, to buy a car. But there are conditions to this."

I feel my mouth fall open, and my eyebrows knit together. The look on my face must be amusing, because Dale starts laughing. "You want to pay for me to get driving lessons and you want to buy me a car?" I repeat what I think he said, but I'm expecting him to laugh and correct me.

"Yes."

"Why?" I place my elbows on the table, and lean in forward toward him. "I mean, why?"

"Because you've worked for us for almost seven years now, and your reviews are always fantastic. Every supervisor you've had has sung your praises, and you're a valued member of our team."

"Oh," I murmur as I look away for a second to comprehend his beautiful and encouraging words. Slowly I bring my hands up to my face and cover them as I sob. I've never, in my entire life, had anyone do something for me as nice as what Dale is offering.

"Hey, before you get all weepy, I said it comes with conditions." He tries to sound all tough, but the crackle in his voice tells me he's affected by my crying, and understands exactly *why* I'm sobbing.

I gather myself, using my hair as a shield to fall around my face so I can calm down and stop crying. When I wipe the tears away, I lift my head and look at Dale. His features are beyond sympathetic, I truly see the concern he has. "What are the conditions?" I ask once I've been able to gain control of myself.

"First, you need to pay back the money for the car, over time."

"And the driving lessons," I interrupt to say.

"No, not the driving the lessons."

"Why not?"

"Let's call it your seven-year bonus."

"My what?" I scrunch my mouth in question.

Dale laughs at me and sits back in his chair. "Your seven-year bonus. Seven years of continuous service entitles an employee to a bonus."

"I've never heard of the seven-year bonus," I quip. If he and Peter are going to do this for me, I'll pay back every cent I borrow.

"You haven't?" He scrubs his hand over his chin and then huffs. "Well, we'll call it seven years of Christmas bonuses."

"I've received them; you can't give it to me twice."

"Geez, Lily. Work with me. I'm trying to give you something, and I'm not quick enough to keep trying to come up with something viable-sounding."

I laugh and so does Dale. "How about this?" I start saying.

"What?"

"You can pay for the driving lessons, but I have to pay you back. Every cent you and Peter put toward me, I'll pay it back."

"For the car, yes."

"Everything, including the driving lessons."

"But we want to give you the driving lessons."

"And I want to stand on my own two feet, and be able to say once everything is paid back, that I was able to get where I am because I had help, but I was still able to pay it all back."

Dale shakes his head, and groans an uncomfortable 'damn it' kind of sound. "Then, you can pay us back for half the lessons. Consider the other half, your birthday present. Which, incidentally I know was only last month and Peter and I missed it."

"Then I'll pay you fair interest on the money you're spending."

"No. That's not part of the negotiations. And might I just add, you should become a lawyer because you can damn well argue."

I snicker at Dale and he's sitting opposite me shaking his head in disbelief. "Thank you, Dale. I accept."

"Thank Christ for that. I thought you were going to make me sign a contract in blood. Phew," he huffs. I laugh again. "But the other part of the condition is this. The car has to be brand new. I don't care what type of car you buy, but it has to be brand new, because then Peter and I will know you're safe."

"Brand new?" Suddenly I start to panic because if I buy a brand new car, I know they can be quite expensive and I don't want to spend the next ten years paying it off to them. "I don't think I can afford a brand new car."

"Peter and I were thinking something dependable like a Ford Taurus or a Toyota Camry. They're both really safe cars and as it turns out; I have a friend at Ford, and Peter knows someone at Toyota, so we can get a good price. If you want something else, like a Honda or Subaru, then we'd need to pay full price."

I must have a weird look on my face because to me, a car is a car. There are big ones, little ones, and super-fast ones, but as long as it's safe I'm not overly worried what type of car I get. "Okay," I slowly add while Dale is trying his best to hold in a laugh.

"Okay what?"

"I'll get a Toyota or a Ford."

"Which one? Or would you prefer time to research them both?"

"If you say they're safe, then I'll go for a Ford. When can we go look for a car?" I'm now super eager and can't wait to get my new car.

"Ha, you've changed your tune." From the excitement, I'm almost bouncing in my chair. "We can go on the weekend if you like."

"Yes!" I shout too loudly. Dale laughs at me again. I'm starting to think I must be like a kid on Christmas morning. I've never unwrapped anything which didn't have an evil ulterior motive behind it. Whatever I've received, it has always come with conditions to benefit the person who's giving it to me. "The weekend sounds so good." I clap my hands together giddily.

"Then Saturday morning I'll come by and pick you up, and we'll go to the Ford dealership."

"Your meals," the waitress interrupts and puts down my soup and Dale's burger.

"Thank you," I almost yell at her, unable to wipe the giant smile off my face.

"I've never seen someone so happy to get chicken noodle soup before. But you're welcome," she smiles a huge smile toward us.

"I'm getting dessert, too," I enthusiastically tell her.

"Then I'll be back for your order." She seems so happy that I'm ecstatic.

Dale attacks his burger with so much gusto, he's eating it like he thinks his wife is about to walk in and catch him. He drips some mustard on his shirt, but he doesn't even realize it. I'd better remind him once he's done. I wouldn't want him to get in trouble with his wife.

Dale and Peter are good men. Like Max, these men are a breed I never knew really existed. I'm sitting here, the happiest I've ever been. It's not because Dale is going to finance a car for me, it's not because he's taking me out to lunch.

I'm sitting here smiling, because for the first time in my life, I have something which was always kept from me.

I have control.

CHAPTER 27

IT'S FRIDAY NIGHT AND I'M sitting in Shayne and Liam's family room looking down at the permit I got today. I have the biggest, cheesiest grin on my face, which has been on my face since Shayne took me to the Department of Motor Vehicles this morning. She took an hour off work, and Peter said I can come in late if I'm going for my permit.

Shayne was trying to calm me down before I took the written test. I was a complete nervous wreck, but she talked sense into me. And now, I have a permit.

"You still smiling?" Liam asks as he walks behind me and ruffles my hair.

"I am," I confirm as I look up at him, still smiling.

"I'll teach you how to drive."

"Um, I've booked three lessons."

"Oh." Liam wiggles his hips at me and says in a shrieking high voice, "Miss Hooty-Tooty wants driving lessons. Look at me, I'm Lily and I'm getting proper driving lessons." He pretends to flick his hair over his shoulder. "Liam's not good enough for me to learn from." He moves his head as if he's flipping his hair at me. We're both laughing, because although I don't flick my hair around, he's got my voice down pat.

"Stop being a woman, Liam," Shayne says as she walks into the room and looks at me, still laughing. "You can only dress in drag in the bedroom." This causes me to laugh even more.

It also makes Liam swing around with his mouth gaping, looking at Shayne. "You promised you'd never tell," he playfully says. "Great! Now you're probably gonna tell Lily how I wear cat's ears and meow for you, too."

By this stage, I have tears streaming down my face. "I love you two," I say through gulping breaths and hysterical laughter.

"Good, so you should," Shayne says as she walks to the kitchen to cook. "'Cause we're damn awesome," she yells once she's in there.

I get up and follow her. "Do you need help with dinner?"

"Nope, I'm good. But Michaela asked when you think you'll be ready with her book. She also asked if she can have your phone number to call you, I said I'd check."

My shoulders stiffen, and automatically I'm uneasy. "Just get her number, and I'll call her to talk to her about it. I'm still reading it, but I should be able to spend all of Sunday on it."

"I have her number in my phone. I'll just get it for you." She goes to her bag, gets her phone and scrolls through it. "Here it is."

"Thanks. I'll give her a call on Sunday. I'll go spend an hour on it now, before dinner is ready. Sure you don't need a hand?"

"Yeah, right. An hour. That means I'll have to call you at least five times, all of which you'll say 'I'll be there in a minute' which will turn into three or four hours."

"Number one problem of a reader, trying to find time to eat."

Shayne laughs, and goes back to making dinner. Liam's disappeared somewhere and I go into my room and open the new laptop I bought straight after getting my permit. I plug the USB drive into the port and start back up a couple of chapters before where I left off.

In the story up to now, the heroine meets the hero and she's torn because she actually has emotions for him, and no longer wants to sell her body as an escort. There have been twists and turns, people coming in from her past, from his past, and from their immediate families. I can't turn the pages quickly enough, and with every chapter that ends, I'm bursting to know what surprise will be presented in the next chapter.

"Dinner," Shayne says as she knocks on my door.

"I'll be there in a minute," I yell back.

"Huh," she sarcastically adds. Even without seeing her, I can tell she'd be rolling her eyes and thinking 'There goes Lily for tonight.'

I keep reading, and of course I get to the end of the chapter, and start the next. Before I even realize, I've finished the book and I'm looking at the screen, breathless and panting. Not because it was crazy sexy, even though parts were, but because the book has left me hungry for more. I'm desperate to continue the story. It's a stand-alone book, and the ending was beyond brilliant, but I want more.

I look down to the right hand corner where the time is and I gasp from surprise. Damn it, I know Shayne and Liam have eaten and are in bed, because it's nearly midnight. As quietly as I can go, I open the door to a dark house. I tiptoe into the kitchen to find a handwritten note, this time by Liam. It reads: 'Slacker. Called you four times. But it's okay, we know you were lost in the book. Dinner's in the fridge. Remember, your boss is picking you up at eight so you can buy a car. Love you, chicken butt.'

I have no idea why he's taken to calling me 'chicken butt' but it's his way of showing affection toward me. Liam is like the brother I've never had, and Shayne is the best friend I've always dreamed about. They're my family, the only real family I've ever had. So if Liam wants to call me 'chicken butt', I know he says it with love.

I heat my dinner, eat it, and go to bed. Tomorrow morning, Dale will be here to pick me up, and hopefully, I'll be the owner of a new car before the day is through.

Waking before my alarm clock goes off, I jump out of bed and go have a quick shower. I'm so excited and jittery, today I'm getting a new car. I dry my hair, throw it back in a ponytail, and get dressed.

"You up, chicken butt?" Liam calls from the down the hallway outside my room. He hasn't realized I'm in the kitchen eating some cereal. I remain quiet and listen to what he's saying and doing. Silently laughing. "Come on, Lily. Get your butt out of bed." I'm eating my cereal, smirking. "God you're a pain in the ass," he mumbles to himself. He knocks again, and huffs because he's not getting a response from me. I of course, am now laughing so loudly, I can't believe he hasn't heard me giggling like a schoolgirl spying on two teachers kissing. "Fine, don't wake up, you're going to miss out." He stomps down the hallway and I lean against the kitchen counter, trying my hardest to hold in the smile. He comes in and jumps when he sees me. "For God's sake, Lily. You scared the crap out of me." He puts a hand to his chest and breathes in deeply.

"You were having such a good time trying to wake me I thought I'd just leave you to your fun."

"Jesus. You could've told me you were awake."

"Who am I to deprive you of your entertainment? I was simply enjoying my breakfast."

Liam squints at me, and I can't help but laugh out loud. "You really are a chicken butt." He moves into the kitchen and begins making breakfast. "I'm making breakfast in bed for Shayne," he says as he gets a frying pan out of the cupboard and begins breakfast.

I hear a knock on the door, and know Dale's here. "I'm out of here." I wash my bowl, place in it in the strainer and go give Liam a kiss on the cheek. "I'll see you when I'm back."

"See ya."

I answer the door and Dale is already walking toward his car. "Good morning, Lily. You ready?" he says as he looks over his shoulder at me.

"I am. Just give me a second to get my bag."

"I'll wait." He gets in the car, and starts it while I run into my room and get my bag. "Bye," I shout to Liam as I run past him, out the front door and into Dale's car.

We make small talk on the way to the dealership, and Dale can tell I'm nervous. We've already established a payment plan before today, and got the insurance for the car all sorted so if the dealership has a Taurus in the yard, I'll be driving it home today (or rather, someone else will). The payment arrangement is more than generous and if I can I want to try and make double payments in order to halve the time I'll be paying. Instead of it taking me four years to pay off, I'm hoping on having it done as close to two years as I can.

"Larry, good to see you," Dale says once we're out of the car and inside the dealership.

"Here's a man who kicks my ass on the golf course every time we play. And now, he's here to kick my ass in my showroom, too," Larry says to me, as he shakes Dale's hand. "You must be Lily. Pleased to meet you." He lets go of Dale's hand, and extends his to me.

"Please to meet you, Sir." I shake his massive, warm hand.

"Pffft. Sir is my great grandfather, I'm just Larry." Larry has to be pushing sixty years old, but he's physically quite fit and his body stands easily a head above Dale. "Come into my office." He guides us over to his office, and I notice on the door is his name with 'President' below it. "Now, Dale said you're in the market for a car. What are you looking at?"

"I've done some research and I like the Taurus."

"Good respectable car, they are. What features do you want on it, so I can see what type of deal I can do for you?"

I go to speak, but Dale slightly touches my leg and shakes his head. I shut my mouth and watch them talk business. "Are you seriously going to try that salesman crap on me? Larry, I've known you and Sue for how many years?"

Larry's lips curl up into a very controlled smile. "I need to know what the young lady wants. It's only fair."

"She wants the top of the range model. The SHO, with every possible extra there is."

"They're forty thousand dollars, and come with everything."

"They're forty thousand for regular folks. Not for me, who can easily make one phone call to Sue and get her to have you doing yard work, even in this snow."

Larry laughs and sits back in his chair, placing his hands on his head. "This is why we're friends. You should come work for me, Dale. I think you'd be great on the floor."

"I'm not working for a grumpy, old bastard like you."

I'm smiling, but trying hard not let out a huge belly laugh. "See what I have to deal with, Lily? See?"

I say nothing, because, Dale is here to negotiate something for me. "She's not going to help you, Larry. Back to the car, now give me a price on a SHO."

"Forty thousand," Larry quickly says without missing a beat.

"No, I don't care if you have to lose money on it, which I know you won't. I want it no higher than in the twenties."

"What? That's a ridiculous price."

"I've bought Betsy's last two cars through you, and if you want me to upgrade mine next year to a car from you, you better get the Taurus in the twenties."

"I can't do that price. That means I'll be in the red."

The negotiations continue like this for close to forty minutes. Back and forth, minor playful insults, threaten to call each other's wives and more trash talk on how bad the other's game is on the golf course. The entire time, I sit quietly, chuckle when the insults are funny, and I listen.

"My absolute best price is twenty-eight. That's it, not a dollar below it."

"Make it twenty-five and we'll take one right now."

"Twenty-five is just not going to happen. At all. You can forget about it." He's shaking his head quite seriously about the price. "Twenty-eight, that's my final offer."

"Twenty-five."

The tension is quite thick in the spacious office, and I can feel my eyes widen as I try and remain invisible. "Twenty-seven," Larry finally concedes.

"Twenty-five. And I'll tell you why you're going to give me this car for twenty-five." Dale sits right back in his seat, and starts bouncing his leg up and down, quite casually. "Because this girl right here, has been through enough shit in her life, and now she needs something to go her way. And that something, is one of those Taurus' you have sitting out in the yard. You probably have what, twenty out there? Soon they'll be last year's stock, and you'll be begging people to buy it, so do yourself a favor, and Lily, and give me the car for twenty-five."

"I hate people like you," Larry instantly responds.

"No, you don't."

Then there's silence in the big office. Nothing but the loud beating of my heart can be heard, I assume both Larry and Dale can hear it, because it's so quiet and tense in the room.

"Come pick your color, young lady," Larry says as he stands and shakes Dale's hand.

"Oh my God!" I jump up out of the seat and fly into Dale's arms. "Thank you, thank you, thank you!" I hug him so tight. Dale's body goes rigid, and I notice how uncomfortable he is. I let go and rush around to the desk and embrace Larry. "Thank you, Larry. This means the world to me."

"You're welcome." I step back and Larry looks at Dale. "You better let me win at golf for the next six months."

"No chance."

When I come down from my ecstatic high, I pick the color I want. It takes a couple of hours, but with everything ready, we're finally able to drive my car home. "Thank you so much!" I reiterate to Dale.

"Now, I called Betsy, she's getting a cab here so either you or she can drive it back to your place, then we'll head off home."

Before I know it, Betsy is driving my car home, and I'm sitting beside her in the passenger seat, reveling in the intoxicating smell of my new car.

Dale and Betsy leave virtually straight away, and I go inside to get Liam and Shayne. They're both so happy for me, and we agree Shayne's going to take me practice driving, in addition to the driving school.

It's early afternoon and I'm exhausted. All the excitement has quite literally left me drained. But I still have to finish Michaela's book, *Love Is Perfection*.

I open the laptop and begin the document, fixing the errors and making suggestions for a smoother storyline. It gets to just before five and I go out to find Shayne and Liam sitting on the sofa, lovingly entwined watching a movie. "Hey, can I get dinner tonight? Pizza?" I offer.

"Yeah, sounds good to me."

"Yep, me too," Shayne adds before they both look back to the TV.

I take it upon myself to go order pizza. I call the local place and they say it's going to be about half hour, so I leave money on the kitchen counter, and go back to Michaela's book.

"Hey, pizza's here," Shayne says, as she opens the door to my room and comes in. "Is it good?" she asks as she sits on the edge of the bed.

"Oh my gosh, it's beyond fantastic! I love it. She's really good at telling a story."

"She'll be happy to hear you say that to her. But come on, dinner. And I'm not leaving until you come with me."

"Hang on, I'll just save what I've done and I'll be out." Shayne stands and puts a hand on her tilted hip. "I promise I'll be out."

"I ain't moving, girl, until you come with me."

I hit save and close the laptop. We walk out together and enjoy a family dinner.

CHAPTER 28

I DIAL MICHAELA'S NUMBER AND wait for her to answer. "Hello," she says.

"Hi, Michaela, this is Lily."

"Oh my God! I've been so nervous while you've had my book. I can't believe you agreed to read it. Is it good? Oh my God, it's bad right? That's why you're not saying anything. I'm pulling it, it sucks right? Oh my God, just tell me. Everyone says how good it is, but you can't believe them. My mom said it was excellent. She's lying isn't she? Oh my God, it sucks."

I'm trying to interrupt her, but her panicked rant doesn't let me get a word in edgewise, until I finally say, "Just be quiet for a minute."

"Oh." And she rasps a sharp intake of air. "Sorry. I'm nervous."

"It's okay. Now, I want to talk to you about *Love Is Perfection*."

"Oh God," she painfully moans.

"Michaela, it's really good. You have nothing to worry about."

"It is?" she shrieks in surprise.

"It really is. It's fantastic. You really need to get this story out, and as soon as possible. I've gone over it, and fixed the obvious errors, but I've also added some notes to it, too. There are a couple of areas I think can flow better, and some of the transition scenes were weak, so I added my suggestions to it. You of course don't have to take anything I suggest on board, it's just I identified some areas of weakness that with a few sentences or paragraphs could be made stronger."

"Oh my God. Really? I thought you were going to rip me to shreds."

"Why would I do that?"

"I've been watching the indie book author community, and some people just love to rip others apart. And logically, I know not everyone is going to love my story, but I'm hoping there's more love than hate."

"I think you have a great book on your hands, and I was totally drawn into the world you wrote. It's really fantastic and you should be proud of it. I'll send the USB drive back with Shayne tomorrow."

"Thank you so much. What do I owe you?"

Geez, I've not thought of a price. "Consider this one a freebie, but if you want to use me again, we'll negotiate a price."

"Can I have your number, and I can look at what you did tomorrow and call you?"

Crap. "Um, I prefer not to give out my number, but I'll give you my email address. Just drop me a line, and I'll call you when I get home from work."

"Thank you so much, Lily. I really look forward to seeing what you've done."

"You're welcome."

I'm just about to hang up, when Michaela says, "I want to credit you for what you've done. What's your last name, so I can write it in my acknowledgements?"

I don't want to give her my surname, because what happens if Trent ever comes after me? I think quickly on the spot, and I remember my favorite teacher in high school was Mrs. Richards, my English teacher. "It's Lily Richards," I say. I need to be wary of Trent.

"Well, thank you so much, Lily. I really can't wait to see what you've done with my baby." When she says 'baby' I can almost imagine her hugging the paperback as she dances around the floor, holding it. And I smile. It's sweet for someone to have a passion so intense.

"Bye," we both say together, and hang up at the same time. I'm so happy, everything is going really well. I just hope she likes the changes I suggested and the work I've done on the book.

I lie back in bed, and look at the clock. In two hours I'm having a driving lesson, but for now, I kind of want to call Max.

I sent him a text message when I activated the phone, thanking him and he sent back a text saying 'you're welcome'. Other than that short exchange, I haven't spoken to him since we had lunch last week.

I scroll through the very few numbers I have, and find his, dialing the number. It rings three times before he answers. "Lily, are you al-alright?"

"I am. I just wanted to talk to you, see how you are."

"I-I'm working r-right now. H-how are you?"

"I'm sorry to interrupt, I'll let you go." I sit up in bed, and cross my legs.

"No, don't go. I-I have a f-few minutes. How are you?"

"I'm really good. I just wanted to thank you again for my phone. It really was sweet of you to buy it for me."

"Y-you're welcome. I f-finish in f-five hours. W-would you like to get a d-drink t-tonight, or m-m-maybe d-d-dinner?" His stutter is worse when he's nervous. It's something I've picked up on.

"I have a driving lesson in two hours."

"Oh," he says and I can hear the disappointment in his voice. "M-m-maybe a-another t-t-time."

"What I'm saying is I'd love to go but I won't be back until later in the afternoon."

"Th-that's perfect because b-by the t-time I'm finished you should be d-done, too." His stutter is better and I can tell there's enthusiasm in his voice.

"Great, where should I meet you?"

"I-I can come p-pick you up."

"Um." Again, I don't want him knowing where I live, because I want to remain private. I need to be smarter and protect myself until I'm one hundred percent sure the people I let into my life are going to stay.

"I get it. It's okay, I u-underst-stand. How about I meet you, say at s-seven?"

We agree to meet outside a restaurant downtown and then Max tells me he has to get back to work. I go out to find Shayne and let her know what's happening.

"Shayne?" I call when I go out to the kitchen and don't find her.

Liam comes out of their room. "Hey, Shayne's having a nap. Are you okay?"

"Oh yeah, I just wanted to give her the USB drive to give back to Michaela and to let you guys know I'm going out with Max tonight. We're going out for dinner, so I won't be around."

Liam pulls a chair out in the dining room and sits down, and invites me to sit at one. I know he wants to talk with me. "Lily, Shayne and I really love you. You're like my sister and I know she loves you like you're her own flesh and blood. But what happened last time, I had to pick up the pieces, and she didn't cope too well when you disappeared and wouldn't return any of her letters. She was literally devastated, and I can't watch her go through that again."

I sigh, because I understand what he's saying. "Max is a friend. And you know I didn't get any of Shayne's letters. Trent must have thrown them away."

"Okay, I know that now. But listen, Lily, if Max is just a friend, you need to tell him that. Because he may be hanging around, hoping he'll be more than just a friend."

"He knows."

"No, he wouldn't. Trust me on this. He's a dude, I'm a dude. I know how we think. I know you wouldn't lead him on, but tell him up front and be honest with him. If he wants to stick around and be your friend, then great. Bring him over so Shayne and I can meet him. But if he wants more, then you need to tell him. Because it isn't fair to him, just as it won't be fair to you if he starts expecting certain things from you."

Damn, Liam is hitting on valid points. I'll speak to Max tonight so he knows where I'm at emotionally, and that I'm not in the market for a relationship. I can't give him what he may want, and I know there's no way I can give him what he needs. "I see your point, and you make a lot of sense."

"We don't want to see you get hurt again. Since you've been with us, in just this short time, you're already different. You smile more, you actually laugh and you look happier. You can stay here for as long as you want Lily; you'll always have a place here. No matter what happens, you'll always have a place in our family."

I can't help but let a tear fall. "Thank you," I whisper.

Liam stands and comes around to hug me. He kisses my head, and says, "Have a good night tonight. I'll drop you off and pick you up."

"No, you stay with Shayne, I'm going to get a cab."

"Okay. Hey, before I forget, have fun at your driving lesson, too."

"Thank you."

"Just remember your keys, and let me know you're leaving for your non-date, date with Max."

"I will."

I go back to my room and get ready for my first ever driving lesson.

"So, I hear you're going out for a non-date date with Max," Shayne says as she sits on the bed and watches me go through my limited closet trying to find something to wear.

"I am. And I'm going to tell him I only have room in my life for a friend."

"If he's a good man, and from what you tell me, he is, then he'll be more than happy with that. I mean, why would he have sat with you in the hospital if he didn't have respect for you?"

I shrug my shoulders and keep looking at my lack of clothes. "What am I going to wear?" I ask aloud, but don't really expect an answer.

"Oh, hang on, get your black pants, I have a really pretty sweater that'll go really nicely. And you can borrow my black boots."

"Your black boots? They have a heel. I can't walk in those crazy high heeled boots."

"Hang on." She gets up and dashes out of the room, then is back in a few moments with a gorgeous red sweater hooked over her elbow, and a pair of boots with a very low heel. "Here, try these on. But now I'm thinking about it, you can't wear those black pants, they won't go." She hands me the sweater and the boots and she darts out of the room again. "Here." She lays a pair of black, skinny leg jeans on the bed. "They'll go better and you'll look hot."

"I can't look hot, this isn't a date. This is just two friends going out for dinner."

"You'll look hot for yourself, not Max. Whatever you do, you should do it for yourself. And if other people want to be around you, they should feel privileged you allow them. You're a good person, Lily, don't ever forget that heart of gold you have. But you need to make sure you're happy before you even think of trying to make anyone else happy."

"Thank you," I say, averting my eyes, not really ready to accept what she's saying. "I've made an appointment with a psychologist," I spring on Shayne.

"You have? I'm so happy, Lily. My God, that's a huge step. I'm so proud of you." She hugs me as I keep my eyes down looking at the clothes on my bed. "God, I'm just…" she shakes her head, but has a giant smile on her face. "I'm really proud of you."

"Thank you. Now, get out so I can get changed." I can't deal with any more emotions tonight. I'll end up bawling my eyes out, and I don't want those kinds of feelings. I just want happiness.

Shayne leaves and I get changed. I call her back in so she can tell me how I look. "You look good, girl. Can I do your make-up?"

"Make-up?"

"Yeah, make-up. And I can style your hair, just something different."

"I don't know." I'm beginning to feel like I'm Shayne's doll. "Maybe, just do my hair. Don't worry about make-up."

Thankfully she claps her hands together and runs out of the room, only to come in with what she tells me is a hair straightener. I give her with a quizzical look, because my hair is already straight. "I'll just put a small curl on the ends. It'll look great."

"Okay," I say as I sit on the bed and she plugs it in and turns it on.

When Shayne finishes, there are light curls on the bottom of my mid-back-length hair, and it looks really good. I call a cab and they say they'll be about fifteen minutes. Finishing getting ready, I take my borrowed coat, and walk out to the family room, where Shayne has joined Liam as they watch TV. "Have a good time, and your curfew is midnight," Liam says, pretending to be my father.

"See you tomorrow morning." I give them both a kiss, and then I hear the beep of a horn. I check and see the yellow cab waiting in the driveway.

I go out, get in the cab, and nervously fidget until we pull up in front of the restaurant.

Max is outside the restaurant looking up and down the street. When the cab stops at the curb, Max dashes to the car, and opens the door for me. Before I have a moment to pay the driver, Max has already thrown twenty dollars at him, asked if it was enough then closed the door when the driver said he had to give him change. "Keep it," Max half yelled in perfect speech. "You l-look b-b-b," he pauses as he takes a breath to obviously calm down. "Beautiful."

"Thank you, Max. You're looking very handsome as well."

"Are you h-hungry? B-because I'd l-like to go s-somewhere f-first. A-and our reservation is at eight-th-thirty."

Red flags fly up, and I take a step back away from Max. "Um."

"I-it's okay, we can s-sit at the b-bar and just ch-chat." But he looks really hurt by my reaction.

"What else do you have in mind?"

"J-just down the r-ro-road there's somewhere I want to take y-you. But I understand if you d-don't want to."

I weigh up everything I know of Max, and nothing screams 'run'. These are just my natural reactions because of what I've lived through in my past. "It's okay, we can go."

"Excellent." We begin to walk, and the weather is absolutely freezing. I feel like a snowman as we slowly walk in the direction Max is leading us. My hands have gloves, and are in the pockets of my/Shayne's coat. I have a beanie and a scarf, and I can still feel the cold penetrating through all the layers. It's early December, and snow will start falling soon. We've had a couple of days where we've had very light dusting, but it'll only be a matter of time before the sidewalks are icy and there are snow banks outside.

The conversation is light and easy, and I tell Max how I'm now the proud owner of a brand new Ford Taurus and that I've started driving lessons. Max congratulates me and tells me when I get my license, he expects to be chauffeured around like a prince in a motorcade.

We stop walking when we get to a park that has been flooded and frozen over and converted into an outdoor ice skating rink. "We're here," he eagerly says as he points to the ice.

"Ice skating?"

"Yep."

"I've never ice skated in my life. I don't want to do it."

"You have to. It's a rite of passage for every American." I stare are him. He didn't stutter once.

"It is, is it?"

"Yup," he confirms. "Come on. I'll t-teach you. I won't l-let you fall." He grabs my hand, and pulls me behind him as he goes to the man in the booth at the edge of the rink and pays for us to rent skates. We both tell him our shoe sizes and the guy gives us skates. Max leads us over to where we can sit and put them on.

I put on mine, and can barely stand as I slowly walk behind Max to the

rink.

"It's really f-fun. Here, let me sh-show you." He demonstrates how to stand and skate, pushing one leg back while finding balance on the other leg.

"Looks really easy," I tease as he skates back from the opposite side of the makeshift rink. It's quite busy, with people skating around as if they're professional skaters. By that I mean, no one is falling on their butt making a fool out of themselves. "Yeah, really easy," I mumble to myself.

"Come on. I'll hold your hand so you don't f-fall." He extends his hand to me, and I look down at it, contemplating taking it.

I decide I can't just hold onto the side of the rink for the next hour or so, I have to try and do this. Finally, I take his hand, and Max wraps his arm around my waist, trying to keep me in an upright position. He's not succeeding. I keep tripping over my feet, trying to walk as opposed to skate. "You'll get the hang of it. Like this." He tries to show me, while still keeping hold of me.

I begin to laugh, because I must look like the funniest sight to any poor bystander watching me. My left leg goes one way, my right leg another, and I end up crashing into Max. He's laughing but he catches me, and doesn't let me fall to the ice.

"Like this," he says again, trying to show me for the umpteenth time how to skate. I pick it up and we start to skate around the rink. Okay, I may be stretching the truth a little when I say I pick it up. More like I manage not to fall over.

"This is good fun," I say as I kick off from Max. He lets me go and I manage to skate more than three feet without falling over.

"It is, when you just let go and go for it." I look back at him, and manage to trip over my own feet. This time my feet go in opposing directions again, and I end up sliding on my butt.

I'm in hysterics, because I haven't had this much fun in I don't know how long. I'm laughing so much, I have happy tears streaking my cheeks.

Max skates over to me, and kneels. "Oh my God. Are you h-hurt?"

I shake my head, and try to stand. My feet don't cooperate and they slide everywhere. I'm laughing so much I can't even manage to stand. Max helps me up, and in my clumsiness, I entwine our legs and take his out from under him. I end up on my butt, laughing so hard I can't control myself, and Max ends up sitting on my lap. He's horrified and trying to move, but the ice is making it impossible. "I'm no good at this," I manage to say between gales of laughter.

"No, you're not," he confirms. Max finally gets off me, and offers me his hand. "Here, let me h-help you."

I grab onto it, and finally pull myself up, with Max's assistance, and we head toward the bench where our shoes are.

As I sit and take off my skates, I start laughing again. "I'm not cut out for ice skating. I have no coordination on the ice."

"Hmmm," Max mumbles. "You really do s-suck." He looks at me sideways as he's nodding his head.

That's all it takes to set me off again. We walk over to the guy and hand in our skates, and we start walking back to the restaurant. "Thank you, Max. Although I'm terrible, that really was so much fun."

"You'll g-get b-better."

"I'm not doing that again. I think I was lucky I didn't lose a finger. So I'll quit while I'm ahead."

"I'll wait for summer and take you roller-skating."

I smile at his words. Just the fact he's planning on sticking around, makes me smile. But it makes me sad, too. "Max," I say in a small voice. God, I don't want to lead him on, so I have to be as up front as possible with him.

"Yeah?"

I stop walking under a street light, about a block from the restaurant, and turn to face him. "I can't be with you."

Max tilts his head to the side, in question. "I don't understand."

"I'm not ready to be in a relationship, and I'm too broken to be able to give any part of me to you. I wouldn't be able to give you what you need. It's not fair to you, if you think this," I point to me, then him, "will go anywhere. I'm not like other girls. I'll never work right. I have too many issues to deal with, and I don't want you to hang around in hope that one day, I'll be okay for you. Because, I don't ever think I'll be normal."

"You've made this decision?"

"What do you mean?"

"You're telling me to leave. To abandon you, just like every other male has."

"They never abandoned me."

"No?" he asks. "They mentally abandoned you and physically abused you. But I'm not them. Please don't make a decision for me. Let me decide what I want." His words have not faltered. Or maybe they have and I just can't hear the stutter anymore. "I have to be worthy of you, Lily, not the other way around."

He has to be worthy of me?

A chill shoots up my back. Not because I'm cold, but because I'm being told, I'm so much more than just an ugly, stupid, broken girl. "Okay," I say, not sure what I'm agreeing to.

"Now, can we go eat?"

"Shayne and Liam want to meet you," I blurt out, like verbal diarrhea.

"They want to meet my friends. They're my family."

He smiles at me and tucks his hands inside his coat pockets. "I want to meet them."

And just like that, I accept Max as a friend. He's a good guy, and I need a good guy in my life.

CHAPTER 29

I HAD DINNER WITH MAX a week ago, and we've had several dinners together since. Christmas is nearly here, and after my driving lesson, I need to go Christmas shopping to buy presents for everyone who's important to me.

It's Thursday morning, and I've just gotten into work. It's been so busy, just like every other December leading up to Christmas. As I sit at my desk, I open up my to-do list for the day when my cell phone starts ringing. I dig it out of my bag, and see Shayne's smiling face looking up at me. "You just dropped me off, why are you calling me? Is everything okay?"

"Michaela just called me, and asked me to get you to call her."

"Oh, okay, thanks. I'll do it in a few when I get myself organized."

"Okay, now, you sure you don't need a ride to the mall?"

"No, I'll cab it. Thanks though."

"Catch ya, girl."

I put my phone down, and look at the schedule. Peter's not in yet, but that's because he's spending the morning doing Christmas shopping for his family. He's a man who has integrity and dignity. When I walked into his office to thank him for everything, including financing my car, he simply nodded and said, "Just keep working hard for us, Lily." He's a man of few words, but he's also a man who, when he speaks, everyone stops to listen. He runs his stores with precision and good management techniques. There's nothing happening he doesn't know about, right down to the floor. And when he walks through the store, all the staff members tremble with fear, but they all respect him.

I run the first lot of reports I need to run, and while they're printing, I call Michaela.

"Hello?" she answers.

"Michaela, it's Lily. Shayne said you needed to talk to me."

"Oh my God. I just wanted to tell you a few things. First, I made all the changes you suggested, and you're right with everything you said. The other thing is, it went live this morning," she almost shouts and squeals at the same time.

"Congratulations, I hope it does well for you."

"I have to tell you, review copies went out, and reviews have already started filtering through. *Love Is Perfection* is getting stellar feedback. Thank you for everything, Lily. Your comments made my book so much better."

"You're welcome."

"And, I've made some friends in this process, and one of them is looking for a proofreader, can I give you her details and maybe you can contact her through social media, and talk to her about it. I told her what a great job you did on my book, and she's really interested in talking to you."

"That's great, thank you."

"She asked me what you charge, and I told her you'd give her a price. Her book is romance too, but I think it's longer than mine."

"Your book was so much more than romance. And you deserve all the success it brings you."

"I'll be happy if I sell ten copies to anyone outside my family." She laughs at her own silliness and I can't help but smile.

"I'm positive it'll do well. Keep me updated on the success of it."

"I will, I'll email you or I'll…" she pauses, and I'm sure she wants me to give her my number. But I won't.

"Email will be perfect. Just give me your email address and I'll send you one so you have my address." I want to create a new one with the name Lily Richards, instead of Lily Anderson. Although I'm not divorced yet, there's no reason to continue using Trent's surname.

"Okay. And thank you again, Lily." She rattles off her email and I jot it down. We say our goodbyes and I continue with my work. When I have a few moments to spare, I create a new email address and shoot a quick note off to Michaela. She responds with a smiley face, so I know she has my email address.

It's just before lunch and Peter walks in clutching several bags from different stores.

"Did you have a productive time?" I ask as he walks past my desk.

"Why do people leave their Christmas shopping to the last minute? It makes it difficult for us to go do Christmas shopping at the last minute," he grumbles as he walks into his office.

"Would a coffee help?" I ask as I stand and follow him into his office. "And wouldn't that mean you should've done your Christmas shopping along with all those people you're complaining about?"

"Stop using woman logic on me. My wife tries that. My daughters try that, hell, even my granddaughters have started. I don't need it here, too." His lips turn up in a smile, and I know he's just joking. "How are the driving lessons going?"

"Good, I have another one when I finish here. It's my third one. I may try and go for my license in early January."

"You can do it, Lily. Have faith in yourself." The words jolt me, as if he's referring to more than just my driving. "Now, I'll have that coffee." Peter is a man's man. He's direct when he speaks, and incredibly fair. But he doesn't often use words like 'please' or 'thank you.' That's okay, because it's just him being direct and getting to the point. Even though I've only held this role for a couple of weeks, Peter's strong reputation filters down to the floor. Before my time up here, I was one of those staff who was intimidated by him. Now I know he just demands excellence, and rewards it when he finds it.

"I'll get it for you." I go downstairs and buy a packet of cookies, Peter's favorite ones, and go back up to the staff room to make him a coffee, while putting two cookies on a small plate and taking it in to him. "Here you go." I place the coffee and cookies down on his desk.

"I only get two today? Have I angered you? Or are you waiting for me to give you your Christmas bonus?" he jokes.

"Please, Peter I don't need a bonus, so I really hope you're joking. And no, you only get two because on Monday you came in saying your wife called you 'cuddly' and I think I may have been adding to you becoming 'cuddly' by giving you cookies."

"Pfft." He waves his hand at me dismissively, and I smile. "I'm not cuddly." He is. Very.

"Okay, well, it was the last two in the cookie jar."

"Really?" He shoots his eyebrows up at me in question. He then turns and goes to his messy desk and sits. "So you just running down there and buying cookies has nothing to do with these?" He points to the small plate.

He misses nothing, not a single thing. "Guilty."

"I have work to do, and I believe you're leaving early so you can go do what every other nut job, myself included, does just before Christmas."

"Yes, Peter, that's exactly right."

He flicks his hand at me, and that's my cue to leave and close his office door.

The next two hours fly by as I do the rest of the day's work. I barrel through it, and by the time I'm ready to leave, I only have a small amount of work left undone.

I look at the time and know if I'm going to make the driving lesson this afternoon I need to get going now. I grab my/Shayne's coat, and head downstairs. There's a cab stand half a block down, and when I get there, there are two cabs waiting.

I'm on a tight time schedule and only have Shayne, Liam, Max, Dale and Peter to buy for. First place I head is to Target to buy me a coat, so I can give Shayne hers back. As it turns out, I find an identical one, so I merely replace hers with a new one. Then I try and find her something for Christmas. But I can't find anything, and as I'm walking around, I come up with a brilliant idea. As a way to say 'thank you', I'm going to send her and Liam on a weekend away. A small vacation, somewhere away from winter and me.

Next, I go to the liquor store and buy both Dale and Peter a bottle of nice, aged scotch. I've bought them both the same, because they've both been incredibly kind to me.

For Max, I'm struggling. I'm unsure what to get for him, because I don't want to buy him something too personal and give him the idea I'm even remotely ready for an intimate relationship, but I also want to get him something that tells him how much I appreciate him for being him.

I wander around, not really sure what to get him. Eventually I make my way to a counter which has perfumes. And I find a scent, a men's aftershave which is quite appealing. Although it's well over one hundred dollars, I buy it for Max and hope he likes it.

I'll have to get Shayne and Liam's present when I get home. I can do that all online. I get a cab home, and hang the new coat on a hanger, and put it on the door handle of Shayne and Liam's room. I quickly change, and get ready for my driving lesson.

As I pull up in front of the house, Shayne and Liam's car is here, beside mine and I know they're home. I walk in with a smile on my face. "Hey, how was your driving lesson?" Liam asks when I come in through the front door.

"Really good. He said I'm quite confident and I'll definitely be ready for my test early in January. He's surprised how far I've come with only a few lessons."

"Good for you, chicken butt. You have that sexy car sitting out in the driveway, and soon you'll be able to drive it. I'm really proud of you."

"Thank you. Hey, can I make dinner tonight or have you or Shayne started it already?"

"Shayne started it. You know how much she loves to cook."

"I do." I smile and walk into the kitchen to find Shayne moving her butt, singing a song in the worst possible voice as she dances around the kitchen cooking. "Hey, can I help?"

"You can pour us a wine, and tell me where that sexy coat came from."

I grab three wine glasses, and the wine that's opened from the counter, pouring us each one. I take Liam's out to him and then come back into the kitchen and sit on one of the stools. "Well, I went to Target and found it.

It's exactly the same as the one I've been borrowing, so I bought it, and gave you the new one. Isn't that okay?" I sip my wine slowly.

"No, it's not. I'll take the one I gave you, and you can take the new one." She stirs what's cooking on the stove stop.

"I've been wearing the coat for a little while now, it's only fair you take the new one, and I'll keep yours."

"Yeah…No. I want my original coat back."

"Why? It's just a coat."

Shayne turns around to face me and says, "You deserve new, not hand-me-downs. You've had plenty of hand-me-downs. Now take something new." She turns and keeps cooking.

I choke up and I'm not sure I can answer her without tearing up and crying. "Okay," I manage to croak.

"Good. Dinner will be ready soon. Michaela said she was so happy with what you did with her book. She even said she's got someone else who's interested in using your services."

"She told me today. I have to figure out what I'm going to charge."

"Michaela said the work you did is worth quite a lot. You did what an editor would do. Not that I know what she's going on about, but she said she would've paid you five hundred for what you did. She also said others charge heaps more than that."

"Yeah, but I'm sure they're qualified."

Shayne's shaking her head. "She said there are people out there who've been beta readers, whatever that is, and go on and say they're editors and charge too much. Some aren't even good. Well, that's what she says. I have no idea." She shrugs her shoulders at what she's saying.

"I don't know, five hundred seems a bit excessive."

"Hey, first rule of business is don't *ever* undervalue your product. If you do, people will think it's crap and won't buy it. It's what I've learned at the tire shop. You have to value what you offer."

"Makes sense," I say as I pick my glass up and sip some more of my wine. "You think five hundred is reasonable though?"

"Well, how about you do an introductory price of three hundred and fifty. Then, if they use you again, you can charge five hundred. If they recommend you to someone new, then the person who's referring you gets fifty dollars off their next book?"

"That may be too confusing for everyone. But I do like the idea of charging them less for the first book"

"Michaela said a lot of editors and proofreaders charge per word, so really five hundred is not unreasonable, especially if the book is large."

"Hmm." I focus on the pot Shayne is stirring and start to really think about a reasonable amount to charge.

"Anyway, dinner will be ready soon."

"Okay, I'll be back in a bit. I'll just go get my laptop." I go into my room, get my laptop and go back into the kitchen, sitting at the counter. I open it up, and while Shayne is cooking, I click onto the vacation destination I've chosen for them, and get everything organized. I'm so excited, and I know they will be, too.

Then I open my email and find a message from someone new, saying she's Michaela's friend and has a book she wants me to look over.

I email her back and tell her my introductory fee is four hundred dollars, and it's fifty percent up front and fifty percent upon completion. She instantly emails me back and asks for bank details to secure me. She also says she'll be ready to send me the book early next week.

"Shayne, she's asking for my bank details."

"Who is?"

I explain to her about the referral and how she wants to secure me, so she's asked for my bank details. "Use PayPal," she says.

I look at her and tilt my head, not really knowing what the hell she's talking about. "What?"

"Here." She walks around, types 'PayPal' into the search engine. "Follow the instructions, it's really quite simple."

I go through and set it up, and before I know it, I have a PayPal account. "That was easy. So I get paid through PayPal, and can then transfer the money into my bank account."

"Exactly right. Now, come get your dinner."

"Hang on, let me send her an invoice and I'll come get it." I create an invoice, and send it to her. Within seconds, I get notified of payment. "Whoa," I say as I smile.

"What is it?"

"I just got paid. Two hundred dollars."

"You go girl. Here." She puts a bowl on the counter and takes hers and Liam's bowls and silverware out to the family room.

I pack my laptop up, feeling on top of the world. Actually, I'm giddy. I just got paid to proofread a book. Correction, I just got *half* paid for a book. Actually, someone wants me, *Lily Anderson AKA Lily Richards*, to work on their book.

As I come back from my room, I do a little dance.

CHAPTER 30

IT'S FOUR DAYS BEFORE CHRISTMAS, and I've been so busy. I've been taking driving lessons, and I've been proofing the book I was paid for. It's nearly time to go home from work, and I've been so busy here too. Tomorrow is Peter's last day before he takes two weeks' vacation. Dale is stepping up, and filling in while Peter is away. I've got both their Christmas presents safely hidden at work, because I want to give their gifts to them after the Christmas staff lunch tomorrow.

Peter is putting on a lunch for all the office staff, and has arranged to give all the floor staff a bonus, in lieu of the outing. He's truly a great boss, and keeps everything running so well, he easily inspires me to be better at my job.

I start shutting everything down, and have a few moments to check my own personal emails. There's an email from Michaela saying she absolutely needs to talk to me as it's a matter of urgency. Panicking, I dial her number.

"Hello?"

"Michaela, are you okay? What's happening?"

"Oh my God!" she shouts at the top of her lungs. So loud, I have to remove the phone from my ear. "Lily. Oh my God!" she screams again. She's not hurt though, I can tell by the tone in her voice she's excited and not in pain.

"What is it?"

She starts talking at speeds which are humanly impossible. I'm picking up some words like "bestseller" and "publisher", but I still have no idea what on earth she's saying.

"Michaela, stop and take a deep breath. Don't say another word, just breathe in and out." I can hear her breathing heavily doing as I'm asking. "Now, are you calm?"

"Yep." Her tone is still filled with mirth.

"What is it?"

"Okay. Guess what? *Love Is Perfection* has hit the *New York Times* and *USA Today* bestseller lists. It debuted in the top ten for both. ARGHHH!" she screams.

"Oh my goodness. Congratulations! That's just fantastic news. I'm really happy for you."

"I had a publisher contact me, they want to negotiate a deal," she says the sentence so fast it sounds like a jumbled mess.

I quickly manage to decipher her words and say, "Wow, that's just phenomenal. And it's your first book, too. What an amazing feat!"

"I really wasn't going to write another book, it really was just a story that came to me and had to be told. Lily, thank you. I know you didn't write my book, but because of your suggestions, it is so much better than what it originally was."

"It's all you, Michaela, I simply tweaked it. Nothing more. And you're welcome." I sit back in my chair, smiling, because I'm truly really happy for Michaela and all her success.

"Um…" she wants to say something, but seems she's stuck for words.

"What is it?"

"I want to pay you, Simone said you're charging her four hundred for her book, so I want to pay you the same."

"No need. We already discussed this." Although her offering is generous, I'm not going back on my word and taking her money now, regardless of the fact she's a bestselling author now.

"Please, I really want to pay you."

"No, consider it my Christmas present to you."

"Then I'll pay you for my next book. But you need to charge me five hundred for it." I look at the phone like she's crazy. Who does that? Insist on paying, and paying more than what has been asked of them.

"Just write the next book, and we'll discuss it when it's done," I say. I won't charge her five hundred, I'll charge her what I charge everyone else. Regardless, my success with her book may be a fluke. Maybe I'm not as good as she's giving me credit for. I'm sure Trent would agree with me, that I'm not as good as she's saying.

"Okay, deal. I'm starting it straight after Christmas. Have a good Christmas, Lily."

"You too." I hang up really happy. The smile feels like it's permanently etched onto my face. It also gives me the oomph to get home and finish with the manuscript I'm currently working on.

"Tomorrow we have the staff lunch. You'll be there won't you?" Peter stops by my desk and asks on his way out.

"I will be. Is there anything you need from me?"

"You've booked the café down the road?"

"Check, and double check."

"You've got everyone's bonus check ready?"

"Check."

"And you've let downstairs know we'll all be out for a couple of hours?"

"I have, I've got Carl on the floor for that time, in case anything is needed. I've made sure there's extra staff to cover the time we're away in case we get busy, like we usually do for the three days before Christmas, I've already triple-checked attendance and let the café know. They were only too happy to close for the general public for those two hours seeing as we're taking up the entire café."

"You really do an excellent job, Lily. I'll see you in the morning."

"Bye," I say as he walks out.

That's Peter for you. You won't hear him say thank you, but you will hear him pay you a compliment on your work.

I finish closing everything down, and walk out toward the cab stand to get a ride home. It's been snowing, and the roads are constantly being ploughed for snow.

From inside my handbag, my phone starts ringing. I take it out, only to miss the call. I look and see Max was trying to call me. I return his call.

"Lily, how are you today?" The past couple of weeks I've been seeing Max quite a lot. I don't even hear his stutter anymore, so I'm not even sure if he still has it or if I've become so accustomed to it I just don't notice it.

"I'm very well, and how are you?"

"You sound so formal."

"So do you." He chuckles, and I smile. He has a really deep, throaty laugh, and I love hearing it. "How can I help you, Mr. Max?"

"Mr. Max? You make me laugh. You may as well call me Mr. Sterling. It sounds better than Mr. Max. Mr. Max makes me sound like a crazy man."

I laugh out loud, "So tell me, how can I help you tonight?"

"Would you care to join me for dinner? I was thinking of trying that new sushi place downtown."

"Hmm, I have some work to do tonight. I want to finish the manuscript I got. Oh guess what?"

"What?"

"You know that first book I proofread?"

"Yes, I do."

"It's a top ten bestseller on both the *New York Times* and *USA Today* lists."

"Wow. And it was her first book too, wasn't it?"

"It was. Hey, the cab driver has just pulled up at home, can I call you back in a few?"

"I look forward to it."

I pay the driver and go inside, to find Liam home, but Shayne out. "Hey, chicken butt. You're home later than normal." I've been taking cabs to and from work, because I finally managed to convince Shayne and Liam that since Trent hasn't tried to get in contact with me, he likely won't. I need to start living life, instead of fearing it. My appointment with Katherine isn't until the day before Christmas. It was her earliest available time. And although that's only days away, I'm quite nervous about it.

"I just took my time. Where's Shayne?" I ask.

Liam's still in his clothes from work, and about to head into the shower. "I'm not sure, she said she had to go to the store. Probably to buy me my Christmas present. I'm not sure what we're doing for dinner tonight, either."

"Hey, do you think it'll be okay if I invite Max over? Maybe I can buy Chinese and you guys can get to know him."

"I'm definitely up for it, I've been saying for a while I wanna meet this guy. Call Shayne and check with her. I'll just have a quick shower."

I go into my room, sit on my bed and call Shayne. Why do I feel so nervous asking her? Maybe because her opinion is very important to me. What if they recognize a trait in him I can't see? What if they see him for something he hasn't shown me yet? What if he wants to control me or raise his hand to me?

My heart is beating out of my chest, and I quickly hang up before Shayne answers the phone. My entire body is shaking from nerves and on my forehead beads of sweat gather. Moisture rolls down my spine, and suddenly it feels like I've got an elephant sitting on my chest.

My phone rings and I know it's Shayne calling me back. But I can't get my heart to settle enough for me to be able to answer the phone. Black spots are dancing in front of my eyes and I can't grasp any control over my own body.

What if he's really not who he seems?

What if he wants to hurt me?

What if...?

"Lily?" Liam bangs on my door. "Lily!" he yells. But I can't speak, I can't say anything because cords tighten around my throat and block my breathing and my voice. "Lily, I'm coming in."

I'm balled up against the bed, and rocking back forth as I try and focus on Liam, who's kneeling beside me.

"I don't know what to do, she's curled into herself and rocking. She's not responding." Liam's in sweats and sitting beside me. He puts a hand on my leg and I start screaming.

"He's touching me. He's touching me," is all I can manage to say.

There's a logical part in my brain, which is screaming at me to be quiet and not say anything. But there's another part which has gone into complete flight mode. They say it's fight or flight, and although I'm not running away, I'm having a hard time coping.

"Lily. Shayne wants to talk to you. I'm just going to put the phone on speaker, and put it down. I'll be standing over here."

I feel Liam move away from me, and I can hear Shayne. "Hey, girl. What's going on?"

"He was touching me."

"Tell me about the book you're working on." I stop rocking, and turn my head to the phone. I begin to slowly tell her, and as I'm talking I can feel myself calming down. A few moments later, I let go of my legs and pick the phone up turning off the speaker.

"I'm okay now."

"What happened?"

"I panicked."

"Why?"

"I wanted to ask you if it was okay for Max to come over for dinner. But I started freaking out, thinking what if he's not as good as I think he is. What if I introduce him to you and he hurts you or Liam? What if he hurts me?" I can hear the whir of the car in the background and know she's on her way home.

"I think that's a brilliant idea. Invite him tonight."

"What if…"

"Then we'll deal with it. Call him and invite him. And Liam said something about Chinese food?"

"I was going to order some." I stand from the floor and go to the door, where Liam is standing. I wrap my arms around him, silently thanking him for being the best brother anyone could ever have. He kisses my forehead, pushes me back slightly and winks. He then walks away.

"Dumplings for me, and sweet and sour pork. Liam will tell you what he wants. I'll be home in about twenty minutes. The roads are slippery, so I'm taking it easy."

I hang up and go out to find Liam. "Hey, thank you for that."

"You're welcome, chicken butt. We getting Chinese or what?"

I smile and hug him again. "Yeah, and I'm going to call Max and see if he wants to come over."

"Good idea. Here's the menu of our favorite place, but call Max first." He walks over to a drawer in the kitchen and gets the take out menu. I leave his phone on the counter and go into my room to get my phone.

There's a missed call from Max, and I return his call. "Hi there, Lily. Fancy hearing from you tonight."

"I'm wondering if you'd like to come to dinner tonight? Liam and Shayne would like to meet you."

"I'd love to." We chat for a few moments, and I hold it together. He has no idea at all, less than half an hour ago I freaked right out. If Shayne and Liam are willing to give him a go, see if he really is a good guy, then why am I panicking so much?

I've ordered the Chinese, Shayne is home and the moment she comes in, she shoves a small bag in my hand and quietly whispers to hide it in my room. I smiled and hid Liam's present. Well, I assume it's for him. I really hope she hasn't bought me anything.

The doorbell rings and I know it's either the Chinese, or Max. I take a breath and steal a small look at Shayne who's nursing a wine and smiling at me. She gives me an encouraging look, one which screams at me, 'It's okay. We're here to support you.' I weakly smile, and go to the door. The moment I open it, I'm hit with the freezing cold of the night air, and I'm floored by the tall man standing in front of me.

"Hello, Lily," Max's deep, gruff voice says. He's holding two things. One is a bouquet of yellow roses, and the other is a bottle of white wine.

"Max," I say, as I step to the side to let him in.

"For you," he hands me the yellow roses, and leans in to kiss me on the cheek.

"Thank you, they're beautiful." I bring them to my nose to smell. I'm not even sure if roses are available through winter, so where he found these, I have no idea.

"You're welcome." I can tell he's jittery, and as on edge as am I.

"This way, please, come meet Shayne and Liam." I lead him through the family room to where Shayne and Liam are standing in the kitchen. "Shayne, Liam, this is Max."

"Pleased to meet you," he says, as he extends his hand and leans in to kiss Shayne on the cheek, then shakes Liam's hand.

By the time introductions are done, there's another knock on the door and I go to get the Chinese food I ordered. As I reach into my pocket to take the money out, a hand darts out, holding the cash. I turn to see Max standing to the side of me with the cheekiest smile on his face.

"What are you doing?" I ask as I try to snatch my money back and give the delivery driver my money. "Don't you dare take his," I growl toward the delivery driver.

"It is an injustice to have a beautiful woman pay for my food. Take my money, young man," he says in that deep, gravelly voice.

The kid looks at me, and then at Max. Deciding Max is more intimidating, he takes Max's money and offers me a consolation prize of a weak smile. "Sorry, lady, I can't break the dude code," he says, then hands me the food.

"You've never let me pay. And besides, you're my guest here. You should not pay for the food." I take the bags, and close the door.

Max takes the bags out of my hands, and walks off toward the kitchen where Shayne and Liam are.

"Dinner, ladies and gentleman," Max says as he places the bags on the counter.

"Bring them in the dining room, we'll eat there," Liam says, carrying bowls and chopsticks, and a fork for me.

Max pulls my chair out, and waits until I'm seated before he sits beside me.

Shayne smacks Liam in the chest and says, "See, that's how a gentleman treats a lady. He pulls her chair out and waits until she's seated before he even thinks about moving. Pull my chair out." I'm chuckling at the banter between them, and I can see Max is holding in his laugh, too.

"Good one, buddy. Next thing I'll have to open her car door, too. Thanks," Liam sarcastically says as he rolls his eyes.

"Damn straight," Shayne adds.

Max and Liam open all the different foods I ordered, and Shayne takes the sweet and sour pork and the dumplings and puts them in front of her. "You going to share those?" Max asks as he pointedly looks at the food.

"Never come between a woman and her dumplings and sweet and sour pork." She nips the ends of her chopsticks together toward Max.

Max put his hands up in surrender and says, "My apologies."

Liam opens the bottle of wine, pours us all a drink and we casually sit around the table, talking easily.

Max effortlessly blends into our dynamic. He's not trying too hard, and he's openly talking with Shayne and Liam. There are questions being asked, and answered, and the conversation couldn't be any smoother if I tried.

I take a moment and look around the table. I'm surrounded by my family and my friend. "I'll make coffee," Shayne says at the end of the meal, as she stands and begins to gather all the containers and bowls.

"I'll help you clear," Max offers.

"Oh no, you stay here with Liam. Liam, take Max out in the family room and talk to him. I have to give Lily my opinion on Max," Shayne truthfully blurts.

"Shayne," I half whisper-yell.

"He knows we're going to talk about him. It's insulting to him if I lie and say I need help in the kitchen. So I may as well tell the truth. Now come help me, so we can girl talk."

I duck my head down, and look at Max, who's smiling. "I'm so sorry,"

I say, though my apology really doesn't have merit. He knows it, and I know it.

"Go, and tell me what she thinks. I may need to up the ante," Max says, as loud as Shayne said her words.

"Oh God, there's two of them," I say looking to Liam.

"Hey, I'm married to one, and if I agree she'll hold out on me. So I'm not saying anything." Liam stands. "Come on Max, let me tell you a few secrets about our chicken butt."

"Oh crap," I sigh.

Shayne takes some things, and I gather up the rest and we go into the kitchen. "Girl, he's fine," Shayne says as she scrapes the bowls into the trash.

"He's really nice."

"That stutter of his is pretty bad. At first I had to concentrate on what he was saying just to try and comprehend him, but the more he talked, the easier it got for me to understand."

"Huh, really." I stop what I'm doing and look at Shayne. "Isn't that interesting? I don't hear his stutter anymore. To me, he speaks like us."

"Really? Because he is hard to understand. Virtually every word he stutters on. I wonder why he's never had speech therapy to correct it. I wonder why he stutters." She's not asking me, she's just talking out loud. Of course I know, but it's not my place to say anything.

"You like him? You think he's good people?"

"I do. And I think you should certainly let him be your friend and if, over time, anything happens, I think he's a good guy. Tell him not be a stranger around here, let's see how he is when he gets comfortable with us."

I hug Shayne. She means the world to me. "Thank you," I whisper. "Just, thank you."

She makes the coffees and takes them out to the family room, where Liam and Max are laughing at something. "What's so funny?" Shayne asks, as she hands Liam his coffee and sits on his lap.

"Nothing that concerns you ladies," Liam retorts. Shayne lifts her eyebrows and tilts her head. "Okay, Max was telling me a guy went into the ER because he had been bitten by his pet ferret on his…" He points to his penis.

"What the hell was the ferret doing near… *that?*" Shayne asks, and scrunches her nose in disgust.

"The ferret sleeps in the bed with him, and the guy sleeps nude."

"I doubt that ferret would be sleeping in the bed anymore," I mumble. And everyone 'ewws' at just the thought.

After everyone has their coffee, Max stands and tells us he needs to get home because he has an early shift at the hospital. Both Shayne and Liam say goodnight to him, and give him an open invitation to come back whenever he wants. They both leave, allowing Max and myself a few moments together before he goes home.

"Thank you, Lily. I enjoyed your family's company."

"They've seen me at my worst, and they're really protective of me."

"I understand why." Max moves toward the front door. "But I like them, and I hope it's okay with you if I come to dinner again."

"Only if you let me pay."

"Like that's ever going to happen." He rolls his eyes. "Before I leave, may I ask what you're doing on Christmas day?"

"Um, Shayne and Liam invited me to go to Liam's mom's place, but I think I'll just stay here. I've never really been into Christmas."

"But the house is so nicely decorated, I'm surprised you're not into the Christmas cheer." He looks around at the green and reds, which are everywhere.

I shake my head, and look down at my knitted hands. "I've never really had a reason. And I'm not ready to do a big family thing. I'll just stay here, and veg out."

"I see. Then I insist on joining you in the 'vegging out' process. How does ten in the morning sound? I'll bring some movies, and you can cook?"

The way he says it, he's not giving me an option to say no. I like the thought of not being alone, but I also don't want to drag him away from whatever his plans were. "I can't ask you to drop your plans."

"I was going to ask you to spend the day with me regardless."

"You were?"

"Of course."

Smiling, I answer, "Ten is perfect."

"Great. I'll see you on the twenty-fifth at ten in the morning." He leans down, and gently kisses my cheek. "Goodnight, Lily."

"Bye," I say as I open the door and let him out. I watch as he goes to his car, gets in and leaves.

As I walk back toward my room, I notice Shayne and Liam have gone to bed. Smiling to myself, I declare tonight's gone fairly well. I may have had a panic attack, but I managed to pull myself together and have a lovely dinner, with the most important people in my life.

I take my pajamas into the bathroom, strip, brush my teeth and get changed for bed. When I get in my room, I turn my alarm on extra early so I can have a shower, and turn the light off, crawling into bed.

There's a smile tugging at my lips.

And when I close my eyes, I'm instantly dragged into the world of a young Lily, and a little blond-haired boy named Wade.

I love having this dream. It reminds me how one day, I'll be as joyful as I am in my dreams. And right now, I know I'm on my way to a happy life.

CHAPTER 31

IT'S THE DAY BEFORE CHRISTMAS, and also my very first psychologist appointment with Katherine. I'm not sure what to expect of her, or even what will happen in just the hour and a half I've scheduled.

I've finished work for the next two days and I'm on my way to her office. It's downtown, about a half hour from home. I don't mind the cab ride, because it gives me time to just think about the last few days.

We had our Christmas party for work, and when Peter handed out all the envelopes with the employees' bonuses, he gave me one too. I wasn't expecting it, so I slid it into my bag with full intentions of returning it to him while we were alone. I didn't for one minute want to appear ungrateful, so through lunch, while everyone was merrily talking, I was trying to formulate my answer.

When lunch was finished and we all slowly walked back to work, I went ahead, and put the envelope on Peter's desk. Moments later he came in, went into his office and called me in.

"Yes, Peter?" I asked as I stood at his door.

"What's this?"

"That's my Christmas bonus. You and Dale have done more than enough for me, including financing the car. I can't accept anything else."

"Hmmm," he said as he sat as his chair.

I felt a victory, because he wasn't going to debate it with me, or pull rank and tell me I had to take it. "Is there anything else you need?"

"Me? No." He shook his head. "But you can take this envelope and drop it off at the local church." He pushed my envelope toward me on his desk. My shoulders sunk, and I started to consider what it is he was actually offering. "Someone will appreciate it there, if not, oh well." He lifted his shoulders as if to say 'too bad.'

"Wait." I felt myself begin to question my decision.

"Yes?" He looked up at me, with not one ounce of judgement.

"Can I take it back?"

"You can do as you please with it."

I walked over and picked up the envelope. "I'm sure the local women's shelter will need it over Christmas."

"The choice is yours and yours alone. No one else can make that decision for you, Lily. What's in this envelope is for you to do with as you choose. If you want to keep it, keep it. If you want to donate it, that's your choice." He pointed to the envelope and smiled.

I stood for a moment trying to wrap my head around this gift. "If I take this…"

"Then you're declaring yourself worthy," he said. The words tear at me. And they've been playing on my mind since that day.

I look down at my bag, and slide the envelope out, looking at it and deciding what I'm going to do with it. I haven't opened it. I don't need to know what's inside, because it's been made abundantly clear to me that Peter and Dale are beyond generous.

The cab pulls up in front of a store, next to which is a flight of stairs, leading up to some offices. Katherine Scott's name is on one of the wall plaques, and I buzz the practice.

"Hello," answers a lady in a croaky voice.

"Um, I have an appointment with Katherine…er…I mean Doctor Katherine…er…"

"Come up, dear." She buzzes the door and I go up to find her office. When I find it, I push the door open and I'm greeted with an older lady, maybe in her sixties, sitting behind the reception desk. "You must be Lily Anderson. Katherine won't be long. Could you fill these forms in, so Katherine has a better understanding of you?"

She gives me a clipboard with a few sheets of paper. Some questions are generic and some are more personal. Before I get to finish, a lady comes and stands in front of me. "Lily?" she asks.

I look up to see an older woman with wild, brown hair, dressed in 'new age' clothing, smiling down at me. "Um, yes." I stand and she has me follow her into her office.

"In here, everything discussed is confidential." She sits crossed legged on her winged arm chair and offers for me to sit. As I look around the room, I notice a bean bag, a regular chair, and a sofa. I opt to sit on the sofa, and put my bag snug up against my body. "So, tell me Lily. When did it start?"

I get a frightening jolt. I realize now maybe I should have checked Katherine out a little more thoroughly. But the way she's looking at me, smiling, and inviting me to pour my heart out breaks me.

I burst into sobs.

Uncontrollable tears fall from my eyes. The heaviness that has always weighed on my chest suddenly lifts and every emotion I've had, rushes to the surface.

An ocean of shame, embarrassment, resentment and weakness spills from me. The tears are clearly my way of me dealing with so many years of abuse, repression, and helplessness.

The next ninety minutes go by in a complete daze, full of the intense agony I've felt for so many years.

Nothing specific is discussed, but I can sense that Katherine knows all about me just by the way I react to her words.

The hour and a half flies by, and we accomplish nothing. Or so it feels to me. At the end, Katherine says to me, "Have you got someone to take you home?" I shake my head. "You can't be on your own."

"Shayne and Liam are staying at his parent's place tonight, so it's only me."

"Lily, I want to see you straight after Christmas. I really believe you're ready to let everything go, and move on with your life. But tonight, a nice hot bath and one glass of wine." She winks at me, and I barely manage to crack a small smile. "Are you sure there's no one you can ask to take you home?"

"Um, maybe. I need to call him and ask."

"I'll give you a moment, come out to my mom's desk when you're through and we can make another appointment." Her mom? I don't even know why, but it gives me even more comfort to know her mom works here. Maybe it's because they're a family, and I've never really had anything like that in my life.

Taking a few deep breaths, I finally manage to settle myself. I'm still hurting, not physically, but emotionally. But I'm more myself than I've ever been. It's cathartic, cleansing even, knowing I'll be able to talk to someone I already have a connection with.

I take my phone out, and scroll to find Max's number. It rings a few times before he answers it, "Lily, what a wonderful surprise."

"Can you please come pick me up?" My voice sounds unsteady, even to my ears.

"Are you safe?" he asks immediately.

"Yes, I'm at my psychologist's and I need…" What do I say? What do I need? I need more than someone to take me home, I just need *someone*.

"I'm on my way. What's the address?" I give him the address and tell him I'll be waiting outside for him. "You will not wait outside, I'll come in. I'll be there soon."

"Thank you, Max." We hang up and I go out to find Katherine, and her mom.

"How are you, dear?" her mom asks me.

"I feel like I've been run down by a train. My head's still reeling, and I can't seem to regulate my heartbeat," I honestly admit.

Katherine wishes me a good night, and a good Christmas, and tells her mom to set another appointment for me for early next week, when they re-open after Christmas.

"You know," her mom starts saying as she perches her glasses on the end of her nose and squints at the computer. "Katherine always gets it right."

I look at her in question, not really understanding what she's saying. "Okay," I say as I hand over money to pay.

"I'll see you next week, dear. You have a lovely Christmas," her mom says. And I'm left wondering what on earth her cryptic clue, 'Katherine always gets it right' means.

The door buzzes and I hear Max telling Katherine's mom he's here to pick me up. "Thank you. Merry Christmas," I say as I leave.

Going downstairs, Max is waiting for me on the curb. The moment I see him, every raw and exposed nerve sparks to life, and the tears begin again.

He engulfs me in his arms, he wraps himself around me, as he gently strokes my hair and tells me, "Everything's going to be okay."

We stand in the isolated street for a long time. Snow begins to fall and small flakes softly land all over us and around us.

My ear is pressed into Max's chest, and his arms are tightly embracing me. I can hear the constant thump of his heart, and match my breathing to the nice easy pace of the rise and fall of his chest. When the severe, sharp anguish finally eases, I let go of Max and step back to look at him. "Thank you." I breathe in, and then out trying to find the right words. "I needed that."

He smiles, and with his leather clad hand, he wipes some snowflakes from my face. "Anytime." He leans down and kisses my forehead, then leads us to his car.

Max drives in silence, and when we get home, he doesn't try to come inside, he leaves the car idling and waits for me to take the lead. "I really…" I huff and nervously look down at my hands. "Shayne and Liam are spending the night at his place home, and I don't think it'll be a good idea for me to be alone."

"Oh," Max says as his eyebrows rise in surprise. "Um…"

I gather the words I need to say. "Max, I've been alone my entire life. Even when I was living with Dad, even when I was living at Trent's parent's place, even when I was married, I was alone. I never had a family, and I've never felt like I've belonged. But now I do, and tonight, I just need to feel like someone who cares for me is close. I'm not talking about sex. I don't know if I'll ever be ready for that again. I just need to know someone I have a connection to, is close to me."

Max's eyes light up as he gives me a small nod, he understands what I'm saying. "I've been thinking about how comfortable that sofa is," he says, breaking the tension surrounding us. He turns off the car, opens the glove department and takes out a small gift bag. "I had it in here for tomorrow, doesn't mean you'll get it tonight," he says once he sees me eying the Christmas gift.

"Come on," I encourage as I get out of the car and go to the front door.

Max follows. He takes off his coat and sets it on the sofa. "Have you eaten?" he asks.

"No, I haven't had a chance. But I've got a giant headache, I might just go have a bath and go to sleep."

"How about I make us something to eat?" He puts his hands up, as if surrendering. "Don't get too excited, I meant something like an omelet, nothing too fancy."

When he mentions eggs, suddenly my stomach growls and I feel famished. "Thank you, that'll be great. I'll just go put my things down and grab my laptop. Do you need help or will you be okay?"

He accesses the kitchen, and turns to me. "I've got this. You go do what you need to, I'll cook us an omelet."

I go to my room, put my bag down, take off my shoes and grab my laptop. I literally feel as if I can lie down and sleep a lifetime. My head is hurting, but the constant ache sitting on my chest feels like it's lighter.

Max is cooking and I sit at the kitchen counter, firing up my laptop.

Checking my emails I have one from Michaela telling me her book has moved up to top five on the *New York Times* and *USA Today* bestseller lists. She's also said she's recommended me to three more authors.

The second email is from my first paid proofreading job, wishing me a Merry Christmas. She loved what I did with her book and she's taken every suggestion I offered her. She'll be uploading her book between Christmas and New Year.

The third, fourth, and fifth emails are all the enquiries from the recommendations Michaela gave. The great thing is, these three books will all be ready at different times, so I can take all three jobs on.

I shoot them a mail with my prices, and a Merry Christmas picture I've found, then close down the computer.

I finish, just as Max serves up an omelet each. My stomach appreciates the smell of the hot, perfectly cooked eggs. "This looks so good." I pick up the fork and start eating mine. Actually, I think a more apt term is inhaling.

"Slow down. You'll give yourself a stomach ache," he says, as he watches me destroy the omelet.

"When I was a kid, I'd have a tummy ache all the time. Not because I'd eat fast, but because I was starving."

"How so?" He squints his eyes and knits his eyebrows together.

"My mom died when I was young. She killed herself. Well, I suppose a drug overdose is killing yourself. All I remember of her is she always told me how ugly I was, but she was constantly slurring her words. Her eyes were dark, she lost heaps of weight and her skin was pasty. I don't remember much else."

"Why would she say such things? How old were you?"

"I was nine when she died. I don't know why'd she say it, all I knew was she hated me."

"Jesus." He picks at his omelet.

"Dad wasn't much better. At first he'd just say the same type of things. Then, when Mom died, it got worse. He'd beat me sometimes, sometimes he left me all alone. The beatings weren't that bad at first…"

Max interrupts me to say, "Any beating is bad."

I nod, understanding what he's saying. "You're right." I look away from his intense brown eyes, because I can see anger brewing behind his irises. "He was drinking more, and he started to neglect things, like food."

"He was an alcoholic."

"A functioning alcoholic. Went to work, then came home and drank into oblivion. Actually…" I half chuckle a humorless laugh. "Sometimes he didn't come home at all. I was left to eat whatever was in the house. Sometimes I'd go a couple of days, sometimes less or more."

"How did social services, or the school never identify a problem?"

"Because I learned how to get to school, and how to get home. I worked hard and I studied. I got so used to being hungry, I was eventually able to put it behind me and just concentrate on school."

"Jesus, Lily. I just don't get how no one noticed."

"Because I was able to hide. Not literally, but I blended into the walls, I suppose I fell through the cracks. I never complained; I never told anyone. Until Shayne, who I met at my first job, I never even had a friend."

Max slumps his shoulders and drops his fork onto the plate. "I'm speechless, but I'm also shocked how not one person took the time to get to know you."

"I never wanted anyone to know, so I put a barrier up, and I hid behind it."

"And this is all from when your Mom died?"

"No, it was before that, but I can't say how much before her death this started. You know, if you get told enough times how ugly, stupid and useless you are, you tend to believe it."

Max picks his fork up and pushes his food around on his plate. "But it's not true."

I shake my head, and look to the drops dripping out of the faucet in the kitchen sink. It's something other than Max to focus on. I shrug my shoulders and feel myself choking on tears. "That's open for interpretation."

"You've never had a normal functioning, and healthy relationship. Until now with Shayne and Liam, and me."

I eat the last few bites of my omelet and then look at Max. "I don't think I'll ever be able to understand what love is. Or even have a bond beyond a friendship. I've been ruined. I've been shattered, and I doubt all my pieces are even findable, much less mendable."

"That's not true, Lily. It's simply not true. You really are…hang on, wait." He darts out of the room and comes back with the small Christmas bag. "Here," he says as he gives me the bag.

"Christmas isn't until tomorrow. And besides, you shouldn't be spending your money on me."

"I'll do as I like with my money. Besides, I'm sure you bought me something, too." I try desperately to remain impassive, but the huge smile on my face proves him right. "Aha, see." He points at me, and playfully taps me on the nose. "Please open it, but open the card first."

"Thank you, I love it," I say as I look at the gold little gift bag.

"You don't know what it is yet. You might hate it."

"No chance. Up until I left *him*, I never got anything unless it came with a condition, or it was actually what the giver wanted. So, thank you, I love it," I reiterate, as I slip the back of the envelope open and slide the card out. I look at the card, and it's a handmade gold card with one beautiful and perfect snowflake.

I open it and the inscription says, *To my Snowflake, I wish you a Merry Christmas, and look forward to more. Max."*

"Snowflake?" I ask in curiosity. He nods his head and his smile shines so bright. "I don't understand?"

"You're the most unique, beautiful and interesting person I know. And just as there's no two snowflakes alike, there's never going to be another Lily. Not to me. Not now, not ever."

"But, I'm only half a snowflake, I'll never be whole; I'll never be perfect."

"I won't believe that, Lily. Never. You may be damaged now, and I say damaged not broken, because you are choosing how you want to live. And if you were broken, you'd give up on life, so you're not broken."

Wow, how intense has the air become? "Thank you," I say and then pick up the small box and unwrap it. When I open it there's a gorgeous, delicate, gold bracelet with a single, small snowflake charm. "Max," I exclaim with happiness. "It's so beautiful! Thank you. Please help me put it on." I take it out, and Max clips the clasps together.

"You're welcome, Lily."

I stand for a moment admiring the most beautiful thing I've ever seen. It's subtle yet stunning. And I can't wipe the smile off my face. "Thank you," I say again as I throw my arms around Max and hug him.

We stand embracing for a few moments, then he pushes me away and looks down at his feet. "I'm tired, Lily. I need to go to sleep. And by the way, we're having pancakes in the morning. I've been known to make the best *mancakes* in the world."

"Huh," I tease. "And who has said these *mancakes* are the best?" I air quote.

"Gee, that one's easy. I say they are." We both smile, and silence fills the room.

"Goodnight, Max. Thank you for being here. I really needed everything you've done for me tonight. From the food, to just your company. I'll bring you a pillow and some blankets." I walk toward the hallway closet and take down a few blankets and a pillow. "Here you go." I take them out to the family room.

"Goodnight, Lily. Sweet dreams."

I forgo having a shower tonight, I'm just too drained to even try and stay awake long enough to have one. I strip and get in my pajamas and crawl into bed.

Sleep is incredibly welcoming. And so are Wade, Mom and Dad.

The sweet smell of pancakes makes my tummy grumble and wakes me from my sleep. I stretch in bed and smile because I know I have a friend who cares about me in the kitchen, making *me* pancakes, and waiting for me to get up.

Last night I went through the emotional wringer. The burden of it all still sits lodged in my chest, but it feels as if it has become lighter. It's as if I'm finally able to breathe without having my lungs completely constricted. It may be months, years, or even decades before I'll be able to let anyone into my heart again.

As I lie in bed, looking up at the stark white ceiling, I make a decision to start divorce proceedings at the beginning of next year. I can't stay married to Trent. I need to sever all ties with him, including the one we made when we married.

I drag myself out of bed, and go brush my teeth before heading out to the kitchen where the aroma of hot pancakes is strong and tempting. "Good morning, and Merry Christmas," I say to Max who's flipping a pancake.

He turns, smiling, and when he sees me, his mouth falls open in a gape and his eyes pop out of his head. "Oh my God," he says staring at me.

I'm still in my pajamas, and my hair's a mess. I cross my arms in front of my chest and back away from the kitchen. "I'm so sorry. I must look a mess," I quickly say as I turn away.

"No don't go," he calls after me. Turning back, I give Max a questioning look. "I'm sorry, you just, took my breath away. You're simply so beautiful."

I beam at his complement, and ordinarily it would be difficult for me to even accept it, let alone hear it. But with Max, I know he means it. He turns back and continues making the rest of the pancakes. "If madam would care to take a seat, I have prepared for her a hot chocolate, and I even found the marshmallows, so it has extra. And I shall serve you your breakfast." He puts on this very rich and fancy accent.

"Why thank you, kind sir," I say, as I sit at the kitchen counter, watching Max.

He's humming to himself, and of course he starts singing, "Jingle Bells", followed by "Rudolph the Red-Nosed Reindeer". "Your breakfast, madam," he carries on with the pretentious accent and places a stack of pancakes in front of me, and one beside me for himself. He then brings over my hot chocolate. "Enjoy," he says and bows.

He's so silly, but he makes me happy. "Thank you."

He sits beside me, leans over and kisses my temple. "Merry Christmas, Lily." He starts to eat.

Once we've finished with breakfast, I go into my room and get his present. He's cleaning the kitchen, and stacking the plates in the dishwasher. "I can do that," I say as I place the present on the counter and go to help him.

"Go away, I'm doing it," he playfully snaps. He eyes the present then looks back at me. "What's that?" He jerks his chin out toward the innocent package sitting on the counter.

"Well, there's this guy I know. He's kinda cool, and I thought I'd like to give him a Christmas present," I tease.

"Huh. A guy you know, you say?"

"Yep. Wanna come with me later to give it to him?"

He jokingly flicks water at me. "I think it's for me."

I gasp at him, and bring my hand up to my chest in a mock shocked look. "What? Why would I do that?"

He wipes his hands on a tea towel, then taps me on the nose. "Because I'm your friend. But hang on." He darts out of the room and comes back with an envelope. "If I take that." He points to the present I've got for him. "Then you need to take this." He holds out a plain white envelope.

The mood shifts, and it's now serious, not playful as it was just moments ago. "You already bought me something."

"And this is something extra. It's not big, just something little. Besides, I got a kick out of buying it for you. Made me laugh while I was thinking about it, made me laugh while I was driving to get it, and made me laugh because I anticipate your reaction won't be…hmmm, well it'll be interesting."

He's piqued my interest. I'm struggling with accepting more than the delicate gold bracelet, but this is really getting my curiosity riled up. And besides, I want him to have his cologne. "Okay, I must admit, I want to know what it is that made you laugh so much." I hold my hand out for the envelope.

"We open them together?"

"On three?" He nods. He picks up the present, and to me he's like a kid in a candy store. Well, what I assume a kid in a candy store would be like. "One," I pause and he scratches at the tape on the side of the present. "Two." He stands in a way that looks like he's about to take off in a sprint. "Three!" I open my envelope and take out what's inside. But I'm watching him as he rips the paper clean off the box.

"Oh wow," he roars in happiness. "Thank you, Lily, I love it!" He puts it down and bear hugs me. "Now, open yours." He places me back on my feet, and steps back to look at me. I read what's inside and start to laugh.

"Do you like it?" The look on his face is priceless. I wonder if kids look like this when they give their moms necklaces made out of pasta.

"You're so cheeky," I say. Inside is a gift certificate for five ice skating lessons. "Really, cheeky," I add. "Thank you." I hug him, too.

"Merry Christmas, Lily." He kisses the top of my head.

"Merry Christmas, Max."

CHAPTER 32

THIS LAST WEEK HAS BEEN a complete whirlwind. I gave Shayne and Liam their present and told them to open it Christmas morning, and she called me screaming, saying they can't wait to use their present. I bought them a four-day vacation to Disneyland, staying at the Disneyland Hotel. They got me an iPad, and said it was for me to read all my books on. Already on it was a copy of Arthur Miller's, *The Crucible*. When Max left late on Christmas night, I got into the bath and took my new iPad with me, and I read *The Crucible*. It was a perfect day.

I also had an extra driving lesson, and the instructor thinks I'll be ready within a week or two to go for my test. So, I've increased the lessons to twice a week because I'm anxious to get my license and not rely on others any more. It's been something I've always wanted, but never been allowed to have.

I've had another appointment with Katherine, and this hour and a half turned into two hours. I walked out emotionally drained again, and completely exhausted from it. But there was one thing she said to me, and it's been monopolizing my thoughts. I was describing to her how the beatings only happened when I couldn't make Trent happy, and she stopped me from saying anything more.

She looked at me in all her seriousness, and said to me, "Stop right there, Lily. Before you go on to say another word, you need to be made aware of something. Something most survivors of domestic abuse take a while to fully comprehend."

"What's that?" I asked as I sat on her sofa and watched her curiously.

"You are not responsible for his behavior."

Those simple words caused an icy chill to goosebump my entire body. From the tips of my toes, to the top of my head, an avalanche of emotions prickled my skin. I couldn't respond, I couldn't say a word because at the time her sentence made no sense at all, yet also struck me as to how accurate those words were.

When I was finally able to speak, the only thing I was able to whisper was, "I'm not responsible for his behavior."

Katherine's face remained passive as she regarded me, and my reaction to those all-important words. It took me a good portion of the two hours to wrap my head all the way around what Katherine had said, and still, today, on New Year's Eve, I'm rocked at how significant her words actually are.

As I sit in my room on my computer, an email comes through for me. It's my very first paid proofreading job, and she wishes me a Happy New Year and tells me her second book will be written by end of January and can she book me in now? She also says in her email, she made top 100 on Amazon, and she's been asked to go to an author signing in Texas mid-next year.

Quickly, I type out my congratulations, tell her I can do her book and send her an invoice for half. Since I started proofreading, I've managed to line up nine books in total, and I'm completely overwhelmed by the positive responses I've been receiving from the authors.

I close my laptop and start getting ready, Shayne and Liam have a few friends coming over for New Year's Eve. Max will be joining us, too. I change into the new blue dress I bought, and put on my black boots. I apply some very simple make-up and straighten my hair.

Going out, I find Liam and Shayne both in the kitchen getting some finger food ready for the guests. "Do you guys need help?" I ask.

"Sure do. Take those corn chips and put them in those bowls." She points to the counter and I see the chips and bowls sitting there. "We're making buffalo wings, so they should be ready soon. And we've ordered two six-foot subs Liam is going to go pick up soon. Oh, and there's drinks in the fridge out in the garage, can you go get them and stack them in this fridge? We also have wine, and champagne. Um…" she stops talking, and looks around the kitchen as if she's forgetting something.

"Everything will be great, Shayne," Liam says as he leans over and gives Shayne a kiss. "Another year, baby. Maybe this year?" He waggles his eyebrows and I know exactly what he's asking.

I turn away, giving them some privacy as I empty the chips into bowls. The doorbell rings and I go to answer it. "Hello," Max says standing at the door. "Wow, I'm sorry, Lily, but you're br-br-breathtaking." It's the first time in a while I notice his stutter. He must truly be nervous if *I* even notice it.

"Thank you, Max. May I take your coat?" His hair has got snowflakes in it, and he shakes it off before he comes in.

He hands me his coat, and kisses me on the cheek. He's also holding a bottle of champagne, and by looks of the brand, it's expensive. "For us to enjoy at the stroke of midnight," he says and hands me the bottle.

"Shayne and Liam are in the kitchen." I lead him toward the kitchen.

"Max, it's good to see you. I'm just on my way out to pick up a couple of subs I've ordered," Liam says and shakes Max's hand.

Once Max and Liam have shaken hands, Max goes around to Shayne and gives her a kiss on the cheek. "I'll come with you," Max says to Liam, who's grabbing his car keys. "We can take my car."

"Here." I quickly duck into my room to get my wallet and come out with a fifty and hand it to Max.

He looks at the bill, chuckles and shakes his head. "I'm not taking that," he says, so surely.

"Here," I hand the money to Liam.

He too shakes his head. "If he's not taking it, neither am I." He points to Max, then adds, "Come on, before they decide we need to buy anything else."

"Hats. Don't forget the hats," Shayne yells to the boys.

"Hats, got it." I then hear Liam whisper, "Quick let's get out of here before she has us buying the entire store."

I stay in the kitchen and Shayne and I continue getting everything prepared. "You know," she says as she checks the wings. "He really is nothing like Trent. I have to say, I had my reservations about him, but I like him. He's one of the few I'd say is *good people*. And regardless of whatever is going to happen with you two, I think you need to have him in your life."

"He is a good person, and he doesn't push anything on me at all. He's just so easy to talk to."

"How you understand his stutter is beyond me. Even with him saying to Liam he'll go with him to pick up the subs, I had to really listen to decipher the words."

"I don't hear it. To me he's just Max, perfect as he is."

"Awwww, Lily has a crush." She throws a corn chip at me.

"I do not," I respond.

"It's okay if you do, it's even understandable. No one's going to judge you for it. Max is really a good guy. Just make sure you take enough time for yourself, to discover what it really is you want."

"Speaking of which." This is hard, Shayne and Liam have done so much for me, but I have to do it. "Around February or March, I want to find an apartment on my own."

"What?" Shayne shrieks. "You can't."

"You yourself said to discover what I really want, and I can't do that here. I'm not saying you're restricting me, because you're not. But you and Liam need your alone time, and sooner or later you'll want to start a family, which means I'll need to leave. And besides, I lived the first seventeen years of my life with a man who abused me, and the next seven I lived with the devil. I need time to find *me*."

"Can you afford it, what with your car payments?"

"I've got eight proofreading jobs lined up, and I'm constantly getting more requests. And don't forget, I got that raise at work when they made me Peter's personal assistant. I can't afford it yet, because I'm literally starting my life from scratch, but I'm hoping by March I should be able to buy a couple of pieces of furniture."

"Who needs furniture?" Liam asks as he comes in, followed by Max carrying a couple of bags each.

"Lily is going to move out."

"What? No. She can't." Liam turns to me. "You can't."

I open my mouth to say something, but Shayne goes to Liam, touches his arm and says softly, "It's time."

Liam looks to me, then to Shayne, then back to me. But Max interrupts and says, "Is that a wise move?"

"I'll move into a building that's safe."

"Hmmm," he mumbles, puts the bags down, and walks out of the kitchen.

I look to Shayne, who lifts her shoulders and Liam says, "Go talk to him."

Walking out, I go to find Max standing in the family room with his back to me. "Hey, are you okay?"

"Can we go somewhere to talk please?"

"Sure, we can go to my room." I lead him to my bedroom and once inside, I close the door. "What's wrong?"

"I'm worried, Lily. You've only just left your husband..."

"Nearly two months ago," I interrupt him to say.

"I understand, but you don't know what he may do. I'd just feel better if you stayed here with Shayne and Liam. At least I'd know you always have someone near in case anything happens."

I sit on my bed, and just stare at him. "I can't *not* do things because I'm afraid of Trent. Because if being afraid stops me, I'll never leave this room."

"I understand, really I do. But I think it's too early for you to move out on your own."

"I'm ready to heal, Max. To find out what I like about myself. And I can't do that if I always have someone hanging around me. I'm not saying I don't want Shayne, Liam or even you in my life, I'm just saying I need to figure things out for myself. I'll be thirty before I know it and I won't have any life experience, outside of being under someone else's control."

Max sits beside me and huffs. He runs his hand over his chin, then through his hair all while not looking at me. "Then I have a solution to this, where you can have your independence and freedom, and I know you'll be safe and I won't worry."

"What's that?" *God, please don't suggest I move in with you, because that's the same as staying here.*

"I own an apartment building. It's in the best part of town, it's totally secure, and all the apartments have their own alarm systems. You can rent one of those from me, and in exchange, you'll have your own place and I'll know you're safe."

"You own an apartment building?"

"I own several." The look on my face must scream, 'What the hell?' because he chuckles at me. "I never told you what my biological father did before he passed away."

"No, you didn't."

"He owned the third largest advertising firm in America."

"He did?"

"Yes, and when he passed away, he left me everything. Including the advertising firm, which is now the second largest in America. He also left me several, six to be exact, apartment complexes scattered through America, one of which is here."

"You never told me." *Wow.* "Did you not tell me because you think I may have come after your money?" I ask.

"I need to watch who I tell, because unfortunately, there are plenty of people ready to swoop in and ask for money. But no, that's not the reason. I never said anything, because it never really came up. And I knew you'd never be my friend just because of my money.'"

"You're so normal though. You don't even drive a fancy car."

Max roars out a huge belly laugh and he throws his head back while he clutches his chest. "Normal."

"Wait, why aren't you working at the advertising company?"

"Dad had me working there for a few years, but I was never comfortable. My stutter made it difficult for people to understand me, and they made fun of me. Don't get me wrong, it doesn't bother me, but I prefer the easy life. I don't need to walk out of there stressed *and* have people make fun of me. I took on the job at the hospital, because it really makes me happy when I drop food off to someone, and they look at me with such thanks. They may say it; they may not. But when I'm 'Max the food guy,' I'm satisfied and happy. It also gives me a chance to see who needs help and I give it to them."

"Like when you sat with me?"

"No, you're the first person I ever sat with. You just drew me in, and held me captive." My lips involuntarily turn up at his kind words. "I've helped a lady whose house was in foreclosure, her husband had run off with a younger woman, and she was going through chemo. I had her mortgage paid two years in advance, and all her medical costs paid."

"You did that? What did she say?"

"I don't tell the people I help, I simply help."

"People? As in you've done this before?"

"And since."

"What?" I move my body and sit on the bed in a way where one leg is slightly hitched, not too high, because I am wearing a dress. "Who else?"

"I once helped a young girl, well her parents. They came in, distressed because she wasn't breathing, but their medical insurance had stopped because he'd lost his job. The girl ended up needing an operation to correct a heart defect her parents didn't know about. The operation alone would've bankrupted them and left them on the street. I paid for it."

"You're a saint," I blurt.

"No, I'm not a saint, but I have more money coming in than going out. I want for nothing, so I give where I can."

"Wow. Speaking of giving I still have my bonus money from work, I wanted to donate it to a local refuge for women, who've escaped from domestic violence." I get up, go to my bag and get the envelope.

"How much is it? I'll match it."

"I don't know," I answer.

"How can you not know how much is in it? Did you open it?"

I flop the envelope down next to Max's leg and sit beside him again. "No, I didn't."

"How about this, I will not only match it, I'll double what's in that envelope, and we'll go down to the closest domestic violence shelter and give it to them, now."

"But, Shayne and Liam have people coming over soon."

"What's more important to you, Lily?"

He's right, I've held onto it for far too long. "Deal," I say as I hold my hand out to him to shake it.

"Let's see what's in the envelope." He picks it up and hands it to me. "Wait, before you open it, what do you think is in there?"

"I don't know, really. I thought the fact they financed my car was my bonus. I'm really not expecting much. I know the highest bonus was five thousand and it scaled down from there."

"What was the lowest?"

"The cashiers. They received a hundred dollars each."

"Okay, so it's somewhere between one hundred, and five thousand."

"It won't be five thousand. No way."

"Open it."

I tear the envelope open, and there's a wad of one hundred dollar bills. We start counting it. One, two, three, four, five, six, seven, eight, nine, at one thousand, I look up at Max. I keep counting, eleven, twelve, thirteen, fourteen, fifteen, sixteen, seventeen, eighteen, nineteen and the final one hundred dollar bill, makes two thousand. "Oh my God," I say, clearly unable to say more.

"Not bad work, Snowflake." I look up at him and he winks. "I have to go home and get the money, because I think I only have a few hundred on me. I'll be back, and then we can go."

"Wait," I say as we stand together. "I can come with you."

"I don't want you uncomfortable, I can come back to pick you up."

"You slept on the sofa, and you were a perfect gentleman, I'm sure."

"Okay let's go."

I go out to Shayne and tell her what we're doing, she gives me a kiss and tells me to be back soon because Michaela will be here and wants to meet me.

Max and I go to his apartment, and when he pulls up outside, I instantly recognize it as the building he was describing earlier. "This is where you live?"

"Yeah, come on. I'll show you my place." He rounds the car, and opens the door for me, then with his hand to the small of my back, he leads me up to the entry, which is manned by a young man with a hat and a suit.

"Good evening, Mr. Sterling. Ma'am." He tips his hat to me, and opens the door.

"Charlie," Max says, and nods.

We walk into the grand foyer, and there's a security guard sitting behind a concierge desk, looking down at something. But he stands the moment Max and I approach him. It feels so opulent and sinfully decadent. There are large gray tiles on the floor, and the entire lobby is so lavish with its deep green and red hues. "Mr. Sterling, on the way up?" the security guard says as he removes a small plastic card and waves it over a black box near the elevator.

"We are, but we'll be down in a few minutes."

"Yes, Sir."

The elevator doors open, and I'm taken back by the crisp and clean lines of the elevator. I look around in total disbelief. "I've never seen anything like this before. It's just so…" I lose the word I want to say. I shake my head, trying to understand it all. "Overwhelming."

The elevator travels to the top, and it opens up to a sunken family room, the size of Shayne and Liam's house. There are floor to ceiling windows completely overlooking the city. As if I've been hit by a tractor beam, I float over to the window. "Oh my God," I say, as I look over the entire city. "Why did your mom and dad never work out?"

"What's that?" Max yells from…somewhere inside this palace.

"Why did your mom and dad never work out?"

"I used to wonder the same thing," he says as he comes to stand beside me, looking out over the city. "It took me a long time, *a long time* to work out that some people just aren't meant to be together. Mom and Dad were so different. But it wasn't until just before Dad died, he told me the truth, he never knew I existed, until the courts located him and told him he had a son."

"What?" I turn and slump my shoulders in disbelief.

"He never wanted me to know Mom had kept me from him. They had a short fling, lasted a couple of months."

"Wow," I whisper, as I turn back to watch the glittering lights, and the soft snowfall. "Just wow."

"You ready to go?" He places a hand on my shoulder.

"This is the apartment building you were talking about, wasn't it?"

"Guilty," he sheepishly answers. "Come on, so we can get back to Shayne and Liam's."

We go down the elevator, and are back in the car heading toward town. "Do you know where you're going?"

"I researched it a while back, in case you disappeared and I needed to find you."

"You know, there's no way they'd let you in there? It's a safe haven for women and their kids. And just having a man in there, might cause damage and would definitely shatter any trust the women may have in the administrators of the home."

"Yes, I'm aware. I'll wait down the road. I'll park, and watch you go in. I'll be pacing around down the street, waiting patiently for you."

"How do you patiently pace?"

"Hmmm, good point. I'll just wait."

"Max, this is the apartment building you were talking about, right?" He nods his head. "There's no way I'd be able to afford the rent on a car spot, let alone the rent on an apartment."

"Hmmm, I do see your dilemma." He pauses for a moment, and I can see a cheeky smile start to form. "But, lucky for you, I know the owner. I'm sure I can get you a good price."

"Max."

"No, hear me out. You'll have the same rental contract as the rest of the tenants, but I'll make yours so I can't interfere at all. It just means I know you're safe. And if you happen to need a cup of sugar, you already know one of the tenants."

"You mean the owner."

"That, too. Please Lily? This is for my peace of mind to know you're safe."

I exhale loudly, as if to say 'I don't like this'. "I'll think about it."

"That's all I can ask for."

We get to the shelter, and Max parks, watching me walk toward it.

I knock, and I'm screened to make sure I'm not a threat. I talk to the lady through the door and tell her I'm here to offer a donation, and it's a large sum of money. There are my two thousand dollars, and an envelope Max gave me. The envelope from him is bigger than the one with my two thousand, but he could've put twenty or fifty dollar bills in there.

The lady allows me into her office and we chat for a few moments. "I have two thousand here, and a friend of mine has sent a donation, too."

She opens the envelopes and quickly glances in mine, then glances in Max's. "No, I think there's a mistake." She hands me Max's envelope back. I look inside, and I find the thickness is all hundred dollar notes. At the very least, there's five thousand dollars in here.

"There's no mistake." I say.

She hugs me and cries, telling me there are women and children here who'll really benefit from this money. I know we should've followed proper procedures and done it officially, because it could've been a tax deduction for both Max and me. But I don't care about that. I just want to help someone who is where I was two short months ago.

When I leave I know, absolutely, I did the right thing. "We can go," I say to Max as I approach him.

"Are you okay?" he asks as he opens my door and lets me get in before closing it.

I sit quietly as we drive, not having answered him. When we reach home, I place my hand over his and smile. "I was lucky I was able to get away. Some aren't so lucky. What we gave them is just a small amount, but at least it'll give someone a fighting chance. So for that, yes, I'm okay."

"Come on, Snowflake, let's go enjoy our New Year's Eve."

We go inside and already there are a few people here. I can't help but stay close by Max. "Oh my God." I recognize that voice from my phone calls with her. "Oh my God. You're Lily!" This tiny, dark-haired, and slightly overweight woman bowls me over in a hug. "I'm Michaela," she says as she keeps hugging.

"Pleasure to meet you. This is Max, a good friend of mine."

"Hi, Max," she says and looks back at me. "I have something for you. Lame, I know, but you helped me so much I just wanted to give you something." She hands me a box which is nicely wrapped. "Please, open it."

I tear the paper, and open the box and inside is a copy of her book, which she's signed to me at the front. There's also a mug, a book mark, and a keychain. "Thank you, so much. These are my first-book related souvenirs. And my first autographed book by a *New York Times* and *USA Today* bestselling author."

"It's called swag, all of this, except the paperback. It's all called swag."

"Thank you, I'll cherish it."

"You're welcome. Anyway, I have to get back to my husband. Really nice meeting you, Lily. And you too, Max."

"My pleasure," Max diplomatically says. "Wow, she was like a very excited tornado," he whispers and chuckles.

"I'll just go put these in my room. I'll be a minute."

"Don't be two, because you'll miss the countdown. I'll get us some champagne."

We head in separate directions, and then meet up at the back of the family room. Everyone is standing around, watching the TV and waiting for the ball to drop in Time Square.

"Here you go, Snowflake." He hands me a flute with champagne.

"Ten, nine, eight, seven, six, five." Max puts his arm around my waist, drawing me into his side and his warmth. I look up at him. "One…Happy New Year," everyone yells.

For one brief second, I hear nothing, I see no one but Max. "Happy New Year, Snowflake." He leans down and brushes his lips against mine. The kiss is sweet, the warmth of his lips stay on mine, and slowly, he parts his mouth and gently asks for my permission to allow him to kiss me. It's more than a peck, and more than anything I've ever felt before. He brings me in tighter to him, and he sprinkles a few kisses from my lips to my ear. "You're wrong, you know," he says as he places one more kiss below my ear and pulls back to look at me. My heart's beating wildly, and my pulse is thumping quickly.

His brown-flecked eyes hold such fierce passion. "About what?" I say, as I get lost in the intensity of his orbs.

"You're not half a snowflake. You're whole, and you're perfect to me." He leans down and kisses me again. I feel the moisture of a tear roll down my cheek. But I close my eyes, and enjoy the purity of the man standing in front of me.

CHAPTER 33

I CAN DRIVE MYSELF AROUND now. I went for my driver's test two weeks ago, and I passed. It's the last week of January and it's gone by in a blink of an eye.

I've been working on all the books I get sent, and I can't believe I'm booked solid until the end of February. I've taken on new clients, and I've managed to be able to save half that money for when I move out. The other half I've been giving to Dale for the loan on the car. Today I have another thousand dollars to give to him.

I walk to his office and knock on his door. He looks up and smiles, "Come in, Lily. Close the door."

I close the door and sit down opposite him. "I have some more money for you." I slide the envelope across the table at him.

"You do?" He takes out his book he's been keeping track of the payments. He has me sign it, and he signs it when I give him the money. "How much is it?"

"A thousand this time," I proudly announce with a huge smile.

"Huh," he mumbles as he opens the envelope and counts out the ten hundred dollar bills. He stops and starts adding all the payments together. "You've had the car nine weeks, and you've paid the one hundred and seventy-five a week we agreed to, plus you've given me, in addition to that, another three thousand, four hundred dollars. That makes it." He double checks his figures. "You've paid four thousand, nine hundred and seventy-five dollars." He tucks his pen behind his ear and sits back in his chair. "Should I be worried?"

"What? Why would you be worried?"

"Because I know what you earn, and it's not enough for you to have paid off an additional three grand."

"I've taken on another job, and it allows me to have extra money. I want to try and have the car paid off by the end of the year."

"By looks of things it'll be paid off well before then. You've already paid off almost one-fifth in just over two months. That's amazing."

"I'm fortunate. I live rent-free with my best friend and her husband. But I'm looking at moving out within the next couple of months, I just want to be able to save some more money before I go."

"If you need more money, Lily."

"No, Sir. I'm fine, really I am. But I'd like to have my car paid off by the end of the year."

"Tell me about this other job of yours." He picks his water bottle up and drinks from it.

"I've been doing proofreading for some authors. Actually, it's turned into editing. I've always had a love for English and I wanted to become a teacher. But truthfully, I'm really enjoying the editing and proofreading I'm doing."

"Does it pay well?"

"If I compare it to my salary from here, on par. I get four hundred a book."

"Four hundred? Regardless of size?"

"Yes, it doesn't matter."

"Hmm, have you researched what other editors get?"

"Not really. I have a good client base, and it's increasing daily. I'm booked solid until the end of February. Several of my authors have made bestselling lists."

"Really?" he asks as he rolls his neck from side to side.

"My very first one I did for free. Her book was her debut novel, and it went to top ten in the *New York Times* and *USA Today* bestseller lists. It's still up there."

Dale's eyes widen and he smiles. "So you must have talent."

I shrug my shoulders and look down at my knitted hands on my lap. "I don't know."

"How big are the books you work on?"

"They differ. The smallest was just under sixty-five thousand words, the largest just over a hundred and fifty. "

"And you charge them all four hundred?"

"Yes, sir."

"If you're being sought after, that means you have a talent for the work you do. Don't undersell yourself."

I smile at his words. "That's what Shayne says, too."

"You should charge per page, as opposed to a flat fee. Because if you have a standard, say even three dollars a page, and the words are a common size and font, then that'll be fairer to the person writing less, and to the person writing more."

"Hmm," I mumble as I think about his words.

"And make it a minimum amount of pages. That way, it's fair for you, too."

I start trying to do some figures in my head, but I'm English savvy, not so much mathematics savvy. "I'll give it some thought, thank you." I go to stand to leave, having taken up way too much of his time already.

"Before you go," he says, and he motions for me to sit again. "Have you had any problems with your husband?"

"Not one word. I've started divorce proceedings. And I've found a psychologist who's helping me deal with everything that's happened in my life."

"You have?"

"I have, I'm just happy he isn't contesting it. I haven't made a fuss about the money he took, or what he did to me. I just want the whole thing put behind me."

"And that right there," he points to me, and the hair on my arms stand to attention. "That right there, Lily is why you're going to be so successful in life. You may have been dealt a shit hand, but you're ready to fight for the future you deserve, not the one that was handed to you."

Wow, just wow. He's so observant and also so encouraging. "Thank you."

"Now, get out of here," he playfully says, with the biggest, cheesiest grin. "But keep up the good work."

I leave his office and go back to my desk. No sooner do I sit down when Peter calls me into his office. "Peter, do you need something?" I rack my brain to try and figure out what it is I've forgotten.

"Here." He hands me an envelope.

I step closer to his desk, and take the envelope. Peter keeps looking down, doing his work. "What is this?"

"I got given a couple of tickets to some movie premier, but I hate movie theatres. They're filled with young kids."

"Okay, who would you like me to give these to?"

"You take them. Or if you don't want to go see whatever movie it's for, give it to someone else. I don't care, just take them."

"Thank you, Peter." I open the envelope, and these aren't *just* movie tickets, these are for the red carpet premier of the new Josh Harlon movie. Josh is one of the hottest action-romance actors in the world. The movie *Love and Guns* is apparently his best movie yet, and there's a lot of buzz around it. "Peter," I half mumble as I keep looking at the tickets.

"Yes?"

"Are you sure you don't want to give these to one of your daughters? Or maybe Dale's daughters? These are really rare tickets, and apparently the actor himself will be there. I can give them to Dale for his daughters."

Peter stops working and looks up at me. He does this funny twisty thing with his mouth as he narrows his eyes at me. I feel like I'm in trouble. "If

I told you I'd bought these for you to go out, you would've rejected them. I tell you I got them given to me, and you still reject them. You've been working hard, I wanted to give you something."

"But you gave me two thousand at Christmas."

"I gave everyone a bonus. I gave everyone what I thought they deserved."

I tilt my head to the side, still looking between the tickets and Peter. "These were intended for me?"

"Yes, they are."

"You and Dale keep doing things for me, I've never experienced anything like this before."

"Close the door, Lily." He stands from where he is sitting and he rounds the big, ugly desk in his office. I close the door, and when I turn he indicates for me to sit at the chair opposite him. "Do you know why Dale and I are so on top of this?"

"No Sir, I don't."

"My daughter got herself involved with someone who we thought was terrific. He had a good job, worked hard, and was the best man she could've met. And really, he was. He took care of her so well. And when they had their daughter, my granddaughter, he doted on her. He was a terrific husband, and a terrific man."

"Sounds like she's one of the luckiest people in the world."

"She was. Until it all changed."

"How did it change? Did he start to hurt her?"

Peter shakes his head. "No, not at all."

I squint my eyes and scratch my head, unsure at where this is going. "I don't understand."

"My daughter wanted to lose weight, and she heard that the drug ice was good for doing that. What she didn't know was just how highly addictive ice is."

"Oh my God," I whisper. Suddenly, sickness rushes to the base of my throat, I'm not sure I can handle what he's going to say.

"At first she was always happy, and bouncing around everywhere. No one suspected she was addicted to anything. She was great with Jojo, my granddaughter, and everything was going well. Until the drugs took over her life. Sean would come home from work and find nothing had been done, Jojo would be left in her dirty diaper all day, and she'd be crying and hungry. The first time that happened, he scooped Jojo up, and brought her to us."

"Oh my gosh."

"We kept her and cared for her, while he looked after our daughter. Don't get me wrong, we were involved with her care, too. But Jojo needed a loving home, and my daughter wasn't able to provide it because of the addiction. Sean, my wife, and I decided we'd provide the financial support to get our daughter the help she needs, but we'd give Jojo all the care and love she deserved."

I'm speechless, other than a gasp, I really have no words.

"Sean tried doing it on his own, but, then she became abusive. He knew it was the drugs, and it wasn't her, but she started lashing out and hitting him."

I clap a hand to my mouth as he tells the story.

"You see, Lily. Domestic abuse touches everyone, and when I know it's touched someone who's as beautiful a person as you are, I need to help. For my daughter, for my son in law, for every survivor."

I sit in silence for a moment, until I think of something he said just a few moments ago. "You said when you first started telling me, you thought your son in law was a terrific person, why only thought it?"

"Because now we know, he's so much more than terrific. He's her savior. She needed saving, and he was the saint who stepped up and did it. He loves her so much, he risked it all just so he could get her healthy again. And we all supported him. To me, he can do no wrong."

I take a few deep breaths and just take in everything Peter has told me. "May I ask how they're doing now?"

"She's been clean for two and a half years. And they're together, stronger than ever."

"I'm really happy to hear that."

"My point, Lily, is no one gave up on her. And I won't give up on you."

I relax my shoulders and let the weight of the entire conversation fall over me. "Thank you," I say as I stand and take the tickets. "I'm sure I'll be able to take Shayne with me. She'll love it."

"You're welcome." Peter goes back behind his desk, sits and continues with his work.

I leave his office, and go sit at my desk, sliding the envelope into my bag in the bottom drawer of my desk. I take my phone out and message Shayne:

Keep the 27th of Feb free. I have a surprise. Lx

Right away she replies:

Tell me now, I hate/love surprises.

I message back:

I'll tell you tonight.

Her response:

Girl, it better be good.

I say:

Oh, it is.

Just as I hit send, Max calls me. "Hello," I answer.

"Hi Lily. I know you're at work, and I don't start until late today. Do you want to have lunch?"

"I'd love that. I go to lunch at twelve-thirty."

"I'll meet you downstairs."

"Okay, bye."

We hang up and I get to work, pushing the excitement of today to the side and concentrating on what I need to do.

I grab my coat and walk downstairs. The cold has started to ease, and we're not getting as much snow now as we have been. It's still cold and we still have snow, just not as much.

I can see Max standing near the checkouts waiting for me. The moment he sees me, his eyes light up and he comes toward me. "Hello, Snowflake," he says, as he leans down and gives me a quick kiss on the lips. "How's work?" he asks.

"Today's been surreal," I say as we begin to walk toward the café we go to.

"How so?" He moves his hand to link our fingers together, and it momentarily startles me. "Is this okay, may I hold your hand?" he asks, as we slow our walk and he looks to me.

Why does it not bother me? Is it because I'm comfortable around Max and just know he'll never hurt me? "It's okay," I say as he tightens his grip around my fingers. "You're not working until late?"

"No, I'm only on from four until nine tonight." We walk to the café, and he opens the door for me. I step through and he then ushers us to the table we've pretty much claimed as our own. Max pulls the chair out for me, then once I'm seated, he sits opposite me. "So, I have something to tell you."

"Hi Lily, hi Max," Katie, the regular waitress says as she comes to stand in front of the table. "Hot chocolate and a coffee?" She knows our beverage order.

"Yes please," both Max and I answer in unison. Then I add, "I'll have the chicken, mayonnaise and lettuce on a white roll."

"And I'll have a burger and fries," Max says.

"Be back in a few," Katie says and walks away.

"What is it you have to tell me?"

Max reaches for my hands, and plays with my fingers. "One of the apartments downstairs opened up. It's not yet vacant, but it will be in a couple of weeks. It's yours when you're ready to move."

"Oh, wow." I look away.

"You don't look happy. I already told you I'm not going to interfere. Not once."

"It's not that." Gosh, I feel so dumb even worrying about it, and even stupider at the fact I have to tell him.

"What is it then? Because I can assure you, it's the safest building in town."

"No, it's not that." Yep, I feel *really* stupid. "I don't have furniture yet. And I'm not sure I'll be able to afford a fridge, let alone everything else for probably another month or so. I've got a few editing jobs lined up, but until I get paid from them, I doubt I'll be able to move in." I take a deep breath. Although I really want to move in, because it is so safe, I'm going to have to do the right thing. "Just rent it out, it's not fair for you to have to wait for me to have the money to furnish it."

"No need to worry about that. All the apartments come with a fridge, a washing machine and dryer, bar stools for the kitchen, and a TV and DVD player. The kitchen is fully equipped with plates and everything, and all you need is a sofa and your bedroom furniture."

"The kitchen is equipped with everything? How does that work?"

"When a tenant moves in, it's part of the contract they sign. I provide a certain amount of cutlery, plates glasses, things like that. When they move out, we donate them to different charities and replace them with new. It's part of the fees they pay."

"I've never heard of anyone ever doing that." Is this too good to be true, or is he wrapping me up in cotton wool because he thinks I'm delicate? "Are you being real with me? Because I've never heard of this."

He looks up at the ceiling, laughing at me. "It is real. It's part of the reason I can charge what I charge. Just like I offer security at the front door and at the garage below. It's one of the things I've put in place. Look, I'll stay here and you can go right now and ask the other tenants. I promise you, it's how I run this complex, along with all the others I own."

"Huh," I sigh. Katie brings over our drinks, and sets them on the table. "Well then. Thank you, I accept," I say once she leaves.

"It still needs to be painted and the carpet replaced once the tenant leaves, so I'd say about six weeks it should be ready."

Katie's back within a few seconds, carrying our food. She places it down, smiles sweetly at us, and leaves. "I wanted to tell you something." I pick my sandwich up and take a bite.

"What is it?" He starts eating his fries first.

"I've started the ball rolling for a divorce. It should be final by the end of February if Trent doesn't cause me any problems."

"Are you doing it yourself?"

"No, I went to a lawyer and got it started. I don't anticipate too many glitches, because I haven't heard a peep from him. Nothing. It's as if he's completely disappeared."

"Let's hope he never comes near you again. Because truthfully, Lily, I'm not sure he'll like the consequences if he does."

"What's that supposed to mean?" I ask as I take another bite of my sandwich.

"It means someone hurting someone I'm very fond of, doesn't play too well in my books. Not at all."

The rest of lunch is spent talking about the movie tickets, the books I'm editing, and just about everything and anything.

But Max's words of 'someone I'm very fond of' are at the front of my mind. They don't seem to bother me, actually, I like knowing Max is protective of me.

Something I'll need to talk to Katherine about tonight after work.

CHAPTER 34

I CAN'T BELIEVE THIS LAST month. Trent didn't cause me one single problem. The divorce went through smoothly and with that part of my life over with, I'm finally able to breathe. Truthfully, I've waited for something to occur. A phone call, a text message, a disturbance at work. But nothing has happened. My lawyer called me to tell me my divorce petition had gone through and there was no contest filed by Trent. I'm now officially divorced.

What a relief! It was like the sun has finally broken through the dark clouds and showed me her sweet rays. Imagine, being in the worst drought of your life, and water pouring from the sky and filling all the catchment areas. It was the biggest sense of relief I'd ever felt.

I was, officially, Lily Anderson again.

The night my lawyer told me I was a free woman, I lay in bed and tried to think about the good times I had with Trent. Looking back, it's as if I was looking on at the life of a person I didn't recognize. Almost as if I was an outsider watching the cruel maiming of an animal and was powerless to step in and help. A glass wall was in front of me. I couldn't touch it, but could only watch and feel everything happening to the broken, wounded girl on the other side.

Of course, every time I was happy with Trent, it was soon overshadowed by the times he hurt me. Those were most painful for me to look back on and watch. I was so frail, so weak yet so strong.

The only sadness I felt, and still feel, is for Trent's mom, Lina. I can see now she's as much a victim of domestic abuse as I was, and I have to wonder if there's anything I can do to help her. But Katherine told me, I need to help myself first, and find who I am before I can even think about Lina. I see her point, and I understand what she's saying.

I hope one day, Lina will want to save herself, because I'll be there to help her.

I went to sleep that night with one chapter of my past ended. But something kept playing on my mind. I tossed and turned all night, instead of the closure of ridding myself of Trent, I had a gaping hole I had no answers for.

Why was I treated so badly by Mom, and then Dad? What happened that made them so resentful they'd hurt their only child? I was no closer to finding the answer. And up until now, I'm unaware why they felt so much hatred and hostility toward me.

I'm about to finish work for the night, and Max has said he wants to take me out. Our relationship is progressing at a tortoise's speed, but I'm nowhere near ready to take it to any intimate level beyond kissing and holding hands. It's crazy, I know. Here I am, twenty-five years old and not ready to have a physical relationship.

Max is by far the most patient and beautiful man I know. He's got his own struggles with his stutter. He's not much into going out and being in public where he has to communicate with many people. I of course, have stopped hearing his stutter. To me, he speaks like everyone else around me, but I know others find it difficult to understand him. Max has become a regular feature at home, and Shayne and Liam both say how he's the nicest guy they know.

The two of them are taking the vacation I bought them for Christmas at the end of March, and I'm hoping I'll be able to move into my own apartment by then.

It's the end of the work day and I duck into Dale's office to give him another thousand dollars. I took his advice, and reworked what I charge. I get several emails a day from people who want me to edit their work. I take no more than two books a week, and I'm booked flat until April.

"Hi, Dale, do you have a moment?" I ask as I rap on his door.

"Sure thing, come in. Sit." He stands and goes over to the little fridge in his office. "Water? Soda?" he asks me as he grabs a soda for himself. "Don't tell Betsy," he whispers as he holds up the soda and looks around the office.

"I won't. I can't stay, but I have some more money to give you. It's a thousand." I hand him the envelope.

"You're unbelievable, Lily. You really are doing well. You do realize, with this amount here, you've paid almost seven thousand on your car."

"Yes I do. I've been keeping track as well. I'm proud of myself."

"And so you should be." He takes the money out, counts it in front of me, then writes it in the notebook. "Here, sign this." He shoves the book toward me, and I sign saying I've given him more money. "How's the car? Are you still enjoying it?"

"Oh my gosh, it's perfect! I love it. I wish I could thank you again without sounding pathetic and whiney. I really do appreciate it."

"I know you do, Lily. Even if you never said a word, I know you're serious and value it, because you're making an amazing dent in the loan." I smile broadly at Dale. "Right, get out of here. I still have work to do."

"Thank you," I say and leave his office.

I head back to my desk, and pop my head into Peter's office. "Do you need anything, Peter? I'm just about to leave for the day and I want to make sure you're okay."

"Yes, yes. I'll be fine. My daughter's birthday tomorrow, so we're all taking the day and doing whatever she wants. And by 'she', I mean Jojo. She dictates what we're all going to do, and we all go along with it."

"It's sweet you can do that. Enjoy your day. I'll hold down the fort." I wink teasingly.

"I'll leave some work on your desk, if you have any problems with it, either ask Dale or leave it and I'll show you when I return to work."

"I can stay behind and you can show me now if you like."

"No, no. You can go. I'll see you in a couple of days."

"Have fun tomorrow."

I get my bag and go down to my car and head home. When I arrive, Shayne's home but Liam had to stay behind and do some last minute things at work. "Hey, Max and I are going out to dinner, do you want to join us?" I ask when I come in and find Shayne watching TV.

"Nah, Liam will be home soon, and I think we're going to go out for pizza and then a movie. Hey, how much fun was that premiere we went to last weekend? Such a shame you can't get tickets like that again." She sips on some water.

"Yeah, that was crazy fun. Who knows, maybe we'll get to do it again. Anyway, I'm going to get changed 'cause Max will be here soon. Will you let him in if he comes while I'm in the shower?"

"No, I'll make him wait outside." She laughs at her own sarcastic sense of humor. "Yeah, of course I'll let him in."

"Thanks." I go into my room, quickly grab some clothes then head into the shower.

"Wow, this is a nice restaurant. I've only ever been to somewhere this nice once. And that didn't go too well," I whisper to Max.

The maître 'd shows us to our table, pulls my chair out and waits until we're seated before he stands in front of the table, and with his very proper pronunciation says, "Your waiter will be with you in a moment. The wine menu, sir." He hands Max the menu, tips his head to me and leaves.

"Correction, I've never been somewhere as nice as this." I feel awkward here, and I'm fidgeting in my chair when Max looks up from the menu and smiles.

"Would you like a red or a white?" I shrug my shoulders in answer. "I'll order one of each then."

"Max, I'm happy to drink water. Please, don't order any wine. You're driving and I have work tomorrow," I beg him. "Please?"

"No wine." He closes the menu and lays it flat. "Do you know what you'd like to eat?"

I'm perusing the menu, but everything looks so good. "Have you been here before?"

"Yes, a few times."

"Will you order for me then? I don't know what to get, everything looks great."

"I will." He keeps looking over the menu.

When our waiter comes and Max starts relaying our orders, I notice how Max slows his pronunciation down so he's understood. This is the first time I've picked up how Max speaks when he's outside his comfort zone.

The waiter takes the menus and leaves. "Do you know, it only now occurred to me I don't know much about you," I say to Max.

"Ask away, I'm an open book."

"How old are you?" I ask as I sip on the water the waiter bought to the table.

"I'm thirty-three on September fourteenth."

"You're only six years older than me?"

"Don't sound so surprised. Thanks for the confidence boost." He looks away, clutching at his chest in mock hurt.

"Sorry," I mumble though really I'm laughing. "Have you been married before?"

"No, never married. Came close once, until I discovered she was more interested in my money than me. I've had two other long-term girlfriends."

"What happened with them?"

"We drifted apart. We didn't end on bad terms, just each went in different directions. And I had one girlfriend, who was a friend before; we thought we'd try to see if we could be a couple, but it didn't last because we're better as friends."

"You're still friends with her now?" I ask in surprise.

"We are. She works for me."

I dart my eyes away and can feel numerous questions starting to form just from his statement. "Um." But I'm not sure where to start.

"She runs one of the branches of the firm." I'm not sure how I feel about this information. I can feel something unsettling in the pit of my stomach, the feeling is foreign and unknown to me. "Hey, don't worry. She's married now, and has been for over a year."

"Worry?" I ask, but my crackling voice deceives us both.

"You looked worried, maybe even jealous." *Is that what I was feeling?*

Jealousy? "I must admit, it's kinda sexy."

"I've never felt anything like this before. Is that what it is? Jealousy? Because I feel like I want to scream and shout and tell her to back away."

"Yep, sounds like jealousy to me."

"Hmm," I groan. This is completely uncomfortable. This physical reaction is logically stupid. He's not with her, and I've made no commitment to him, nor has he made one to me, so it feels unjustified.

"Anyway, tell me about your day?" Max picks up his glass and drinks his water.

"Actually, I've been thinking about something."

"What's that?"

"I need closure on my Mom and Dad. More specifically, my Dad. My mom died when I was young, so I can't get anything from her, but my Dad, he's the biggest part of my life I remember, before Trent. And I really want to know what happened for him to treat me so poorly."

"Have you tried asking him?"

"I'm not sure I can face him. And besides, I left when I was seventeen, and I never looked back. Though I still don't know who was worse, him or Trent."

"Do you know where he lives?"

"I know where he used to live, I have no idea if he's still there. I don't know anything. It's been so many years, anything could've happened to him."

"I can help if you like?"

"How?"

"I can hire a private investigator, get them to find your dad and see what information they can get."

The waiter approaches and places our meals in front of us. He asks if we'd like cracked pepper and when we both decline, he leaves us.

"Can I think about it? Although I'm ready to close that door from my childhood, I'm just not sure I'm prepared to find out they did and said all those things to me just because they didn't want me. I mean, they could've given me away, they could've put me up for adoption, or they could've handed me to the fire department. I just need some time to really consider your offer."

"My offer is there unconditionally. And once I find a private investigator, I can put him or her in touch with you and you can deal with it directly and share with me the information you choose."

I cut into my succulent steak and exhale. "You really are something else."

"Now, can I ask you a question?" I nod as I chew the delicate and juicy piece of meat. "Do you want kids?"

The question takes me by surprise. Considering my past and the number of miscarriages I've had, I'm not sure I can put that kind of strain back on my body or my mind. "I was pregnant. Many times. Five to be exact. But…" I put my knife and fork down and feel myself starting to tear up. "He beat me, and I lost every one of the babies."

"I knew of one." Of course he does. He sat by my bed and fed me.

"I haven't grown up in a loving environment. I don't know what it is. I don't understand it. Would I like a child? I'm not sure I could show her or him what love is, because I don't know how to convey it. I'm not even sure if I'll ever be able to have sex again. Trent was my first, and he wasn't very nice to me." I smile, however I know there's no joy in the hurt I'm showing.

"I want to be your last, Lily." Max reaches out to hold my hand. "I want to show you what it feels like to love and be loved. I want to be the one you wake up to for the rest of your life."

"It's been months already, and all we do is kiss and hold hands."

"I don't care."

"But?" I add, waiting for the condition. The 'you better be ready soon or I'll go elsewhere.'

"But what?"

"The catch to your *I don't care*, what is it? You'll give me until Christmas, then you'll start looking elsewhere?"

"I'm not Trent, Lily. If it takes you five lifetimes to simply lay next to me in my bed, then I'll wait those five lifetimes. I don't want anyone else. I'm not even interested in anyone else. I'm not a player. I never have been. I want a family, I want a wife, and I want those things with you."

"You want to marry me?" *What on earth is going on?*

"Not right now, but eventually, yes. You have a long way to go, but I have no intention of not being by your side for every step you take."

He is the sweetest man I've ever known, and as I sit and eat dinner I keep looking up at him. "You really are perfect," I say.

"So are you, Snowflake."

CHAPTER 35

THE WEATHER IS WARMING UP, and I'm moving. I can't believe it's the middle of March already, and today is moving day for me. I've bought a sofa and bedroom set and arranged to have them delivered to my new apartment.

Shayne is in my room, helping me pack my clothes and shoes. "Are you looking forward to next weekend?" I ask Shayne as she transfers my clothes from the drawers into a borrowed suitcase.

"Oh God yes. Liam's dad told us he wants to buy another tire shop, and give it to Liam and me."

"But you two run the one you're in now."

"Yeah, but apparently that was our trial, to see how we'd do. He said," she lowers her voice and puffs out her chest. "*You kids have proven to me you can run a place at a profit. I want to buy you your own, what do you say?* Geez, Lily. It's good, you know? But at the same time, I don't want to have to go through all the stress of going into a rundown place and building it up from scratch. Liam and I can do it, because we work well together, but you know…," she stops talking and looks at me. I'm nodding in support of her. "We've been trying for a baby for a while now, and we can't get pregnant. And if he buys a rundown workshop and expects us to get it up from scratch, I'm not sure I'll be able to cope with the pressure." She stops folding the clothes and sits on the bed.

"You should talk to him, Shayne. Tell him how you feel." This is the most vulnerable I've ever seen Shayne. She's never worn her heart on her sleeve like this.

"I don't know," she says wistfully. "I don't want to disappoint him, because he really has done so much for Liam and me. But at the same time, I'm at the stage where I want to start a family, too. I'd like to have a baby before I'm thirty-five, because time is just too short. I mean, it was only yesterday I was living in the garage which was converted and babysitting. And today I'm sitting in the bedroom with my best friend, crying because I can't have a baby."

"Shayne," I say as I move to hug her. She lets her head fall to my shoulder and she cries for a moment. There's nothing really I can say, or if there is, I don't know the words.

"How dumb, huh? I was tossed aside by a mom who didn't want me, because her new husband didn't like how she came with baggage. And now, all I want is to have a baby of my own, so I can show her how much she means to me, and how much I love her."

"It's not dumb if that's how you feel. You and Liam deserve to be happy."

Shayne returns my hug, sits back, and wipes the tears from her eyes. "I'm just emotional. My best friend is leaving me today, and I feel like I'm losing a part of me. I know where you're going, you'll be happy, but you've lived with us for five months and I've loved having you every day you've been here." She leans in and gives me another hug.

"I can never thank you enough for what you've done for me. You opened your heart, and your home, even after all those years where we didn't talk."

"You don't need to thank me, girl. It's what we do for each other." *Damn it, I promised myself I wouldn't cry.* But, that promise has been thrown out because now, Shayne and I are blubbering like fools.

"Oh my God, who do I have to beat up?" Liam says as he stands inside my room. "Max and I can go teach someone a lesson."

Shayne and I both wipe our tears and laugh. "We're just being girls," Shayne says. "You don't have to beat up anyone."

"Good." Liam throws a punch in his hand, "'Cause I so would."

"Come on, let's get me packed. I have an apartment to move into."

"Holler when you're ready and I'll take stuff out to your car," Liam says as he leaves my room.

"You know," I start saying as I pack what's in my wardrobe. "You two are going to make the best parents." I look over to Shayne who's beaming at me. Her smile is so bright and her eyes sparkle.

Before we know it, I've packed my life into two suitcases and three boxes. That's all I have to show for myself. But, I also have my life. I'm not entirely sure if I stayed with Trent I'd even be alive today. Looking at my packed car, I'm alright with the fact I have virtually nothing. Because I have my freedom.

"Right," Liam starts. "Don't forget to write, and come home on all the important holidays," he teasingly says as he wraps me in a hug. "You've been a good kid, chicken butt. Play nice with the other kids, and make sure you get to class on time." He lays a kiss on my forehead. But I can tell this sarcasm is his coping mechanism.

"I will. I won't go to any parties on campus either." I let go and head straight into Shayne's arms.

She's crying, and then I start crying. "You have a home here anytime you want or need it."

I start that whole ugly crying thing. My eyes are constantly dripping, and I can't seem to be able to breathe right. Shayne and I are both crying loudly as we hold onto each other. "I love you so much."

"I love you, girl."

Finally, I let go and step away from Shayne.

Liam steps in and hugs her, consoling her as she cuddles into his chest.

I step up to my car, and smile. "To the rest of my life," I say under my breath. As I get in and back away, I know this is the right move for me. I've gone as far as I can staying at Shayne and Liam's house, now it's time I push myself further.

I drive to my new home, and don't look in my review mirror. Not because I don't want to be sad again, but if I look behind me, that's where I'll end up. I need to keep looking forward, and live.

I unpack some of my clothes into my new chest of drawers, and once I'm done then I take the clothes which need hanging and hang them in the closet.

I can't believe I've unpacked everything in under three hours. It gives me time to sit, relax and tackle one of the books I've been working on.

Max has stayed true to his word, and not interfered at all. He didn't come help me move, and he hasn't once come into the apartment. I send him a text letting him know I've arrived and asking if he'd like to join me for dinner. As if he was waiting beside the phone, he replies with a smiley face emoticon and says he'll be here soon.

Pizza it is. Because I still have to finish the final read through and get it sent to my client. And if I can, I want to start on another manuscript I have.

I get my laptop, open it up and sit on my new sofa, which I bought with my own money, and I pick up where I left off. Before I know it, my phone rings from beside me. "Max?" I answer knowing it's him from his name popping up on the screen.

"Do I have to wait outside for the entire night?"

"Crap." I get up and go to the door, where Max is leaning against the opposite wall with a bottle of Dom Perignon Rose. "I'm sorry, were you knocking for long?"

"Oh, only half an hour," he teases. "Not really, just a few moments." He holds up the bottle. "Welcome to the building," he says and comes into my apartment, and heads straight for the kitchen.

"Champagne and pizza will go well together. But I doubt you welcome every tenant to the building with a bottle of Dom Perignon."

"Busted." He turns to look around. "But I don't like every tenant like I like you." He winks at me. "I like what you've done with the place." He indicates toward my new sofa. "Unfortunately, it's one of the smaller apartments; all the bigger ones have had the same tenants in them for years. Sorry, it's so small."

I look around and wonder what on earth he's talking about. It's as big as Shayne and Liam's house. "Um? What? My bedroom is bigger than the one I had at Shayne and Liam's house."

"Regardless, sorry it couldn't be one of the bigger apartments, as long as you've unpacked and are settled."

"I am, but I can't find my diary."

"It's got to be somewhere. Maybe it's back at Shayne and Liam's."

"Yeah, I'll go through the week and have a look. Anyway, let's order pizza."

"My treat," Max jumps in and claims. "Considering this is your first night here, I can't expect my tenant to buy her own pizza after all the hard work of moving."

I roll my eyes at Max and stand with a hand on my hip. "Are you ever going to let me pay?"

"Nope." He wraps his arms around me and brings me in tightly for a hug. "Never." He kisses my nose, then gently kisses me on the mouth. "I'm really happy you're here," he adds.

"I'm happy to be here."

"Pizza. I'll order." He lets me go, takes his phone out of his jeans pocket and walks in toward the second room, which I'll eventually convert to a study, and orders pizza.

When he comes out he asks if he may sit on the sofa, then picks the remote up and starts flicking through the channels. I sit with my laptop on my lap and finish the book I'm working on. The security guard from downstairs buzzes just as I send my final edits through to the author, then open another manuscript waiting for me.

"That'll be pizza. I'll get it." Max gets up and goes to the door, waiting for the delivery of dinner. "Come get it," he calls from the kitchen. He's laid the two pizzas out, got two plates and is pouring the champagne. We sit at the breakfast bar and he holds his flute up, ready to make a toast. "To new beginnings, and to new memories. May the best of your past be the worst of our future." He clinks his glass to mine.

I smile, because it doesn't escape me how he said 'our future' as opposed to 'your future'. And I like what he said. "To our future," I say and take another sip. We begin to eat and I want to broach the subject of my father with Max. "I've been considering your offer, and had many discussions with Katherine about it, and I'd like to take you up on it."

"Which offer is that?" He takes a huge bite of his pizza and chews.

"About you hiring a private detective to find my dad, and whatever else they manage to uncover."

Max nods once, and says, "Consider it done. I'll pass your number onto whoever I hire and you can talk to them directly."

"I prefer you be with me if they do manage to find any information."

"Your wish shall be granted. Now, eat while it's still hot."

Everything is right. My life is really good. "Thank you, Max." He nods, then shoves more pizza in his mouth.

CHAPTER 36

IT'S MID-APRIL AND THE weather has certainly given us all something to revel in. The nights are crisp, but the days have been fantastic.

Max spends most of his spare time in my apartment, only dragging himself home to sleep. And I've got several manuscripts in queue, just waiting for me to give them my undivided attention.

Today's Friday and the last day of the work week. It's nearing the end of the day, but before I go I check my emails and find one from the sixth largest publishing company in the world. They're based in New York, and have highly popular and acclaimed authors signed to them. The email reads cryptically. It says they'd like to get in contact with me, and can I call on them at my earliest convenient time. The name of the person is Jolene Grace and she'll be waiting for my call.

Huh. I walk into Peter's office, and he's standing by his large window looking down at the floor. "Peter, am I interrupting?"

He turns on his heels and looks at me. "Not at all. Please come in."

"I won't take long. Um, this is going to sound strange, but I got an email from a publishing company who wants me to call them. Would you mind if I use Dale's office and do so? I know Dale's not here today, but I'd like for you to okay it first."

"Of course, go ahead." He flicks his hand at me as he says 'go ahead.'

I walk down to Dale's office, with the number and the name of the woman I'm to ask for, close the door and sit at his desk. I'm not entirely sure what's happening, but I'm so nervous. My heart's beating quickly and my hands are shaking. I feel as if I'm in trouble, though I know I'm not.

A lady answers the phone with the company name. "Hello, may I speak with Jolene Grace?" I ask.

"May I ask whose calling?" she sounds so proper and snooty.

"My name is Lily Richards. She's waiting for my call." My voice sounds fragile, like I'm waiting to be reprimanded for something.

"Ah, yes Ms. Richards. Jolene *is* waiting. I'll just put you through."

Holy crap, I *am* in trouble. If I hang up now, then she can't yell at me. *Snap out of it, Lily.*

"Lily Richards, it's an absolute pleasure to finally be able to talk to you."

"It is?" Suddenly the butterflies in my stomach disappear and I look around the office, searching for I don't know what.

"You, young lady have been a hot, hot topic of late."

"I have?" I nervously tap my finger on the desk.

"Oh my God, yes. We're all very interested in meeting you."

"You are?" Why am I answering everything she says with a question?

"We are. And I'd like to personally invite you to the offices here in New York. All expenses paid, for a weekend."

"Why?"

Jolene laughs into the phone, but I'm more confused now than I was when I first received her email.

"We've been tracking a few authors, and we've noticed these authors all have one thing in common – you. You see, we've signed two of your clients, and we've spoken with three others. When we asked them who does their proofreading, they answered with the same name, yours. Then we asked them who edits their books, and all of them said you. You do everything, which in-house we call a big picture editor. We have proofreaders, we have editors, but we need more. And your name keeps popping up."

"I don't have any formal education, though. And really it's the author who does all the work."

"Oh yes, I agree. But here's the thing, the author can have the best story in the world, but if it's not proofread and edited correctly, they'll be forgotten quite quickly. An editor polishes it and makes the story shine, makes it stand out, and makes it easy for people to remember it. You are crucial to readers suffering book hangovers."

"I do that?"

"The authors you've been working with are incredibly talented, but you my friend, also add a lot of punch to their words. And for that, we'd like to fly you here, from wherever you are in the country or the world, and have a chat with you about working for us."

Is it wrong that I want to jump up and down and scream with happiness? *Maybe, but I'll be doing it once I hang up.* I've heard of big corporations head hunting the best in their industry, offering them ridiculous payments and incentives to work for them. But I'm just me. "Aha," I say way too happy to be able to form a comprehensive sentence.

"Can I make the arrangements for you? Say next weekend?"

"Um, I um. Um." *Crap, what do I say?* "Can I think about it, and let you know tomorrow?"

"Lily, I look forward to your call."

"Thank you." We hang up, and I sit back in Dale's chair, looking around the office as if the most surreal thing just happened. I suppose it *is* the most bizarre thing to happen to me.

Me. I've been headhunted! I can't believe it. Finally, once the phone call actually sinks in, I walk back to my desk in a dreamlike state. "Lily," Peter calls me in. When I'm at his door, he drags his eyes over me and furrows his brows together. "Everything alright?" he asks.

"I'm really not sure. It was freakish and unreal, but euphoric, too."

"What happened?" he asks concerned.

"I think I'm being headhunted by a publishing company."

"You think? What did they say?"

"They want to fly me out to New York, all expenses paid, to have a talk with me."

"Wow." The way Peter drags 'wow' out, it gives me goosebumps and makes me smile. "What an opportunity. And to do something you love. You have to go."

"What?"

"You have to go. Take that nice young man with you, the one who stutters, and go to New York. If for nothing else, just to hear them out." I regard Peter. I've always said he has his finger on the pulse, and for him to refer to Max, tells me just how much he knows.

"She offered to set it up for next weekend."

"Did she? You have a day off next Friday, and the following Monday," he says with certainty.

"No I don't." I shake my head while mentally thinking about my schedule. But my days are set, Monday to Friday.

"I'm giving them to you. You have next Friday and the following Monday off. You can't let this opportunity go. It may be what you want, it may not, but you have to go and discover that for yourself."

"But, what about my job here?"

"Are you kidding me, Lily? You've been, hands down, the best personal assistant I've ever had, but this place isn't for you. It never has been. You need to do what you love."

"But I owe Dale money."

"Yes, and from what he's told me, you're barreling along paying your car off. You'll still pay it off, you won't abandon your responsibilities. And besides, Dale will kick your ass out of the office next Friday once he finds out you've been offered this opportunity."

"What if I don't like what they have to say?"

Peter stands from behind his desk, and comes over to me. He places his big, wrinkly hand on my shoulder and smiles. "Then you say 'thank you, but no thank you' and come back here. But don't *not* do it for fear of what may happen. Because you'll always look back and say 'what if'. Your job is secure here, it's not going anywhere. But truthfully, Lily, it's time you do what you love."

I feel a tear flow down my cheek, and I simply nod. "Thank you, Peter."

"You're welcome. Now go home and I'll see you on Monday, when you'll come in here with the prettiest smile you've ever had, because your work-week will be short, and you'll be going to New York."

My whole life I've been surrounded by men who never cared about me for anything more than their own benefit. Now I'm in a sea of gentlemen. They not only care, but they push me to be the best version of myself I can be, without any worry of the consequences for them.

"I'm so proud of you," Max says as he sweeps me up and spins me around once I tell him about my phone call. "You're going to go, right?" He places me on my feet and rubs his hands up and down my arms.

"Peter says I need to, if anything, just to hear them out."

"Smart man your boss. Hang on, I've ordered Thai for dinner."

"Thank you. I don't know, what do you think, should I go?" I walk over to the sofa with my water bottle and curl up on the edge with my feet tucked under my body.

"Of course I think you should go. It may be the opportunity of a lifetime, it may be a stepping stone to something bigger, or it may just end up being a weekend trip to New York. But in any event, you shouldn't let this chance pass."

I take a deep breath and look out over the city. We're in Max's apartment and the view is nothing short of breathtaking. I huff, still unsure what to do.

"What's the problem? What's stopping you?"

I shrug my shoulders. "I suppose it's the unknown. What if it ends up being something I can't do?"

"That's a logical feeling. But look at it this way. You've been doing this since when? December? We're in April, and four of your authors have made both the *New York Times* and *USA Today* bestseller lists. *Four.* And one of them hit with their debut novel. If publishers are taking note of them, then they'll see your name attached to their books. And that makes them sit up and take note, because they believe you'll improve the manuscripts you work on and make them money. You're obviously already doing something right."

I open my water bottle and take a sip. "That's logical." *Can't argue with that.*

"What's the worst thing which can happen? You'll take a job with them, it won't work out, and you'll need to go back to the supermarket. You'll still have the authors who aren't with a publishing company, and you'll still be doing what you love. So really, I don't see a risk."

"Will you come with me?" I ask.

Max's jaw twitches and I can tell he's holding in a smile. "Oh yeah, I can come," he says casually. I know he's playing me and wants me to ask him again.

"You don't have to. I can go on my own," I tease him.

He leaps up off the sofa, and scoops me up hugging me tightly. "I'd love to go, Snowflake. Thank you for asking me." His phone starts ringing, and he lets me go to get it. "Oh," he says in a deeper tone as he looks at the phone. "I'll be back in a moment." He disappears down the hallway and closes the door.

I go to the kitchen and get a couple of bowls, and forks and spoons out, ready for dinner.

When I finish, Max emerges from where he was, looking quite distraught. "Are you okay?" I ask and go over to him.

"That was the private investigator. She's on her way over. She says she's got a packet for you to read."

"A packet?"

"She didn't sound great, Lily. Like something's up. I called down to security and told them to send her up. She'll be here soon."

Suddenly my appetite disappears and I feel like I have fingers tightening around my throat, preventing me from breathing properly. "Okay," I say to no question asked.

I go to sit on the sofa again, and stare out at nothing. No words, no pictures. Absolutely nothing is making sense.

"Lily, are you okay?" I shrug my shoulders slowly. *I'm not sure.* "She'll be here soon."

"Okay," I say aimlessly.

"I can stay here while you open whatever she gives you, or I can leave."

"No," I say too enthusiastically. "I need you here. Please, don't go."

"Then I won't." He comforts me by sitting beside me and drawing me protectively into his side.

We don't have to wait for long before the elevator doors open and a woman is standing inside his foyer. I take her in, and I'm surprised by her appearance. She's wearing gothic clothes, has a lot of piercings on her face, and tattoos everywhere. We both get up, and walk over to her.

"Max, here you go." She hands him a thick yellow envelope and she looks at me and smiles, "You're really pretty," she says. I'm not sure if she's saying that to lessen the impact of what's in the thick yellow envelope, or if she actually thinks I'm pretty.

I stare at the envelope, my eyes are fixated on it. I can feel my blood turning to ice as it rushes around my body, and my skin is covered in tiny goosebumps. Every hair on my body is standing at attention, and part of me wants to tear the envelope up and never look inside it.

"Thank you," I finally manage to say, acknowledging her compliment. I hear Max thank her and the elevator ding, indicating she's left. I'm not sure what will happen next, all I know is I'm being led by Max to sit on his sofa.

"Are you ready?" he asks. He places the innocent-looking, though I'm sure life-altering envelope down on the coffee table.

"I'm ready," I whisper. I pull my shoulders back and sit tall. Max hands me the envelope, and I tear it open.

Sliding the stack of papers out, I flip through it and try to read as much as I can. But all I'm seeing is newspaper clippings, headings of "accident" and "overdose" and "family mourns". There's a lot of paper, but nothing makes sense.

I look up at Max, close my eyes and take several deep breaths. If I'm going to know, I need to begin at the start and go to the end. It's the only way I'll be able to understand.

"I'm ready," I say aloud, maybe it was for Max's benefit, or maybe for my own. Opening my eyes I look at the first piece of paper.

It's a copy of my dad's death certificate. He died from severe liver disease; caused by chronic alcohol abuse. Dad died four years ago. He didn't show up to work for five days, and they went to his house to see what was happening. They found him decomposing in his favorite chair.

It goes on to show Dad's employment record, his complete medical history, everything about Dad. Once I've sifted through many papers on Dad, all held together with a paperclip, I get to another stack of papers. This one is all about Mom.

Her coroner's report shows she died from a massive overdose of sleeping pills. There were many drugs in her system, but the sleeping pills were essentially the cause of her death. And it was deemed 'accidental'. The papers on my mom reached back to high school, it even showed Dad and Mom were high school sweethearts.

I keep flicking through her stack, and find she had a love for English like I do. She wanted to be an elementary school teacher and had completed two and a half years of college when she became pregnant with her first child, Lily Anderson – me.

But my eyes keep looking over the line, 'first child.'

If I was her 'first' child, then there must have been a second. But I don't remember anyone else. In my dreams, I have a brother whose name is Wade, but growing up there was never any mention of him, or even any pictures of him. So I always thought he was merely a dream, a fantasy I'd created to help me cope with all the bad times.

I scan the rest of Mom's papers, looking for anything to tell me about any other child she had.

The next bundle is me, but I'm not interested in me, I need to find what else there is.

The last bundle has a newspaper article attached to the front with the heading, "Toddler dies in tragic accident." I drop the rest of the papers and focus on this one article.

'A heartbreaking accident has left a family in mourning when three-year-old Wade Anderson was hit by a car outside his family home. In a catastrophic turn of events, his father, Stanley Anderson, was the one who killed his son. He was driving home from work and Wade ran out the front of the car. Mr. Anderson, unable to stop the vehicle in time, collided with and instantly killed his son.'

I look up from the newspaper article and search for something, anything. "Are you okay?" Max asks as he sits beside me. I can hear him and I know he's asked a question, but my brain can't interpret what he's asked, nor can I respond.

I look down at the newspaper article. *'Liliana Anderson, Wade's mother had ducked inside to check on the family's older daughter, Lily, who had fallen and was calling out for her mother.'*

"Oh my God." I drop the paper and bring my hand to my mouth. "I remember. I remember everything."

A movie is playing around in my mind, and I remember every moment; every sound, every smell, as if I'm living it right now. I stand from the sofa and absentmindedly walk over to the window overlooking the city. The lights of the city below twinkle beautifully as the harsh reality of the recovered memory plays in my head.

"Mom was outside with Wade and me, but I had to go to the toilet. We were playing in the backyard. Dad had made us a sandpit, and Wade, Mom and I were in it building sand castles." I smile, remembering how cranky I got when Wade kept knocking my castles over. The warm sun was on my face, and Mom was laughing every time he'd put his little hand or foot through my castle.

"I went inside and went to the toilet while mom stayed outside with Wade. When I finished washing my hands, I slipped in the bathroom because I had splashed and there was water on the floor. I yelled out for Mom, because I'd hurt my elbow. She came rushing inside and while she was cleaning the cut, we heard a screeching of a car's brakes." Absentmindedly I begin rubbing my elbow, remembering the pain.

"Oh shit," Max says. I look at him in surprise, momentarily stunned he's still here with me.

Then I look back out over the city lights. "Mom went running out the front, and I was right behind her. Wade was lying under the car and Dad was on his knees, crying. Mom started screaming and crying, and I just stood there, not sure what was happening. The neighbors came out of their houses, looking to see what all the commotion was about. Before I even knew it, there were police and an ambulance there."

"How did he go from the back to the front?"

"The side gate had a latch, if you moved it just right, it would open. Dad was always supposed to fix it, but he never did. That night was the worst night of my life. They told me Wade had died. A few days later we buried Wade with his favorite teddy bear, and I gave him my favorite socks. He always wanted to wear them. That was the night everything changed at home."

"How old were you, Lily?"

"I was six years old."

"How did it change?"

"We were sitting at the table having dinner, and Mom was a mess. I remember her eyes were always red from the tears. But Mom said to me that night, 'if you hadn't screamed for me, he'd still be alive. It should've been you who died. From now on, we'll feed you, but don't think we'll ever love you.' She stopped crying when she said that to me, and from that day on, I was never talked to again."

"Oh my God."

The next thing I feel is Max's warm body against mine. He's holding me, giving me support in any way he can. "From the time I was six, until only very recently, I've never been part of a family. I've never been loved; I've never been wanted."

"That's because they weren't worthy of your love. It was a heartbreaking accident, they shouldn't have treated you the way they did. You were only a child, and none of that was your fault."

"I know," I cry into his chest. "But how do I handle this now that I remember what happened?" I look up at Max and his sympathetic brown eyes look deep into my soul.

"We handle it, together. Call Katherine and make an appointment with her, and I'll come with you."

I lay my head on his chest again, and tighten my arms around his body. "Thank you, Max. For everything."

He kisses the top of my head, and tightens his arms around me.

With dinner long forgotten, we stay knitted together. "Can I sleep here tonight?" I ask.

"Of course, I have a guest room set up. You can take my bed, and I'll sleep in the guest room."

"No, not tonight, I need you close to me. Can we sleep in the same bed, please?"

He leans down and chastely kisses me on the lips. "Anything my snowflake needs."

"Can we go to bed now? I'm not sure I can be an adult for the rest of the night. I just need to let everything sink in."

Max quietly leads me to his room, gets a t-shirt and some boxer shorts for me, and points me in the direction of his bathroom. I strip and just stand under the shower's stream of hot water. Still in a haze, I get out, dry myself off, and change into the clothes he's given me.

Max is in bed with his shirt off, wearing only boxers. His chest has intricate tattoos, but I'm still in a daze. I don't even bother trying to decipher what they say or mean. I just crawl into bed, into Max's arms, and simply close my eyes.

My dreams tonight aren't happy. They aren't of a blond-haired little boy. There's nothing to rejoice about. My nightmare tonight is of me, alive in a see-through casket, trying to scratch my way out. But my mother is throwing spades full of dirt over me while saying, "I'm glad it was you."

I haven't really slept. I've dozed, and I've tossed and turned, but I haven't actually slept.

Finally, after two in the morning, I drag myself out of bed. Max is snoring, quite loudly at that. I go out into the family room and look through the papers that have essentially changed my life. *Or maybe they haven't.*

I pick up the only bundle of papers I know won't affect me. Mine.

I take the paper clip off, and go through everything in the papers. My marriage to Trent is there, as is everything from my work history right back to school. At the back of the stack is a sealed white envelope with my name messily scrolled in black ink.

I take the envelope and place everything else on the sofa next to me. I rip the side and slide out the letter.

DEAR LILY,

THIS IS THE HARDEST THING I'VE EVER HAD TO DO. AND I HOPE YOU FIND IT IN YOUR HEART TO ONE DAY FORGIVE ME AND YOUR MOTHER FOR THE WAY WE TREATED YOU.

WADE'S DEATH WAS THE SECOND WORST THING TO EVER HAPPEN TO OUR FAMILY. THE WORST THING, WAS THE WAY

WE TREATED YOU, OUR DAUGHTER. WE HELD ONTO OUR HATE TOWARD YOU, BECAUSE WE WERE TOO GUTLESS TO LAY THE FAULT ON WHO ACTUALLY DESERVED IT, YOUR MOM AND ME. i SHOULD'VE FIXED THE GATE; i KNEW iT WOULD OPEN EASILY. BUT i NEVER DiD.

YOUR MOM SAW YOU AT FAULT BECAUSE YOU CALLED HER iN, BUT SHE KNEW SHE SHOULDN'T HAVE LEFT WADE iN THE BACKYARD ON HiS OWN. SHE STARTED DRINKING, AND POPPING PiLLS, THEN STARTED DOiNG HARDER DRUGS iN ORDER TO COPE. MY CHOICE OF ADDiCTiON WAS ALCOHOL. YOU KNOW THAT BECAUSE YOU OFTEN WERE THE RECiPiENT OF THE ANGER UNLEASHED WHEN i'D DRiNK.

i COULDN'T COPE WiTH WHAT i DiD TO WADE. i DiDN'T SEE HiM RUN OUT, AND i HiT HiM. WHEN i GOT OUT OF THE CAR, HE WAS CRYiNG AND CALLiNG FOR YOU. THE LAST WORDS ON HiS LiPS WERE „LiLY", AND i HELD HiM iN MY ARMS AS HE DiED. i COULDN'T COPE AND i WANTED TO FORGET, BUT EVERY TiME i'D DRiNK, THE ONLY THiNG i DiD WAS REMEMBER THE WAY HE TOOK HiS LAST BREATH iN MY ARMS.

i'M AFRAiD „SORRY" WON'T EVER BE ENOUGH FOR EVERYTHiNG i DiD TO YOU. iT'LL NEVER BE ENOUGH. BECAUSE NO FATHER SHOULD EVER TREAT HiS DAUGHTER THE WAY i TREATED YOU. i'M NOT A MAN, LiLY, i'M NOT EVEN A MONSTER. i'M LOWER THAN THAT.

BY THE TiME YOU'LL READ THiS, i'LL BE DEAD. AND SO i SHOULD BE.

i WANTED YOU TO KNOW THAT ALTHOUGH i BLAMED YOU, iT WAS NEVER YOUR FAULT. YOU SHOULD NEVER HAVE BEEN SUBJECTED TO THE HORRIBLE THiNGS i PUT YOU THROUGH.

i'VE HEARD THROUGH THE GRAPEVINE YOU'RE MARRiED NOW AND LiViNG iN A DiFFERENT STATE. i'M NOT SURE HOW MUCH OF THAT iS TRUE, BUT i HOPE iT ALL iS, AND i HOPE YOU ARE HAPPY. i HAVEN'T TRiED TO FiND YOU TO BEG FOR YOUR FORGiVENESS, BECAUSE i'M NOT WORTHY OF YOUR CLEMENCY.

BUT i WANT TO TELL YOU THiS. i AM SORRY AND i LOVE YOU. YOU WERE NEVER STUPID AND YOU CERTAINLY AREN'T UGLY. BUT MOST iMPORTANTLY, YOU'RE WORTHY. YOU'RE WORTHY OF LOVE, YOU'RE WORTHY OF RESPECT AND YOU ARE WORTHY OF HAPPiNESS.

i LOVE YOU, LiLY.

DAD.

PS: YOU ARE WORTH iT.

Tears are falling on the aged, yellowing paper and I re-read it over and over again.

A warm hand is placed on my shoulder, and I nuzzle into it. Max doesn't need to say anything. And I don't have the urge to speak either.

Instead, I sit on the sofa, cross-legged and just stare out the window.

CHAPTER 37

I HAVE NOT LEFT MAX'S apartment. I've stayed curled up on the sofa, or in his bed the entire time. Max invited Shayne and Liam over, and they came on Tuesday night. Shayne read the file, and all I could hear from her was an occasional gasp or an odd 'damn'.

Max called Peter and told him I won't be in to work for the week, and why. Peter offered to come see me, but Max diplomatically declined.

And last night, Max had arranged for Katherine to come talk to me. She was here for hours, Max was nothing less than the gentleman he'd always been. He gave us privacy by going to my apartment, and brought me food when she left.

Today, I've started to eat again. Finally, after the intensive talk with Katherine, I'm finally able to start comprehending it all.

"I still want to go to New York," I say to Max who's making me something to eat.

"We can go next week."

"No." I stand from where I've been lying. "We're going this weekend." I see Max's lips turn up into a smirk. "I'm going to call Jolene."

"Okay, but I'm not traveling coach. If they can't fly us first class, I'll pay to fly us first class. And tell her…actually, just tell her I'll take care of the flights and the accommodations."

"Okay," I say as I head to Max's bedroom, where he brought my laptop in case I wanted to do some work.

I open up the emails, and jot down Jolene's number, then call. The receptionist puts me through immediately.

"Lily, I thought you weren't interested," Jolene says when she answers the call.

"My sincere apologies, but I had some family matters come up. But I'm back now, and I'd like to take you up on your offer to come speak to you in New York. But I'll make all relevant arrangements regarding flights and accommodation."

"Great, do you think you can come into the office on Saturday?"

"Yes, that's fine."

"Okay, well how about we make it ten in the morning?"

"Fantastic, thank you."

"I'll email you the address and a list of hotels nearby."

"Thank you." We hang up and I go out to find Max watching TV. "I told her we'd be taking care of the hotel and flights."

"Great, I'll make the arrangements."

"She's sending me an email with the address and nearby hotels."

"Okay. Come sit here." He taps the sofa beside him then lifts the remote to turn the TV off. "You look better." I go and snuggle into his side.

"I feel better, almost like I'm normal. At least I know now I did nothing wrong. But, I want to go see all their graves. I think I need to in order to put that part of my life to rest."

"When do you want to go?"

"Now, after I have a shower." I stand from the sofa and stretch. I pick up the paper that has the address of the cemetery.

"I'll go get ready, too. But you do realize, it's a good five hours away." He stands and starts to walk in toward his room.

I nod my head. "I'm going to go back to my apartment. I need to wash and get changed and just start to feel like myself."

"Do you want to wait and I'll come with you?"

"No, I need to go and do it on my own. I'm seeing Katherine tomorrow morning, and I want to be able to say I've been there. I can't keep holding onto this, I need to move forward." I tilt my head to the side and lift an eyebrow. "Or at least start to move forward."

"Whatever you need, I'll be here." He kisses my temple and leaves me to leave.

I stand and look down at the three small grave markers that have been destroyed by graffiti. Max has his arm wrapped around my waist.

"This is strange," I say as I continue to look at the three graves. "I've never known them to be loving, or even really coherent, but I feel something."

"What do you feel?"

"Like my heart has broken, as if a part of me has been ripped apart and I can't put it back together. It's weird, because I don't even know them, especially Wade, but I love him."

Max remains quiet, but he holds me closer to him, allowing me to use his body to steady myself. Eventually, I sit on the grass, and just stare. Max moves away, giving me privacy to do what I need in order to deal with this entire situation.

"I've never known you, Wade. Actually, I've never known any of you. I lived with you, Mom and Dad, but now I know the version of you I lived with wasn't really the people you were meant to be."

I wipe a stray tear from beneath my eye and keep looking at the memorials. "I dream of you." I let out a humorless chuckle. "I dream of all of you. We're usually out having a picnic and playing. You and Dad go exploring while Mom and I sit and play in the tall wildflowers. You like playing with my hair, Mom. You're always touching it, and braiding it." I smile at the thoughts of my beautiful dreams.

"Wade, you and Dad go off and find things, and you're always calling for me when you return."

I wipe more tears away from my eyes.

"I remember some things. Like how your blond hair glowed in the sun, as if you were wearing a halo. I remember you couldn't say the 'L's in my name, so you'd call me *Wiwi*. In my dream I love hearing your laugh, but now I know it's not just in my dream."

I move so I'm sitting up on my knees and start to pick the weeds from around their graves. "What happened to you, Wade, I know now it was an accident. You weren't supposed to run out on the street, and Dad wasn't meant to kill you. It's no one's fault. Not mine, not Mom's, not Dad's and certainly not yours."

I take a deep breath and gather myself so I can tell them what I need to.

"My whole life I thought I was worthless. When I left you, Dad, I went to live with Trent. He turned out to be a monster. I thought I was broken before I met him. I thought I needed him to make me whole. But he ended up ruining me. Breaking my spirit, and tearing apart my soul."

I look up to the darkening sky and watch as the clouds rapidly move in. The sky is beginning to turn gray and the sun has retired for the day.

"But I don't blame you, Mom and Dad. I wanted to. I wanted to say it's because of you I was caught in an abusive relationship. But I can't. It's not your fault. We all suffered from that day forward, and we all suffered differently. You lost your life, Wade. Mom and Dad lost their minds, and I lost myself. But now it's time for me to move on, because out of the four of us, I'm the only one who's still breathing and has the option to move forward. I won't make the mistake you made, Mom and Dad. I won't let this consume me until it finally claims me. For that, I thank you. You've taught me a lesson, a valuable one."

"Lily, we've been here for a few hours, we need to head back," Max says as he kneels beside me.

"Just a couple more minutes."

He nods and kisses me on the lips. "I'll be waiting by the car."

I go back to looking at their plain tombstones and decide I'll do what they never could. I'm going to honor them in death, and pay them respect as their last living family member should. "I want you to know, no matter what you did to me, I always loved you."

I stand from the ground and brush loose grass off my legs. "Next time I return, I'm going to make sure you have decent headstones. Bye Mom, Dad, and Wade." I blow them all a kiss. "I wish I knew all the people who died on that day."

Turning, I head toward Max with tears streaming down my face. "You ready to go home?" Max asks as he leads me back to his car.

"I am, but I'd like to get them proper headstones, not just those small insignificant ones."

"I can arrange that for you. And once they're ready we can come back out if you like."

"Thank you. I'm not sure I'd be able to handle this without you."

"You would, because you're the strongest person I know." He opens my door, waits until I'm in, then he walks around the front of the car. Max gets in the car and silently sits looking at me. I think he's checking to make sure I'm okay. After a few moments he starts the engine and we leave.

Although I've done nothing since last week, I'm mentally exhausted and drained. During the five-hour car ride home, I sleep the entire time.

"Wake up, Snowflake." Max nudges me gently.

"Hmmm," I mumble, unable to open my eyes or keep them open. Suddenly I feel weightless as I'm being carried. I put my arms around Max's neck and nuzzle into his neck. "Thank you," I whisper. I inhale deeply and I'm wrapped in the beautiful scent of Max.

"Shhh, I've got you, Snowflake," he softly sighs. "I've got you."

I know we're in Max's apartment, because I feel the vast difference in size between my bed and his. His mattress is firmer and his bed is the biggest bed I've ever laid eyes on. Although I'm fighting sleep, I'm also suddenly very awake.

Strange, yes I know. I'm somewhere between awake and sleeping, that space where if you close your eyes, your mind will begin to race. But if you keep your eyes open, all you want to do is sleep.

Max takes off my shoes and lays them beside his. "Do you want to take a shower?" he asks.

"I'd like to have a bath," I say as I stretch my arms over my head.

"I'll go draw it for you." He goes to his huge bathroom, and I can hear the water running. He comes back in, gets me a t-shirt and boxer briefs, then takes them into the bathroom. I watch as he does all these things for me.

When the bath is ready, he comes and sits on the bed beside me, stroking my face. "Your bath is ready. I've dimmed the lights and put on some soft music for you. I want you to eat something, too. So I can either make you some toast, or I can call for take-out?"

I look up at him and admire him. The way he's looking at me, the tenderness of his touch and his protective nature, his wanting to care for me, all of that pushes me further into the zone of love. He truly is perfect. "Thank you, Max. I know I've said it to you before, but thank you. You truly are amazing."

He leans down and kisses me. "You're my snowflake. I'd do anything for you."

"I'm understanding just how much of yourself you give to me."

"And I want to give you so much more. But for now, I want you to go enjoy your bath." He holds his hand out to me and helps me out of the bed. "I'll make toast," he adds even though I didn't give him an answer. But toast is perfect, because it's all I can stomach.

I go into the bathroom, strip and sink into the large bath. The warm water embraces me, and soothes everything. Why is it soaking in a hot bath, with soothing music and dimmed lighting, actually feels good? I have no idea, but I revel in the decadence and comfort of this moment.

When I get out, I feel so much more relaxed and calm, as if every problem has been erased and all I'm left with is a warm, fuzzy feeling I can identify as happiness. I go out to the kitchen and Max is preparing toast and hot chocolates. "Extra marshmallows," he says as he looks down at one of the hot chocolates.

"Thank you, just what I need." I sit on a stool at the breakfast bar and I watch Max spread peanut butter on two pieces of toast. "Thank you," I say, as he slides the plate over to me.

"I'd prefer you to eat more. You haven't eaten much since you got the envelope, and I was beginning to worry."

"I have you taking care of me."

He grins at me, and we eat in silence, just relaxing to the soft sounds of the mellow music Max has playing throughout the apartment. When we finish, we opt to leave everything as it is, and we head to bed. Once we brush our teeth, we climb into bed together.

As my eyes begin to drift, Max holds me tight against his warm body.

"One day, will you tell me about your tattoos?" I ask as I rest my head on his chest and he drags his fingers softly through my hair.

"There's nothing to tell. I wanted them, and I got them. The tiger I got because I find the tiger a noble and strong animal, and the phoenix I got because I like how it can rise from its ashes and become stronger than its past."

"Wow. For you it's all about strength."

"Mental strength. Now shh, you have to be up early tomorrow. You're seeing Katherine and we're flying out to New York."

My eyes are already closed and I can barely make out any sounds.

The exhaustion of today has knocked me out. I drift off to sleep and have the most peaceful slumber I've had in a long time.

"I love you," Max tells me in my dream.

"I love you," I respond.

CHAPTER 38

"HOW WAS YOUR SESSION WITH Katherine?" Max asks as I try and settle in my seat.

"Um." I'm so nervous. This is the first time I've ever been on an airplane. "You sure these things are safe?" I ask, completely forgetting Max even asked me a question. Logically I know the chance of crashing is virtually non-existent, but that doesn't stop my nerves from tap dancing inside my body.

"Relax, it'll be fine." Max grips my hands. "You're shaking," he says as he squeezes my hand in comfort.

I look around the plane, making note of all the exits, and looking above to see where my life jacket is. "I've never been on a plane before."

"It may be your first, but it won't be your last. Take it easy. When the plane takes off, I'll get you a drink."

My eyes are darting around everywhere. "Okay," I say and finally sit back in my seat.

"Ladies and gentleman, please prepare for takeoff," the captain says over the loud speaker.

I react violently to his announcement. I feel like I'm going to be sick, my heart is racing right out of my chest and there's a knot the size of Texas sitting in the pit of my stomach. "Do you need a sick bag? You're looking really white," Max offers as he indicates for the air hostess to come over.

"I think that may be a good idea. I'm not feeling my best," I say.

"Sir, can I help you?" the cute blonde says to Max.

"An air bag please."

She looks at Max and squints as if he's speaking an ancient language. It's times like this I realize how bad Max's stutter can be. She doesn't know what he's saying, even though I no longer hear it. "I'm going to be sick," I say before Max repeats himself and feels bad because she's struggling to understand him.

The air hostess comes back with two, very thick, white bags and hands them to me. "Anything else I can help you with?" she asks sympathetically. I shake my head and go back to concentrating on my breathing.

Within a few moments the plane is taking off, and I'm gripping onto

Max's arm as if we're about to fall out of the sky. We're up and gliding before I know it, and my ears are desperate to pop. I yawn, and yawn and try everything. Finally, holding my nose and sealing my lips, I blow air out and my ears pop. "That's better," I say relieved my head has been depressurized.

Max has been sitting beside me, wordlessly suffering as my nails dig into him and watching me as I try to acclimatize myself to the cabin pressure in the plane. He of course has a wicked smirk on his face, and he looks completely amused at my total inexperience with flying. "Better?" he asks once my ears pop.

"Yeah. But I could do with a drink. Some water."

Max presses the buzzer and when the flight attendant comes, I order us two waters. She returns fairly rapidly, and I open my bottle and drink virtually half of it in one go. "Thirsty?" Max pointedly looks toward my water bottle.

"Nervous," I answer.

"Now, tell me about Katherine. How did it go?"

"Really well. I told her about everything, showed her the letter Dad wrote me. She says I'm doing well, and you know what? I actually feel like I am. She says it's because I'm ready to move on with everything, but I just need some help along the way. I don't think I'll ever have a time without seeing her, but I may be able to cope with not seeing her every week. But for now, I really think I need her and how she helps me understand things."

Max sips on his water. "But you've always been far beyond your years. Maybe that day will come sooner, rather than later."

I half chuckle and look around me. The seats in first class aren't too close together, but they're close enough for other people to hear if we're speaking at a normal tone. I lower my voice and answer, "That's because I was forced to grow up and become as self-sufficient as I could be from a young age. I may be mature, but I've missed out on so many things, too. Up until now I've never been on a plane, or a boat for that matter, or even a train. I've never been to an amusement park, or the theatre or even a museum. I never went on any field trips at school, or my high school prom. I haven't experienced any of the things that mold us to be the adults we are. Instead, I was making my own lunch at the age of six. After Wade died, Mom took me to school for a week then told me to find my own way there and back. When I got head lice at the age of eight because it was going around school, I cut my own hair because I didn't know how to get them out. I had the same toothbrush for years, and finally got a new one when Mom died, because I took hers. These aren't things a kid should ever go through, but I did."

Max lifts his hand and cups my face, delicately running his thumb under my left eye. I close my eyes and lean into his gentle and warm touch. "You're so strong, Snowflake."

"Thank you."

I open my eyes to his own heated, darkening gaze looking at me. "I'm glad you asked me to come along. Because I also have something planned we'll be doing over the weekend. New York City is beautiful and busy. It's like nothing you've ever seen before. There are people everywhere, and yellow cabs, my God, cabs as far as the eye can see. I've got a busy few days lined up for us. But tonight, once we get to our hotel, it'll be nice and easy. A massage, and then dinner."

I smile at Max. "You're going to give me a massage?"

Max shifts in his seat, obviously uncomfortable. "Ahh…no. I arranged an appointment for you with the hotel's masseuse. I'm not sure I'd be able to touch you like that," he openly admits to me.

"I'm sorry," I say.

"Anyway, I do have a few things planned for us."

"Thank you."

Last night's massage was the best thing I ever felt. The woman, I forgot her name, was absolutely magic with her hands. When she started working on my back and shoulders, my eyes closed in bliss. Then she started on my legs and I swear I fell asleep.

When I went back to our room, I was drifting on the most perfect of waves. I loved it, every moment of it. And though Max had made a reservation at the restaurant in the hotel, we ended up ordering room service and going to bed early. Max got us a suite with two rooms and two beds, saying he didn't want me to think he was taking the situation for granted.

And now we're sitting, waiting for Jolene to introduce herself. Max offered to stay at the hotel, but I feel better knowing he's here for me. We're waiting in the meeting room on the fifteenth floor, and I'm nervous. I wipe the sweat from my hands down my pants and then pick up the water we've been offered and take a sip. "It'll be okay," Max reassuringly says.

"I know, I'm just nervous and kind of excited."

This tiny woman, no taller than five feet barrels into the office. She has a severe bob haircut and she's wearing red-rimmed glasses. "You must be, Lily. So pleased to meet you," she says as she approaches me and extends her hand so I can shake it.

I stand and welcome her out reached hand. "Jolene?" I ask.

"So good to meet you. And who would this very nice-looking man be?"

she says, eying Max. She may be small, but she's a force to be reckoned with. She has to be pushing sixty, but I can tell she's a 'take no crap' kind of person.

"Max Sterling, ma'am," he carefully and slowly introduces himself.

"Oh I like this one, he calls me ma'am. Keep that up, young man." She sits beside me and puts a file on the glass table. "Now, about you Lily. You're younger than I thought."

"Oh, um, okay." I look sideways at Max, unsure on how to respond. "Thank you?" It's more a question than a statement.

"It's a good thing, a very good thing." She opens the file and starts reading it. Again, I'm lost at what to think. Bizarre is most certainly a word I would use. "These are a list of your books, yes?" She hands me the paper and I see them all.

"They're my books, well the books I've worked on," I correct myself.

"Every one of these books has made a list. And I sit up and take notice when I see the same name being thanked for her proofreading and editing. And it appears it's your name."

"I've been fortunate. All my clients have been exceptional."

"See this is what I do. I look out for someone who's going to be a star. Authors, editors, cover artists, you name it. I watch and learn. Now, take Michaela. *New York Times* and *USA Today* bestseller with her first book, and I do believe you've finished editing her second book, is that correct?"

"Yes, ma'am."

"This is what I know. We've signed her, actually, she only flew out just two weeks ago and signed all the paperwork. I asked her for the original manuscript prior to it being sent to you, then I asked her for your notes on both books. She was only too happy to provide them to me. I looked at her book, looked at your notes and I took notice. Her book was good raw, but what you did to it, the suggestions you made were terrific, and truthfully, I found one error once you were done."

"You found an error?" I ask horrified. "Oh my God!" I clasp a hand to my face, instantly ashamed of myself.

"It's okay," Max whispers, as he grasps my knee below the table.

"Ha," Jolene laughs. "Dear, Max it's more than okay. Because we'd send the manuscript to no less than three editors, then two proofreaders and sometimes there's still errors. You did it all, and that takes a lot of talent."

I smile. "Thank you," I say.

"Oh no, darling, you don't get off that easy. I thought possibly you just fluked it, so I had my team rip apart the other books you did. I needed to make sure if I offer you a job, you're actually as good as I think you are. I had all your books edited, torn to shreds. Each line, each error, each word."

The hair on the back of my neck stands, and I feel ill. Suddenly I have a feeling it wasn't such a great idea to come to New York. "Oh," I say, unable to form anything comprehensible to say.

"And this is what I found. Out of all these books," She taps the paper on the table, "you made a total of fifteen errors."

"That's embarrassing," I whisper.

"No, it's not. It's fantastic. It means you have an acute eye for detail, and you do a very good job. I've been in the industry a long time, if you haven't noticed, and I've seen it change on a dime. It's constantly evolving, but the one thing that is consistently rare to find, is an editor who has the eye for detail, and the know-how of where to steer the story to change it from good to exceptional. And those are the reasons I want you. I'm willing to negotiate."

"You are?"

"Yes, so tell me, Lily Richards, what do you want?"

"Actually that's not my name. Lily is, but Richards isn't. I had to go under a pen name." It's the only way I can describe it without giving away why I don't use my actual name.

"Makes sense, because when I did a search for 'Lily Richards' I did not find any information on you. Back to the reason you're here. Wherever you're working now, I'll give you ten percent more than you're currently earning."

"I'm a personal assistant."

Jolene rolls her eyes and flicks her wrist. "And your talent is being wasted there. I want you, Lily. I want you to work for us, and do what you've done here." She taps twice on the glass table on top of the list of books.

"But I don't have the qualifications to be an editor."

"You, my dear Lily, have something much more valuable than qualifications. What you have can't be taught; it can't be learned. You have the most elemental understanding of a story and where to improve it. So, what do you want? I'll give you your own office and a personal assistant."

"Wait, I'm not moving here," I say. Abruptly I've gone from a high, to a low. Because there's no way I'm moving. "I'm sorry, I must've misunderstood our initial phone call, but there wasn't any mention of moving."

Jolene sits back and casually hooks her left arm over the back of the chair. "I had thought if you weren't local, which I found out from Michaela you weren't, you may refuse to move here. I think I can come up with an alternative. You can do everything via phone or email, fly out once a month so we can touch base, and I'll have a personal assistant here for you." She smiles triumphantly at me.

"It's a generous offer. If I was to take it up, would I be able to still edit away from here, I mean take on my own jobs which I'd ensure doesn't interfere with my work here."

"No. You'd be working for us, and all your work would come through us alone."

"I see," I say. "Thank you for your offer. I think I'll need some time to consider it."

I stand, Max follows, then Jolene stands. "If you get approached by anyone else, make sure you come back to me and let me know of their offer." She extends her hand and shakes mine, then Max's.

"Thank you."

"Thank you," Max says, and we both leave.

We walk outside and I take a deep breath, "Wow," I say and turn to Max as we walk toward our hotel room.

"How do you feel about it?" he asks.

"Truthfully, the compliments were quite difficult for me to hear, actually. And her offer I think is okay."

"Just okay?"

I shrug as we walk along the sidewalk. "She's offering ten percent more than I earn now, and I can't take on any jobs for myself. So I think I may end up earning less than what I make now."

"I sense a 'but'."

"The 'but' is I'll be doing something I love. And something she thinks I have talent in."

"Then ask for more money."

"I can't do that."

"Here, let's go have a coffee. Or in your case, a hot chocolate." Max points to a small deli, and opens the door for me. We find a seat at the back and Max goes to the counter to order our beverages. I sit and look out at the city.

It's Saturday morning and the street looks so busy with people coming and going everywhere. As I wait for Max, I wonder if this is a place I can move to. It's obvious there's opportunity here, but can I actually pack up, leave the only family I know and move here?

"Penny for your thoughts," Max says as he sets the take-away cups down. "They don't have marshmallows."

I look at him as if he's speaking a foreign language. "Who doesn't have marshmallows in their hot chocolate?" I ask as I pick up the cup and blow on it before sipping it. "I was thinking how Jolene offered me a job here, in New York. And I was wondering if I could actually move."

Max's face doesn't falter, though I'm sure he wouldn't be happy. "Would you?" he asks as he stirs his coffee. I shake my head. "Because it's too busy, right?"

I shake my head again. "No, although I'm not keen on just how hectic it seems. I mean, we've been in the deli for only a few minutes and I already feel exhausted looking at everyone rushing around. But no, that's not the reason."

"What is it?" He lifts the cup and tastes his coffee. "God, that's awful."

I smile but then I answer, "Because I've never really had a family. And now I do, and I don't ever want to let them go. I have Shayne and Liam and you."

Max reaches over and cups his hand over mine. "Thank you," he says.

I smile at him, and turn to watch the bustle of a city that never sleeps.

I took a nap after lunch, and then had a soak in the bath in our room. Max went downstairs because he 'had something to do' and said he'd be about an hour or so. I took advantage of that and used the bath.

When he returned he was quiet and not his usual self. But I didn't pester him to find out what was wrong. I've learned with Max he's big on communication, and when he needs to say something he will. Pushing him to tell me what's wrong, will result in him saying he's fine.

"Come on, we're going to be late," he says. I come out and Max's eyes light up when he sees me. "You look beautiful." He comes toward me looking quite suave in his tailored suit.

"Thank you."

"Have you got a jacket or cardigan you can take?" I'm wearing a black pair of pants, low heels, and a top Shayne convinced me to buy, because apparently 'it looks so hot on you'. It's a black corset top with red ribbon.

"I do, hang on, I'll get it."

I put it on, and walk back out to Max. "You sure I look okay?"

"You look so much better than okay." He leans down and kisses me on the lips. "Come on, Snowflake, let's go."

"Where are we going?" I ask as we get in the elevator and travel down.

"I can't tell you that, but you'll enjoy it."

He leads me out the front, and we cross the road, to where a horse-drawn carriage awaits. There's a man in a top hat and suit holding the carriage door open. "Good evening, Mr. Sterling, Miss Anderson. I hope you enjoy Central Park."

"Central Park?" I squeal in delight as I half skip to get into the carriage.

"Central Park," Max confirms as he gets in and sits beside me.

The ride starts, and my eyes are wide open as I watch all the sights. The outer loop of Central Park is nothing short of breathtaking. I feel like a princess as Max pours us champagne and the horses trot along in all their majestic glory. "This is like nothing I've ever seen before," I say in awe.

"It's the most perfect sight I've ever seen." I turn to see what Max is looking at, and it's me. "I want to tell you something, Lily. And I want to tell you now, so I know you'll remember it for as long as you live."

"What's that?"

"I love you. I think I've loved you from the moment I first saw you, I may have even loved you before then. You're perfect, beautiful and rare. Just like a snowflake." I run my hand down his cheek, feeling the scruff of the stubble already coming through. I open my mouth, but Max holds his hand up. "Please, don't say anything. I just need you to know how I feel." He leans in and kisses me sweetly.

I understand what he's saying. He knows I've been through a lot, and he also recognizes how I'm not quite ready to say those three important words. Because once I say it, I'll mean it for the rest of my life.

"Thank you," I whisper.

"We're going to the theatre to watch Matilda and then, I'm taking you out to dinner."

"Won't it be too late?" I ask as I rest my head on his shoulder.

"It's not a school night," he chuckles and kisses my temple.

I lay against Max, watching the city go by, and know I'm the happiest I've ever been.

CHAPTER 39

"LILY," PETER CALLS ME INTO his office.

"Peter, you need me?"

"Two things. Did you make a decision about New York? And there are two police officers downstairs who want to see you."

Cold instantly blankets me and I suddenly feel ill. "What?" I say as I quickly back up to hold onto the wall.

"My God, Lily. Sit down," Peter says as he rushes from behind his desk and helps me over to the chair opposite his. "Do you want some water?"

"Police? Why are they here? Oh my God, Max, I need to call him make sure he's okay. And Shayne, and Liam." I'm starting to go into a panic, and I can't believe how badly I'm reacting.

"Calm down. It's okay. I can get them, and be here with you."

I nod my head vigorously unable to actually say anything.

Peter goes around to his side of the desk and picks his phone up. "Dale, there's two police officers who need to talk to Lily, down by the cashiers. Could you go and get them and bring up a bottle of water? I don't have any in my fridge, I've run out." He listens for a second, then adds, "In a moment."

"What do they want?" I ask Peter. Of course, my asking him is useless. I know he's not aware, because he would've told me if he knew.

"Lily, do you want me to call your boyfriend and have him here, too?"

"He's working, but what if it's him? What if something's happened? Oh God, I feel sick." I clutch my stomach as I take deep, short bursts of breath.

"Lily, this is Detective Harris, and Detective Jones, they have some questions to ask you," Dale introduces the two female police officers. "Peter." Dale flicks his head, telling Peter to leave.

"NO!" I shout too loudly. "Please, they don't have to go, do they?" I ask Harris and Jones.

"Ma'am, if it's more comfortable for you to have them stay then that's fine by us. But what we have to ask is of a very delicate nature," the one identified as Harris says.

"They can stay." I look at Peter and Dale and beg them, "Please, will you stay?"

"Of course," Dale says and goes and stands in the opposite corner of the room. Peter sits down in his chair and the two police officers step inside.

"Would you prefer to close the door?" Jones asks as she looks behind her.

"No one comes up here except for me and Lily, and sometimes Dale," Peter answers.

"Okay, are you alright, Lily, you're looking really pale?"

"Are Shayne, Liam, and Max alright?"

The two women look at each other then back to me. "We're sorry; we don't know who they are."

Instantly, I relax. My shoulders slump and I exhale a big breaths. "Please, go on," I say after the few seconds it takes me to calm.

"Do you know Trent Hackly?" one asks.

And as quickly as I relaxed, it takes less time for every single muscle in my body to tense again. "He's my ex-husband," I say as I look between them.

"Lily, you okay?" Peter asks. I nod my head, but I'm feeling ill.

"Can you tell us about the relationship you had with Trent?"

I'm shaking my head before she even finishes the question. "I don't want to," I whisper. "I can't…go through that again."

"Go through what, Miss Anderson?" Harris squats down in front of me and asks in a gentle voice.

"Why are you asking me about him?"

"We need to know some details, because it'll help us with our investigation."

"Investigation?" I ask and look at Peter then Dale. "Am I part of this investigation? Have I done something wrong?"

"No, not all. Trent's gotten himself into trouble, and we need to know how he was with you."

I shake my head and shrug my shoulders. "I don't understand, what's he done?" I won't tell them anything which can cause me further embarrassment without knowing what they're actually doing here.

Harris turns to look at Jones, and Jones gives her a small nod. "Trent beat his wife."

"Wait, what? His wife? Our divorce only went through about two months ago. Who…how?" The questions I'm asking are more like me thinking out loud. I don't actually expect a response.

"Do you know an Audrey Miller, now Audrey Hackly?" Harris asks.

"Oh my God." I feel ill. "I knew her from high school." I suspected she and Trent were having an affair back then. "She married him?"

"They've been together for a number of years. She moved out here to be with him."

"While we were still married," I whisper as all the pieces of the puzzle begin to fall into place.

"Yes. I'm sorry," Harris says from the other side of the room.

"Lily, anything you can tell us which can help us in our investigation against Trent would be helpful."

"What did he do to her?" I ask in a soft voice as I look the detective straight in the eyes.

"He broke her jaw, her pelvis, lacerated her arm, and smashed her head to where she needed stitches."

"Don't tell me anymore," I whisper. "I can't hear what he did." Instantly I'm hurtled back to memories of the last beating he gave me, the way he kept hitting my head against the fridge. I lift my hand and touch the spot I had stitches on my head. "I feel sick," I say as I stand and run for the bathroom.

"Lily," Peter calls after me. But I keep shaking my head as I run to the bathroom, open the toilet stall and vomit into the toilet. I vomit again, and again. And when there's nothing left in my stomach, I sit on the floor, curled into myself and cry.

"Lily," Jones says softly as she comes into the bathroom.

"Go away; give me a few moments," I manage to say as I sob.

"I just want to tell you a story. Is it okay if I do that?"

Through the tears I mumble, "Yes."

"I want to tell you about a girl I know who in high school fell in love with the school's sports star. He was popular and good looking and all the girls wanted to be with him and, as the saying goes, all the boys wanted to be him. But he had his eyes set on the geeky girl, and they ended up together."

"This is a nice story," I say through the door as I pick myself up and sit on the lid of the toilet.

"It was, until he decided he wanted her to do something and she didn't want to."

"What did he want her to do?"

"He wanted her to sell her body, and pimp herself out because he thought she'd make him a lot of money."

"Oh my God," I say as I come out of the stall and go wash my face and hands. "What happened to her?"

"She started doing it, because she thought he'd love her more. But then she wasn't making enough money for him, and he started beating her to make her work harder."

"Oh my God," I say as I look up from the running tap to her.

"But after a couple of years of him bullying her around, and beating her, she finally realized what he was doing was the furthest thing from love there was."

"Did you save her?" I ask as I wipe my hands and then lean against the wall in the bathroom.

"No, Lily I didn't save her. She saved herself. She made a conscious decision to change her life, accept her past, and move on with her future. She also finally grasped how strong she was as a woman and had that miserable son-of-a-bitch arrested. She went to court for his trial, stood with her shoulders straight and her head held high, and she gave the court her testimony."

"Wow." I look down at her shoes avoiding her eyes then look back up at her. "Whatever happened to her?"

"Why aren't you asking what happened to him?"

"Because I have faith he was dealt with by the court."

Her mouth twists up in half a smile and she says, "You're looking at her."

My arms break out in goosebumps and I get ambushed by admiration for her. "Wow."

"You can do this, Lily. If there's anything you can tell me to help me put him behind bars, please I need you to be brave."

I open the door and walk back to the room where everyone is waiting for me and Jones to return. "I have something I can say, but I have something which may be even better."

"What's that?" Jones asks.

"I have the diary I was writing. But it's at my best friend's house and I need to go find it."

"A diary? As in a journal?" I nod my head. "Does it have details?"

"I can give you some details," Dale interrupts. "Lily showed up here freezing cold, with blue lips because she'd left him with nothing more than the clothes on her back. I wrote it down, kept a note of what happened in case there were repercussions."

"You did?" I ask Dale.

"Yes, I'm sorry, Lily. I didn't mean to deceive you, but I kept a record of it."

"You were protecting me. I'm not mad."

"I'll go get it." Dale darts out of the office and comes back a few moments later with an envelope. "I've kept a copy for myself, but here's the original."

"Thank you. Lily, when can you get your diary?"

"I can go after work tonight and get it."

We make arrangements for me to go tomorrow morning down to the police station and give them my journal. They also tell me if I need to give evidence, they'll speak to the DA and ask if I can do it via videotape, so I don't have to face Trent.

When they leave, I sit, emotionless, in Peter's office. "Are you okay?" he asks.

I shake my head, then nod. "I don't know. I feel numb."

"Look, I'm going to call that guy of yours and get him to come pick you up. Take the rest of the day off, and tomorrow morning go to the police station. Just come in after that."

I nod but I'm not sure what I'm nodding for. "Okay," I say in an automatic response.

Like a jumbled blur; I hear Peter talking, and Dale talking, but I'm completely zoned out and not sure what's happening. I just sit in Peter's office, staring, at nothing.

My mind goes around and around. I'm numb, but I'm also confused. I'm not sure how long I sit here, because everything is quiet. I can't hear anyone. Maybe they're talking, or maybe they're not. I'm stuck in limbo, somewhere between hell and earth. Every emotion, every feeling, everything is bubbling just beneath the surface. Like an active volcano waiting to erupt.

"Lily," Max's serene deep voice calls me.

Blankly I look into his dark brown, green-speckled eyes. *Did he say something? Is he actually here?*

"Lily," he says again, as he lifts me from my seat and hugs me.

"He did it again," I flatly say. "He hurt someone else."

"I know, Snowflake. Peter told me. I came the moment he called me."

"They want my diary. I need to give them my journal. We have to go." Suddenly I feel an extreme amount of urgency as I leap out of Max's arms and go for my desk to get my bag.

Max is right beside me and walking me down to my car. But I'm in no shape to drive. "Here," I say as I give him my keys."

"I've got my car. We can come back later and get yours, okay?" I nod my head, tuck my keys back into my bag and walk in the direction of Max's car.

"Is Shayne home yet?" Max asks. "So she can let us in."

"I still have keys. They told me when I left I could keep them, because it'll always be my home." I get into the car and stare at nothing, everything is a blur. Before we reach Shayne and Liam's house, Max calls them to let them know what's happened.

In a daze, I stare out the window, really not comprehending what's been happening. I feel like I'm so unsure of everything. I'm a mess. I feel a tidal wave of strength, then it dissipates to uncertainty and anguish.

"I have to do this," I end up saying to myself. "If I don't, he'll always be able to hurt someone else. He shouldn't think he has that right."

We pull up outside Shayne and Liam's house, and we go inside to the room I was staying in. I look everywhere and can't find the journal. "It's useless, he's going to get away with it because I can't find the journal."

Max hugs me and lightly rubs his hands up and down my back. "Lily, when was the last time you wrote in it?" he ask in his beautifully hypnotic, deep soothing voice.

Instantly his lull completely relaxes me. "It was when the divorce went through," I automatically respond as my eyes close.

"And where were you sitting when you wrote it?"

I think for a moment, and an image flashes in my mind. "On my bed. I put the journal down and went to sleep. Oh my God," I yell. "It's under my bed." I get down on all fours and look under the bed. There it is, with a dust bunny over it, right down the back of the bed. "Thank you."

Max pushes the bed, and I grab my journal, wiping off the clump of dust. "There you go," he says smiling broadly at me. "You just needed to relax."

"Can we go home now? I just need to switch off and not think about anything."

He takes the journal, and links our fingers together, leading me out to the car. "I think you need a bath, some dinner and a really stupid comedy to make you laugh."

"Let's not worry about my car tonight. A bath sounds perfect."

He opens my door and tosses the journal on the back seat. As we drive home I keep looking back at it. "Don't worry about it," he says, obviously sensing the weight my diary is imposing on me.

"I can't help it. What I have in there may send him to jail."

"No, you can't look at it that way. If he goes to jail, it's because of what he did not because of what you wrote."

He's right. I didn't beat Audrey. I didn't do all those terrible things to her. He did them. And for that, he needs to face the consequences.

CHAPTER 40

"ARE YOU READY?" MAX ASKS as we stand on the sidewalk outside the police department. I nod my head. "I have the journal. I kept copies of every page. You can do this, Lily. I'm right next to you, the whole way."

I look up at the building and smile. I *can* do this. We walk in and go to the front counter which is manned by two people. "Can I help you?"

"I'm here to see Detectives Harris and Jones."

They look me up and down, then pick up the phone to ask either of them to come down.

A moment or so later, while my pulse quickly thrums through my body I hear, "Lily," Harris says as she approaches us. "Come with me," she leads us to an office and closes the door. "You're looking better than you were yesterday. You are?" She directs her attention to Max.

"Max Sterling."

She gives him a slight nod, and looks back to me. "Did you bring the journal?"

"I did. Here." Max hands her my diary. "I also took copies of everything in case anything happens."

"Nothing will happen. We'll read it and take copies of what we need. Once Trent's trial is over, we'll return it to you."

"Can I ask a question about Trent?" I look at Harris and silently plead.

"If I can answer it, I will. There are things I can't discuss with you, obviously."

"When did he beat Audrey?"

"Three days ago."

"Is he in jail?"

"He was granted, and made bail."

I shiver at the thought he's around and could come after me. "Should I swear out an order of protection against him?"

"It'll be a good idea, considering he's out on bail, and now we have something that shows he's a perpetual offender."

I look at Max and he nods his approval. I can tell he wants me to get one. "Okay, how do I go about doing that?"

She explains it to me, and tells me under the current circumstances, they should be able to get a judge to approve it fairly rapidly.

Max and I leave after filling out paperwork for the restraining order, and Max takes me to work. "You sure you don't want to spend the day at home? I can have a masseuse to come over, maybe even have someone come and give you a manicure and pedicure?" he asks.

"No, I'll be okay. I need to keep busy, and I need to call Jolene and speak to her. I should've told her on Saturday I wasn't going to accept the position. I don't want to move, even though I would like to be doing what I love."

"Okay, well the choice is yours. I'm working late tonight. I won't be home until around eight or nine."

He pulls up in front of the store and leans over to kiss me. "I'll see you tonight," I say.

As I go upstairs, I stop into Peter's office. Dale's there and they're drinking coffee and laughing. "Lily, come in," Peter says. Dale gets up from the chair, and moves to lean against the small expanse of wall between the large windows overlooking the floor.

"I just wanted to let you both know what's happening."

"And what's that?" Dale asks.

I give them a run-down of everything that happened this morning, and both say how they're pleased Trent's finally being held accountable for his actions.

"I also wanted to say, to both of you, thank you. You've not only shown me kindness, but you've also been patient with everything. I really appreciate it."

"Peter told me you had your interview with that publishing company," Dale says changing the conversation. *Obviously they both find it as difficult to accept compliments as I do.*

"I did, but I'm going to decline their offer."

"What?" they both half yell at me. "Why?" again they both say.

"First they wanted me to move to New York so I could go into the office, but I told them I'm not moving. So they offered for me to do it all by email, phone, courier and fly into New York once a month. But I don't want to do that either."

"Was the money good?" Dale, the numbers man, asks.

"It was ten percent more than I'm earning here, but the catch is I can't have any personal clients."

"Ten percent is weak," Peter says and Dale nods his head.

"It's really a combination of things which made me decide to decline the offer."

"You've not declined it yet?" Dale asks.

"What with what happened yesterday, I really didn't have a chance to."

"Do you want to take it?" Peter says as he finishes his coffee.

"It's what I'd like to do, but at the same time, I like it here. And I'm booked up for the next three months and I have five on a waiting list. So really I don't need them, but it would be nice to do what I love."

"You know, Lily," Peter starts. "You've been headhunted by one publishing company. I can guarantee it, you'll have more offers." I laugh and remember what Jolene said to me. "What's funny?" He looks at me quizzically.

"Jolene, the lady who offered me the position, said to go back to her with any offer I receive. I'm sure she was being nice, and I most likely won't receive another offer like hers again."

"There she goes again," Dale murmurs to himself, but obviously loud enough for me to hear.

"What is it, Dale?"

"You, Lily. You still don't get it."

"Get what?"

"You're worth what she offered times a million. She wanted to meet you because you, my dear Lily, are worth it. Every penny, every dollar. And her offer won't be the last. It's only a matter of time, and someone will give you what you want and you'll be an asset to their company, just like you're a precious commodity to ours."

"Thank you," I say and accept his beautiful words. "But I'll be rejecting it because frankly, air travel and I aren't the best of friends."

Peter and Dale both laugh, and understand what I mean. "Tonight we'll need a hand with counting inventory out the back. Can you stay late and help?" Peter asks.

"Of course. Around what time do you think I'll be done, so I can tell Max?"

"No later than eight to eight-thirty."

"Great, I'll let Max know."

I get up and go to my desk. First thing I do is call Max and let him know I'll be working late, and he says for me to wait at work because he'll come by and take me out to dinner. Seeing as the hospital is close by, there's no sense in me driving home, only so we can come back out this way for dinner.

And then I call Jolene and reject her offer. She tries to offer me another ten percent, but I've made my mind up to not accept. The biggest drawback for me is being unable to take on new clients, who could potentially be another *New York Times* or *USA Today* bestseller.

"I'll be getting off right at eight, so just wait for me, okay?"

"Yep, we're busy with an inventory check anyway. I'll just have to go get my sweater from my car when we're done."

"Alright, I'll see you when I get there." Max hangs up and I go downstairs to start helping with the stock counting out the back.

The hours fly by, and before I know it, Peter's telling me Max is waiting in the store out in front. He tells me to go home and thanks me for all my help.

"Hey," I say to Max as I go to him. "I've gotta go get my cardigan from my car. It's parked around the back."

"I'll come with you."

"How about you bring the car around the back? I'll go straight there, see you in a few minutes."

"Okay."

I give Max my bag after I take the keys out, and head out through the back exit as he goes to get his car. I walk toward my car in the back parking area, and it's quiet and isolated out here at this time of the night.

When I reach my car, I unlock it with the fob when I hear the one demonic voice I know I'll never forget, "Lily."

I turn around and I get punched in the face. Startled, I fall back against the car. "Trent," I scream.

He lays another punch into my stomach, winding me. I buckle over in pain, and try to scream, but he's knocked all the air out of me. Instead I desperately gasp for air, trying to get something other than pain into my lungs.

He grabs me by the back of the head, and smashes my head against the door. "Help," I scream.

"You should've just minded your own damn business, bitch. But you had to give them your fucking immature, stupid little diary."

"Help," I yell again, fighting the urge to throw up. I'm fighting, with everything I have in me. I begin to lash out with my arms, and I manage to swipe at Trent's face.

"I should've done the world a favor and killed you when I had the chance. Looks like I'll have to do it now."

"Help," I yell as I keep punching toward Trent.

Suddenly he's dragged off me and I see him being flung, like trash, to the ground. "Keep your damn hands off her," Max yells at Trent and lays a few swift kicks into his side.

"Fuck, you broke a rib," Trent yelps in pain as he holds his side.

"Are you okay?" Max cradles my face in his hands, then kisses my forehead. "The police are on their way."

"Max," I mumble as I watch Trent writhing around on the parking lot concrete in pain.

Max looks toward Trent and shelters me from looking at him. "Don't bother looking at him," he says while standing over me, protectively.

As I hug Max, I peek from around his broad shoulders. Max barely touched Trent. Yet there's tough guy Trent, twisting around as if he was beaten to within an inch of his life. Much like he'd actually done to me, and most likely Audrey.

The police are here within moments, and Trent is screaming at how Max beat him.

Peter comes out to see why there are police cars and an ambulance out behind his store.

"What happened?" he asks as one of the police officers whose separated Max from me and is taking his statement.

"Trent attacked me, told me he was going to kill me." Although I can see Trent lying on the ground, I feel nothing for him. He's rolling around, yelling and crying, but I don't feel a single thing toward him. I don't feel the knots in my stomach I used to feel when he hit me. I don't even feel my pulse hammering through my veins in anticipation of the next blow. I'm completely numb toward him. I have no inclination to go to him and to make sure he's alright. He's nothing to me, and I feel just that toward him. *Nothing.*

"How's the head, Lily? Your eye looks bad."

I can already feel my eye swelling, and I know within an hour or two, it'll be much worse. "I've suffered worse."

"No more suffering." He walks over to the police officer who's cuffing Trent and he says something to him. He shakes hands with him, then heads back over to me.

"What happened?" I ask.

"Look up there." Peter points to the back of the building and I look in the direction. And I see them. A cluster of cameras. "You see them."

"I do," I say, as I smile and shake my head.

Max stops talking to the police officer and comes over to me. "You need to get looked at," he says as he points to my eye.

"No need, it's not that bad," I say. "But Peter just gave me some great news."

"Which is?" he turns to Peter and asks. Peter just points to the cameras and Max lets out a chuckle. "But you still need to get looked at. Come on, I'm taking you to the hospital."

"But the police?"

"We can go down after you've been looked at and give them your statement." Max leads me to his car, and Peter is already walking with an additional police officer back toward the store.

"I'll be glad when today is over," I say as I relax back in the plush black leather seats of Max's car.

"So will I," Max adds as we drive toward the hospital.

CHAPTER 41

WHAT A DIFFERENCE A MONTH makes.

As it turns out, Trent didn't break anything of mine. Max, however, did manage to break two of Trent's ribs. With the surveillance out in the back of the store, and what Trent said to me, he was arrested for attempted murder.

In turn, it all fell apart for Trent. Audrey pressed charges against him, and he ended up losing his job at the hospital where he was working. They didn't want a felon working for them. His trial isn't until toward the end of the year, and Trent is being held in prison until then.

Katherine has been such an integral part of my recovery. She's been working with me extensively and I'm managing to get through it all.

Peter and Dale were right. I ended up receiving three more offers from publishing companies. And in an hour, Max and I are going to go see the one I'm most interested in. "Are you nervous?" Max asks as he brings me over a hot chocolate.

"You know what? I'm actually not. I've been approached by a lot of publishing companies, and I either have to travel, or I can't keep working on my own list. And if I don't get a job with one, well I'm busy enough to be able to leave the store if I want to. I'm booked three months in advance with now over twenty on a waitlist. So, no, I'm not nervous."

"It makes me happy to see you happy, Snowflake."

"You'll have to think of a summer name for me, and alter them when the seasons change." I put my laptop on my lap and finalize the last part of a read-through before I need to send it to my client.

"Did you hear what I said?" Max asks.

"Huh? Were you talking?"

Max stands and goes into the kitchen. "We're going to be late," he says as he points to the wall clock above the TV.

"Crap," I holler as I place my laptop down and run into my room to get changed. Where did that forty minutes go? I change and go out to the family room where Max is chuckling to himself, leaning up against the kitchen counter. "Come on, stop standing around," I tease as I head out the door. Max follows, laughing at my complete disarray.

We get down into the parking garage and Max jogs ahead, opening my door and waiting for me to get in before he jogs around and reverses out of the spot. "You don't need to be nervous."

"I'm not." *But really I am.*

"Ha. You could've fooled me. You're fidgeting and you keep fixing your hair. You look beautiful, and I'm sure they'll be a good fit for you." I nonchalantly shrug my shoulders, as if it's not a big deal. "There you go again, pretending you don't care."

I look at him and smirk. "When have you gotten to know me so well?" It's a rhetorical question. Max laughs and repeats my casual shrug. "Yeah, right," I mumble under my breath.

We pull up in front of the address Miriam gave me, and I look up at the small building. This publishing company is really small. It's made up of Miriam who's the Director, one editor, one proofreader, and a personal assistant. "You ready?"

"I am."

"Would you like me to come in with you?" Max asks. I silently nod my head. "Then let's do this."

We get inside and the personal assistant greets us. Her name is Xena and she's young and full of life. Her hair is all different shades of pink and she has a piercing above her lip. She asks if we want anything to drink, Max and I both decline.

"Lily," a relatively young woman says as she comes toward us.

Both Max and I stand, "Yes, hi, I'm Lily and this is my partner Max."

"Pleased to meet you, ma'am," Max says as he extends his hand.

Miriam looks at Max and smiles. "The pleasure is all mine." Right away I look at her and stare blankly. I've had no problems understanding Max and his stutter, but I know all new people at first really struggle with him, which is why he's content to not introduce himself. But Miriam responded to Max and answered him as if she understood. Or maybe she *did* understand him. Either way, her reaction is already marking her high on my list.

"Please, come into my office," she pauses and laughs, "And my boardroom," she pauses again, turns to look at me with an amused look, "And our staffroom."

"It's an all in one. Cozy," I say looking around and noticing the stacks of paper down the other side of the conference table.

"MML Publications is only fairly small in comparison to the top five. But I'm expanding and always in need of editors. However, I don't hire easily. I have one editor, one proofreader and our PA."

"I've done my research, and I've also seen the authors you have."

"You have?" she asks as she tilts her head and looks at me. "She's a smart one," Miriam says to Max.

"She certainly is," he agrees.

"I've also done my research, which is why I approached you. I've been keeping track of the books you edit, and every single one of them has made a bestseller list somewhere. And that is impressive. This is what I can offer you."

I put my hand up to stop her. "Before you tell me what you can offer me, I'm going to tell you what I want."

Miriam looks at Max again and winks at him. "What would you like, Lily?"

"I've had a lot of offers, and I've rejected each and every one of them. But these are my terms. I want you to match what I get now for being a personal assistant at the store where I work, and I'm still able to work for clients of my own away from here."

"I can't agree to the last part," Miriam interrupts to say.

"Here's the thing, Miriam." I cross my legs in a dainty way, knit my fingers together and place them on the table. "If I can still keep doing edits personally, then I can keep an eye out for new authors. And you never know where you'll find the next big thing. You yourself have said every book I've worked on has gone on to place on some bestseller list somewhere. Wouldn't you like me to bring them to you, so you can grow your company to be one of the 'big five'?" I air quote 'big five' then sit back in my seat and watch her reaction.

I see her visibly swallow hard. "Are they your only conditions?"

"I'll work from home when I want and in six months we'll renegotiate my pay."

"Well, this has certainly not gone as planned. This is what I was proposing. I'd match the pay you're getting now. You'd work out of this office Monday to Friday, you wouldn't be allowed to take on outside work, and we'd renegotiate in twelve months."

"Hmmm," I say nodding my head. "Seems you have a way to go to match my conditions." Inside I'm nervous as anything. But Peter, Dale and Max keep telling me I'm worth so much more than I'm asking for, so stick to my conditions and don't falter. And if I'm not a fit for MML Publications, then I'll be a fit somewhere else.

Miriam stands and goes over to the door, which she opens and says to Xena, "Get a welcome package, with all the relevant forms." I'm doing an internal dance, and I'm trying my hardest to contain my smile. "Welcome to MML Publications," she says as she holds her hand out for a congratulatory shake.

When we finish talking, Max and I leave and we head home.

"Oh my God, can you believe it?" I say in the car, still on cloud nine from the happiness coursing through me.

"Of course. It was bound to happen." He places his hand on my thigh, and I cover it with my hand. "Tonight, we'll go out to celebrate."

"Where are we going?" I ask.

"Actually, when we get home, I want you to change into something comfortable, because we're going somewhere before we go out to dinner."

"Where?" I ask excitedly.

"I'm not telling, but I'll give you fifteen minutes."

We pull up in the garage and I'm out the door before Max even pulls the hand-brake up. I'm pressing the elevator button, I'm in and the doors close as I see Max running to make it. I hear him yell, "Okay then I'll wait here."

I go put jeans, a t-shirt, and sneakers on, then go back down to the garage where Max's very attractive, tall, broad body is leaning against his car. Suddenly I see him for so much more than he's ever been to me before. He's always been statuesque, a perfect marble carving of a Roman or Greek God. But right now, I'm completely floored by his casual, incredibly sexy appearance.

"Are you ready?" his silky voice asks.

"I am," I respond. What I don't say is I'm ready for so much more than just this outing he's taking me on. I'm ready for him. "Where are we going?" I ask, suddenly completely aware of the beautiful man sitting beside me. Don't get me wrong, I've always felt attraction toward him, but now I'm ready to take it to the next level. And I have no idea how to tell him.

"Somewhere you said you've never been."

"Huh, care to give me another hint?"

"Nope," he says and then starts to whistle.

About twenty minutes into our trip, Max pulls up outside a small, barn-like house. There's a scratchy old sign hanging up outside which reads 'Strawberry Museum.' Of course, I can't help but laugh. "A museum," I say as I get out of the car and close the door. *He remembered what I said in New York.*

"I want to take you to the Louvre, but seeing as that's over five thousand miles away and you'd need to get on a plane, I brought you to the world-famous Strawberry Museum," he happily says as he points to the sign like one of those game-show girls. "Come on, let's go see all things strawberry."

We walk in, hand in hand and we look around the tiny museum. By tiny, I mean it's an old house which has been converted into a museum. The back of the house leads out to an open courtyard which has tall trees and flowers and planter boxes filled with strawberry plants. There's a small café attached which makes all things strawberry-related.

"Have you ever smelled anything as sweet as this?" I ask as the common fragrance of strawberries assaults us the moment we're outside. "It smells like they're making strawberry jam." The smell of sugar cooking with the strawberries is undeniably one of the most fragrant aromas I've ever sensed.

"How about we share a strawberry sundae?" Max is already heading over to the café to get it before I even say anything.

We're the only ones here and so I pick the best seat, the one with ribbons of sunlight touching my skin, but also the one closest to the planters of strawberries.

"The girl will bring it over when it's ready." He sits opposite me and looks around. "I did some research on museums, and this one was one of the most obscure ones I could find. It was either this or the toothbrush museum."

"There's a toothbrush museum?" I scrunch my nose at it, thinking of what could be on display there. Used toothbrushes?

"Yep, but when I saw they have strawberry sundaes, it brought me back to when Dad would take me out for ice cream after I came to live with him. It was a way for him to get me to talk. And I wanted to share with you how it felt for me as a kid to do something with someone who loved me."

I lower my eyes and feel the tears starting. But these are happy tears. I feel so alive, and finally, after twenty-seven years, I'm finally starting to understand myself. "I love you, Max." I look up to find him staring at me. "It's taken me a while to allow myself to feel it, and realize I'm worthy to be loved. But I know I love you with everything I am. I've never known love before. I thought I did at one time, but I now understand that was a coping tool. You've been by my side and asked nothing of me, yet given me so much of yourself."

"Snowflake," he whispers as he draws his eyebrows together.

"It's taken me a long time. But now I know I am worthy of love, and I'm in love with you." Max is quiet for a scary, long moment.

"That's all I've ever wanted to hear," he says.

"That I love you?"

He shakes his head. "No snowflake, to hear you say you're worthy."

I stare into his hungry, loving eyes and break down.

The ice cream sundae ended up being the most delicious thing I'd ever eaten. Not because it was sweet and gooey. Not because it had an abundance of strawberries and strawberry sauce. But because I shared it with the man I love.

We're heading home now, forgoing dinner at some restaurant and opting for take-out instead. My cell phone rings, and I take it out of my bag.

"Girl, you sitting down?" Shayne says before I even have a chance to say hello.

"Max and I are on our way home, so yes ma'am, I'm sitting down."

"Put me on speaker, I want to tell you both something."

"Hang on," I say and turn to Max. "Shayne wants me to put her on speaker, she wants to tell us something." Max nods his okay. "You're on speaker, Shayne," I say and hold the phone between Max and myself.

"You know the trip to Disneyland you got Liam and me for Christmas?"

"I do," I answer.

"You know how Liam and I had the best. Time. EVER?" she yells.

"Yep, I do. You kept sending me pictures of all the rides you were on. And even one with you trying to feel up Prince Charming."

Max laughs and so do I.

"Hell yeah, girl. That man was F.I.N.E."

"I'm right here, you know," I hear Liam grumble in the background.

"Be quiet you," she says to Liam playfully. "Anyway, you know how Liam and I had a heap of crazy-ass monkey sex?"

I slap my hand to my forehead and shake my head. "Yes, I do recall the messages telling me how many times you and Liam were having sex." Max laughs again.

"Seems one of those times worked."

It takes me a split second, less than a split second to know what she's saying. Suddenly, without my control I start screaming. Shayne starts screaming, and Max pulls over to the side of the road.

"Oh my God," I say through the hysterical crying and screaming. "Congratulations."

"Congratulations, Shayne. And to you too, Liam," Max says as he grabs the phone before I drop it from all the excitement.

"So, anyway. Barbecue, our house, next Sunday," Shayne manages to say once she's stopped screaming. "You're going to be the best auntie in the world, Lily."

"We'll be there," Max responds on behalf of us both.

Then the realization hits me. I'm going to be an auntie. Not to my brother's child, but to my best friend's child. "Yeah, we'll be there," I say, mustering as much happiness I can.

"Bye, guys," Shayne says and hangs up.

"Are you okay?" Max asks as he puts the phone down between us. I smile and nod, then my nod turns into a shake. "What is it?"

"I'm so happy for them to have a baby. Really I am. But she said I'm going to be an aunt. How can I be? I'm..."

Max moves so he's cupping my face in his hands, his thumbs tenderly stroking my cheeks. "You'll be the best aunt in the world to that child. You know why?" I shake my head. "Because you were chosen." I feel my lips twist up in a slight smile. "And one day, you may even want to give their little son or daughter, a cousin to play with." I rapidly blink at Max.

"I'm worthy," I finally sigh.

"Yes, you are." He leans over and kisses me.

We stay entangled for what seems like hours, but I know it's not. "I'm hungry," I finally say.

"Let me take my snowflake home and feed her."

When we get home, we head to my apartment, where Max orders dinner for us.

We sit cuddled together on the sofa, not really watching TV, not really talking, just enjoying our own company. Dinner arrives and we eat while still watching TV. "I have to go in to work on Monday and tell Peter and Dale I resign."

"They'll be happy."

I flash a look over to Max, and he starts laughing as he's eating his spaghetti. His laugh turns into a choking fit, and I pat him on the back to help. "That was the funniest look you've ever given me," he says after he sips on his soda. "But I meant, they'll be happy you're doing something you love."

"I know what you meant. I was just playing."

I finish my dinner and tell Max I'm going for a shower.

"I'll clear everything away," he says as he takes my bowl and his to the kitchen.

As I stand under the hot stream of water which is pelting me on the back, I think about what's happened today. It seems like today is one of the most significant days of my life, apart from the day I walked out on Trent.

In such a short time I'm finally discovering who I am, and what it is I want from my life. But the one thing which will never waiver, is the desire and love I feel for Max. He's always been there, my beacon of hope from the first time I saw him in the deli, to right now as he's cleaning away our dishes. He's always been there, and always will be.

I get out of the shower, dry off and head out to my bedroom, where Max is lying in bed. "Did you shower already?" I ask.

"I ran upstairs and had a quick shower, because I wanted to be here when you came out."

I crawl into bed, and snuggle against Max.

My heart's beating rapidly, and I can feel the nervous butterflies flapping around in my stomach. I want to take this to the next level, but I'm unsure on how to communicate it. I lean up on my elbow, and kiss Max's beautiful, full lips.

Slowly I begin to reach my tongue out, drawing a fine line around his mouth. Max returns my hunger, and soon has me on my back as he hovers over me. "Are you sure, Snowflake?" he asks.

I nod my head, and drag my hands through his hair. "I'm sure," I whisper.

"Sit up for me," he instructs. I do and he grips the hem of my t-shirt and lifts it over my head. I'm left wearing just my panties and nothing else. His heated gaze greedily rakes over my exposed breasts. "You're so beautiful," he whispers as he darts down and swirls his raspy tongue over my nipples.

Insatiably, he sucks on my right nipple, and when I violently grip his head, he moves to my left one. Inside me something is happening. Pure elation begins to steadily bubble away inside me.

Max's fingers slowly brush down my stomach, stopping to circle my belly button, then follow the line of my panties. He removes his warm mouth from my breast, and looks up at me. "May I?" he asks and pulls slightly on my panties.

Breathlessly I say, "Yes."

He moves on my bed, and hooks his thumbs into the sides, then carefully drags them down my body. "I was right," he says as he stares at my body. "Beautiful." His mouth connects with my tummy. He licks and laves his way further down until he's nestled between my legs. "Just relax and feel me."

I lay back and close my eyes, enjoying Max and what his tongue is doing to me. All thoughts drift away. Nothing but pleasure and joy courses through my veins. I can feel a heat burning through my body, touching every part of me, waking parts I never even knew I had.

My breath becomes erratic, and small moans escape my lips. *What is happening to me?* Oh God, this is bliss. My body begins to shake uncontrollably as more strangled noises erupt from the back of my throat. "Oh God," I cry, my voice husky. My hips tilt and gyrate on their own, trying to get more of the delicious feeling from Max's mouth. "Oh God," I half shout as I latch onto Max's hair and drive myself vigorously further into his face.

"Ahhh," I scream in ecstasy as my body violently spasms in response to Max and his clever mouth.

Max crawls up the bed toward me, and when he reaches my face, his dark eyes tell me everything I need to know. He slides into me and I let out a breath as I accept him.

"I love you so much," I say.

Max and I are in each other's arms and Max is drawing figures on my back. "Will making love with you always be this good?" I ask as I kiss his chest.

"No." *Crap, what?* "It'll get better." He leans down and kisses the top of my head.

I smile and know he's right. "I've been thinking about something," I say. I hook my leg over his and turn so my chin is resting on his chest.

"What's that?" he asks while staring hungrily into my eyes.

"I've found somewhere else to live, and I'm going to give up my apartment."

Max's jaw jumps and I see it tense. "Aha," he says and lifts an eyebrow at me. I can already tell he's not entirely pleased with me moving away from him. "Where is this place? And is it safe?"

"It's not too far from here. I think you'll like it," I say as I lean down and pepper kisses across his chest.

"Don't try to distract me, Lily. Where exactly is 'not too far from here'?"

"Seriously, Max. You should be happy I'm moving."

"Why is that?" his voice has a distinct twinge of developing disappointment.

"Because I'm moving to your apartment."

His look automatically eases and he's doing his best to contain his huge smile. "What am I going to do with you?" he asks as he flips us and starts nuzzling my neck.

"I have a couple of ideas," I say as I spread my legs to accommodate his tall frame.

EPILOGUE

IT'S BEEN TWO YEARS SINCE Trent went to trial and was convicted, and he's eligible for parole in another eight years. I was given the option to give my testimony via video conference so I didn't have to face him in court, but I decided I needed to face my fears.

I walked into the courtroom with my head held high, my shoulders squared, back straight, and with all the composure of a skilled surgeon about to undertake surgery on the President. Inside though, I was praying I could keep calm and get the job done. I was nervous and I felt like I was going to be sick, but when Trent called me a slut under his breath as I approached the witness stand, it was then I decided. In order for me to move forward, I must face my past and flip it the bird.

And that's what I did. I looked at the attorneys asking me questions, I answered them all, and I read from my diary about all the horrible things he did to me. Once I'd finished reading passages of my journal, I looked over and saw some of the jurors were wiping tears away. When I was excused from the witness box, I walked out the same way I walked in. With my head held high and my shoulders back and straight. I had nothing to be ashamed of. He put me through hell, brainwashed me, and kept me prisoner in my own mind by convincing me I was worthless. It didn't take long for the jury to reach a verdict and convict him.

As I walked past him, I turned, smiled and gave him a nod. Then I walked out, and left my past exactly where it deserved to be.

Max was pacing the corridor, waiting for me outside the courtroom and the moment I made it outside the doors, I collapsed into his awaiting arms. It was by far the most difficult, yet liberating thing I had ever done.

I looked at the man who beat me, and told the court what he did to me.

"Hey, Snowflake, are you going to get up today," Max says as I lay in bed, reminiscing about the court case.

"I'm thinking about it," I answer as I stretch and look out our bedroom window to the beautiful city below us. The gold bracelet Max gave me catches a sparkle of light, and I smile, remembering and honoring our past.

Max places my hot chocolate on the bedside table and lays down beside me. He leans down and kisses my ever-growing tummy. "You know, little man, mommy and I can't wait until you decide to join us," Max says to my tummy as he kisses it again.

I lift my arms and place them beneath my head, and watch Max as he talks to my baby bump. The moment I told him we were pregnant, he got on line to find the best OBGYN in the state. Luckily, the second best is someone Max knows through the hospital. It was really cute how he automatically went into this protective mode. Protective of me and of our son.

"I think I want to give work up once Wade is born," I say to Max. When we were thinking of names Max's first choice was Wade. Of course, I cried.

"I've been telling you the same thing ever since you told me we're pregnant." He gets up and helps me sit up in bed. He hands me my hot chocolate and begins getting changed. "I think you should write a book. Miriam can promote it." He turns and cheekily winks at me.

MML Publications has tripled its sales in two years, and has some of the hottest, most talented new authors around. I've found some exceptional gems, and I've been able to introduce them to Miriam and get them signed.

I sip my hot chocolate and follow Max's taut muscles and firm lines as he strips out of his sleep pants and t-shirt into jeans and a shirt. "Stop looking at me like that," he teases. "I have to get over to Liam's and help him set up for Sophia's birthday. Poor Liam's copping it from Shayne, apparently she's been quite hard to live with through this pregnancy." He chuckles, then quickly adds, "Don't tell her I said that. I don't want to get Liam, or myself in trouble."

I smile at him. "I won't."

"Anyway, you really should think about writing a book. Give it some thought."

"Actually I have," I answer, as I struggle to get up and go to my husband so I can give him a kiss before he goes.

"I'll be back to pick you up in a couple of hours." He kisses me on the lips. "But you have thought about a book? Really? You haven't said anything to me about it."

I waddle out to the kitchen, where Max has pancakes prepared for me. "Mancakes," I say as I start to eat them.

"Yep, I know how much you love them. But, tell me about this book." He leans up against the kitchen counter and picks his mug up to drink.

I finish chewing what's in my mouth. "Well, I think I have a title."

"Yeah? What is it?"

"I'm going to call it...Ugly."

THE END

FOR HELP

Australia: Reachout – national service. 1800 Respect

U.K: National domestic violence hotline. 0808 2000 247

USA: National domestic violence hotline. 1800 799 SAFE (7233)

ACKNOWLEDGEMENTS

DOMESTIC VIOLENCE AFFECTS PEOPLE WE may know who are too ashamed or frightened to speak up.

When you look at the person next to you on the bus, or the train, or even at school or work, ask them if they're okay. A kind word may be all they need to get through the day or even make the courageous decision to seek help.

Lily's story completely consumed me. She came to me one night while I was lying in bed. A vision of a blonde-haired teenager popped into my mind. She was huddled in the bath, with her arms wrapped around her boney knees and she was crying. She looked up from the blood-soaked water and she whispered two words to me. "Help me." From that day on, more and more of her came to me. It took her months to tell me her entire story, but when she finally gave me her soul, I knew I had to write her story for every person, female or male, who's suffered or is suffering at the hands of an abuser.

Lily, for your heart, I hope I did your story justice.

I must thank some incredible people who've been my sounding board for Lily's story.

To my very good friend Jodi. You were the person I'd call when I wrote a scene I loved, or hated. And you helped me form some of the characters to be as evil as they are.

To Karen, I asked you on the fly to read the story for plot holes and flow. You told me how much you loved it. I've included most (insert LOL) of your suggestions, and the story is stronger for it.

To my darling, Cheryl. You praise my talents often, and I thank you for the beautiful confidence you have in me.

To my sweetness, Mandy. You are such a terrific person, who makes me laugh. Thank you for your help.

To Kellie from Book Cover by Design. Amazing. I told you what I wanted, and you got it straight away. You have an amazing talent, my friend…amazing!

To my very good friend, Melinda. Your proofreading skills are exceptional. I gave you my Lily, and you've treated her with the utmost respect.

To Editing Vixen. Your work is always outstanding. Thank you for everything. (THAT – hehehe)

To Al. Thank you for your proofreading expertize.

And to my editor, Debi. You're so much more than an editor, you're my friend too. You put up with all my 'Americanizing' questions, and you always treat my books with so much integrity and respect.

And to all my readers. Thank you for buying my books. I do hope Lily has been able to give you a voice. Because if she can overcome her past, you can open your heart to your future.

Bound by custom or unique by choice.

Margaret X

ALSO BY
Margaret McHeyzer

Chef Pierre

Holly Walker had everything she'd ever dreamed about – a happy marriage and being mum to beautiful brown-eyed Emma - until an accident nineteen months ago tore her world apart. Now she's a widow and single mother to a boisterous little 7-year-old girl, looking for a new start. Ready to take the next step, Holly has found herself a job as a maître d' at Table One, a once-acclaimed restaurant in the heart of Sydney. But one extremely arrogant Frenchman isn't going to be easy to work with...

Twenty years ago, Pierre LeRoux came to Australia, following the stunning Aussie girl he'd fallen in love with and married. He and his wife put their personal lives on hold, determined for Pierre to take Sydney's culinary society by storm. Just as his bright star was on the upswing, tragedy claimed the woman he was hopelessly in love with. He had been known as a Master Chef, but since his wife's death he has become known as a monster chef.

Can two broken people rebuild their lives and find happiness once more?

Smoke and Mirrors

Words can trick us.

Smoke obscures objects on the edge of our vision.

A mirror may reflect, but the eye sees what it wants.

A delicate scent can evoke another time and place, a memory from the past.

And a sentence can deceive you, even as you read it.

Grit

Recommended for 18 years and over

Alpha MC Prez Jaeger Dalton wants the land that was promised to him.

Sassy Phoenix Ward isn't about to let anyone take Freedom Run away from her.

He'll protect what's his.

She'll protect what's hers.

Jaeger is an arrogant ass, but he wants nothing more than Phoenix.

Phoenix is stubborn and headstrong, and she wants Jaeger out of her life.

Her father lost the family farm to gambling debts, but Jaeger isn't the only one who has a claim to the property.

Sometimes it's best to let things go.

But sometimes it's better to fight until the very end.

Yes, Master

**** This prologue contains distressing content. It is only suited for readers over 18. ****
Also contains M/M, M/M/F, M/F and F/F scenes.

My uncle abused me.

I was 10 years old when it started.

At 13 he told me I was no longer wanted because I had started to develop.

At 16 I was ready to kill him.

Today, I'm broken.

Today, I only breathe to survive.

My name's Sergeant Major Ryan Jenkins and today, I'm ready to tell you my story.

A Life Less Broken

Contains distressing content. 18+

On a day like any other, Allyn Sommers went off to work, not knowing that her life was about to be irrevocably and horrifically altered.

Three years later, Allyn is still a prisoner in her own home, held captive by harrowing fear. Broken and damaged, Allyn seeks help from someone that fate put in her path.

Dr. Dominic Shriver is a psychiatrist who's drawn to difficult cases. He must push past his own personal battles to help Allyn fight her monsters and nightmares.

Is Dr. Shriver the answer to her healing?

Can Allyn overcome being broken?

My Life for Yours

He's lived a life of high society and privilege; he chose to follow in his father's footsteps and become a Senator.

She's lived a life surrounded with underworld activity; she had no choice but to follow in her father's footsteps and take on the role of Mob Boss.

He wants to stamp out organized crime and can't be bought off.

She's the ruthless and tough Mob Boss where in her world all lines are blurred.

Their lives are completely different, two walks of life on the opposite ends of the law.

Being together doesn't make sense.

But being apart isn't an option

HiT Series Box Set

HiT 149

Anna Brookes is not your typical teenager. Her walls are not adorned with posters of boy bands or movie stars. Instead posters from Glock, Ruger, and Smith & Wesson grace her bedroom. Anna's mother abandoned her at birth, and her father, St. Cloud Police Chief Henry Brookes, taught her how to shoot and coached her to excellence. On Anna's fifteenth birthday, unwelcome guests join the celebration, and Anna's world is never the same. You'll meet the world's top assassin, 15, and follow her as she discovers the one hit she's not sure she can complete – Ben Pearson, the current St. Cloud Police Chief and a man with whom Anna has explosive sexual chemistry. Enter a world of intrigue, power, and treachery as Anna takes on old and new enemies, while falling in love with the one man with whom she can't have a relationship.

Anna Brookes in Training

Find out what happened to transform the fifteen-year-old Anna Brookes, the Girl with the Golden Aim, into the deadly assassin 15. After her father is killed and her home destroyed, orphan Anna Brookes finds herself homeless in Gulf Breeze, Florida. After she saves Lukas from a deadly attack, he takes her in and begins to train her in the assassin's craft. Learn how Lukas's unconventional training hones Anna's innate skills until she is as deadly as her mentor.

HiT for Freedom

Anna has decided to break off her steamy affair with Ben Pearson and leave St. Cloud, when she suspects a new threat to him. Katsu Vang is rich, powerful, and very interested in Anna. He's also evil to his core. Join Anna as she plays a dangerous game, getting closer to Katsu to discover his real purpose, while trying to keep Ben safe. Secrets are exposed and the future Anna hoped for is snatched from her grasp. Will Ben be able to save her?

HiT to Live

In the conclusion to the Anna Brookes saga, Ben and his sister Emily, with the help of Agent rescue Anna. For Anna and Ben, it's time to settle scores...and a time for the truth between them. From Sydney to the Philippines and back to the States, they take care of business. But a helpful stranger enters Anna's life, revealing more secrets...and a plan that Anna wants no part of. Can Anna and Ben shed their old lives and start a new one together, or will Anna's new-found family ruin their chances at a happily-ever-after?

Binary Law (co-authored)

Ellie Andrews has been receiving tutoring from Blake McCarthy for three years to help her improve her grades so she can get into one of the top universities to study law. And she's had a huge crush on him since she can remember.

Blake McCarthy is the geek at school that's had a crush on Ellie since the day he met her.

In their final tutoring session, Blake and Ellie finally become brave enough to take the leap of faith.

But, life has other plans and rips them apart. Six years later Blake and his best friends Ben and Billy have built a successful internet platform company 3BCubed, while Ellie is a successful and hardworking lawyer specializing in Corporate Law.

3BCubed is being threatened with a devastatingly large plagiarism case and when it lands on their lawyers desk, it's handed to the new Corporate Lawyer to handle and win.

Coincidence or perhaps fate will see Blake and Ellie pushed back together.

Binary Law will have Blake and Ellie propelled into a life that's a whirl wind of catastrophic events and situations where every emotion will be touched. Hurt will be experienced, happiness will be presented and love will be evident. But is that enough for Blake and Ellie be able to live out their own happily ever after?

Printed in Great Britain
by Amazon

80745666R00183